Mary H Carpenter
17 Hall Ave
Newark, OH 43055

W9-BUC-005

MIRACLE CURE

MICHAEL PALMER

MIRACLE CURE

BANTAM BOOKS

NEW YORK TORONTO LONDON SYDNEY AUCKLAND

MIRACLE CURE
A Bantam Book/March 1998

BOOK DESIGN BY DANA LEIGH TREGLIA

Library of Congress Cataloging-in-Publication Data
Palmer, Michael.
Miracle cure : a novel / Michael Palmer.
p.   cm.
ISBN 0-553-10523-X
I. Title.
PS3566.A539M57   1998
813'.54—dc21   98-4884
CIP

Published simultaneously in the United States and Canada

Bantam Books are published by Bantam Books, a division of Bantam Doubleday Dell Publishing Group, Inc. Its trademark, consisting of the words "Bantam Books" and the portrayal of a rooster, is Registered in U.S. Patent and Trademark Office and in other countries. Marca Registrada. Bantam Books, 1540 Broadway, New York, New York 10036.

PRINTED IN THE UNITED STATES OF AMERICA

BVG   10 9 8 7 6 5 4 3 2 1

TO JUDITH PALMER GLANTZ

FOR YOUR TALENT AS A MOTHER AND YOUR GRACE AS AN EX.

AND

IN LOVING MEMORY OF MY FATHER.
WE MISS YOU, POP.

.   ACKNOWLEDGMENTS

My name is on the cover of this book but it was hardly written in a vacuum. My deepest gratitude goes once again to my tireless editor, Beverly Lewis, assistant editor Christine Brooks, and my incomparable agents, Jane Rotrosen Berkey, Don Cleary, and Stephanie Tade.

In addition, thank you—

Dr. Anthony Zietman for the evening at the King's Rook;

Drs. Michael Fifer and Igor Palacios and the gang at the MGH cath lab for your skill and hospitality;

Dr. Jerry Faich for the inside stuff;

Dr. George Allman for sharing knowledge and experience;

Dr. Michael Czorniak for the articles;

Dr. Bob Smith and Bill Wilson for the tool kit;

Beverly Tricco, Sam Dworkis, and Mimi Santini-Ritt for the readings;

Matt, Bekica, Daniel, and Luke for the inspiration and the help in solving problems;

And special thanks to Dr. Cary Akins, Renaissance man and mender of broken hearts.

The people named above have contributed mightily to the color and flavor of this novel. Any errors or other misrepresentations of fact are purely mine.

M.S.P.

THERE ARE THREE KINDS OF UNTRUTHS:
LIES, DAMN LIES, AND STATISTICS.

—Attributed to Benjamin Disraeli by Mark Twain

MIRACLE CURE

PROLOGUE

IT TOOK EVERY BIT OF HER STRENGTH, BUT SYLVIA Vitorelli managed to force a third pillow under her back. She was nearly upright in bed now. Still she felt queasy and hungry for more air. It was the dampness and the mold, she told herself. If she were in her apartment in Boston rather than her son's farmhouse in rural upstate New York, this would not be happening. Not that her breathing had been all that great in Boston, either. For months her ankles had been badly puffed and her fingers swollen. And now, over the past few weeks, she had been experiencing increasing trouble catching her breath, especially when she lay down.

Sylvia cursed softly. She should never have agreed to make the trip to Fulbrook. She should have told Ricky that she just wasn't up to it. But she had really wanted to go. The ghost of her husband, Angelo, had made living in their apartment a constant sadness. And the dust and noise surrounding construction of Boston's central-artery tunnel had made living in their part of the North End unpleasant. Besides, her daughter-in-law, who had always acted as if her visits were an inconvenience, had actually made the call inviting her to spend almost two weeks away from the city. *The kids ask for you all the time, Mama,* she had said. *And autumn is so beautiful up here.*

Sylvia checked the time. Ricky, Stacey, and the children would be at church for another half hour or so and then were going to stop by to see some friends. She had begged off going with them, citing a headache. The truth was, she didn't feel as if she could even get dressed. She should try to get up, maybe make something to eat, watch Mass on TV, but when she tried to move, she suddenly was seized by a violent, racking spasm of coughing, accompanied by a horrible liquid sound in her chest.

For the first time, she began to panic. The dreadful gurgling in her lungs persisted. Now she was gasping for breath. Sweat began to pour off her forehead, stinging her eyes. Her purse was right next to her on the bedside table. She fumbled through it for her pills with no clear idea of what she would do once she found them. Her fingers, which lately had remained somewhat swollen most of the time, were now stiff, obscene sausages, bluish and mottled.

The air in the musty room seemed heavy and thick. An extra fluid diuretic pill might help. Maybe one of the nitroglycerins, too. Desperately, she emptied her purse out onto the bed. Alongside several vials of pills was an appointment card from the clinic at Boston Heart Institute. Drops of perspiration fell from her face onto the ink. Her next appointment was a week from tomorrow. In order to fly to Ricky's for the eleven days, she had had to skip a Vasclear treatment—the first one she had missed in almost a year. But the missed medication couldn't possibly be the reason she was having so much trouble breathing now. She was down to only one treatment every two weeks, and was due to drop to one a month before much longer. Besides, her cardiologist had told her when she called that it was perfectly okay for her to go.

Oh, my God, she thought, as she frantically gulped down one pill from each of the medication vials. *Oh, my God, what's happening to me?* Suddenly she remembered that the nitroglycerin, which she had not had to take since the early days of her Vasclear treatment, was supposed to be dissolved under her tongue, not swallowed. She tried to get a tablet into place under her tongue, but her hands were shaking so hard that she spilled the tiny pills all over the bed and onto the floor.

Her left ring finger was beginning to throb. The gold band she had worn for over fifty years was completely buried in her flesh. The finger itself looked terribly swollen and dark violet, almost black in color. *Oh, please God, help me. . . . Help me!*

Drowning now, she struggled to force air through the bubbling in her chest. A boring, squeezing pain had begun to mushroom outward from beneath her breastbone and up into her neck— angina, just like before she had begun the treatments. She had to get Ricky on the phone. Or was it better to call 911? She had to do something. Her nightgown was soaked with sweat. She was breathing and coughing at the same time, getting precious little air into her lungs. There was no telephone in the guest room.

Gamely, she pushed herself off the side of the bed and lurched across to the bureau. Her feet were like water bottles, her toes little more than nubs above the swelling. Another spasm of coughing took away what little breath remained. She clutched the corner of the bureau, barely able to keep herself upright. The cough was merciless now, unremitting. Perspiration was cascading off her. Her head came up just enough for her to see that the mirror was spattered with blood. Behind the scarlet spray was her ashen face. She was a terrifying apparition. Her hair was matted with sweat. Bloody froth covered her lips and chin.

Seized by fear unlike any she had ever known, Sylvia turned away from her reflection, stumbled, and fell heavily to the floor. As she hit, she heard as much as felt the snapping of the bone in her left hip. Sudden, blinding pain exploded from that spot. Her consciousness wavered, then started to fade. The agony in her hip and chest began to let up. *Ricky . . . Barbara . . . Maria . . . Johnny. . . .* One by one her children's faces flashed through her thoughts. The last face she saw was her Angelo's. He was smiling . . . beckoning to her.

PART ONE

Two Years Later

CHAPTER ONE

THE BOSTON GLOBE

**Jungle Drug Holds Promise for
Heart Disease**

Researchers at Boston-based Newbury
Pharmaceuticals are heralding what they
say may be a major breakthrough in the
treatment of heart disease, now America's number one killer. . . .

"YOU CAN'T THROW THE SEVEN OF HEARTS, BRIAN. I
just picked up the eight of hearts three cards ago."

"I'm betting you've got eights."

"Okay. . . . Bad bet. . . . Gin."

Brian Holbrook watched his father score up gin plus nineteen and sweep the cards together with practiced ease. The hands that had once been thick and strong enough to crush walnuts were spotted from sixty-three years in the sun and bony from almost a decade of infirmity. But they could still handle cards.

Jack Holbrook—*Black* Jack Holbrook to many for as long as Brian could remember—wasn't a professional gambler. But he dearly loved to bet. He called it wagering, and he would do it on anything from the Super Bowl to whether the next car coming around the corner would be foreign-made or domestic. Two bucks, ten, a hundred—it really didn't matter to Jack. The game was the thing. He was, and always had been, the most fiercely competitive man Brian had ever known.

Careful not to let his father see, Brian glanced at his watch. Three o'clock. They had been playing gin for almost two hours. At a penny a point, they kept a running score until one of them, invariably Jack, reached ten thousand. Brian was currently down over seventy dollars.

"How about we quit and watch the ball game?" he suggested.

"How about we ride into Boston, have an early dinner, and see that new Van Damme movie?"

"I've got to be at the club at nine."

"There's plenty of time. I don't remember the last time we spent a whole day together like this."

Jack was right about that. With two jobs and his weekly super-vised visitations with the girls, Brian was usually either on the move or dead asleep, facedown on the bedspread. The club was Aphrodite, one of the Day-Glo rock spots on Lansdowne Street, across from Fenway Park. Brian was a bouncer. At six three, 215, he fit the part well, though at thirty-eight he was a bit long in the tooth for the work. Then, of course, there was the matter of his education. An M.D. degree with board certification in internal medicine and cardiology made him an oddity among the bouncers. But without a license from the Board of Registration and Discipline in Medicine, those certifications were useful only for the bottom of a birdcage.

It was a rare totally free Sunday afternoon for him. Becky and Caitlin were away for the weekend at Phoebe's parents' place, so his weekly visitation was postponed until Tuesday. And for some reason, his boss at Speedy Rent-A-Car hadn't noticed that he failed to slot Brian for yet another Sunday in the office. A career man at Speedy, Darryl loved exercising power over people—particularly the new college grads who used the agency as their entry into the job market. He hadn't found out until well after Brian started work at the place that he was an M.D., but since then, Darryl had done his best to make up for the lost time.

Bouncer . . . car-rental gofer . . . supervised visitations with his daughters . . . living with Dad . . . Brian knew that after eighteen months of hard work—counseling, Narcotics Anonymous meetings, and endless hours with his NA sponsor, Freeman Sharpe, a building maintenance man with twenty years of recovery from heroin addiction—his internal demons were pretty much under control. But his external life still left a lot to be desired.

Brian's Saturday-night stint at Aphrodite had ended after three, so it wasn't until ten that he had gotten up. He had planned to go for a run, and then maybe hook up with some of the kids playing touch football in the park. They loved having him in their game, especially when he sent one of them deep and threw a fifty- or sixty-yard bullet spiral to him. But one glance at Jack had changed his mind. The man who had been Brian's football coach from Pop Warner to high school and on to college was wrapped in an afghan in his favorite chair, where he had been sitting up for most of the night. On the table next to him were several cardiac medications and others for pain. He looked drawn and in need of a shave.

"Got any plans for the day, Coach?" Brian asked

"Yeah. The sultan of Brunei is supposed to stop by with his harem. I told him just three for me, though."

"How about I make you some breakfast?"

Jack's gray crew cut, chiseled features, and lingering summer tan helped him look younger, *and healthier,* than he was. But Brian knew that his cardiac condition was worsening. Portions of his six-year-old quintuple bypass were almost certainly closing. Brian picked up the small vial of nitroglycerin tablets and checked inside. More than half were gone.

"How many of these did you take yesterday?" he asked.

Jack snatched the vial away and put it into his shirt pocket.

"To tell you the truth, I don't remember taking any."

"Jack, come on."

"Look, I'm fine. You just tend to your business and let me tend to mine."

"You are my business, Jack. I'm your son and I'm a cardiologist, remember?"

"No. You're a bouncer in a bar. That and a car salesman."

Brian started to react to the barb, then caught himself. Jack was probably operating on even less sleep than he was.

"You're right, Coach," Brian responded, willing his jaw to un-clench. "When I'm back to being a cardiologist again, then I can give advice. Not before. Let me toast you a bagel."

The living room of the first-story flat that Jack had owned for the ten years since his heart attack was, like the rest of the place, devoid of a woman's touch. There were sports photos on the walls and trophies on almost every surface that would hold one. Most of the awards had Brian's name on them. They were the trappings of a man who needed gleaming hardware and laminated certificates to pump up his self-esteem. When Brian had first moved in, being surrounded by all those trophies had been something of a problem for him. But Freeman Sharpe had helped him deal with his issues. *Remember, your dad loves you and he always wanted more for you than he ever wanted for himself. And if he pushes your buttons, just tell yourself that he's a master at doing that because he's the one who installed them in the first place.* And in the end, as with so many other things that had seemed like a big deal, the trophies meant nothing more than Brian chose to make them.

As he headed into the small kitchen, he glanced at one of the photographs on the wall by the doorway. It was the official photo of the UMass team taken just before the start of his fateful junior season. He was in the middle of the next-to-last row. Number 11. Then, for the first time that he could remember, his eyes were drawn to a face at the right-hand end of the very last row. Dr. Linus King, the team orthopedist. Brian had looked at the photo any number of times before—where it hung, he had no real choice. It was curious that he had never noticed the man until now. Over countless therapy sessions and countless recovery meetings, Brian had come to accept responsibility for his addiction to prescription painkillers. But if there was anyone else who bore accountability, it was King.

Brian repressed the sudden urge to slam his fist into the photo. Over the year following his reconstruction of Brian's knee, Linus King, a sports-medicine deity, was always too busy to conduct a thorough reevaluation of his work, to say nothing of sitting down to talk with his patient about persistent discomfort in the joint. Instead, he had preached patience and rehabilitation, and had prescribed hundreds of Percocets and other painkillers. Finally, a repeat MRI had disclosed a previously undiagnosed fracture. A cast and three months of rest took care of the cracked bone, but by then Brian had acquired a string of harried doctors, each willing to dash off a prescription in exchange for not having to listen. His addiction was full-blown and well-fed years before he violated the law and his own principles by writing the first prescription for himself.

"Jack, do you really think you're up for a trip into the city?" Brian asked now.

"I don't know. I think so. I'm going slightly stir-crazy, son. And beating you at gin isn't what I'd call the most challenging activity in the world."

"I'll tell you what. I'll cut cards with you. You win, it's Jean-Claude and the restaurant of your choice."

"And if I lose?"

Brian could tell his father knew what was coming.

"You lose and we still go into Boston. But you've got to promise me you'll go back and see Dr. Clarkin."

"I'm fine."

"You're not fine. It's been six years since your operation. Clarkin can revise those grafts or replace them."

"No more Clarkin, no more surgery. I've told you that a thousand times. I've had my last catheter and my last tube."

As often seemed to be the case with a physician or a physician's kin, everything that could have gone wrong postoperatively for Jack did. Heart failure, infection, graft revision, reinfection. A total of eight miserable weeks in the hospital which, in the era of managed care, spoke volumes as to how spectacularly ill he was. For many of those weeks, he literally begged to die. True, Black Jack was more stubborn than most. But having seen the man every one of those fifty-six days, Brian could hardly blame him for taking such a hard line against any return to the OR.

"All right," Brian said. "But I've never seen you chicken out of a friendly wager before."

"That's because I have a reputation for always paying up on my losses. And I know I'd end up welshing on this one. Tell you what. How about one cut: the seventy-one bucks you owe me versus you treating for dinner and the movies."

"Deal." Brian turned over the queen of clubs. "Hey, maybe my luck is changing."

Jack cut the three of diamonds. He stared at the card for a few protracted seconds.

"Maybe mine is, too," he said.

He pulled on his favorite sweater, a frayed orange cardigan

Brian's mother had given him just before her death nearly thirteen years ago.

"You gonna be warm enough if I put the top down?" Brian asked.

"Sure. . . . Um . . . son, there's something I gotta get off my chest before we leave."

"Go ahead."

"I . . . I was out of line saying what I did this morning about you not being a cardiologist."

"Don't worry about it. Besides, I never paid any attention to anything you ever said before. Why should I start now?"

"I'm frustrated, that's all. And I don't understand how you could have let this happen."

"I know, Pop. I know. Sometimes we have to hit bottom before we figure out how to really enjoy life."

"I'm sure something will come along."

Brian looked away.

"I'm sure it will," he said.

Actually, he was reasonably certain it *wouldn't*. The Board of Registration in Medicine had determined six months ago that he was in good recovery and ready to resume practice, but it was their policy in drug and alcohol cases to insist on a physician having a work situation in place with tight on-the-job monitoring and random urine testing before a license would be issued. No job, no license. It was the board's immutable law. Brian had argued that in Boston, with three medical schools and a plethora of teaching hospitals, cardiologists were more plentiful than cod. Why would anyone take a chance on hiring someone without an active license?

Two children and Jack's shaky medical situation made a move too far away from eastern Massachusetts out of the question. So Brian had done what he could, responding to ads in the cardiology press and the *New England Journal of Medicine* and sending out at least two dozen resumés. He had networked until he had absorbed more than his quota of rejections, and had seen colleagues he thought were his friends turn away. He had even placed an ad himself.

Former chief of cardiology and cath-lab director at Boston-area hospital seeks group practice in eastern Mass, Rhode Island, southern New Hampshire.

No job, no license. No license, no job. Catch-22.

Now, for the past month, he had simply stopped trying. He had stepped back and begun to mull over other directions in which his life might be ready to go. The process hadn't been easy, but there was one saving grace. Rarely, in all these frustrating months of rejection and disappointment, had he thought about drinking or taking pills.

"You ready, Pop?"

"You go on and get that top down. I'll be right there."

Jack Holbrook headed slowly toward the bathroom. When he heard the front door open and close, he quickly braced himself against the wall, fighting to slow his breathing as a skewer of pain bored up to his jaws from beneath his breastbone. He fumbled the vial of nitroglycerin from his shirt pocket and dissolved one under his tongue. Half a minute later, the pain began to subside. He wiped beaded sweat from his upper lip and took a long, grateful breath.

"Jack, everything okay?" Brian called from the front steps.

"Yeah, fine, Brian. Everything's fine."

The Towne Deli was a trendy little place on Boylston with a fine salad bar and nine-dollar sandwiches. Brian dropped his father off in front and spent ten minutes finding a parking space. Jack's condo was in Reading, a working-class suburb that straddled Route 128 northwest of the city. The ride in, beneath brilliant late-afternoon sun, was as much of a joy on Sunday as it was a nightmare during the typical morning commute. And Brian's three-year-old red LeBaron, by far the best thing he retained after the divorce, was the perfect car for the day.

During the drive, Brian knew that Jack wanted information. Any job prospects? Any new word from the board? Any interesting women? But perhaps in honor of the warmth of the day and the peace between them, his dad kept his thoughts to himself. Brian, too, avoided the inflammatory topic of his father's health. Instead, they alternated between sports and silence.

Brian entered the Towne Deli and spotted his father at a small table in the corner. For a few seconds, he stood by the front door, studying what remained of the man who had so dominated the first two decades of his life. From almost the day Brian took his first step, Coach was there, monitoring his diet, social life, and workouts, creating what he believed would be one of the great quarterbacks. And save for one play, he might have succeeded.

Jack sat motionless, staring down at the menu. Then, almost subconsciously, he began rubbing at his chest and up toward his neck. Brian hurried across to him. Beneath his tan, Jack was ashen. His eyes were glazed.

"Jack, what's going on? Are you having pain?"

Jack Holbrook took a breath through his nose and nodded.

"Some," he managed in a half-grunt.

Brian checked the carotid pulses on either side of Jack's neck. They were regular, but thready. A sheen of sweat had formed across his forehead.

"Jesus," Brian whispered. "Jack, do you have your nitro?"

Jack produced the bottle from his shirt pocket.

"Shouldn't have come into Boston," he said hoarsely.

"Nonsense," Brian said, sensing the strange, paradoxical calmness that for many years now had been his response to a medical crisis. "It wouldn't have made any difference. Come on, Pop. I'm going to sit you over here on the floor and give you one of your nitros. Do you still have that aspirin I put in your wallet? Good. Let me get it out."

Either Jack was having a bad angina attack—not enough blood flow to a portion of his heart—or he was having a full-blown coronary: a myocardial infarction in which the heart segment was getting no blood at all. If the problem was an artery obstructed by a clot, the extra aspirin might help dissolve the blockage before there was permanent damage.

"Is there a problem, sir?"

Brian looked up at the balding restaurant manager. *Of course not, I always put my father on the floor in restaurants.*

"He's a heart patient and he's having chest pain," Brian said instead.

"Should . . . should I call an ambulance? Ask if there's a doctor here?"

"I *am* a doctor," Brian said, for the first time in a year and a half. "And I think an ambulance would be an excellent idea."

Silently, Brian cursed himself for giving in to the Boston trip. Jack's internist, cardiologist, surgeon, and all his records were at Suburban Hospital, way on the other side of Route 128. It was an excellent hospital, well known for its orthopedics, rehabilitation medicine, and in some circles, for a former chief of cardiology named Brian Holbrook.

He checked Jack's pulses once again and mopped his brow.

"How's your pain, Jack? One to ten."

"Six. The nitro's helping. What are the odds it's a coronary?"

"Fifty-fifty."

"Bad odds."

"Just hang in there. The EMTs'll get a little oxygen going and give you some pain medicine, and you'll feel much better."

"Ten bucks says one of the EMTs in the ambulance is a woman. Deal?"

"Deal. Just stay cool. Do you want to lie down flat?"

"I couldn't."

In the distance, they could hear an approaching siren. Brian kept a constant check of the pulse at Jack's wrist. The perspiration, so typical of a cardiac event, seemed less heavy.

"Everything's fine, Pop. How's the pain now?"

"Ten."

"The pain is up to a ten?"

"No, you owe me ten."

Jack nodded toward the door, where a young brunette in blue EMT coveralls was on the pulling end of a stretcher. Brian introduced his father and gave a capsule summary of the situation and the limited treatment he had instituted.

"You a doctor?" The young woman asked immediately.

"A cardiologist. Brian Holbrook."

"Well, we got no pride on this team, Dr. Holbrook," she said, doing, it seemed, a dozen things at once, and doing them all well. "If there's anything we overlook, just call it out."

"Thanks. Jack's a patient at Suburban Hospital."

"Well, in a few minutes he's going to be a patient at White Memorial. That okay with you?"

White Memorial was not only the best hospital in the city, it was the home of Boston Heart Institute, one of the foremost centers of its kind. Brian flashed on the interview he had blown when applying for cardiology training there. The subsequent rejection letter was hardly a surprise. Given all that had happened to him since then, he mused, it seemed the interviewer had shown pretty good judgment.

Brian noted Jack's immediate improvement with a bit of IV morphine and some oxygen.

"Actually," he said to the young EMT, "Boston Heart is precisely where I was going to ask to have him taken."

CHAPTER TWO

BRIAN SQUEEZED INTO THE AMBULANCE FOR THE SHORT ride from Back Bay to White Memorial. His father's pain was down to a two or three by the time they left the Towne Deli. Still, throughout the ride Brian kept a watchful eye on the monitor. The absence of extra beats was a good sign, but the shape of the cardiogram wave pattern strongly suggested an acute coronary.

Jack's cardiologist at Suburban was Gary Gold, one of Brian's former partners—the only one of the four partners who had believed that Brian was recovering from an illness and should be readmitted to the practice as soon as he was ready. Silently, Brian cursed himself for not insisting that Gary be more aggressive with

Jack in pushing for a repeat cardiac catheterization and surgical evaluation. But then again, with Jack so adamantly against repeat surgery, what was there to do?

White Memorial was an architectural polyglot of a dozen or more buildings crowding four square blocks along the Charles River. All around, as with most large hospitals, there was construction in progress. Earth movers and other heavy equipment were as much a part of the scene as were ambulances, and two towering cranes rose above all but the tallest building. A new ambulatory care center, one sign proclaimed. The twenty-story future home of the Hellman Research Building, boasted another. Like the patients within, the hospital itself was in a constant cycle of disease and healing, decay and repair, death and birth.

The vast ER was in noisy but controlled disarray. The two triage nurses were backed up, and the waiting room was full. Brian took in the scene as they rushed Jack to a monitor bed in the back. The drama and energy of the place were palpable to him—his element. Merely walking into the ER made him feel as if he had been breathing oxygen under water and had suddenly popped through the surface. He had anticipated heightened emotions at reentering this world, but he was still surprised by the fullness in his chest and throat, and the sudden increased moisture in his eyes. Not that long ago he had been part of all this and his own actions had caused it to be taken away. Now, there was no telling when, or even *if,* he would ever get it back again.

"How're you doing, Jack?" Brian asked, taking his father's hand as they waited for a clean sheet to be thrown over the narrow gurney in room 6.

"Been better. The pain's gone, though."

"Great."

"Two bucks says I don't get dinner."

Brian glanced at the monitor. The elevation in the ST segment of the cardiographic tracing was less striking—definitely a good omen.

"If this place serves typical hospital food," he said, "you stand to win twice."

He helped the team transfer Jack to his bed, then stood off to one side as a resident named Ethan Prince began his rapid preliminary evaluation. Brian grudgingly gave the young man high marks for speed and thoroughness. Then he remembered where he was. Suburban was a decent enough hospital, but not one of the interns or residents there would ever get a call-back interview at White Memorial. Slip below the top ten percent of your medical school class and you didn't even bother applying.

"You know anybody here?" Jack asked Brian.

The resident, listening through his stethoscope, shushed him.

I hope not, Brian thought.

"I don't think so," he whispered.

As if on cue, he heard his name being called and looked over at the doorway. Standing there, hands on hips, was Sherry Gordon, not much older than Brian, but a grandmother several times over. She was right up there with the sharpest ER nurses Brian had ever worked with.

"Hey, you're a Suburban girl," he said, crossing to her and accepting a warm hug and kiss on the cheek. "What're you doing here?"

"Cream rises to the top. They'd had my application on file for years. Openings don't come too frequently in this place."

"You like it?"

She gestured to the chaos and smiled.

"What do you think?" She studied him intently. "So, how about you? Are you okay?"

Brian held her gaze.

"It took three months in a rehab," he replied, softly enough that only she could hear, "and about a billion AA and NA meetings, but yeah, I'm okay."

"I'm happy to hear that, Brian. Real happy. That's your dad, right? I remember that nightmare he went through at Suburban."

"Six years ago. He had an MI four years before that, then gradually his angina became too severe to bear and we went for the surgery. And you're right. It was a nightmare. And to make matters worse, the bypass wasn't even that successful. He's probably having a small MI now."

"Well, he's got a crackerjack resident going over him. Kid reminds me of you."

"I wish."

"Tell him to look into getting your dad put on Vasclear. Everyone around here has started talking about it. Listen, I've got to get back to help Dr. Gianatasio. He's got a real sick lady down the hall."

"Phil Gianatasio?"

"That's right. You know him?"

"From years ago, when we were interns, then residents, together. I had no idea he was even in Boston. This is like old home week for me. Please tell him I'm here, Sherry. I'll stop by when I'm certain my pop's stable. Would that be okay?"

"I don't see why not. Got to run. Good luck with your dad."

Vasclear. Brian knew next to nothing about the drug, and most of what he did know he had learned from the newspapers. He wasn't as medically current as in the days when he was attending cardiology rounds twice a week and reading or skimming a dozen different journals. But he had kept up fairly well through tapes and two courses, and Vasclear, the latest in a long line of experimental drugs aimed at reducing arteriosclerosis, simply hadn't been written about widely.

Ethan Prince freed his stethoscope from his ears, reviewed Jack's EKG again, then passed it over to Brian. Brian accepted it calmly, consciously trying to keep his eagerness and gratitude hidden from the younger physician. There was still a persistent two-millimeter elevation in the ST segment in several of the twelve standard views in the tracing.

"Looks like some persistent anterior injury," Brian said.

"I agree. I'll get the wheels in motion for his admission. Meanwhile, we've got to decide whether to attempt to melt the blockage. Before we do that, I'll try and get him a cardiologist. Dr. Gianatasio is on first backup, but he's got all he can handle with a very sick woman in four. I'll have to find out who's on second call." He turned to Jack, whose color had improved significantly. "Mr. Holbrook, it appears you're having a very small blockage, and as a result a part of your heart is not getting enough blood."

"A heart attack," Jack said. "It's okay. You can say it."

"Actually, we won't be certain it's a full heart attack until we see some blood tests and another cardiogram."

"Two bucks says it is."

"Pardon?"

"Never mind him," Brian said, taking Jack's hand again. "He was a football lineman in school—offense *and* defense. Too many blows to the helmet."

"I see. . . . Well, I'd better get going. I need to find out who's on cardiology backup and I need to get back in with Dr. Gianatasio."

"Just one quick thing. Sherry Gordon said I should look into Vasclear."

The resident shrugged. "You probably know as much about it as I do. It's a Boston Heart research drug. Rumor has it the results have been really promising."

"Thanks."

"Anesthesia," the overhead page sounded . . . *"Anesthesia to the ER stat. . . ."*

"That lady in four must be going down the chute. I guess they're calling anesthesia to intubate her."

Ethan Prince hurried away, leaving a nurse tending to Jack. Brian shifted uncomfortably from one foot to the other, aware of feeling impotent and embarrassed. Just down the hall a cardiac patient was in serious trouble. Brian was another pair of skilled hands, another cardiologist for Phil Gianatasio to bat ideas off of.

Yet for all the good he could do anyone at this point, he might as well be a high school dropout.

"Dr. Holbrook?"

The stocky, dark-haired nurse standing by the door had the bearing of someone with authority. Her expression was grim.

"Yes?"

"Dr. Holbrook, I'm Carol Benoit, the head nurse down here. I'm sorry to interrupt, but Dr. Prince told me your father was quite stable. Could I speak with you for a moment?"

"Of course."

"Dr. Holbrook, there's a critically ill woman in room four. Dr. Gianatasio asked if you'd mind going in there."

Brian felt an immediate adrenaline rush.

"I'd be happy to," he replied, perhaps too eagerly.

He glanced at Jack, who was resting comfortably, eyes closed. His respirations were not at all labored and his monitor pattern was regular. There would be no problem in leaving him for a short while. Brian took a step toward the door, but the head nurse continued to block his way. She motioned him to a spot in the hall, out of earshot of both Jack and the staff.

"Before you go in there," she said in a stern half-whisper, "I want you to know that I insisted Sherry Gordon tell me who you are and at what hospital you are working. She told me you had lost your license."

"So?"

"And when I pushed her for an explanation, she told me why."

Brian's reaction to the woman had blossomed from a kernel of wariness into full-blown mistrust. He pulled himself up to his full height plus half an inch or so.

"Get to the point," he said.

"I don't want anyone without a valid license practicing medicine on any patient on my emergency ward."

"Frankly, I don't see where sharing my experience and ideas is practicing medicine."

Carol Benoit's eyes were hard.

"I'll be in there watching," she said.

Brian stepped back into the room to reassure Jack that he'd be nearby and would be right back. Then he flexed a bit of tension from his neck and headed over to room 4.

It had been ten years since Brian and Phil Gianatasio were in training at Eastern Mass Medical Center. They had worked well together during those two years. Phil seemed at ease with Brian's flamboyance and self-confidence, and Brian appreciated that Phil, more steady and meticulous than brilliant, always worked within his limitations and was never afraid to ask for help. After residency, Brian had won a cardiac fellowship at one of the finest hospitals in Chicago, and Phil had temporized by enlisting in the service—the Army, Brian thought. At first, they had exchanged a few letters and calls. Gradually, though, their connection weakened, then simply vanished.

Phil greeted him from the far side of the gurney. He had always been overweight, but since residency he must have gained twenty pounds. His dark hair was yielding to an expanding bald spot on top and was longer in the back than Brian remembered. One thing that hadn't changed a bit was the warmth and kindness in his face. At this moment, though, Phil looked worried. It was not difficult to see why.

On the gurney, unconscious and clearly toxic, was a disheveled woman with graying red hair in her late sixties or early seventies. Her grunting respirations were barely moving air, and the paleness around her eyes and mouth were a frightening contrast to the crimson of the rest of her face. Also in the room were Dr. Ethan Prince, Sherry, another nurse, the anesthesiologist, and, over in one corner, an older man with a rumpled suit and a stethoscope protruding from his jacket pocket. The woman's private physician, Brian guessed. It was just a snap judgment, but the man seemed ill at ease in the face of such a crisis. Just inside the doorway, observing more than participating, stood Carol Benoit.

Monitor pattern . . . cardiac rate . . . pulse oximeter reading . . . complexion . . . fingernail-bed coloring . . . cooling blanket. . . . By the time Brian had gone from the doorway to the bedside, his mind had processed a hundred bits of information. He breathed in the action and the urgency. It would only be for a few fleeting minutes, but for now that didn't matter.

"Brian, you're a sight for sore eyes," Phil said. "Like one of those gods in Greek tragedy who pops out of the wall of the theater just when he's needed."

"Hey, careful. I'm through doing the god thing. It ended up causing me nothing but trouble. What's the scoop here?"

"Well, Mrs. Violet Corcoran is a sixty-eight-year-old patient of Dr. Dixon's. That's Fred Dixon right there. Fred, Brian Holbrook." Brian and the older doctor exchanged nods. "As far as Fred knows, she's never been really sick before this week."

Something in Phil's tone suggested that merely having Dixon as one's physician carried with it certain health risks. But the man *had* come in to see his patient on a Sunday afternoon, and in Brian's mind, that negated a certain amount of clinical incompetence.

"He was treating her with some erythro for an upper-respiratory infection," Phil went on. "A couple of hours ago her husband called in that she wasn't looking so good. Her temp's one-oh-four. Pulse one-forty. She's got a pretty dense left-lower-lobe pneumonia. BP was one-sixty. Now it's down to one hundred."

"Septic shock?"

"Probably. But look what she's doing."

Phil indicated the cardiac-monitor screen, which now showed a heart-rhythm pattern Brian was almost certain was sustained ventricular tachycardia. V. tach of this sort was very unstable in most situations, and was often a precursor of full-blown cardiac arrest.

"I read V. tach," Brian said.

"We all agree. She's been in and out of it since she arrived. Short bursts at first. Now, more prolonged."

"Treatment?"

"We're working our way through the pharmacy. So far we've tried Xylocaine, bretylium, and Pronestyl, and we're about to give her a hit of digitalis. Nothing's touched it."

"She's going too fast to guide her out of it with a pacemaker."

"Exactly."

Brian motioned toward Phil's stethoscope.

"May I?"

Carol Benoit had seen and heard enough.

"Dr. Gianatasio," she cut in, "I'm sorry to have to remind you, but Dr. Holbrook has no license to be treating or touching our patients."

For a few seconds there was no movement in the room, no sound save for the soft gurgle of the oxygen bottle. Then Gianatasio slipped his stethoscope from his neck, rounded the gurney, and handed it to the head nurse.

"Okay, then, Ms. Benoit," he said without rancor, "suppose you evaluate this woman and give us your considered opinion."

Benoit's face grew pinched and flushed. She pushed the proffered instrument back at Phil and moved away.

"Suit yourself," she said. "But I'm holding you responsible for whatever happens."

"I'll take my chances. Brian, if you don't come up with something we haven't tried, I'm going to have Sule, here, intubate her and we'll take a crack at shocking her out of this."

Brian took Phil's Littmann stethoscope and moved to the bedside.

"Without figuring out the underlying reason she's in that rhythm and doing something about it," he said, "I don't think zapping her with a lightning bolt would make any difference."

"It could be just massive infection in a woman with some preexisting heart disease."

"Maybe."

"Whatever it is, be quick, Brian. She's in it again."

Brian first scanned Violet Corcoran, head to feet. There was something about her, something that reminded him of a case he had seen somewhere in his training. *Where? What was it?* He felt over her heart, then her neck, then the arterial pulses at her elbow, wrist, and groin. Finally, he slipped the earpieces of Gianatasio's Littmann into place, and worked the diaphragm side of the stethoscope over her heart, chest, and neck. Next he repeated the exam using the bell side.

"Sule, go ahead and intubate her," Phil said. "Then we've got to try shocking her. Damn! This is getting out of hand fast."

Brian didn't respond. He was completely immersed in a sound—a sound coming from the front of Violet's neck. And suddenly, he remembered. To his left, the anesthesiologist had slipped in an endotracheal breathing tube so smoothly that Brian had not even realized she was doing it.

"We'll try two hundred joules once, then go right to three-fifty," Phil ordered.

"Wait!" Brian said, indicating the spot on Violet's neck. "Phil, listen to this."

The easily heard humming sound, Brian was nearly certain, was a bruit—the noise of turbulence caused in this case, he believed, by blood rushing through a markedly overactive thyroid gland.

"Pressure's dropping," Sherry Gordon said. "Ninety."

Phil listened for a few seconds.

"I heard that sound when I first examined her, but I thought it was a murmur transmitted up from her heart."

"I don't."

"Thyroid?"

"I'm almost sure of it. I've only seen one case of thyroid storm in my life, but this looks just like it. High temp, wild pulse, coma, increasing stretches of V. tach."

Gianatasio listened to the sound again.

"Could be," he said excitedly. "Dammit all, it just could be. Fred, does this lady have any history of hyperthyroidism?"

Fred Dixon flipped through his office notes and lab reports.

"Eighty," Sherry called out.

"Well," Dixon said, his voice a bit shaky, "I noted a slightly elevated thyroid level at the time of her physical a year ago. But people her age get *underactive* thyroids, not overactive, and besides I didn't think——"

"Brian, where do we go from here?" Phil cut in.

"Call an endocrinologist. But I would say in the meantime, massive doses of steroids, high doses of IV propranolol to block the effect of the hormone on her heart, and then some sort of specific chemical blockade of thyroid hormone production as well. The endocrinologist or a book can tell us what and how much."

"Let's go with it," Gianatasio said. "Ms. Benoit, find out who's on for endocrine and get 'em down here or on the phone as quickly as possible. If it's the phone, put Dr. Holbrook on. Then get over to the residents' lounge, please, and get me Harrison's *Principles of Internal Medicine* and the fattest endocrinology textbook you can find. If there's none at least two inches thick, go to the library. The rest of you, listen up, please. We're sailing into some uncharted waters. . . ."

CHAPTER THREE

"NO AUTOGRAPHS. NO AUTOGRAPHS, PLEASE. I'M SORRY, but Dr. Holbrook won't be signing any more autographs today."

Fending off an imaginary crowd, Phil Gianatasio backed into room 6.

Brian, alone in the room with Jack, watched from the bedside, amused.

"If you don't stop that shit," he said, "I'm going to autograph that butt of yours."

"Ah, and what a butt it has become!" Gianatasio exclaimed, slapping himself on the behind. "A rhino rear. Hippo hindquarters. Magnificent! Why, you could sign your autograph and write your autobiography, and possibly still have room for a sonnet or two. God, Holbrook, what a save you just pulled off. What . . . a . . . save! Ol' Violet hasn't just dodged a bullet, she's dodged a friggin' howitzer shell!"

"What's going on?" Jack muttered, rousing from a Valium twilight.

Jack hadn't totally dodged his bullet, but it appeared he had suffered no more than a flesh wound. His initial blood tests had confirmed that, in fact, he had suffered a myocardial infarction—a coronary—although all indications were that the heart attack was a small one and not immediately life-threatening. But at sixty-three, with his history, Jack was definitely functioning on borrowed time.

Even though Brian was thrilled over the Corcoran save, he remained determined to keep his feelings in check and to allow Gianatasio to display enough exuberance for both of them. He motioned Phil to sit down.

"What's the latest?" he asked.

Gianatasio sank down gratefully.

"The latest is that this guy just wandered down from the last row of the bleachers with the bases loaded and two outs in the bottom of the ninth inning and struck out the grim reaper on three pitches. That's the latest."

Brian turned to his father.

"Pop, this overgrown child here is Phil Gianatasio. You probably don't remember, but we were residents together back in the dark ages."

"Of course I remember. Father owned a restaurant. Pretty dark-haired wife."

Jack pushed his hand though the side rail of the gurney, and Phil took it.

"Your memory's absolutely amazing," Phil said. "Dad's still got the restaurant, and Joanne is still the pretty, dark-haired wife . . . but alas, not mine.

"Brian's divorced, too," Jack said, making no attempt to mask his dismay.

"No more Phoebe?" Phil cocked an eyebrow.

"Separated two years ago. Officially divorced a little over a year ago," Brian said, feeling his elation start to fade. "We have two little girls."

"Doesn't sound like you're too happy about it."

Brian shrugged. "The breakup certainly wasn't my idea, if that's what you mean. Phoebe married me expecting little doc on the prairie, and she ended up with little doc in the rehab."

Phil laughed ruefully.

"Joanne got big doc in the hospital—all the time. Especially since I landed here three years ago.

"Kids?"

"Maybe next time. But enough about me. Mr. Holbrook, do you know what your son just did? In those few minutes while you were snoozing away, he plucked an incredibly obscure diagnosis out of thin air and saved a sweet little old lady's life."

"That's nice," Jack said, with no enthusiasm.

He rolled over and faced the wall.

Phil looked over at Brian, who could only shake his head. He should never have mentioned rehab. Jack was tough as nails in most areas, but not that one.

"Later," he mouthed.

Phil nodded sympathetically. He was a doctor. He had a father. He knew about the pressure of expectations.

"Well," Phil said, clearing his throat for transition, "as you can tell, the news from next door is good. Real good. Endocrine is with her now. He totally agrees with the diagnosis and treatment. The thyroid-storm buzz has already started zipping throughout the hospital. This place absolutely lives for cases like this one. And there I was, right in the middle of it, and I missed it."

"You were too close. You had to worry about keeping her alive."

"You always were kind."

"It's the truth."

Brian was interrupted by his father, who answered the question about his wakefulness with an Olympian snore.

"You used to sound just like that in the on-call room," Gianatasio said. "I had no idea it was genetic."

"Phil, tell me about this Vasclear."

Gianatasio's expression became intense.

"It's the real deal, Brian. The closest thing medical science has come up with to a fountain of youth."

"What is it?"

"Part phospholipid, part enzyme. Originally taken from a tree bark this guy Art Weber found in South America. Now it's been synthesized by the chemists over at Newbury Pharmaceuticals on the south side of the city. Brian, it unplugs arteries."

"For real?"

"The before-and-after arteriograms are stunning."

"What's the downside?"

Gianatasio shook his head.

"I know this is hard to believe, but Boston Heart is just nearing the end of tightly controlled, double-blind Phase Two clinical trials, and so far, there *is* no downside."

Brian sensed his pulse quicken. He was like an oncologist suddenly hearing of a universal cure for cancer with none of the side effects of conventional chemotherapy. Despite Jack's sonorous breathing, he lowered his voice to an urgent whisper.

"Phil, how can I get my father put on it?"

"I'm not sure. Who's his doctor?"

"He hasn't got one yet. The resident was phoning the guy on call after you."

"Oh, God, no. Bart Rutstein takes private patients only because he can't get enough research money to keep his gene-splicing lab going *and* feed his five kids. I'll take care of your dad if you want. But I have a better idea. Carolyn Jessup is the clinical director of the Vasclear program. She has a huge private practice, and a lot of her patients are in the study. We should see if we can get her to accept your dad as a patient."

"Carolyn Jessup! Getting her to take care of Pop under *any* circumstances would be great. I took her cardiac-cath course a couple of years ago. It was the best one of its kind I've ever been to."

Brian flashed on the tall, elegantly dressed woman of fifty or so, striding confidently across the stage of the lecture hall before 150 cardiologists from all over the world—a consummate teacher and clinician, still graced with the cool good looks of a high-fashion model.

"That course fills up the day it's announced," Phil said. "For good reason. Jessup's a bit on the distant side, she can be a little intimidating at times, but she's a really fine doc. When I came here, they were searching for a new chief of the institute. Everyone thought she was a shoo-in for the job. I still don't know why she didn't get it. Maybe her manner—she can be pretty aloof—maybe her gender, maybe she's not political enough. Goodness knows she's published enough."

"Ernest Pickard got the job, right?"

"From the NIH. Exactly."

"Well, he's no small fish, himself."

"Hardly. And he's actually done a great job with this place. It's to both their credit that there's been no acrimony between them since he took over. And you know the hospital grapevine as well as I do. If there'd been so much as a sideways glance from one at the other, someone would have picked up on it and started the drums beating."

"Could you call her?" Brian asked.

"I could and I will. If she's not around this evening, she'll surely be in tomorrow. However, I ought to explain that although I *am* up for tenure, and she certainly knows who I am, I'm still a few dozen rungs below her on the academic ladder."

"Hey, tenure at the world's greatest medical school and Boston Heart! God, Phil, that's great. I'm really proud of you."

There was a moment of awkward silence.

"Brian, I wasn't shoving that tenure business in your face," Phil said finally. "I hope you know that."

"Believe me," Brian replied, "if I know nothing else, I know that. Besides, I had my chances and made my choices just like you did. I maybe could have gotten help sooner, but I never thought there was anything wrong, or at least anything I couldn't handle. I don't ever want you or anyone else walking on eggshells around me because of what's happened. For as long as I can remember, I was leading my life in fast-forward, like one of those space rockets that has to go a certain speed to break free of the earth's gravity. Now, I've gotten to see that the trick for me is learning how to achieve breakthroughs in my life by going *slower*. I'm still not very good at it—my lowest gear is still higher than most people's highest—but I'm getting better."

"I can tell," Phil said. "I can see it in your eyes. Listen, about Vasclear."

"Yes?"

"Like I said, the drug's still in a double-blind study of three treatment strengths—low-dose, high-dose, and placebo. The treatment groups are labeled alpha, beta, and gamma, but because the double-blind code hasn't been broken yet, nobody knows for certain which is which, not Jessup, not even Art Weber, the guy who discovered the drug. He's the project director from the pharmaceutical company."

And Brian knew that was as it should be. A double-blind study was the only completely valid way to evaluate a new drug. To eliminate bias as much as possible, neither the patient, nor the treater, nor the evaluators of the treatment knew whether the medication being given was active or placebo. That information belonged only to the computer that set up the treatment groups and dispensed the drug. Ideally, there would also be a crossover mid-way through the study time frame, when the group being treated with placebo and the group getting the active drug would be switched, still maintaining secrecy as to which was which.

"But if the drug is doing as well as you say," Brian pointed out, "surely everyone must have an idea which group is which."

"There's no question in our minds that the beta group's on the high dose. That's where most of the remarkable results are coming from. But the computer hasn't seen enough data to authorize breaking the code. I think that's because the number of patients is still so low. Since they went to Phase Two a couple of years ago, there've only been about six hundred patients. That's two hundred in each treatment group. But even so, I've been hearing rumors that the code may be broken soon. I've even heard the drug may end up on the market before long—the results are that good."

"Well, that'll be great for the world, but maybe too late for Jack. Make it happen if you can, Phil. Please. The poor guy's been through a lot."

"So the resident tells me." Gianatasio checked the time. "Well, I'd better see how things are going with Stormy. That's how Violet Corcoran will now and forever be known at WMH. Jack's going up to the CCU soon. I'll be up to see him as soon as—"

A softly cleared throat from the doorway got their attention. A tall, angular, well-dressed man was standing there.

"Ernest," Phil exclaimed.

"I was doing some work in the office when word filtered up to me of a remarkable save down here. I came down to thank the men responsible for it."

Phil introduced Brian to the BHI chief as the man who really deserved the credit for what went on in room 4.

"I'd love to take the bow," Phil said, "but the only truly brilliant thing I did was to call in my old friend here for a consult."

"Sometimes, calling in the right consult is the only truly brilliant thing one *can* do. I'm pleased to meet you, Dr. Holbrook." Pickard's handshake was confident, his speech measured and cultured. "But unless I'm mistaken," he continued, "we've met before."

"Excuse me?"

"In a manner of speaking, that is. I was at the Harvard game when you threw five touchdown passes against us. That was you, yes?"

"It was."

"Well, that was quite a performance."

"Maybe, but your guys had much higher SAT scores than we did."

Pickard's bass laugh was genuine.

"Probably so," he said. "Probably so. The day I saw you play, I thought for sure you'd end up in the pros, you were that good."

Brian exchanged a glance with Gianatasio, then said simply, "It didn't happen."

"Well, that was medicine's gain, and our gain in particular, if what I've been hearing is true. So, please, tell me what went on in there."

"If it's all right with you, Ernest," Phil interjected, "I'll go check on the lady in question. Come down after you two have had the chance to talk."

Pickard pulled the two chairs in the room away from the bed, and motioned Brian to one of them.

"That's your father, I understand."

"He was our coach during that game you watched."

"He must be very proud of you."

Brian wondered how much Pickard knew about him and his situation. He glanced at Jack, then at the monitor screen.

"Sometimes," he said.

"He's stable right now?"

"For the moment."

"Excellent. Well, I've been told you diagnosed thyroid storm after just a two-minute exam in a lady who was in extremis."

"I saw a case during my fellowship. She looked exactly like that one."

"Remarkable. Take me through what you saw."

For a man of his stature and responsibilities, Pickard seemed relaxed and unhurried. Brian took him step-by-step through his evaluation, noting the clues in Violet Corcoran's history, cardiographic pattern, and physical findings that led him to the diagnosis.

The BHI chief listened intently. When the tale was completed and a few clarifying questions answered, he stood and shook Brian's hand.

"That was a wonderful piece of deduction under pressure," he said. "I congratulate you, and hope you'll repeat your part in this case when she's presented at Grand Rounds."

"Of course."

"And if there's ever anything I can do, please feel free to ask."

Pickard turned to leave, then turned back when Brian said, "As a matter of fact, there is. I've been told that Dr. Jessup is the director of the Vasclear study."

"Correct."

"I wonder if you could prevail on her to take my father on as her patient."

"I believe I can do that. Carolyn is at home right now. I spoke to her not an hour ago. But I must caution you that I have no influence whatsoever as to who gets put in the Vasclear program and who doesn't. That's strictly up to Dr. Weber and Dr. Jessup."

"I understand."

"Very well, then," Pickard said. "I'll give Carolyn a call as soon as I've seen this patient of yours."

Again he turned to leave. Again he turned back when Brian spoke.

"Dr. Pickard, there is one more thing," Brian heard himself saying.

"Yes?"

"If it's at all possible, I really need a job."

CHAPTER FOUR

THE GLEAMING, STATE-OF-THE-ART CARDIAC CATHETER-
ization laboratory of the Boston Heart Institute was located on the
basement level. Brian walked alongside his father's gurney as Jack
was wheeled through the corridors of White Memorial and over to
Boston Heart.

Two days had passed since Jack's small coronary, and as his new
doctor, Carolyn Jessup, had predicted, he had encountered no complications. Now it was time to take a look at the status of his
coronary arteries and to make some decisions about his future
treatment. The one treatment option that would not be available to
them was Vasclear. Through Ernest Pickard's intervention, Jessup

had agreed to take Jack on as a patient. But the protocol for the Vasclear study, which was being followed to the letter, specifically excluded patients with a history of bypass surgery.

"Five to two says she kills me down there," Jack said.

Jack groused constantly about having the catheterization, but Jessup had met surprisingly little resistance in talking him into it. It seemed to Brian that the coach might be developing something of a crush on his elegant physician. The notion made him smile.

"Nonsense," Brian replied. "She's the best there is at this."

"I thought *you* were the best there is."

"That doesn't count."

Although the prospect of getting Jack treated with Vasclear seemed dim at the moment, Brian's chances for a job at BHI were getting a bit brighter. Yesterday, between his shifts at Speedy and Aphrodite, he had gone up to Ernest Pickard's fifth-floor corner office, overlooking the Charles, and had spent nearly half an hour with the BHI chief, talking about his life, his addiction, and his recovery. In the end, Pickard gave no indication of what he was thinking, but later that evening Brian had found a message on his answering machine from his former partner Gary Gold, saying that Pickard had called to get Gary's opinion of him.

The man from transportation wheeled Jack to the holding area. Brian, invited to observe by Jessup, went to the carpeted locker room, changed into scrubs, and then entered the lab. Of the many areas of cardiology, he had always enjoyed catheterizations the most. There was an energy and tension in performing the procedure he had always found akin to what he used to feel playing quarterback. There was the need for steady hands and a delicate touch, plus the ability to transpose the two dimensions seen on a TV monitor into the three dimensions of a patient's heart. And of course, there was the ever-looming specter of a cardiac crisis.

Now, alone in the lab, he mentally walked himself through the cath that Carolyn Jessup would be performing on his father. The first step would involve local anesthesia to Jack's right groin and the "blind" insertion through the skin of two long, thin, hollow catheters—one into his femoral vein, then up the vena cava, and into the right atrium and ventricle of the heart; and the other right next to it, into his femoral artery, then up the aorta, and into the two corresponding chambers on the *left* side of the heart. The separate catheters were necessary because, except in certain congenital and disease conditions, there was no direct connection between the right chambers, which pumped blood to the lungs, and the left, which received blood from the lungs and pumped it through the aorta to the coronary arteries and the rest of the body.

Once the catheters were in place, as verified by a squirt of X-ray dye, blood pressures would be measured in the various chambers and vessels. Next, the left-side catheter would be repositioned inside Jack's right, then left, coronary arteries, the two main vessels that branched off the aorta to supply blood to the heart muscle. X-ray contrast material would be injected into the arteries while a video camera recorded the flow and simultaneously projected it onto the monitor screen. The arteries would then be viewed from eight different angles.

Grateful to be back in his milieu, if only as an outsider, Brian examined the mechanized table, the powerful X-ray camera, and the various types of catheters hanging in sterile cellophane packets from labeled hooks along one wall. He was looking over the crash cart when his father was wheeled into the room by the cath tech, a tall, rail-thin black man who introduced himself as Andrew.

"Dr. Jessup left word to expect you," he said. "She'll be down shortly. Welcome to the lab."

"How about you put me down as a no-show and take me back to my room," Jack said.

"Is your father always like this?" Andrew chided.

"Oh, no. Not at all. He's probably this mellow because he's been premedicated."

The room, which seemed quite spacious when Brian wandered it alone, began filling rapidly. The console-room nurse arrived next, took her place behind the glass wall, and began readying her monitoring and recording equipment. Moments later, the scrub nurse entered from the women's dressing room, gowned herself, then pulled on a pair of gloves and began preparing her instrument tray. Brian helped Andrew move Jack from the gurney to the mechanized fluoroscopy table.

"Jesus, Brian, this is like being set down on a slab of ice. There's no reason they couldn't put a little heating coil in these tables. None at all. A little cushioning, too. Don't X rays go through cushioning? Hey, Andrew, how about a pillow. I can have a pillow, right?"

Brian knew that Jack's machine-gun speech and litany of complaints meant only that he was scared stiff. Andrew, apparently appreciating the same thing, put his hand reassuringly on Jack's shoulder. Brian knew his assessment was right when Jack made no attempt to move it away.

"Good morning, everyone."

Carolyn Jessup entered from the women's lounge and took command of the room instantly. She wore a paper hair-covering and mask, loose scrubs, and tennis sneakers, and looked as engaging in that outfit as she did in her lecture suit. Her first stop was at Jack's side.

"Have you been behaving, Jack?" she asked.

"Complaining, but behaving. You look very mysterious, with just your eyes showing like that."

Brian groaned inwardly. Suddenly, Black Jack Holbrook, the man whose glare set 270-pound linemen onto their bellies for twenty push-ups, was a puppy dog.

"All women look alluring and mysterious in this getup," Jessup said. "That's why there's such a clamor for jobs in the OR. Before we begin, do you have any questions?"

"None, except what am I doing here?"

"Without these pictures, we're just about blindfolded in trying to figure out what to do to help you."

"As long as one of the choices isn't surgery."

Brian had discussed with Jessup the aftermath of Jack's catastrophic post-op course.

"He'd probably be willing to go along with just about anything," Brian told her that first night, "except repeat bypass."

The expression in Jessup's eyes was knowing.

"We'll see," she said.

Now, she bent down to whisper a few words of encouragement and then crossed over to the scrub nurse, who helped her glove and gown.

Let the games begin, Brian thought, noting how small and frail his father looked, sandwiched as he was between the table and the massive fluoroscopic camera.

Gloved, gowned, and masked, Carolyn approached the table, polled the console nurse and each person in the room with her eyes to ensure they were ready, and began. Her movements were economical and assured. Her skill at inserting the large-bore guide needles into the femoral artery and vein was unerring.

"Brian, I've sent for his old films from Suburban," she said, threading the long catheters up without breaking tempo. "They should be here later today."

"It's been about four years since he was done last, so I'm not certain how much help the films will be. You know, I don't think I've ever seen an arterial catheter quite like that."

"That's very observant of you. It's a prototype from Ward-Dunlop, the surgical supply people. We've been working on the development of this catheter with them for three years. Right now, we're one of several institutions evaluating it. It's all we use here."

"I can see why. It looks like a definite improvement over the one that we were using."

"It is. In another year or so, we expect every cath lab in the country to be using them. Hey, Jack, are you still with me?"

"I'm with you. . . . But I'd rather be with you in Hawaii."

Jack's speech had slowed and thickened. His eyes were closed. The pre-op medication had kicked in right on schedule.

"Good," Jessup said. "If anything hurts or bothers you, just shout out."

"I will."

"Now, Jack, I want you to know that I've asked another doctor to stop by and look at these arteries of yours with me."

"Fine by me. Whatever you say."

"His name is Dr. Randa. He's the chief of the surgical unit here at BHI."

"No surgery," Jack managed.

"I understand that's how you feel, Jack," she said with, it seemed to Brian, a hint of flirtatiousness in her voice, "and right now I'm not suggesting anything. Just a consult. He's just going to look at the films and say hello. Okay?"

"If . . . you . . . say . . . so."

Brian was pleased to hear his father capitulate so easily, although he was well aware of the role sedation was playing in Jessup's small victory. He was also elated that Laj Randa was being called in on the case, even though he had once heard the surgeon described as two velvet hands on a 130-pound asshole.

As Jessup advanced the catheters into Jack's heart, she checked their position by shooting in a small burst of X-ray opaque dye and turning on the X-ray camera for short exposures using a toe pedal on the floor. Brian was not surprised that she checked much less frequently than most operators. She performed the pressure measurements and brief injections of the chambers on the right side of the heart, then turned her attention to the more important left side, and Jack's coronary arteries in particular.

"Okay," she said. "Let's start with the right coronary. Left anterior oblique view, please, Andrew."

The tech adjusted the position of the huge camera to the first of what would be eight different views, and Carolyn Jessup did the first injection of dye. In between glances at the EKG monitor and at his father, Brian studied Jack's coronary arteries on the video display. With each injection, the arterial tree lit up bright white against the pulsating gray of the heart itself. Although the main vessels followed a similar pathway from patient to patient, the overall pattern of the arteries was actually as unique and individual as fingerprints.

Jack's vessels were as bad as Brian had feared. There were arteriosclerotic plaques blocking portions of nearly every artery that mattered. Two of the grafts from his previous surgery appeared to have closed. For three decades of marriage, Jack and Shirley Holbrook had drunk and smoked to excess. After her death from alcohol-induced jaundice and kidney failure, Jack had stopped drinking altogether. He stopped smoking a year or two after that, but much cigarette-related damage had already been done.

After the final injection of the left coronary—the so-called Widowmaker Artery, Brian whistled softly through his teeth and looked away. Jessup turned from the table to face him.

"Not a pretty picture," she said softly.

Jessup was withdrawing the catheters when the door to the men's locker room burst open, and Laj Randa strode into the cath lab, followed at a respectful distance by two of his fellows. The surgical chief was no more than five feet four, with café-au-lait skin, a short black beard, and piercing dark eyes. He wore a royal blue silk turban and had a steel bracelet on his right wrist. *A Sikh,* Brian thought. *Mystical, deeply religious, persecuted in the Punjab of northern India for centuries.* He had trained with a Sikh during his fellowship. The man was as determined, as opinionated and intense, as anyone he had ever known. If Randa was equally fervent, the hair beneath his turban had never been cut, and most of his beard was actually rolled up tightly beneath his chin.

"So, Carolyn," Randa said, breezing past Brian, "this man is how old?"

His accent was a mix of British and Indian.

"Sixty-three. He—"

"And who did his previous surgery?"

"Steve Clarkin at Suburban did a quintuple bypass six years ago," Brian said.

Randa stopped short and turned slowly to Brian, who towered over him.

"And you are?"

"Jack's son, Brian Holbrook. I'm a—"

Randa had already turned away.

"Carolyn, could you have your nurse run the film for me."

Jessup nodded to the control-room nurse, who could hear everything they were saying. Surely Randa knew that, too, Brian thought. He could have simply asked the nurse himself. *A 130-pound asshole*. Whoever had made that assessment obviously knew what he was talking about.

Moments later, Jack's catheterization began to replay on the monitor.

"See," Randa said to his sycophants, "only three grafts are left open and one of them is nearly closed. Typical result for Clarkin."

The remark was inappropriate under any circumstances, but doubly so in the presence of Clarkin's patient. Jessup, obviously used to the surgeon, seemed unfazed.

"So," Randa said as soon as the screen went dark, "are you planning on treating this man with your magic juice?"

"Laj, let's not get into this here."

"I read an article about your drug in the *Boston Herald*. The *Herald*! Why not the *National Enquirer*?"

"I don't know where the lay press is getting its information about Vasclear," Jessup said patiently.

"Obviously someone is feeding it to them. I don't like getting my medical information through the tabloids. From the beginning of science, methods have evolved to inform the scientific community of a new discovery. They do not include the *Boston Herald*."

"I've got half a dozen academic papers on the drug accepted or already published in very prestigious journals. The FDA has thousands of pages of our research documentation and dozens of our angiograms. Now please, Laj. Let's discuss this someplace else. As for your question about this patient, our double-blind research protocol bars anyone from Vasclear treatment who has had bypass surgery, so Mr. Holbrook doesn't qualify."

"Whatever you say."

Randa walked past her to the table. Brian could see Jack's eyes open, then close. He was awake and very much aware.

"I am Dr. Randa," the surgical chief said, not bothering to shake Jack's hand or even to ensure that he was awake. "Your arteriograms show a great deal of arteriosclerotic blockage throughout the arteries of your heart. You would benefit from bypass surgery as soon as possible. Dr. Jessup will go over the details with you and set up a time. I would suggest if there is an opening in my schedule, that you have the procedure done before you go home. Otherwise, you should be at bed rest until something can be arranged. One of my fellows will be up to see you later today. Good day, Carolyn."

"Thanks for coming down," she said as he was heading out the door.

Brian went immediately to his father.

"You okay?" he asked.

"No surgery," Jack said.

"We'll do our best. But listen, Pop, I don't want to lose you, and the girls would be devastated. I'll do my best to protect you from surgery, but whatever it takes, I'm going to recommend, including a repeat bypass. I need your promise that you'll go along with that. Jack?"

There was a prolonged silence.

"I don't like that guy," Jack said finally.

"You don't have to like him, Jack," Jessup said. "You just have to believe us that he's one of the very best in the world at what he does."

She motioned Brian across the room and out of Jack's earshot.

"Randa's an absolute boor, I know," she said. "But trust me, he really is a wizard in the OR. Lately, he's even more unbearable than usual because of our research. I can't believe he isn't feeling very threatened by the Vasclear results we've been getting."

"If what I've been hearing is correct, I understand why. He'd be like a blacksmith watching a Model T Ford rumbling up the road. Dr. Jessup, about putting Jack on Vasclear—"

The cardiologist shook her head.

"I'm sorry, Brian. In almost three years of research we haven't broken protocol once. Not once. The only thing I can promise you is that I'll mention the situation to Dr. Art Weber, the project director from Newbury Pharmaceuticals. But you know, even if he said yes, which is doubtful, Jack would have to be randomized into the study like every other patient. That gives him only a thirty-three percent chance of getting into the maximum-treatment group and an equal chance of getting placebo."

"I understand, but please, do what you can. If we really push, there's a possibility we could talk Jack into surgery. He's taken to you like no other doctor he's ever had. But if we can manage him with medications alone, we really owe it to him to try that."

"Well, we might be able to buy some time by juggling his meds. I have a few ideas that might help the situation, especially after seeing his pressures on this cath. And I will speak with Dr. Weber, I promise you that. But I'd have to say that as things stand, surgery is my recommendation."

"Okay. I'm not arguing. But I need time to think and to discuss this with Jack. I haven't seen many patients go through the hell he did after surgery. We nearly lost him."

"I know."

"Well, thank you. There's no need for you to wait around here. I'll stay with my dad until he gets back upstairs."

Jessup smiled at him enigmatically.

"Actually," she said, "there *is* a reason for me to wait around. Come back into the lab."

Brian followed her back into the cath lab, where Jack had been transferred from the table to his gurney.

"How're you doing, Pop?"

"That wasn't much fun, if that's what you mean. What was that guy—some sort of Arab?"

"Indian. He doesn't have much of a bedside manner."

Carolyn Jessup cut in, speaking to the staff.

"If all of you could repair to the dressing rooms for a couple of minutes, I'd like to speak to these two gentlemen alone. Thank you." She waited until the doors had closed, then took a plain white envelope out of her pocket and handed it to Jack. "Dr. Pickard, the chief of this hospital, had this brought to me just before I came down here. It was delivered to his office late this morning. He sends his regrets that he can't be here to do this personally. But I'm glad I'm here in his place. Go ahead, Jack, open it."

His hands a bit shaky, Jack tore open the envelope and extracted a small, wallet-sized card. He stared at it for half a minute at least, then said softly, "Oh, my God." He looked up at Jessup. "This is for real?" She nodded. "Carolyn, this is going to do more for me than any operation or any pill ever could. . . . Here, son."

He passed the card through the side rail of his gurney. It wasn't until Brian had it in his grasp that he realized what it was.

COMMONWEALTH OF MASSACHUSETTS
BOARD OF REGISTRATION IN MEDICINE
David Connolly, Governor
ISSUES THIS LICENSE TO

Brian's name and address followed. There was an addendum printed at the bottom that the license was provisional, but that made no difference. Brian stared at the card, afraid that if he tried to speak he'd end up crying.

"You start here as a postdoc fellow next Monday," Jessup said.

"Tuesday morning you'll be assisting me here in the cath lab. Pass that test and you'll be doing caths by yourself within the month. Just promise us all one thing."

"Anything," Brian said. "Anything at all."

"Promise us you won't show up the faculty with any more diagnoses like that thyroid storm."

———

Angus "Mac" MacLanahan had always prided himself on having a good attitude about life. As a machinist in Glasgow, then later, after immigrating to the States, as a mechanic fixing the upper crust's Jaguars, he had always been upbeat—content with his lot, but willing and anxious to do what he could to improve it. Now, every step was an effort as he trudged up the hill from the clinic to an empty apartment, battling the consuming sadness that came from no longer being healthy.

It had been great for him for a long time. He was a gentle bull, known for his strength and stamina. They had made him chief mechanic at Back Bay Jag. He had an angel of a wife and three terrific kids. Then Mary had gotten the bad news about the lump in her breast, and everything seemed to go sour—her surgery, the doctors appointments, the horrible, poisonous chemotherapy, and still, ultimately, the bone pain, weight loss, and at last, the merciful end.

It wasn't six months after Mary's death that Mac had his first episode of chest pain. He was working under a hood when the pain hit—an ill-defined burning pressure that started beneath his breastbone, but seemed to be everywhere in the top half of his body at once—his shoulders, his neck, his jaws, his ears. Deep down inside, he knew it was his ticker. But his mind wouldn't accept it. He simply got a glass of water, sat down, wiped the sweat from his forehead and face, and breathed slowly until the pain let up.

He told no one about the episode—not his sons, not his coworkers, not his doctor. And for a couple of months, he paced himself and took a break the moment he sensed the fearsome ache coming on. But finally, his tongue loosened by a pint or two at The Tartan, he made the mistake of mentioning the symptoms to his friend, Marty Anderson. The very next day, with Marty at his side, he was at his doctor's office.

Now, two years later, he wondered whether or not he should have just said the hell with it and let them cut on him.

The walk to his apartment was just five blocks, but Mac was only at the 7-Eleven store and he had already had to stop three times. The doctor at the clinic, a woman who looked to be in her teens, had brought in a dietician to go over the low-salt diet for the umpteenth time, and had bumped up the fluid pills to two twice a day. Mac reminded her that he already kept a bottle by the bed to pee in the three or four times he had to go each night, but the doctor just laughed and assured him that the ankle swelling and shortness of breath would be better if he would eat fewer chips and drink less beer.

"Why not just give me the black pill," Mac had responded, only half in jest.

He shuffled into the 7-Eleven and picked up some milk, ketchup, a package of vanilla sandwich cookies, and a small bag of Doritos. The effort left him panting.

"You all right?" the man behind the cash register asked.

"I'm okay," Mac managed. "Just a little . . . winded is all."

"You sure?"

"I'll be fine in . . . just a minute. . . . Here."

He paid the clerk and forced himself to stop leaning on the glass countertop. Then he shuffled from the store.

"You sure you don't want me to call someone?" the man called after him.

A block and a half, Mac told himself. He was hardly at his best, but hell, he could walk on broken glass for a block and a half if he had to. If he didn't improve soon, though, he was going to have to make some decisions about living alone. But a home was unthinkable, and he had no desire to become a burden to either of his kids.

Maybe Dr. Babyface was right, he told himself. Maybe the change in fluid medicine would help.

His feet ached by the time he reached his building. All he could think of was getting his shoes and socks off and getting into the recliner. The last obstacle between him, a glass of milk, some cookies, and the ball game was a single flight of stairs. He unlocked the front door and the inside security door. Clutching the plastic bag of groceries with one hand and the banister with the other, he ascended step by step.

Finally, at the second landing, he leaned against his apartment door, gulping air as he fumbled with the key. The apartment, as always, was pitch black. Not once that he was aware of had he left a light burning unnecessarily. As he stepped inside, he became aware of the distinct odor of gas. The pilot in the stove must have gone out, he thought as he closed the door behind him. He'd get a window open right away and then fix the damn thing. He threw the living-room light switch by the door, but he would never see the spark that resulted from the slightly widened gap in the contacts.

The gas-laden atmosphere instantly turned the neat apartment into an inferno. Mac MacLanahan's eardrums imploded moments before his eyes melted and his clothes burned away. By the time his body slammed into the wall by the door, his skin and the lining of his lungs were charred. And by the time the wall began burning on its own, the last of his consciousness had begun to fade.

———

Brian left the hospital at five and walked to the Methodist church in the South End. When he had first returned from the Fairweather Treatment Center in Greenville, North Carolina, fifteen months ago, he had been too self-conscious to go to NA or AA meetings anyplace where he was likely to run into an ex-patient. He preferred the anonymity of Boston.

During a coffee break at his third or fourth meeting, this one in the Methodist church basement, a slightly built black man had approached him. He wore tortoiseshell spectacles with tinted lenses, and would have looked professorial except for the letter F in thick scar tissue over his wiry deltoid, and homemade blue tattoos on the bases of his fingers that read HARD LUCK when he balled his hands into fists.

"You know," Freeman Sharpe said that night, in his mellow baritone, "this isn't Acne Anonymous. This disease we're doing battle with is lethal. It's cunning, powerful, and above all, patient. You persist in sitting on your hands in the last row and keeping to yourself at the break, and sooner or later, probably sooner, you're gonna crash."

It was then Sharpe had volunteered to be Brian's sponsor, helping him to meet people and guiding him through the ins and outs, the dos and don'ts of recovery. Even now they still spoke on the phone nearly every day. Whatever Brian's problem, Freeman had a reasonable solution. Whatever his question, there was an answer.

Tonight, though, Brian felt his question was perplexing enough to test even Sharpe.

He had no more Aphrodite, no more Speedy Rent-A-Car, no more Darryl, decent money about to come in, and he was three days from being back taking care of patients. It was all there—all of it. Why, then, was he feeling so ill at ease?

Brian's inexplicable apprehension began to lift as soon as he set foot in the grungy church basement. Although most of the support groups he attended were Narcotics Anonymous, he had no problems going to AA meetings, either. A drug is a drug, he had been taught at Fairweather, and the decision to stay away from mood-altering substances had to include alcohol.

Freeman Sharpe waved to him from across the room and greeted him with a handshake, a hug, and the appraising eye Brian had come to expect.

"Pardon me for saying it, young Holbrook," Freeman said, "but you don't look like a man who's just had the weight of the world lifted from his shoulders."

"That obvious, huh?"

"That obvious."

"I think I'm frightened."

"Of what?"

"I don't know."

"I don't believe that. Why don't you take a stab at it?"

"Well, Boston Heart Institute is like the top of the line."

"So?"

"With my history, people will be watching me very closely."

"So?"

"I . . . I don't want to screw up."

Freeman cleaned his glasses with a tissue, then tightened his fists and stared down at his HARD LUCK tattoos.

"I see," he said.

People were settling in for the start of the Friday meeting, so Freeman led Brian outside into the cool late-summer air. Brian's misgivings about starting at BHI had to connect with an important lesson for Sharpe to insist that he miss part of a meeting.

"Okay," Freeman said, leaning against the building and crossing his arms, but never taking his eyes from Brian's, "you're afraid of screwing up at mighty Boston Heart Institute. Tell me, exactly who was it that hired you for this job?"

"Pickard. Ernest Pickard. He's the director."

Brian already sensed what was coming, but he was grateful that Freeman was going to lead him there.

"The director . . . and he hired you."

"Right."

"He went over your papers, your resumé, and your test scores and such?"

"Yes."

"And he checked your references?"

"He did."

"And he still decided to hire you?"

"He did."

"Is he an intelligent man?"

"Very."

"So, the way I see it—correct me if I'm wrong—is that you're not the one responsible for bringing you on board at the hospital. A very intelligent man, who knows what the job's all about, and who knows how to evaluate medical talent, and who went over all your stuff, determined you could do the job."

"I guess so."

"So, what'm I driving at?"

Sharpe, arms still folded, peered up at him. The man was a master at knowing when it was time for an answer and when it was time for a question.

"My only job is to do my best," Brian responded, not daring to allow a singsong, this-is-child's-stuff insinuation into his tone.

"Not to *be* the best. By now, I hope you've realized that all that be-the-best shit has to go. 'Cause if screwin' up on this job is the best you can do, that's not your problem, my man, it's Ernest Pickard's. He picked you."

CHAPTER FIVE

Dr. ALEXANDER BAIRD GLANCED OVER HIS SHOULDER at the cameramen and reporters crowding the press section of the hearing room. Immediately, two flashbulbs popped off. Then another. The Senate Committee for Government Affairs' Subcommittee for Oversight of Government Management was in a five-minute recess. Baird, the Food and Drug Administration commissioner, was wishing he had emptied his bladder before entering the hall. The notion of plowing back through the milling crowd to the men's room held absolutely no appeal.

It was the oversight subcommittee's mandate to determine that the FDA was carrying out its functions in a proper fashion. Of course, "proper" had a distinctly political flavor. Over the two or three days before he was to appear at this gathering, Baird had heard rumblings from his staff that there was more than the usual amount of interest in the session. No one seemed to know why. Now, after three-quarters of an hour of fielding softball questions on a variety of subjects, Baird still had no explanation for the inordinate amount of media attention and observers.

"Teri, I can't shake the feeling they all know something I don't," he whispered, glancing up at the paneled dais that enabled the subcommittee members to loom above the witnesses.

Dr. Teri Sennstrom, group leader for cardiovascular drugs, poured a glass of ice water, which her boss declined.

"That makes two of us," she said. "The Little Bighorn's mighty pretty this time of year, don't you think, General Custer?"

"Very funny."

"Very serious. I smell an ambush, but I just can't figure out where it's going to be coming from."

Over the ten months that he had been FDA commissioner, Baird had come to rely heavily on Teri's opinion. She was thirty-six, the same age as his daughter. But unlike Margaret, who had bounced through graduate schools in education and business and still didn't know what she wanted to do with her life, Teri, who had already been with the agency three years when Baird took over, was as focused and resourceful as she was loyal. Deputy director positions in the FDA didn't open up that often, but when the next one did, Teri Sennstrom would be high on his list of candidates. Today, she sat at Baird's right hand as his clinical adviser. To his left was the FDA attorney, a hawk-nosed veteran of the political wars named Barry Weisman.

The subcommittee meeting, chaired by the powerful Republican senator from Massachusetts, Walter Louderman, was the second one before which Baird had appeared as head of the Food and Drug Administration. His first appearance, just after his appointment, had turned out to be little more than shadowboxing—a get-acquainted session in which a constantly smiling Louderman skillfully let Baird know that even though Baird was the President's man, liberal through and through, Congress and all the committees that mattered were controlled by the GOP. This time Louderman, a moderate Republican with undisguised national aspirations, had yet to say a word.

Originally a small-town family practitioner, Baird was a professor at the Medical College of Missouri when he was summoned by the President to Washington to straighten out the FDA. The agency had been badly mismanaged throughout the last administration and had been rocked by a number of scandals, including one ugly episode involving payoffs to cover up the fraudulent labeling of baby food. Blunt and outspoken on social issues ranging from smoking to gun control, Baird was already being criticized for lacking the social grace, political savvy, and even physical stamina to survive long in his office.

He leaned over to Teri and shielded his mouth from the microphone.

"What on earth do you think Harvey Wiley would say if he witnessed this circus?" he asked.

Wiley, a turn-of-the-century chemist and consumer-rights advocate, had led the legislative battle to pass the Pure Food and Drug Act of 1906, and was generally regarded as the father of the FDA.

Teri smiled at Baird's image.

"Wiley was a politician," she said. "He'd understand this show perfectly. And from what I've read, he was also a bare-knuckles fighter when he had to be. But one slight correction, Dr. Baird. Circuses have a stated purpose to thrill and entertain. I prefer to think of these oversight subcommittee hearings as theater—theater of the absurd." She motioned up at the senators returning to their seats and automatically reached up to smooth her pale hair. "Act Two," she said.

Barry Weisman flipped off his and Baird's microphones.

"Well, Alex," he said, "here we go again. I'm right here beside you. Even if all you need is a break in tempo, feel free to put your hand over the mike and whisper something in my ear. It looks great on TV, too. And just remember, no matter how many compliments they shower down on you, no matter how many pearly whites they flash you, don't let your guard down. Not for a moment."

"Not for a moment," Baird echoed.

"One other thing. The more you can get the camera on Dr. Sennstrom's face, the better the agency looks."

"Do I detect reverse discrimination?" Teri asked.

Weisman grinned. He had been a close friend of Teri's for several years, since the day he had finally accepted that she had no interest in dating him.

"Just a biological truism," he said.

"Okay, then, Dr. Baird," Louderman began, "suppose we get on with our business. My esteemed colleague from Texas, Senator Harrington, has a few questions for you regarding some of the recent situations your agency has encountered."

Teri covered the mike and whispered, "You know about this guy, yes?"

Baird nodded. Senator Bart Harrington was Louderman's stooge, and sometimes his muscle. Whatever Harrington had to say had doubtless been fed to him by the committee chairman. Baird thought he knew what was coming. One of his first acts as FDA commissioner had been to pull Kinethane, a controversial weight-loss drug, off the market three years after it had been approved for general use. The product, which had made hundreds of millions of dollars for a Texas-based company, appeared to be causing an unusual, sometimes lethal, form of pancreatitis in a small but significant proportion of the many millions who were taking it.

Twenty-five deaths had been attributed to the product, and a class-action suit was in the works. The manufacturers had countered the charges with expert testimony from a team of highly paid hired-gun statisticians showing that, given the improved health accompanying even a modest decrease in obesity plus the "natural" occurrence of this form of pancreatitis, the benefits of Kinethane far outweighed its risks. But the FDA had statisticians of its own. And in the end, Baird had felt he had no choice but to pull the drug.

Baird knew that the most brutal oversight-subcommittee hearings often revolved around the agency's approval of a drug later found to be harmful. He expected to have to answer questions about why it had taken the FDA so long to appreciate the Kinethane hazard and respond to it, so he was well prepared with data *and* with Teri Sennstrom. He pulled out the half-inch-thick file from the stack in front of him, in anticipation of an attack. But *that* attack never came.

"Dr. Baird," Harrington began, "I want to congratulate you for the excellent job you are doing putting the FDA back on its feet."

Baird glanced over at Barry Weisman, who merely rubbed at his chin and shrugged.

"Thank you, Senator," Baird responded. "We're certainly trying."

"What I'm particularly interested in today, Dr. Baird, is having you share with us some of your data regarding investigational new drugs."

"Such as?"

"Well, for instance, how long does it take for a new drug to make it to the public?"

"From animal testing?"

"Yes."

"Well, of course that varies greatly depending on the drug, the thoroughness of the pharmaceutical company sponsoring it, and many other factors. But from beginning to end, the process can take from five to as long as ten years or even more, and cost upward of one hundred and twenty-five million dollars."

"There are three phases of human testing in drug research, is that correct?"

Baird was startled by the specificity of the question, but answered it in tempo.

"Essentially, yes. Each of the three human-testing phases involves more patients than the previous one and usually more investigating institutions as well."

"Do promising, life-saving drugs ever get approved for public use while the human research is still in Phase Two of the customary three phases?"

"Yes, Senator Harrington, there have been such occasions."

Harrington, whose heavily veined face and W. C. Fields nose strongly suggested to Baird that he might have a drinking problem, consulted his notes then cleared his throat.

"Dr. Baird, could you tell us something about the drug lovastatin?"

"Such as?"

"Just a brief history of the drug from the FDA's point of view."

Teri covered the mike.

"Any idea where he's headed?" she whispered.

Baird shook his head.

"In that case, tread lightly," she warned.

"Lovastatin is a wonderful cholesterol-lowering agent developed by Merck and Company. It was approved for prescribing to the public in August of nineteen eighty-seven."

"Approval of a new-drug application, also known as an NDA, is the last step before a medication is released for general use, yes?"

"That's correct, Senator."

"Well then, could you tell us, please, Doctor, how long after the lovastatin new-drug application was submitted was it approved?"

"Before answering," Baird said, picking his way along as if he were in a pitch-black room, "I feel I must explain that a new-drug application is submitted to our agency only after Phases One, Two, and Three are—"

"Yes, yes, I understand, Doctor. Could you please answer my question?"

The interruption and the edge in Harrington's tone immediately put Baird on red alert.

Easy does it, Weisman jotted on the legal pad set between them on the table.

"Nine months after the NDA for lovastatin was submitted," Baird said, "it was approved. But the research on that drug was—"

"Thank you, Doctor."

"No, Senator, if you please, I'd like to finish my sentence. The Merck company did meticulous clinical studies of their drug and submitted remarkably comprehensive data. Their work on lovastatin actually began in the late seventies."

"Then tell us, if you will, precisely how much time elapsed from the beginning of Phase Two human trials until the NDA for lovastatin was approved?"

"I really don't have that information at my fingertips. But I'd be happy to—"

"It was just three years, Dr. Baird. Just three years from the beginning of Phase Two human trials until approval of the drug."

Harrington, his smug expression almost comical, turned to Walter Louderman and nodded that he was passing the baton. Louderman, a husky, graying Harvard Law grad, shuffled some papers. Then he took a slow drink of water and cleared *his* throat before fixing his pale blue eyes on Baird.

"Dr. Baird," he said, "there's another drug I'd like you to tell us about. Correct me, please, if my pronunciation is off. The drug is zidovudine."

"Your pronunciation is perfect, Senator Louderman." *Why wouldn't it be? You probably practiced saying the word a hundred times before you'd chance it in front of all these cameras.* "The drug you ask about was originally and perhaps more commonly known as AZT."

Barry Weisman motioned with his hand for Baird to hold up and turned the microphone toward himself.

"Senator Louderman," he asked, "do you think we might be given some idea as to where this line of questioning is leading?"

"If you can be patient just a bit longer, Mr. Weisman, I think you will have your answer. Now, Doctor, can you give us the same sort of capsule summary about AZT that you did for lovastatin?"

Baird searched for a trap behind the question, but could find none.

"AZT is an antiviral agent developed by Burroughs-Wellcome and Company, now Glaxo Wellcome, and has been a valuable treatment against the virus that causes AIDS."

"And when were clinical studies begun on *that* drug?"

"I'm not sure. Sometime in the mid-eighties."

"Actually, Doctor, Phase One trials of AZT began in June of nineteen eighty-five. Phase Two began seven months later. The human testing was terminated in September, nineteen eighty-six, just eight months after Phase Two studies were begun. There never were any Phase Three studies."

Baird was aware of his bladder now and silently cursed himself for not addressing that situation during the break. Just the same, whether out of fatigue, irritation, anxiety, or some combination of the three, he took several swallows of the ice water Teri had poured for him, and then motioned for her to respond to the statement.

"We're not certain we follow you, Senator," she said. "The FDA is certainly proud of the speed with which we got both lovastatin and AZT approved for public use."

"And well you should be, Doctor Sennstrom. Because both those drugs had huge lifesaving potential for a large number of people. . . ."

Louderman paused, looked up at the bank of cameras, then once again shuffled the papers in front of him.

Here it comes, Weisman wrote, filling the O in with a frowning face.

". . . Dr. Baird and Dr. Sennstrom," Louderman said finally, "are you aware of a drug named Vasclear currently under Phase Two clinical studies?"

"We are aware of the drug, yes," Baird responded.

"Could you tell us all what the drug does?"

"I can tell you what it's *purported* to do. It is being investigated for properties it *may* have that reportedly enable it to dissolve arteriosclerosis."

"Dissolve arteriosclerosis. . . . Do you mean it can cure hardening of the arteries?"

At that moment, Baird remembered that Newbury Pharmaceuticals, the small drug firm developing Vasclear, was based in Boston, Louderman's home turf. Suddenly, he understood the why and wherefore of the entire session. An ambush, indeed. He covered the microphone.

"Barry," he whispered, "we know where Louderman's going now. If we feel he's squeezing us too tightly on this, I want you to go out in the hall, see if you can reach the President, and have him put a stop to it."

He turned back to Louderman.

"From what I know of the drug, Senator, and I admit that is not a great deal at this point, curing hardening of the arteries is a possibility. I would caution you and everyone watching this hearing that research on Vasclear is quite preliminary."

"A drug that cures hardening of the arteries and you don't know a great deal about it?"

"A drug that *may* cure hardening of the arteries, Senator. We have literally hundreds of investigational new drugs we are currently following. And as I said, research on Vasclear is quite preliminary."

"I beg your pardon, sir," Louderman countered, "but the research on this medication is actually quite far along, and the American people should know that the results to date have been astounding. I know for a fact that the scientists of Newbury Pharmaceuticals have twice submitted a new-drug application to *your agency* requesting the same sort of consideration that was given to *that AIDS drug,* and twice they have been turned down by *your people.*"

Go! Baird wrote on the legal pad. Barry Weisman took the cellular phone from his briefcase, slipped it into his jacket pocket, and hurried from the hearing room. Baird stalled with another sip of water. From what he knew, the Vasclear research did hold great promise. But he also knew that Louderman's staff had been pressuring the team assigned to evaluate Newbury Pharmaceuticals Company's clinical data.

The income from a drug that could eliminate arteriosclerosis would be staggering. Louderman was angling toward the Republican presidential nomination. His early public support of the drug would be a huge political coup, and somehow, profits from the drug were sure to find their way into his campaign coffers.

However, from what Baird had been told by his staff, as remarkable as the early Phase Two data on Vasclear was, more study on humans needed to be done.

"Excuse me, Doctor," Louderman was saying, "but would you please answer my question?"

"I . . . um . . . I'm afraid I'll have to ask you to repeat it, Senator."

"Your agency pushed through both lovastatin and zidovudine because they were lifesaving drugs. Wouldn't you call Vasclear, a cure for a horribly costly, often-fatal illness, lifesaving?"

"At this point, Senator, I wouldn't call it anything but a drug with a great deal of potential."

"And you would be wrong!" Louderman pounded his fist on his

desk for emphasis. "You obviously have not reviewed the research data on this drug personally. If you had, I believe you would be a darn sight more enthusiastic."

"Perhaps," was all Baird could reply.

"This committee is going to reconvene a month from today, Dr. Baird. By that time, I hope you will be ready to tell the American people why a lifesaving, life-giving, life-sustaining drug—"

One of Louderman's aides had come up behind him and handed him a phone. Louderman listened to the caller for thirty seconds, said a few words, and then handed the phone back. His smile was icy. Baird thought he saw a tic fire off at the corner of his eye.

"Well, now," he said. "It seems you have a dedicated protector in the large white house down the street. His wishes are that you be given as much time as you need to evaluate the Vasclear situation, with the understanding that you will make it your highest priority."

Baird met the senator's gaze evenly.

"I will do my best, sir," he said.

"I hope so," Louderman countered. He hoisted himself up as rigidly as he could and looked more at the cameras than at Baird. "And, sir, I also hope that all those bedridden people out there with chest pains and stroke symptoms are as patient with you as our President is."

Without waiting for a rebuttal, Louderman gaveled the session to a close.

Baird waited until the dais had emptied, then turned to Teri.

"I didn't want to tell him that you were the group leader on this project."

"It would have been okay if you did. We've been on top of this drug."

"I know you have. What do you think about what Louderman said?"

"I don't like the subliminal message about how we would go to any lengths to cure AIDS, but we're withholding the miracle cure of the century from Mr. and Mrs. Middle America. Sounds too much like Louderman's running for president."

"Which everyone knows he is. But you agree we should be speeding this drug along?"

"I can't make that judgment yet. But it does look very promising. And there's no question it falls into the lifesaving-drug category."

Baird studied her face for several seconds. Weisman was right, he thought. Teri Sennstrom's intelligent good looks couldn't help but put the agency in a positive light.

"Okay, then," he said. "You know what you've got to do. I don't like anyone pushing me around, but I knew this job was political when I agreed to take it. I'm going to make this drug one of my top priorities, but I'll need your help in bringing the pile of data down to some sort of manageable size for my review."

"You've got it."

"Start putting things together, and we'll meet in, say, a week."

"Fine."

"And Teri?"

"Yes?"

"We can let Louderman flex his muscles all he wants to. That's just politics. But in the end, we've got to remember where our responsibilities lie. I don't want another Kinethane. I don't want another thalidomide. If this drug has problems, we've got to keep it away from the public, Louderman or no Louderman."

CHAPTER SIX

MAIL ROOM, COMMUNICATIONS CENTER, SECURITY, PER-
sonnel, payroll. One by one, Brian ticked off the items on an efficiently designed checklist as he worked his way through the maze
of corridors, buildings, and offices that made up White Memorial
Hospital. It had been more than a decade since his last hospital
orientation, and he was feeling as keyed up and nervous as he had
that day in Chicago when he began his cardiac fellowship.

At the laundry, Brian tried to explain that he would be functioning largely as a cardiology fellow, but his title—postdoctoral fellow—put him a notch above that. After prolonged deliberation, the
bewildered woman at the uniform window settled on two short

clinic coats for the cardiac fellow part of him, and two knee-length lab coats for the faculty part.

"No white pants," she said in a thick Asian accent. "White pants for resident babies."

His final stop was at the employee assistance office, which, at Dr. Pickard's request, had already added Brian to the list of physicians, nurses, and others who were getting random urine testing for alcohol and substances of potential abuse. The nurse running the EAP was kind and reassuring enough, and certainly experienced at dealing with monitoring, but Brian was still quite embarrassed.

The system was that at least once a week, on a day randomly selected by a computer, he would receive a page to "call Dr. Jones." He would then have two hours to report to employee assistance for a test. The only excuse for coming later than two hours to leave a specimen was his being involved with a procedure in the OR or the cath lab.

Unpleasant, but not unmanageable, he acknowledged. And certainly not undeserved.

Brian signed the appropriate waivers and assurances, took the copies and instruction sheet, and headed up to meet Phil Gianatasio at the conference room for a tour of the facility. Phil was there with a small cake in the shape of an anatomically correct heart, and a very pretty, slender brunette in her early thirties. Carrie Sherwood was the unit secretary for the clinical-research ward.

"I brought her here to meet you because she runs the clinical service and I wanted you to start off on her good side. The last resident who did something to get on her bad side ended up throwing himself off the top of the Cromwell Building."

"Philip, stop that."

Brian could tell by the way the shapely secretary reacted to the tease that she and Phil were lovers. After a few minutes of small talk and some cake, she headed back to the research unit, giving each of them a prolonged look at her from behind. Brian nodded his approval.

"Fine lady," he said.

"Best thing about her?" Phil replied. "She doesn't seem to give a shit that I'm waistline-challenged. She's also loaded with friends. I can think of two right off the top of my head who wouldn't mind being fixed up with an M.D. who was a cross between Joe Montana and Alex Trebek."

"I wish."

"Seriously—you seeing anyone?"

Brian shook his head.

"I've been out a couple of times, but my heart just hasn't been in it."

"Well, from what Carrie tells me, these friends of hers sound like they'd manage to hold your attention for an evening or two."

"First things first, okay?"

Brian couldn't believe he was responding to his friend's offer by quoting a twelve-step banner. Had he really become that dull?

"What I mean," he added, "is let me put in a little time here. Then we'll talk to Carrie."

"Great. Well, Dr. Pickard suggested we make our way around the research ward, the labs, and finally the Vasclear clinic. But first, since you'll be covering the Vasclear clinic a lot of the time, he wanted you to see the video."

"Video?"

"The staff calls it *Vasclear Über Alles*. It's an informational video we show to the house staff, visitors, and even the patients. It's pretty good, actually, except it's a bit simplistic for doctors and at least a bit too complex for most of our patients."

Brian's interest immediately perked up.

"I'd like to see it."

"Then see it you shall, my man, provided you excuse me while it's running. After a dozen or more screenings, I've just about got the dialogue of this film memorized. Speaking of Vasclear, though, have you heard anything from Jessup about your father?"

"Not really. I thought I'd speak to her tomorrow when I scrub with her in the cath lab, even though I don't want to start off my first week here by bugging the associate director. She called once after Jack's discharge to see how he was doing. That in itself was really kind of her, but she didn't say anything about Vasclear. Before Jack was discharged, she did promise that she'd speak to Dr. Weber about getting him into the study."

"Well, I'm not sure you should hold out much hope," Phil replied. "Weber's a decent enough guy for someone without a bit of detectable humor. But he's absolutely committed to seeing that every aspect of the Vasclear protocol is followed to the letter. I suppose if I had medical immortality on the line, to say nothing of a few billion dollars, I'd be pretty obsessive, too. So where's Jessup right now, as far as Jack's treatment is concerned?"

"Her recommendation is still surgery."

"Will your father go along with it?"

"Frankly, Phil, having lived through that eight-week nightmare with him last time, we're both still holding out for Vasclear."

"As long as it's the beta group."

As long as it's the beta group. Brian wandered to the window and gazed out across the river at Cambridge. If there was no way he could get his father into the beta group, was he desperate enough to steal the drug? The question burned in his thoughts. He wasn't aware he was clenching his teeth until his jaws began throbbing.

"Roll the film," he said, pulling the drapes. "And give my best to Carrie."

Phil tossed him the remote and left. Brian settled into one of the high-backed, oxblood leather chairs, tilted back, and put his stockinged feet up on the table. Yesterday's *Globe* had had a small article about Senator Louderman pressuring the FDA head to get Vasclear approved for public use. Even if Jack was refused admission to the study, maybe the standard medical management Jessup was using could buy him enough time, provided, of course, Louderman won his battle.

His mind tied in knots, Brian punched *play.*

To say the twenty-five-minute informational video was glossy and big-budget would not have given proper credit to the graphics, music, sound bites, animation, and a script that might have been done by an evangelist.

VASCLEAR
The Search Is Over
The Answer Is Here

First some footage of paintings and lithographs of Ponce de León, searching for the fountain of youth. Next a speed-flight over the jungle, backed up by a score that sounded straight from an Indiana Jones movie, and a litany of some of the most important drugs to come from jungle plants. And finally, a few almost gratuitous shots of South American natives—meat eaters who had found the secret to staving off arteriosclerosis and living, according to the paternal voice-over, a century or more.

Next came a smooth segue to Newbury Pharmaceuticals—a tribute to their modest accomplishments in the past, a tour of their gleaming, refurbished plant in an industrial area of Boston, and a shot of their research laboratories. Finally, to explain the miracle of Vasclear, the voice-over introduced Dr. Art Weber, project director.

Weber, tanned, sandy-haired, and blue-eyed, had a youthful face that was handsome in a Hollywood sort of way. His accent sounded Eastern European. With the help of animation and operating-room footage, Weber described the genesis of arteriosclerosis and modern medicine's efforts to combat what he called the ravages of the number one killer in the civilized world—the diets, the drugs, behavior modification, and finally, the surgical approach.

The bypass operation they had chosen to show was a particularly bloody one, Brian noted. Clearly not Laj Randa. A patient facing such a procedure would have been happy to volunteer to participate in any alternative that offered a chance at avoiding the knife.

"Arterial clearing with Vasclear has been steady," Weber continued. "Here is the actual arterial X ray of one of our patients, and here are the films of that same patient twelve months after the onset of Vasclear therapy. Note the clearing of the blockages of the left main coronary here, the right in these spots, and the circumflex. And did the patient's symptoms respond? Well, let's just ask her."

Strings, angelic horns, and dramatic camera angles, accompanied a cheery woman's voice saying, "I had pain up here in my shoulder and neck. It was pure luck I saw my doctor and had my heart tested. I was a disaster waiting to happen. They gave me a choice: undergo bypass surgery or become part of the Vasclear study. I still don't know what Vasclear concentration the treatment group I was in received, but I suspect it was a good dose, because my symptoms vanished almost immediately, and they haven't returned."

By now the camera had made its way to the subject's face. She was everybody's dream grandmother—expansive, nurturing smile, sparkling eyes.

"At this point," Art Weber was saying, "we cannot claim that Vasclear will work for everyone. But our human trials are suggesting that up to seventy-five percent of patients may derive considerable benefit. At present, Newbury Pharmaceuticals researchers, in cooperation with the physicians at the world-renowned Boston Heart Institute, are searching for ways that even this remarkable percentage might be increased."

The video rounded out with a dramatic projection of what the world had in store with Vasclear. By the time it was done, Brian was obsessed with the drug. Vasclear was the candy that beckoned from the porcelain bowls in Aunt Bea's living room, and Brian was the child forbidden by his father from taking it.

———

The driving late-afternoon rain had Bill Elovitz and a dozen others pinned in the doorway of Filene's department store. With a week until Devorah's birthday, he knew it had been foolish for him to come into Boston on such a day. But a sale was a sale, and his wife had never been so specific about a gift—but only if he could get the robe in pink and at forty percent off.

Across the street, an army of sodden rush-hour commuters jostled their way into the maw of the MBTA's Downtown Crossing station. Elovitz pulled the hood of his rubber slicker up over his head and tightened the drawstring beneath his chin. The olive-colored raincoat had actually been a birthday present to him from Devorah a few years ago, but he had only worn it four or five times if that.

The shallow Filene's entryway offered little protection from the wind-whipped squall. Elovitz was seventy-four years old and retired. There was never anyplace he had to be badly enough to venture out in such a storm. Two boys, laughing and shouting to each other, charged past him and splashed out onto the street.

"It's nice to be young," the elderly woman standing next to him said.

"It's nice to be at all," Elovitz replied. "Well, I don't think this rain is about to stop. Have a nice day."

He adjusted his grip on the large shopping bag and plunged across to the station. By the time he reached the stairway, he was gasping for breath. He braced himself against a wall for nearly a minute before he felt safe descending to the tracks. He knew the wet, heavy air was partly responsible for his difficulty, but he was also certain there was something else going on. For weeks now, his tolerance for even modest exercise had been slipping. Sooner or later he would have to have the problem checked. But right now, what he had to do was to get home.

He started down the stairs. Ahead of him, a woman slipped on the wet concrete. The collision with the husky man in front of her was all that kept her from a nasty tumble. Elovitz was normally quite placid and easygoing. But the crush of wet, harried people and the dense air had him very much on edge.

Charlestown, where Elovitz and his wife had lived and worked for the past twenty-five years, was on the Orange Line, just half a dozen or so stops from Downtown Crossing. By the time he reached the platform, he was experiencing persistent air hunger and an oppressive sense of claustrophobia. He felt frantic to find some space away from the crowd—space where he might be able to draw a deep, satisfying breath.

The concrete platform, an island serving inbound commuters on one side and outbound on the other, was jammed. The smell of wet clothing, wet hair, and perspiration was unpleasant and strangely frightening.

"Excuse me, please. Excuse me," Elovitz panted, squeezing between bodies on his way to the track side. "Excuse me. I'm sorry. Excuse me, please."

The platform was four feet or so above the track. Once Elovitz reached the front row, he was certain he would be able to breathe.

"Hey, watch where you're going!" a man behind him snapped.

"Fuck you," another man growled.

Elovitz clutched his package, kept his eyes on the open space ahead, and pushed on. Finally, at the moment when he thought he might collapse, he forced himself between two women right to the edge of the platform. The air wafting from the nearby tunnel actually tasted light and sweet. Elovitz allowed the crush of bodies to help hold him upright as he gratefully filled his lungs. Off to the right, he could hear the rumble of the oncoming train.

Suddenly, just as the lights of the approaching engine appeared, there was a shift in the crowd. The intense pressure from behind caused Elovitz to stumble forward. His knees buckled as his foot slipped off the edge of the platform. Amid screams from above, he fell, landing heavily on the railbed. The bones in his left wrist snapped, sending white pain up his arm. His head slammed against the rail. Dazed, he rolled over and tried to force himself to his knees. The air brakes shrieked deafeningly as the train careened down the track in a full emergency stop. Thirty feet . . . twenty . . . ten . . . Elovitz lurched to his feet and stumbled several steps backward. Those few steps made the difference. The screeching stopped with the nose of the engine just a foot away.

Now, it seemed, everyone on the platform was screaming at him.

"Stop!" they were hollering. "The third rail!" . . . "Stay away from the third rail!" . . . "Don't move!" . . . "That's high-voltage!" . . . "Don't move!"

Stunned and disoriented, Elovitz turned toward the cacophony, blinking up at the crowd and the lights.

"Don't move!" . . . "Voltage!" . . . "Stay!" . . . "No!"

A man leaped onto the tracks and started toward him. Reflex-ively, Elovitz stepped to his left. His shoe caught on the rail, send-ing him reeling awkwardly backward. The screams from above intensified as he lost his balance entirely and in agonizing slow motion, fell heavily onto the high-voltage rail.

———

Phil still hadn't returned, so Brian took the time to call and check in on his father. Jack could certainly be left alone at times, but with Brian gone most of the day, nutritious meals and inter-mittent companionship were a priority. The steady concern of Jack's friends and neighbors had been astounding. One woman actually made up a coverage schedule and got people to sign up. It was more evidence of how poorly the coach was feeling that he didn't grumble about the arrangement or the attention.

"Pop, how're you holding up?"

"No complaints."

His voice sounded shaky.

"You been up walking and stretching?"

"A little."

"Any pain?"

"Not much."

Jesus, Coach, Brian wanted to scream. *Will you stop the macho act and tell me what's going on?*

"The visiting nurse will be there to check on you in half an hour," he said instead. "Ask her to beep me here to give me a report. You have my pager number."

"How are *you* doing? Saved any lives yet?"

"No, but I haven't killed anybody, either. That's all I wanted."

"Five bucks says you save someone's life in the next twenty-four hours."

"Dad, it really doesn't work like that. Only on TV, where they have to keep their ratings up."

"Five bucks."

"Okay, you're on. You going to watch the Sox tonight? . . . Jack?" The silence was too prolonged. "Jack, what're you doing?"

"Nothing," his father said finally, his voice even more strained than before. "I'm fine."

Brian knew he had just put a nitro under his tongue. Chest pain at rest was not a good sign.

"Just have the nurse call me," he said.

Phil returned with coffee and doughnuts.

"A little sustenance for two starving docs before we finish the orientation tour," he announced.

"Phil, you're a cardiologist. How can you keep eating that junk?"

"What can I say? I'm weak. Just ask Ms. Carrie. But on the bright side, at least I'm not going to lose my license from being strung out on crullers."

"Good point. Once I get settled in on this job, though, we're going on a health-and-exercise kick together."

"If you thought getting off the pills was tough, wait until you try getting me into a gym."

They walked through the clinical ward—a twenty-five-bed unit with excellent staffing, then upstairs and through the surgical unit—Laj Randa's fiefdom.

"Okay," Phil said. "How about we go through the labs? BHI has more than its share of research geeks. I, myself, have a little lab where I am trying to stress and feed a bunch of hamsters into developing coronary artery disease."

"Are you succeeding?"

"Who cares? The publications I've gotten out of those furry little buggers have helped to get me tenured. That's all the experiments are really about anyhow. Academic medicine, my friend. Hamster or perish."

"Got it. Listen, if you don't mind, I'd just as soon skip the labs and go see the Vasclear clinic. I'm on the schedule there tomorrow evening. Besides, one of the reasons I never got too wrapped up in academic medicine was my desire to avoid the research."

"Vasclear clinic it is," Gianatasio said. "Only, if it's okay with you, I'll turn this part over to Lucy Kendall, the head nurse there. I have a packed house this afternoon in the office, and getting a little head start would be a huge help."

"Fine by me. Tell me something, Phil. How much have people been told about me?"

"What do you mean?"

"Well, this Lucy Kendall, for instance. Does she know I just got my license back and why?"

Gianatasio shrugged.

"If the gossip doesn't involve Lucy, I doubt she'd pay any attention to it," he said. "But hospitals are hospitals. People like to grind up other people, and we doctors are prime chuck. I gave up caring who knows about me and Carrie and who doesn't. It's much easier that way. People may be talking about you, especially after your save with Stormy in the ER. But so far, I haven't heard anything. I'll keep you posted if I do."

"Do that, Phil. Please."

The Vasclear clinic was, not surprisingly, a jewel—ten medication-administration rooms, carpeted, professionally decorated, with electronically controlled space-age recliners and individual patient-choice sound systems. Lucy Kendall, the Vasclear nurse practitioner, showed Brian around and managed to fit in a good portion of her life story at the same time. She was married to a GP in the suburbs and had just given birth to her second child—a boy.

Generally, Brian was oblivious to a woman's flirtatiousness. Throughout their marriage, Phoebe was constantly pointing out to him the differences between a woman being sociable and coming on. But even for him, Lucy Kendall was an easy read. She was overly touchy and familiar from the start, and told him more than once how pleased she was with how quickly her figure had bounced back after her pregnancy. She seemed positively giddy when Brian picked up on her heavy-handed hints and agreed with her.

Brian actually was relieved that he would be working with someone so wrapped up in herself that she would likely remain uninterested in him and his background. He also didn't think she realized that, at every opportunity, he was alternating questions about her and her life with queries about Vasclear.

He knew what he was doing as he pumped her for more and more information on how the drug was handled, where it was stored, how it was labeled, how it was administered, and where the records were kept. He knew precisely what he was doing, but it was still hard to accept.

He was casing the place—casing it as he had the pharmacy at Suburban Hospital. He was taking advantage of Lucy Kendall the same way he had taken advantage of the young hospital pharmacist at Suburban, searching for a softness in the system that he could exploit. Only this time, he wasn't looking for pills to feed his addiction. This time, he was developing a plan in case Jessup and Weber refused to admit Jack into the Vasclear study, or in case they did and he was not randomized into the beta group.

Brian felt himself begin to tremble. Less than one day back at work and already he was plotting how to steal a drug. Was there really any difference between stealing an experimental medication to help save his father and stealing pills to stop his own discomfort—his own pain? His recovery program was built on a bedrock of uncompromising honesty. Was he emotionally ready to begin cheating the system again, however worried he was feeling, however noble the reason? After all the meetings and therapy sessions and soul-searchings, was it possible that he really hadn't changed at all—that he had been fooling all his therapists, his sponsor, and worse, himself?

The questions made Brian queasy . . . but they didn't make him stop.

CHAPTER SEVEN

THE WASHINGTON POST

**FDA Accused of Dragging Feet
on Miracle Heart Drug**

Senate Government Affairs Committee
Chairman, Senator Walter Louderman
(R-Mass.) has accused FDA Commissioner Dr. Alexander Baird of dragging
his feet on approval of a drug that
Louderman says could save the lives of
hundreds of thousands of Americans
each year. . . .

AFTERNOON SHADOWS WERE LENGTHENING WHEN LUCY Kendall reluctantly concluded Brian's orientation and headed off to see patients. Through her garrulousness, Brian had learned a great deal about the handling and administration of Vasclear, but there were still some missing pieces—pieces that would be filled in when he actually worked a shift in the clinic.

Outside, from five stories up, he could see that rush-hour traffic was snarled in a heavy rain. The twenty-minute drive to Reading would be doubled or even tripled. The visiting nurse's report gave him no cause for alarm about Jack, and anticipating a long day of orientation, he had asked their neighbor to schedule people until nine. There was no reason to hurry home, and every reason to become more familiar with White Memorial Hospital and Boston Heart Institute.

He was about to call Lexington to say good-night to the girls and to let Phoebe know that he had survived day one, when his pager went off. Phil answered his call.

"Bri, you done up there?"

"Just about. Why?"

"I'm heading for the ER to do a consult and I thought you might want to meet me down there. I want to hear how it went in the clinic."

"I'll just check in with my kids first, Phil. But after that, sure, I'll be down. Whatcha got?"

"Oh, just the usual run-of-the-mill stuff. Seventy-four-year-old gent who fell onto the third rail in the Downtown Crossing T station."

"And he's alive?"

"Not only alive, but apparently ready to sign out of the ER."

"Sounds like my kinda guy. You get started. I'll be down in a few minutes."

Brian punched in the numbers of Phoebe's house, wondering if he would ever do so again without bracing himself for the note of disapproval and cynicism he still detected in her voice.

When Brian and Phoebe first met, he was already dependent on painkillers, although it took her years to realize it. Confronting him with her concerns only precipitated angry rebuttals, followed by additional years of lies, denial, and deception. Few things, Freeman had pointed out, were more powerful than loss of trust. Phoebe had her fears surrounding his dishonesty and her feelings about drug addiction, and there was nothing that would alter them except time—time and the changes in Brian that only continued recovery could bring.

Caitlin answered his call on the first ring. She was nine—bookish and intense like her mother and so similar to her in appearance that Brian sometimes thought it was Phoebe sitting curled up in the chair, reading. Even two years after he left the house, Caitlin was still unwilling to accept the situation and seldom spoke about it. Tonight she was anxious to talk about her French class at school, *Heidi,* which she had just finished reading, and her latest piano piece. She reacted mildly to Brian's news about coming to spend the day with him and Jack. Apparently, Phoebe had yet to explain that because their father's medical license had been restored, Caitlin and Becky were free to go wherever they and their father wished. The supervised visitations were over.

"Je t'aime, Papa," Caitlin said before turning the phone over to her younger sister.

"I love you, too, babe," Brian said, swallowing against the baseball that had suddenly materialized in his throat.

"Knock knock," Becky chirped without bothering with a greeting.

Nearly seven, she was radiant, high-energy, athletic, and as down-to-earth as Caitlin was ethereal. Brian had once asked the girls if they ever agreed on anything. Not surprisingly, one replied yes, and the other, no.

"Who's there?" he responded.

"Ivan."

"Ivan who?

"Ivan workin' on the railroad. Here's Mommy. Bye."

"Becky!" Phoebe called out. "Come back here and talk some more with your father. . . . Gone."

"That's okay. I got a knock-knock joke out of her that was actually a knock-knock joke. I'll settle for that."

"She's doing great."

"I know. They both are. . . . So, I'm officially on board."

"Congratulations. You should be very proud of yourself."

"I get paid next week. Postdocs don't earn too much more than fellows, but the check I'll be able to send you will be increased by almost fifty percent."

"Good for all of us," Phoebe said, out front as always. "My bank account echoes when I deposit money in it. If what you say is true, pretty soon I might be able to cut back a couple of hours a week at work—maybe get involved in Brownies."

"Good idea," he replied, carefully avoiding any reaction to her not-so-subtle reminder of his years of broken promises.

There was silence, during which Brian knew she was waiting for his retort.

"You know," she said finally, "as angry and frustrated as I was with you, I always sensed you could make it through this thing."

It's still a day at a time, Brian wanted to warn her. Instead, he thanked her. The sentiment was one she had never expressed before.

The ER was in a rainstorm-induced lull. Brian crossed the muddied reception area and caught up with Gianatasio in the hallway just outside room 4. Phil was hunched over a man in a wheelchair, listening with his stethoscope inside the man's unbuttoned shirt. His patient, who looked every bit of seventy-four years, had his left wrist in a cast and his arm in a sling. His unruly hair was a pile of silver straw. His thick-featured, deeply etched face had a pleasing quality to it, although at the moment he appeared anxious. A man who had endured hard times and prevailed, Brian thought.

Phil worked the stethoscope from his ears and straightened up.

"Wilhelm Elovitz, meet Dr. Brian Holbrook."

"Bill. Everyone calls me Bill," Elovitz replied with a totally engaging smile and a modest Jewish accent. He gestured to the middle-aged woman pushing his chair. "This is my neighbor, Mrs. Levine. She's here to take me home."

"Bill is going to be on the ten o'clock news," Phil said. "Maybe even on CNN, and possibly in *Ripley's Believe It or Not.* The MBTA platform at Downtown Crossing was so crowded, he got shoved off in front of an oncoming train. The conductor managed to stop just in time, but then Bill stumbled trying to get up and fell right on the third rail. This rubber raincoat kept him from becoming a crispy critter, and all he ended up with was a broken wrist."

"*You* can say 'all he ended up with' because it is not your wrist," Elovitz remarked dryly.

"Why did the ER people ask for a cardiac consult?" Brian asked.

"Oh, partly because they just thought that anyone who fell on ten trillion volts ought to be checked over by us whether he conducted the electricity or not, and partly because he's a Vasclear patient. One of the first, as a matter of fact."

Brian's interest perked up immediately.

"And you're doing okay?" he asked.

"I don't know about *your* okay," Elovitz said, "but by *my* okay I'm okay. Now please. My wife is not well and she's very worried about me. I've got to get home."

Brian noted that the man took an extra breath or two during each sentence.

"Dyspnea?" he asked Phil.

"He's in some early CHF," Gianatasio replied, using the abbreviation for congestive heart failure—fluid building up in the lungs because of a weakened heart. "Listen, Bill. You're a little short of breath. I don't work in the Vasclear clinic anymore, but Dr. Holbrook does, and he would like to check you out. Could you call the clinic tomorrow and make an appointment to see him?"

Elovitz cocked his head and looked up at Brian.

"You're a good doctor?" he asked.

"Pretty good," Brian said. "Yes."

"In that case, I'll call. Thank you, Dr. Phil. Let's go, dear."

Before either physician could say a word, Mrs. Levine had wheeled her charge down the hall and around the corner.

"He's cute," Brian said. "How's his ticker?"

"It needs some buffing up. I don't do really good exams in the hallway on patients who are fully dressed and squirming to get out the door. That's why I told him to arrange to see you. You might want to check with the Vasclear secretary in two days. If he hasn't made an appointment, maybe we should call him. Now, let's repair to the residents' room. I want to know if Juicy Lucy came on to you or not."

Twenty minutes later, Brian walked Phil out of the hospital and then returned to continue his orientation tour. Gianatasio was in no position to determine whether Wilhelm Elovitz was a treatment failure on Vasclear or whether his symptoms were due to factors other than hardening of the arteries. But he did make the point that Brian already knew well—while the drug had so far proved to be wildly successful by any standards, twenty-five percent of patients receiving it did not respond.

Brian wandered back to Boston Heart and made his way past the third-floor operating suite and the second-floor laboratories. Patient registration and the administrative offices were on the main floor, along with the regular cardiac clinic. The basement level housed the cardiac cath lab on one end and the animal maintenance facility on the other. In between them was a mechanized canteen. Brian suddenly realized he hadn't eaten anything since breakfast except Phil's cake.

He picked the stairs nearest the cath lab and descended to the basement. Tomorrow morning he would be taking the same stairway down to scrub in on a cath case for the first time in a year and a half, and with Carolyn Jessup no less. The cath lab and the film library next door to it were locked, and the basement corridor was totally deserted, although there were lights on beyond the twin glass doors of the animal facility. He was approaching the small canteen when a man emerged carrying a small cardboard box with two coffees and some sandwiches. He was Brian's height, or even a bit taller, but with a linebacker's broad shoulders and narrow waist; small, dark eyes; high cheekbones; and acne-scarred skin. He was wearing jeans and a blue button-down dress shirt, and was so startled at seeing Brian that he nearly dropped his food.

For the briefest moment, their eyes met. Brian saw only hostility and not a spark of intelligence. The man grunted a greeting, missed badly at an attempt to smile, and backed away several steps before turning. He then hesitated once more before entering the stairway across from the one Brian had used—the stairs down to the subbasement. Brian checked his map. The floors depicted on the sheet ended with the basement. He tried to place the man into some hospital niche based on his dress, impressive size, and connection with the subbasement. Maintenance? Security? Laundry? Heating plant?

A few moments later, Brian was microwaving a breaded chicken-breast sandwich and sipping from a paper cup of scalding coffee as bad as any he had ever tasted. The strange, moose-in-the-headlights expression on the man's pockmarked face refused to fade from his thoughts. But what could the guy have been doing? Stealing food from the vending machines?

Brian's reflections were cut short by his beeper. The number in the display was his home phone. He checked around for a phone, and then carried what remained of his sandwich and coffee down the glimmering linoleum to the lights at the end of the hall, where

Animal Maintenance Facility was painted in gold across the first of two pairs of glass doors. It wasn't until he was inside the outer set that Brian smelled and heard the animals. Through the inner doors, the odor and racket were a lot stronger.

"Help you?"

The man, his feet up on an old, scarred desk, was gaunt and ill-kempt. Brian took in the gray stubble, scraggly gray-black hair, jeans, and stained knee-length lab coat. An empty pen holder/nameplate on the desk identified him simply as Earl.

"My name's Holbrook, Dr. Brian Holbrook. Today's my first day at BHI, so I'm kind of orienting myself. I also wanted to use your phone if I could."

"Phone's all yours," Earl said with an Appalachian twang. "I heard you was comin' today. Gonna be helpin' with the Vasclear study, right?"

Brian was surprised that this basement dweller knew of him. *People may be talking about you, but so far, I haven't heard anything.* Isn't that what Phil had just said?

The man's teeth were nicotine-stained and in dreadful condition, and he was contributing, not insignificantly, to the odor of the place. But there was a smell other than filth that Brian detected coming off him as well—a smell he had become sensitized to over the last eighteen months—alcohol.

"That's right," Brian said. "I'll be working on the ward and covering the Vasclear clinic some evenings. Were you involved in the animal studies?"

" 'Course."

Brian picked up the receiver, at the same time nonchalantly dropping his half-eaten sandwich into the trash. The man's body odor, plus the alcohol fumes, had killed his appetite. Jack's line was busy. Just a few hours ago, the visiting nurse had reported him stable and in decent spirits. Brian checked the coverage list. Sally was supposed to be there with him. It was most likely something minor, he decided.

"Busy," he said. "Okay if I look around for a few minutes before I call again?"

"Suit yerself. I'll be right here."

"What animal did they use for the preliminary Vasclear studies?"

"Oh, a little of everything," Earl replied. "That's the way they usually do it. First the rats 'n rabbits, then a whole bunch of pigs, a few sheep, some dogs, an' finally some monkeys. They like to work with them pig hearts most of the time. Somethin' about them bein' a lot like human hearts. Doesn't surprise me none. I can show you a lot of humans who are just plain pigs."

His mucousy laugh at his own humor terminated in a spasm of coughing. Brian glanced down at his newly placed TB skin test and made a mental note to have a follow-up done in a few months.

"Any problems arise with the testing?" he asked.

Earl looked at him queerly.

"Why no," he said finally. "Why would you ask somethin' like that?"

Brian grinned, trying to dispel the sudden change in mood.

"Just wantin' to learn about the drug I'm going to be workin' with is all," he said, consciously adding the slight twang to his voice.

"Well, for your information, the animal testing was perfect."

"That's great to hear. I'll be back in a minute to try that call again."

Brian turned quickly and headed through the glass-paneled door to the right of Earl's desk, and down one of the rows of cages.

Earl's territory was actually quite large—and much better maintained than the man himself. From the left side of the facility to the right, the cages and the animals increased in size. Mice, hamsters, rats, rabbits, even some small dogs. Brian had never had pets when growing up and perhaps for that reason didn't feel passionately against animal testing of pharmaceuticals, so long as the animals themselves were well cared for. But looking at them now, in row after row of cages, did affect him.

To the far right, separated from the rest of the facility by a glass wall, was a series of larger cages. Several of them were empty at the moment; two held sheep; two others large dogs; and eight of them housed primates—six wiry gibbons and two chimpanzees.

The primate cages were four feet wide by eight feet deep—tall enough for a man to stand. Brian was pleased to see the swinging bars and children's toys—touches of caring. Several of the monkeys seemed as curious about him as he was about them. Then, one of the chimps caught his eye. It was the smaller of the two, although it was still as large as a six-year-old child. It was slumped against the near corner of the cage, apparently asleep. But its breathing was sonorous and labored, and its abdomen seemed markedly distended. In addition, its hind paws were strikingly swollen.

To Brian's eye, the somnolent animal seemed to be experiencing fairly severe fluid retention. Lungs, kidneys, liver, heart—instinctively, Brian thought through the various system failures that could be causing such a condition, acknowledging that certain hormonal imbalances could produce the same picture as well.

There was a mop resting against the wall nearby. Brian held it at the business end, slipped the pole between the steel mesh, and gently prodded the animal. Nothing. No reaction at all. He repeated the maneuver a little more firmly, touching the end of the pole against the side of the chimp's distended belly. A rheumy eye opened and slowly looked down at the spot. But there was no reaction besides that. The animal was ill, almost moribund. Brian noted down the number in the card affixed to the cage—4386. Then he returned to the desk, where Earl was reading the comics in the *Herald*.

Before mentioning the animal, Brian called Jack once more. His father answered on the first ring.

"Brian?"

"Yeah, Pop. You okay?"

"Of course. I was just calling to see when you were coming home."

Brian winced. Once one of the most fiercely self-reliant men he had ever known, his father was becoming more and more dependent as his illness progressed. Brian had encountered the syndrome in many of his patients, but Jack was only sixty-three. It was as if his natural aging was accelerating. And without any siblings, Brian knew there was nowhere for him to displace the consequences. The coach was rapidly becoming his third child.

"I was going to wait until the traffic let up some," Brian replied. "Seven-thirty, eight, maybe. Can I bring you anything?"

"How about some ice cream?"

"You can't eat ice cream, Jack. . . . Oh, hell. Listen, I'll be home by eight, and I'll bring you a cone from Schiller's."

"Hey, that would be great. That kind made out of cookies, okay?"

"Oreo, Pop. You've got it."

Brian said good-bye and set the receiver down, wondering where it was all going to end.

"Thanks," he said to Earl. "Thanks a lot. Say, listen, I was just watching one of those chimps back there, cage number four-three-eight-six, and I swear he's sick."

"Nonsense. Ol' Jake is fat 'n lazy. But he ain't no sicker 'n you or me."

"Maybe so, but I think he's got pretty severe fluid retention. Come on back and I'll show you."

"I ain't goin' no place except here. I'll look in on him before I leave."

There was clear irritation in his voice.

"Hey, easy does it," Brian said, trying to remain cheerful, but sensing his own temper beginning to click in. "It won't take a minute to come check him." He gestured at the *Herald*. "That'll be there when you get back."

The moment he said it, Brian knew the facetious remark was a mistake.

Earl pushed unsteadily to his feet and confronted him, his face distorted and crimson. The alcohol odor was even heavier than Brian had at first appreciated.

"Look," Earl said, "I told you I'd check Jake in my own time and tha's what I'm gonna do. You're a druggie, ain't you. Everyone's been sayin' that. Well, you just watch your step, 'n watch who you're orderin' around."

Brian was shocked. He warned himself to leave and just let the matter drop. But the quarterback in him wouldn't allow it.

"Earl, I may be new, but I'm still a doctor on the faculty here, and I don't think what I'm asking is so unusual. Look, just tell me what study the monkey's involved in. I'll speak to the researcher myself."

"These are my animals. If they's any reportin' to do, I'll do it myself."

"Hey, I don't know what's with you, but you've been drinking—quite a bit, I think. I'm going to speak with Dr. Pickard about what's going on down here."

Earl jutted his chin out.

"You just go ahead," he said. "Report me to anyone you fuckin' want. My bet is you do that 'n you'll find yourself on unemployment quicker than you can say junkie. Now get out of here."

Brian held his temper in check, but just barely. The fallout of being involved in a major incident with an employee after only a few hours on the job wasn't worth it. Fists clenched, he whirled and left.

CHAPTER EIGHT

BOSTON HERALD

General Release of Wonder Heart Med Could Be Just Weeks Away

Officials at South Boston's Newbury Pharmaceuticals say that patient testing of their experimental heart drug, Vasclear, has demonstrated remarkable clearing of clogged coronary arteries in over seventy-five percent of cases. They have requested lifesaving-drug status for their discovery, which would enable it to become available to the general public without further testing.

BRIAN SLEPT LESS THAN TWO HOURS DURING THE night before his first full day on duty. It was hardly the way he wanted to prepare his mind or body for a morning in the cath lab and the afternoon covering the clinical service. But the emotional roller coaster of his orientation day had refused to slow down.

. . . *Report me to anyone you fuckin' want. My bet is you do that 'n you'll find yourself on unemployment quicker than you can say junkie.* . . .

Jesus! Gianatasio's assessment of the situation notwithstanding, the word about him certainly *was* out. And it was clear that although he might be given responsibility for patient management, resuscitations, performing cardiac catheterizations, and running the Vasclear clinic, he was still very much the low man on the BHI totem pole. But he also felt the strength of his recovery had him ready to deal with whatever life in the hospital held in store.

The moment of truth for him had come nearly eighteen months ago, on his second day at the Fairweather Center. His counselor, Lois, herself a long-term recovering addict, had two small plaques tacked to the wall above her desk.

TIME IS NATURE'S WAY OF KEEPING EVERYTHING FROM HAPPENING AT ONCE.

WHEN WE SPEAK OF TOMORROW, THE GODS LAUGH.

Brian was staring up at the words without really comprehending either message when Lois suddenly snapped a ruler down on her desk.

"Okay, Dr. Holbrook," she said, "it's time for the sixty-four-thousand-dollar question. What are you willing to do to get out from under the shit that's burying you right now?"

Brian, then just a week past the morning when two Drug Enforcement Agency officers had marched into his office with a computer printout of wholesale-drug-house Percocet orders, and a dozen or so prescriptions made out to various members of the Holbrook family, was too frightened, bewildered, and depressed to respond to the woman right away. He had no way of knowing that there was only one totally acceptable answer to her question, and that he was about to give it. Finally, he looked up at her, his eyes glazed and reddened, his face unshaven.

"I'm willing to do anything," he said. "Just tell me what to do."

Where those words came from at that moment, he still didn't know. And at the time, he certainly didn't notice the glow that they brought to his counselor's face. But they marked the beginning of the radical overhaul of his life.

The Fairweather Center specialized in helping alcoholic and chemically dependent health professionals. Many of the seventy or so who were residents there at the same time as Brian were physicians. And almost all of them, Brian included, had to overcome their own arrogance, drive, discipline, denial, and logic in order to free themselves from their addictions. They had to learn that what worked for them in courses like organic chemistry—intellect and sheer willpower—was not going to be enough to bring about lasting recovery, and in fact, was going to be an impediment in the early stages.

For Brian, the teachings of Lois and the rest were like a log floating past a drowning man. He grabbed on and held tight, with no idea where the current was taking him. For others at Fairweather, meetings and sponsors and surrender to a higher power made no sense whatsoever. And while they argued and rationalized and resisted, their log drifted on past. Some of those docs—physicians with so much training, so much intelligence, and so much to give—were already dead.

"For the past three months you've been leading a sheltered existence here at Fairweather," Lois told him as she handed over his discharge plan. "But trust me, real life is waiting for you up there in Massachusetts, and real life can be pretty damn cruel at times, especially for an M.D. with your history. So, just remember, it's a day at a time, an hour at a time, a minute at a time. Whatever it takes to get through a situation without resorting to pills again."

. . . *My bet is you do that 'n you'll find yourself on unemployment quicker than you can say junkie.* . . .

. . . *Real life can be pretty damn cruel at times.* . . .

The words continued reverberating in his head as Brian entered the hospital through the White Memorial lobby. He was still shaken by what had happened in the animal lab the night before, but he knew that whatever he had to endure, he would. All he had ever asked was to get his foot back in the door of medicine. Now, it was time to begin proving himself. And if proving himself meant turning the other cheek to bastards like the animal keeper, that's what he would do. There was simply too much at stake not to—for him and for his father.

At eight-fifteen the previous evening, when Brian arrived home from his orientation, he had found Jack asleep in his chair. Sally Johansen, the neighbor on duty, put a finger to her lips, then pointed to the nitroglycerin vial and put up three fingers. Three episodes of pain. Brian thanked her silently, kissed her on the cheek, and waved her out. Then he gently woke Jack up to give him his Oreo cone. Jack stayed awake long enough to wolf down the ice cream and then allowed Brian to walk him to bed, a concession that was totally out of character. The man was failing. Difficult decisions could not be postponed much longer.

Brian set a stack of cardiology texts and journals on the floor by the couch. Then, suddenly restless, he had pulled on a pair of sweats and gone for a slow three-mile jog through the balmy evening—the first time in months he had run. The encounter with Earl was tough to shuck, but finally, after half a mile or so, he managed to get his mind to drift into hazy images of what life would be like once he had a private practice again and a few years of decent income.

Back at home, he had showered, then settled in for what turned out to be several hours of studying. He was dozing on the living-room couch when he heard Jack groan, shuffle to the bathroom, then back to bed. Brian finished the chapter he was reviewing and went to the doorway to check on him. His father was propped against the headboard, the tiny vial of nitroglycerin in his hand.

"Pain wake you up?" Brian asked, startling him.

"Oh, hi . . . no . . . I mean, a little. Yesterday wasn't my best."

"Mine, either," Brian said before he could edit himself.

"What do you mean by that? You said over the phone that things were going great."

"They're fine. Everything's fine . . . except you and that angina."

"I'll tell you what," Jack said, slipping a nitro under his tongue, "when you level with me, I'll level with you."

He closed his eyes and slid back down on the pillow, waiting for the medication to dilate his coronary arteries and bring a little extra blood to his oxygen-starved heart muscle. In just a few minutes he was asleep on his back, snoring. Brian stood there for a time, looking down at him.

What if I hadn't changed that play that you called? he was thinking.

Brian arrived at the cath lab after making rounds on the eighteen patients on the clinical ward with Phil, a cardiac fellow, two residents, two medical students, and the nurses. He was not surprised that his old friend was an excellent teacher and compassionate physician. Only two of the eighteen patients were part of the Vasclear study, and although both were quite ill from cardiac disease, both were in the gamma group, which Phil said was almost certainly placebo. If anything, the bedside discussion of Vasclear and the consistent lack of side effects in the beta group made him even more certain that Jack would benefit from treatment with it.

The case he would be assisting Carolyn Jessup on was a routine eighteen-month, post-Vasclear cath study in a sixty-nine-year-old woman named Nellie Hennessey. Brian walked down to the basement from the fifth floor, with the faces of Earl the animal keeper and the pockmarked man flashing alternately in his mind like a neon sign.

Before entering the cath suite, he glanced down the corridor at the animal facility. *Number 4386.* Was it worth speaking to anyone about the pathetic chimpanzee, or, for that matter, about Earl's abominable behavior? At this moment in his brief history at Boston Heart, the answer to both questions was a resounding *No.* If he was going to make waves about anything, it would be about getting Jack randomized into the Vasclear study.

Andrew, the cath tech, was changing into his scrubs in the men's locker room.

"Morning, Dr. Holbrook," he said. "Welcome to the staff."

There was genuine warmth in his expression. Brian extended his hand and the man gripped it firmly. When they met at Jack's cath, Brian had liked Andrew immediately. Now, he felt a twinge of discomfort that, like everyone else in the institute, Andrew had probably encountered some version of his life story. *Get used to it,* he thought, paraphrasing something Freeman had said to him more than once. *Get used to it, then get over it.*

"It's Brian," he said.

"Very well, then, Brian. How's your father doing?"

"Well, you saw his cath."

"I did. I hope the show Dr. Randa put on didn't frighten you both out of following his recommendation. He's just like that."

"As a matter of fact, Randa did send me scrambling to get my dad into the Vasclear program."

"And?"

"I haven't heard yet. Apparently his prior bypass surgery is a problem."

"I'm sorry to hear that. Vasclear sure has been a wonder. Mrs.

Hennessey, who we're doing this morning, looked just about as bad as your father before we started treatment. And now, just wait till you see."

"Is she here yet?" Brian asked.

"Right outside in the holding area with Jennifer, the cath nurse. Lauren will be operating the console in the control room. Both of them were here when we did your father."

"Well, I'm ready."

"Dr. Jessup's here, too. I just saw her go into the locker room, so it shouldn't be too long before we're ready to go. That Mrs. Hennessey's a nice lady. Real nice."

Brian entered the cath lab just as Nellie Hennessey was being helped from the stretcher onto the cath table. He had seen her pleasant, impish face before, although it took him a few seconds to remember where. She was the Vasclear poster child featured in the video. Brian remembered her snapping blue eyes.

"Nellie, look at these two men," Jennifer said. "Twin towers. They look like basketball players."

Nellie Hennessey pointed up at Brian.

"Andrew I know, darlin' " she said. "But who's he?"

"A new doctor here. Dr. Holbrook. He's going to be assisting Dr. Jessup with your cath."

Nellie motioned Jennifer to bend closer.

"He's very cute," Brian heard her say in a stage whisper.

"Mrs. Hennessey, it's nice to meet you," he said, taking her hand. "But I think I sort of met you yesterday when I watched the film about Vasclear."

"Oh, yes," Nellie said. "My fifteen minutes of fame. How long have you been a doctor?"

"Quite a while. But I'm new *here*."

She thought about that for a moment.

"Well," she said, "Dr. Jessup's the best. She'll teach you all you need to know about doing this."

"Why thank you, Nellie," Jessup said, sweeping into the room, scrubbed, capped, and masked. "Good morning, everyone. I assume you all remember Dr. Holbrook. Brian, why don't you scrub. We'll be ready to go as soon as you do."

There was a small prep area between the locker room and the lab. Brian donned a mask and hair-cover and did a four-minute scrub over the stainless-steel sink. Despite the fact that he had performed a thousand or more cardiac caths, and even though he was only going to assist today, his heart was doing the flamenco in his chest. He shook the water from his hands, backed into the cath lab, and allowed the scrub nurse to help him gown and glove.

"Okay, gang," Carolyn said, "let's get started. Nellie, are you ready?"

"My back's already starting to ache. So let's get this over."

"Grumble, grumble."

Jessup gave Nellie Hennessey's history as she worked.

"Mrs. H. is a sixty-nine-year-old retired schoolteacher—"

"Sixty-eight-and-a-half," Nellie interjected.

"Sixty-eight-and-a-half, who was referred to me almost two years ago for chest pain—"

"Actually, it was up here in my shoulder and sometimes my neck," Nellie said, her speech beginning to thicken. "Never really in my chest."

Jessup put two fingers over Nellie's femoral artery pulse and smoothly slipped the large-bore needle through the anesthetized skin beneath her fingers and into the vessel. Then she advanced the arterial catheter through the needle and up toward the left-side chambers of Nellie's heart.

"Having Nellie as a patient," she said, "is like being back in school. You get marked off for everything."

"You still get an A, dear," Nellie said, her tongue and mouth now parchment-dry.

"That Ward-Dunlop catheter really is slick," Brian noted.

"I expect you to use it exclusively when you start doing cases on your own."

"No problem there."

"Well, to continue, Nellie's treadmill stress test was positive, and a subsequent cath showed fairly severe coronary artery disease. She was a perfect candidate for randomization into the Vasclear study. Right, Nellie?"

Nellie, eyes closed, was breathing deeply and regularly.

"Jennifer," Jessup went on, "maybe we should be giving her a tad less pre-op medication. If I have to stay awake for this, everyone does." She glanced over at the nurse, her eyes smiling. "Seriously, nice job. She's perfect. . . . Anyhow, Brian, Nellie's symptoms disappeared almost immediately and haven't returned. This is her third and last follow-up cath. Then she becomes an alumna."

"What Vasclear group is she in?" Brian asked, already knowing the answer.

"Beta. Okay, Doc, you're on. Let's switch sides. You do the right heart and afterward I'll switch back and do the coronary-artery shots. Nellie's asleep so you're not being graded on this. Just relax and have fun."

"Thank you."

Surprised and pleased at being asked to do anything other than observe, Brian moved behind Carolyn to take her place at the table.

"Everything on the Ward-Dunlop works pretty much like the one you're used to," she said, "except the controls are much more responsive, and the connections on the ports just click and lock."

"Impressive," Brian said, proceeding with the pressure studies and dye injections.

The nurse, Jennifer, was working beside him now, keeping a careful watch on Nellie, checking her blood pressure and IV.

"Everything okay?" Brian asked her.

"All systems are go," she replied.

Brian took some pressure measurements through the catheter, then injected some dye to check the tricuspid and pulmonic valves. The moment he had thought might never come was here. He was back in the cath lab, regaining control, piece by piece, of his own destiny.

"You seem pretty comfortable there, pardner," Jessup said, returning to her position to do the left heart and coronary-artery exam.

"Just like riding a bike. She's got a pretty healthy-looking heart."

"Wait till you see her coronary arteries. These pictures we're about to shoot are going to be the eighteen-month-afters. The befores are in the cine-library through the door just past the women's changing room. Did security give you a code for the keypad?"

"They did."

"Great. Sometime soon, go and take a look at Nellie's pre-Vasclear films. We've got two Vangard viewers in there. One for backup."

"I'm impressed," Brian said. The viewers, from what he remembered, cost around twenty thousand dollars apiece.

"You'll be even more impressed when you review her films," Carolyn said. "Now, let's take a look at her left heart and coronaries."

The experimental Ward-Dunlop catheter was exceptionally easy to manipulate, and certainly showed up well on X ray.

"Left anterior oblique cranial . . . right anterior oblique caudal . . ."

Jessup called out each angle, waited for Andrew to position the X-ray camera, then injected some dye and activated the camera with her foot pedal. Overhead, one screen showed the bright white of the X-ray-opaque dye as it briefly filled Nellie's coronary arteries before being washed away, and another traced her heartbeat, oxygenation, and other vital signs. In the glassed-in control room to their right, the other nurse, Lauren, monitored duplicate screens, and kept watch over the machine that was recording the injections on videotape. Later, the tape would be reviewed by Jessup, and a report dictated. The width of every significant artery and every blockage would be carefully measured by computer and recorded.

". . . Right anterior oblique cranial," Carolyn said, completing the last of the five left coronary-artery views. "Okay, everyone, if there is anyone with reasons why this woman and this catheter should remain in holy matrimony, let him speak now or forever hold his peace. . . . There being no objections to removal of this line, I hereby do so."

Carolyn withdrew the catheter with the same smoothness, the same confidence, as she had displayed throughout the procedure. But quite suddenly, a brief flurry of extra heartbeats appeared on the screen. Then another burst.

A few moments later, Nellie Hennessey moaned.

Then she opened her eyes.

Then she began screaming.

CHAPTER NINE

"OH, MY GOD! . . . MY CHEST, MY CHEST! . . . OH, God, I can't breathe!"

Nellie Hennessey, wailing piteously, clutched at her chest and thrashed back and forth, slamming her arms and shoulders against the X-ray tube still positioned just above her. Overhead, the monitor continued to record salvos of extra heartbeats, often the prelude to a full-blown cardiac arrest.

There was no doubt in Brian's mind what was happening. The woman was having a coronary occlusion—a heart attack. But why? They had just examined her coronary arteries and they were virtually clear of arteriosclerosis. There were only two explanations that made sense.

"Give her morphine," Jessup ordered urgently. "Three IV. No, make it four. How's her pressure?"

"One-eighty over one-ten," Jennifer replied.

"Brian, what do you think?"

"She's either in coronary-artery spasm," Brian said, "or the tip of that catheter broke off while you were pulling it out. Has that ever happened before?"

"No," Carolyn said, too quickly. "I mean, not here. Not in a while. . . . Nellie . . . Nellie! You've got to try and lie still. Jennifer, where's that morphine?"

"Four milligrams in."

"Hang a nitroglycerin drip up, please."

"Right away."

"Oh, my God!" Nellie shrieked. "Help me! . . . Please help me!"

Brian knew he was just there to assist, and Carolyn Jessup was a seasoned specialist, a professor. Still, Nellie Hennessey's life was at stake. He had spent seven years as a partner in a very active private practice, the last three of them as chief of a busy cath lab. If it became clear that he saw something Jessup didn't, he wouldn't hesitate to call her attention to it. But for the moment, she was handling things flawlessly. And regardless of who was in charge, Nellie Hennessey was in big, big trouble.

"Let's give her seventy-five of Xylocaine to do something about those extra beats," Carolyn said. "Nellie, please, try to hold still! Andrew, give me an LAO caudal angle. I've got to see if the catheter tip has broken off and wedged itself in an artery."

Andrew moved the camera electronically to the left anterior oblique position. Nellie, perhaps responding to the IV morphine, settled back a bit, but continued moaning in pain. Jessup clicked the fluoroscopic camera on with the toe plate.

"There," Brian said.

It took a few moments for the others to see the fragment, but there it was—a small, bright white line on the black-and-white screen. It was three-quarters of an inch long, resting on top of the upper portion of the heart muscle, moving with each beat.

"What do you think?" Jessup asked. "Left main?"

"Hard to say, but yes. That's my guess."

Almost certainly, the catheter tip had broken off and become lodged in the left main coronary artery—the Widowmaker.

"Lauren, call the OR, please," Jessup said to the control-room nurse. "Have them assemble the pump team and whichever surgeon's available. We're going after this, but I want them on standby as quickly as possible."

"Oh, sweet Jesus, I can't breathe!" Nellie was crying. "Do something . . . My chest is being crushed! . . . Please, please, oh God, do something!"

The tension in the room, already bowstring tight, was ratcheted even tighter by the woman's unremitting cries. Brian was impressed and relieved to see that everyone on the team seemed able to handle the strain. For a moment, Andrew's eyes met his. Although outwardly composed, there was no masking the technician's concern.

"Jennifer," Jessup said, "if her pressure's okay, give her another two of morphine."

"Given."

"Brian, what about intubating her? Are you sharp?"

"I moonlighted in an ER for my first few years in practice. If anesthesia can't get down here, I think I can do it."

"Lauren, page anesthesia. Andrew, get things ready for Dr. Holbrook to intubate. Be sure to check the balloon on the tube. Nellie, hang in there. Can you hear me?"—Nellie nodded weakly—"Good. Now listen, please. A piece of the catheter we used has broken off in one of your arteries and is blocking the flow of blood.

We're going to get it out. Understand? . . . Good. As soon as it's out you'll feel much better. Now, who came with you today?"

"My . . . daughter."

"We'll speak with her shortly. Meantime, just tell Dr. Holbrook if your pain's not getting better, and he'll give you some more medicine. Andrew, I need a Microvena snare. Quickly, please."

The snare was a wire loop, threaded up through a catheter, and operated by a finger trigger. It was tricky to use under the best of circumstances. But with Nellie unable to lie still for more than fifteen or twenty seconds at a time, and the fragment of catheter tubing moving with each heartbeat, the retrieval was going to be a bear.

Brian was impressed to see that Jessup was meeting the challenge head-on. But as first one, then another pass with the snare failed to catch the tubing, he could hear the strain creeping into her voice. Her eyes were narrowed. She shook her hand to loosen the muscles.

Nellie's heart attack was evolving rapidly. A large portion of the muscle in the front of her heart was getting little or no blood, and that muscle was reacting to the diminished oxygen supply with viselike pain and electrical instability—continued bursts of dangerous extra beats. There was no permanent damage yet. But soon, almost certainly before she could be brought to the OR, there would be. And if two of the premature beats should fire off at the same time, her heart might well be thrown into electrical standstill—a cardiac arrest. . . . Brian did his best to shelve that thought.

Jessup tried a third time . . . then a fourth. Her fists were clenched with frustration.

"Lauren, are they ready in the OR?"

"Not yet."

"Pressure's dropping some," Jennifer said quietly.

Jessup readied the snare for another try. Then she glanced over at Brian. Her eyes looked flat, defeated. There was nothing to do, her expression was saying—nothing to do but hope the cardiac surgical team sent for Nellie before her heart gave out altogether. But even then, once Nellie was in the OR and on heart-lung by-pass, another battle would be fought—the battle to salvage as much cardiac muscle as possible. With each passing second, the likelihood of her making it without massive damage was diminishing, as was the chance that she was going to make it at all.

"Oh, please. . . . Oh, please. . . . Oh, please. . . ."

Nellie was moaning continuously now.

Brian checked her pupils and saw maximum narcotic constriction. Giving her more morphine would be risky. A narcotic-induced crash in her blood pressure or a respiratory arrest would make a grave situation even worse.

"Any ideas?" Carolyn asked softly.

"Just one," Brian replied. "Try using a biopsy forceps instead of the snare."

"What?"

"Andrew, do we have a BIPAL biopsy forceps?"

"I think so."

"I've used them a couple of times for endocardial biopsies. It has two little prongs to snip off pieces of tissue. I'd like to take a crack at clamping down on the catheter tip with those prongs."

"I have one right here," Andrew called out.

"Do it, please," Jessup ordered, stepping aside to make room for Brian.

"The OR just called," Lauren said through the control-room intercom. "They're ready."

Jessup hesitated. A miss now would consume more time than Nellie had left, but a dash to the OR was chancy at best. For five seconds, ten, there was only silence.

"Brian, I know it's been a while," she said finally. "Are you okay with this?"

Brian looked down at Nellie Hennessey, who lay there, eyes closed, whimpering softly. Tears of pain had tracked down over her cheeks. He knew, as did Carolyn, that this was rapidly becoming the worst of disasters. If the obstruction wasn't removed immediately, the best Nellie could hope for was life as a cardiac cripple.

"I can try," he said.

"Go ahead."

Brian took a single calming breath and guided the two-pronged forceps up the aorta toward the fragment. Over the years, he had spent countless hours studying textbooks and models of the heart, assisting in the OR, and working in cath labs. Now, all that experience was at work, helping him to visualize Nellie's heart in three dimensions—to see through the flat image on the monitor screen and to angle the forceps just so.

The Board of Registration in Medicine has determined that your license to practice medicine be suspended for a period of . . .

Oddly, the memory of the words on the letter from the board flashed through Brian's mind at the moment he closed the prongs of the BIPAL. On the monitor, the catheter fragment twitched visibly.

"I think you've got it," Jessup said in a half-whisper.

Slowly, ever so slowly, Brian pulled back the instrument. For an instant, the fragment seemed to be caught on something. Then, dutifully, it flicked again, indicating it was still locked between the biopsy prongs. One millimeter at a time, Brian withdrew the BIPAL out the left coronary, over the aortic arch, then down the descending aorta. Almost instantly, the dangerous premature beats disappeared from the electrocardiograph monitor screen. And even before the piece was pulled out through Nellie's groin, she stopped her restless, pain-driven struggle.

"Oh, my," she said. "It's better. The pain's beginning to go away."

The cath team members exhaled in unison. Brian's exhilaration exceeded anything he had ever experienced on the football field.

Your license to practice medicine has been suspended . . .

"Thank you, God," Brian murmured under his mask.

"Lauren," Jessup said, her eyes beaming, "call the OR and tell them we won't be needing them."

CHAPTER TEN

IT WAS NEARLY TWO IN THE AFTERNOON BEFORE AN opening in Carolyn Jessup's schedule allowed her to respond to Brian's request to meet with her. She looked relaxed and, as always, elegant in a gray cotton suit and white blouse. Her dark hair was pulled back in a knot. Her office rivaled Pickard's in opulence, with floor-to-ceiling bookshelves covering one wall and various certificates, testimonials, diplomas, celebrity photographs, and letters of gratitude blanketing another. One thing that Brian did not find was a photograph of family or of Jessup in any recreational setting. But with more important business on his mind at the moment, he shrugged off his curiosity about the woman. Whenever he wanted to, he could read all about her in *Who's Who in American Medicine.*

Brian settled into a low-backed leather chair across the desk from her. A pressing appointment of some kind had kept Jessup from spending any time with him after Nellie Hennessey's remarkable save. Now, she fixed her dark brown eyes on him and nodded her pleasure.

"You certainly have had a major impact on this place in a very short time," she said.

Brian gestured to his height.

"I've always had trouble being inconspicuous," he said.

"Did you always want to be a doctor?"

"No. Actually, I always wanted to be a professional football player. I liked science, though. And after I tore up my knee in a game, I knew I still wanted to amount to something, so I decided to take a shot at med school."

"I see. Well, there are two patients in this hospital who should be pretty grateful that you did. So am I."

"Thank you. And thanks for trusting your judgment about me down there."

Brian held off bringing up Jack and Vasclear, hoping that Carolyn would do it herself.

"The truth is," she said, "it wasn't just my judgment about you. I didn't think Nellie would have survived if we had to bring her to the OR. It was quite literally do-or-die. And to tell you the very absolute truth, I really didn't think you could pull it off. But I assume, or at least I *hope,* you didn't ask to see me so that I could tell you what a great job you did."

"No, although it's good to hear. What I wanted to talk with you about is Jack."

"Sure. I'd be happy to go over his situation with you. But first there's one thing I wanted to mention that I neglected to say in the cath lab before I had to run off."

"Yes?"

"At any given time, there are a dozen or more medications and products that are being evaluated at Boston Heart. Sometimes we are one of a number of centers working cooperatively. Sometimes we have sole responsibility for a study. Always, there is a great deal at stake—tens, even hundreds of millions of dollars. Staffing, equipment, research positions, teaching positions, *your* position—all of them are tied up with the economics of research and development."

"I understand that," Brian said, puzzled as to where Jessup was heading.

"Good. Now, one of the policies Dr. Pickard and his predecessor instituted, which we feel is essential for the continued growth of the institute, is that all product problems must be reported to either Dr. Pickard or myself. We will evaluate the situation and decide what, if any action, is called for."

Brian felt his gut begin to tighten.

"I see," he managed.

"The staff in the cath lab, on the ward, and in the clinic all know that discussing any problems concerning the work we do here with anybody—inside the institute or without—is grounds for dismissal. Our reporting system is in place for a very good reason. Many times a manufacturer can correct a problem with a drug or piece of equipment in just a few weeks. But if the bureaucracy in Washington or the FDA in Rockville gets hold of something, it could take years. The staff here all know that this is institute policy, but I'm not sure anyone had spoken to you yet."

Brian felt himself plummeting earthward from a great height.

"Actually, nobody had."

"And?"

"Well, I spoke to Phil Gianatasio about what happened. He and I have known each other since residency."

"I know. That's no problem. Philip is one of the best, most loyal people on this staff. He's up for tenure."

"I'm sure he'll get it. Um . . . there's more. I've always been pretty obsessive about not allowing work to pile up any more than it absolutely has to, especially paperwork. I dictated the op note of the cath before I was even out of my scrubs. The note included the rescue of the cath-tip fragment, although I didn't say that I was operating the BIPAL forceps."

"No problem," Jessup replied. "Once transcription gives you your copy, just send it up to me. I'll do the dictation over myself so you don't have to worry about it."

Brian was beginning to feel genuinely ill about what he still hadn't disclosed. He considered lying by omission, simply not telling her what else he had done. But certainly word would get back to her sooner or later. And when it did, he might well be finished at BHI.

"I'm afraid there's one more thing," he said.

Jessup's expression darkened.

"Go on," she said.

"Well, after I finished the dictation, I noticed there was a stack of FDA MedWatch forms in a holder on the desk. As long as I was tying up the case, I filled one out and sent it in."

Brian could see the muscles in Jessup's face harden.

"Submission of that form is strictly voluntary," she said.

"I know. I've always felt that doctors were too busy or lazy to report most problems with drugs and products, and so I've always gone out of my way to do it."

That was very foolish of you.

Had Jessup actually said those words, Brian wondered, or had he imagined them?

"Exactly what did you do with the envelope?" she asked.

"Excuse me?"

"The envelope. The envelope with the MedWatch report." Jessup's voice was harsh. "Did you mail it?"

"I . . . yes. Yes, I dropped it off at the mail room on my way up to the ward. Dr. Jessup, I'm really sorry. If I had known—"

Jessup had already snatched up the phone and asked the operator for the mail room. After several minutes of waiting in silence, looking anyplace except at Brian, she set the receiver down.

"The mail's gone out," she said flatly. "We had an understanding with Ward-Dunlop that we would allow them first crack at correcting any problem with the catheter. That's the way we do business. That catheter is due for government approval later this year. By January, hospitals all over the world will be using it."

But it's flawed, Brian was thinking. And hadn't Jessup said something about a previous similar episode at another institution?

As if reading his thoughts, Jessup softened a bit.

"Brian, I know you meant well, and I totally approve of physicians protecting their patients from defective or dangerous products and pharmaceuticals. But there's a much better, more efficient, and certainly more cost-effective way of doing it than relying on what may be the most inept, bureaucratically snarled agency in the entire government. What we encountered in the cath lab was probably nothing more than an isolated defect in an isolated product, not a design flaw."

"I understand. Believe me, it won't happen again."

"Well, I hope not. The people at Ward-Dunlop will do what they can to deal with the impact of your report." She checked her calendar and then her watch. "Was there something else?" she asked.

There was no doubt in Brian's mind that she was still peeved.

"My father?" he asked.

"Oh, yes. He seems to be holding his own on the change of medications I instituted."

"Actually, I think he's still somewhat unstable. Certainly the quality of his life's not very good. Looking at Nellie's cath this morning made me wish more than ever that Jack could get put on Vasclear."

"He needs surgery, Brian."

"Dr. Jessup, my father bets on things. It's sort of a hobby. Give him the seventy-five percent chance that Nellie Hennessey had

when she started her Vasclear, and he'd choose Vasclear over surgery every time."

"Brian, please. I'm his doctor, and I'm recommending repeat
bypass. Could I make myself any clearer?"

"You said you'd speak with Dr. Weber."

"I'm sorry, I haven't had the chance. But he's very protective of
the study. I know he'll say that we're not taking post-bypass patients."

"Why can't you start another subset?"

"Even if we do take him, he'll have to be randomized just like
all the other patients. That only gives him a thirty-three percent
chance to get the results you talked about."

"That's the same chance Nellie Hennessey had, and look what
happened to her. Dr. Jessup, I want my father back, and I don't
want him to suffer like he did after his last bypass."

"Dr. Randa, for all of his personality flaws, is definitely a cut
above Dr. Clarkin."

"I'm sure Randa has disasters, too."

"God, but you're persistent. I'll tell you what. Dr. Weber's been
away, but I think he's back now. Will you be around later in the
afternoon?"

"Actually, I'll be covering the Vasclear clinic."

"Okay. For what you did this morning to save Nellie, I'll do my
best. I'll speak to him and get in touch with you at the clinic."

"That's the most I can ask for."

"And no more FDA reports?"

"No more."

"Fine. That'll be all, then."

Brian turned to go, then turned back.

"Dr. Jessup, that persistence you spoke about?"

"Yes?"

"I learned it from my father."

CHAPTER ELEVEN

THE IWO JIMA MEMORIAL OVERLOOKED THE POTOMAC from a spot near the National Cemetery at Arlington. As instructed, Dr. Alexander Baird took the limo that had been sent for him, allowed the driver to decide where he should be dropped off, and walked past the magnificent statue to a particular bench. There, secluded from the footpaths and walkways by a small grove of evergreens, he sat and waited.

Baird's day usually began at six with a jog around the streets of Georgetown, followed by breakfast with his wife. Today, much to his irritation, it was necessary to deprive himself of both pleasures for an early trip to the office in Rockville. Throughout the morning, he had continued his ongoing review of two stacks of paper-work, amounting to nearly five feet of Vasclear-related reports and research results.

It was just after one in the afternoon and except for a few runners, the park was deserted. Across the river, morning sun glinted off the Jefferson and Lincoln memorials and sparkled off the top of the Capitol. From a distance, D.C. was alabaster perfection. But Baird had come to realize that being lulled by any aspect of the city—its appearance, its power, its sense of purpose—was not unlike becoming mesmerized by the beauty, symmetry, and easy movement of a cobra.

Four days had passed since the hearing before Walter Louderman's oversight committee. During that time, as he had promised, Baird had augmented Teri Sennstrom's staff by transferring three additional research examiners from their projects to the job of reviewing the Vasclear research and cardiac-catheterization data. But Senator Louderman, like most of those in Washington, it seemed, trusted no one but himself.

Memos had begun to circulate suggesting that larger, more established pharmaceutical houses than Newbury were pressuring Baird to keep Vasclear out of general distribution for as long as possible while their scientists searched for a compound chemically different from Vasclear, yet similar in action and effectiveness. At the same time, articles began proliferating in the lay press all over the world, extolling the remarkable results of the wonder drug and estimating the loss in lives and health-care dollars for every single day it remained locked in Newbury warehouses. *Fountain of Youth Reduced to a Trickle,* the headline in one New York tabloid declared.

If Louderman's people were to run his presidential campaign as efficiently as they did this one, the incumbent's reelection was in serious trouble. Just enough references were made in the press to the anti-AIDS drug AZT to spur a flood of letters to the editor and mail to congressmen demanding that a medication aimed at healing the heart of America be afforded the same priority by the FDA as one directed at the germ some of the more depraved protesters called God's virus.

The media blitz couldn't have been more effective. Suddenly, even the most medically unsophisticated seemed to know that AZT was approved in 1987 after less than two years of clinical testing and three months of FDA review. And although he was teaching medical students in Missouri at the time, Alexander Baird was being portrayed as responsible for hurrying it through in a manner much different from the way he was handling Vasclear. Finally, not at all to Baird's surprise, White House Chief of Staff Stan Pomeroy had called and set up this meeting.

Baird rubbed at the fatigue in his eyes and then watched enviously as two runners loped along the walkway to his left. It was generally agreed that he had done an excellent job of restoring some of the lost public and private confidence in his agency. Now, political pressure seemed poised to overwhelm the caution that had marked his first nine months as FDA commissioner. And the only weapons he had been able to muster to counter the surge were his own intuition and an unwavering respect for the scientific process.

"Deep thoughts?"

Stan Pomeroy had entered the grove through the trees behind Baird. He took a seat on the bench and extended his hand. Baird shook it warmly. Pomeroy was the first black White House chief of staff and was held in almost universal esteem in a town where true esteem wasn't easily come by. When Baird had waffled on the idea of stepping into the FDA furnace, it was Pomeroy who had flown out to Missouri to convince him.

"Nothing that figuring out the secret of life won't take care of," Baird replied.

"I see. Well, in that case, take a little more time."

"That's all right. I'll take the subject under advisement until tonight in the shower."

"Thanks for meeting with me like this, Alex."

"Did I have a choice?"

Pomeroy shrugged.

"You always have a choice. I told you that when we asked you to take over at the FDA. The President knew what a thankless, controversial job you were walking into. He meant it then and he means it now. You're the boss."

Except we're talking about the President of the United States here, Baird was thinking. *The man even the seven-hundred-pound gorillas step aside for.*

"I appreciate that, Stan," he said.

Pomeroy opened his briefcase and extracted a file stuffed with newspaper articles. A quick flip-through showed Baird that they were from all over the world.

"You've seen these?"

"Enough of them."

"And?"

"Stan, all I can say is that even a cursory search of the lay press will produce dozens—God, hundreds—of articles extolling the latest potential breakthrough in the search for a cure for cancer or heart disease or Alzheimer's or AIDS. The public is desperate for good news in all medical areas, but especially those. Leaking information through the press is the form of extortion that researchers use to push for more grant money, or drug companies use to influence public opinion. The problem is that most of the time there's a reason the researchers and pharmaceutical people have chosen to take their cases to the lay public rather than to pass them through the scientific community first—and that reason is, their work won't stand up to close scientific scrutiny."

"And how is *this* drug standing up to *your* scrutiny, Alex?"

Baird fidgeted for a time and stared out across at the city before he replied.

"The truth," he said at last, "is that the results—as far as they go—are pretty impressive. The Phase Two patients have been randomized into three treatment groups, each with about two hundred people, and it does seem that one treatment group is doing much better than the other two, and that one group is doing much worse."

"Then what's the problem?"

"I don't know, Stan. It's a sense I have—a tingle in the back of my neck. First of all, there's Newbury Pharmaceuticals. They've come out of nowhere on this one. Up until Vasclear, all they've ever produced are vitamins and a few generic copies of drugs. Remember, the FDA doesn't have the budget or the resources to do any scientific or clinical research ourselves. All we can do is evaluate the work the drug houses submit to us. The more familiar we are with the company and their methods, the easier it is to trust that what they're telling us is all there is to tell. And then there's the drug itself."

"Go on."

"Well, the drug is almost too good to be true. Maybe I'm just frightened at the incredible potential for healing that has been laid in our hands by these people—frightened that something *will* be wrong with it. To this point, what we have are spectacular results treating a devastating disease coupled with minimal, if any, side effects. Usually our statisticians are battling the manufacturers over risk-benefit ratios, trying to decide if the scattered treatment successes are worth chancing the terrible side effects of a drug. In the case of Vasclear—provided, as I said, that what we've been given is all there is to the story—it's no contest. The only negative thing of note that I've seen surrounding this drug is that it apparently doesn't work for everybody. About twenty-five percent of the beta treatment group—the group I assume is getting high-dose Vasclear—has had no benefit from the drug whatsoever. But still, a seventy-five percent success rate with minimal side effects would put any medication in the pharmaceutical hall of fame."

"Then I ask you again, Alex, what's the problem?"

Baird sighed and massaged his temples.

"Maybe nothing. But the data submitted to us reflect only two years of treatment involving six hundred patients. I guarantee you that within a few days of Vasclear's approval, tens of thousands of people will be on it. Within a couple of months it will be hundreds of thousands. Millions, maybe. We're not talking about an anti-itch cream here, Stan. This is a drug people have been waiting for—a drug that has the potential to change the civilized world, to add years, hell, decades of healthy living for many of us."

"That's the President's point exactly."

"But only six hundred cases."

"Don't you follow up new drugs for side effects?"

"Of course. But the reporting and follow-up programs are largely voluntary and badly flawed, and this drug is going to be a runaway train. Once it's out there, once those delivery trucks get rolling, if there are long-range adverse effects we don't know about right now, some big-league damage is going to be done before there is any recall."

"But so far no big-league damage."

"Nothing."

"And the study's been well conducted?"

"As far as we can tell. I have one of our best people coordinating the review of Newbury Pharmaceuticals' data. Teri Sennstrom, you know who she is?"

"I think so. Young, sort of blondish hair, kind of pretty?"

"That's Teri, although I think you'd get an argument from a lot of men about the 'kind of' part. She's also extremely bright and very thorough."

"Has she been up to Boston to observe the study firsthand and to meet with the people who are conducting it?"

"Once, but that was a while ago."

"How about sending her up again? Or better still, go yourself if you think it would help you get more comfortable with your decision."

"You mean, with my decision to approve the drug."

Pomeroy immediately sensed Baird's irritation. He turned, resting the side of his knee on the bench so he could face the FDA chief more directly. The intensity in his eyes mirrored his words.

"Alex, if it wasn't important to us, damn important, I wouldn't be here."

"When I agreed to take this job, you promised me total latitude in running the agency."

"And you still have it."

"I do? Then why do I feel like I'm being bounced on the nose of the presidential seal?"

Pomeroy grinned at the image, then tightened the hold his eyes had on Baird's.

"Tell me something, Alex," he said. "The truth. If you were having chest pain right now, which would you choose, Vasclear or bypass surgery? With what you know *right now*—"

The question was hypothetical and not at all fair, and Pomeroy's expression said that he knew it. The real question was, when was any amount of research on a drug, any amount of data, enough? In skilled hands, statistics were as malleable as Play-Doh.

"Give me the numbers," one of the more brilliant statisticians at the FDA had once told him, "and I'll give you whatever results you want without cheating in any way. It just depends on what statistical tests one chooses to use, as well as which tests one chooses *not* to use."

Baird stared off at the city.

"With the data and reports I have now," he said finally, accepting that he was about to capitulate, "and knowing no more than that, I would take the drug."

Pomeroy exhaled his relief.

"Thank you, Alex. Thank you for your honesty. That being the case, you and Dr. Sennstrom have three weeks. At that time the President would like to be standing beside you when you sign the new-drug application and he announces that research partially funded by his administration is about to take a giant step toward curing cardiovascular disease. If, in the meantime, you find any tangible reason why we should put off approving the drug, just show us what it is and you can have all the additional time you need. . . . Alex, I know you're thinking about resigning over this. All I can do is beg you not to."

Baird absently twisted his wedding band.

"Okay, Stan," he suddenly heard himself saying, as if through a distant tunnel, "three weeks it is."

CHAPTER TWELVE

BRIAN MADE SIGN-OUT ROUNDS ON THE SEVENTEEN remaining patients on the clinical ward and headed for the Vasclear clinic. Carolyn Jessup had yet to call him with the results of her meeting with Art Weber, but she had promised he would hear from her before he left the clinic for home. Jack had spent a reasonably comfortable night, but at his best he was still living the life of an invalid. And he knew it. After helping Jack to his room, Brian had sat on the edge of his bed and once again talked with him about surgery and Vasclear.

"I want to die," Jack said. "Look at me. What do I have to look forward to? Christ, I can't even go to the movies, let alone a ball game."

"But don't you see, Pop, you're feeling hopeless because you're sick. You forget about being Gramps to the girls, and seeing me get back on my feet, and maybe meeting someone yourself, taking some trips, doing some Little League coaching. I mean, you're only sixty-three. You have what all the rest of us have, today—no more, no less. I'm telling you, Jack, whether it's Vasclear or surgery, when your body is better, your head will get better, too. You've just got to hang in there."

"I just can't face having my chest cut open again, Brian. All those tubes. I just can't."

Brian took some lanolin-with-vitamin-E lotion and massaged the dry, scaly skin on his father's feet. Jack's pajama shirt was unbuttoned, exposing the huge sternotomy scar, as well as the numerous "dimples," each representing a drainage tube of one kind or another.

"I'm trying to get you the Vasclear, Pop. I really am. But if I can't get you put on the beta strength of the drug, you've got to let me set you up with Dr. Randa. You had a bad time of it with your bypass. I know that. But a lot of people sail through the procedure and are out of the hospital in just four or five days. I agree that Randa may be a jerk, but he's a world-class surgeon."

"No, Brian. Get me put on the drug. I like those odds."

Lucy Kendall had been taken by surprise by Brian's first visit to the clinic. Today she was ready. She wore tight-fitting slacks and a sweater that couldn't help but test the cardiac fitness of her male patients. Complaining about the heat in the seventy-degree clinic, she shimmied out of her lab coat and draped it over the back of a chair. Then several times, while showing Brian those parts of the facility he had missed on his first tour, she made a point of pressing one of her ample breasts against his arm.

"So, how many patients do we have scheduled tonight?" he

asked, not at all in the mood for her sledgehammer-subtle flirting, but determined to use it to learn what he needed to know.

"Five an hour for four hours. That's about average. You said you lived in Reading. Do you live alone?"

"No, with my dad. So, is their medicine brought over each day?"

"Who?"

"The Vasclear patients."

"Oh. . . . No, no. Each week. I send an appointment list over to Newbury each week, and they send over the appropriate vials of Vasclear. So, would you like to stop off somewhere for a drink after the clinic?"

"Thanks, I'd like to, but I've got to get home to my pop. He's recovering from a coronary. Don't you have little ones at home?"

"I've got an au pair to take care of them. I purposely picked a nineteen-year-old beauty queen from Sweden so that Jerry could have something to fantasize about besides me."

"What if someone's a no-show at the clinic? What do you do about their meds?"

"There aren't many of those, but sometimes people can't make it. I just keep their Vasclear locked up. Then, every few weeks, I catalog what's left over and discard it. You like to dance?"

"Sure. I don't get to do it much, and I'm not too graceful, but I like it. Is there a key for the fridge where the Vasclear's kept?"

"Eight-four-nine-oh."

"Pardon?"

"The code for the keypad on the refrigerator. Eight-four-nine-oh. You know, I should have one of those keypads put on the refrigerator at home. Maybe Jerry would take the hint and realize that a forty-inch waist just isn't going to do it. You're a thirty-six, right?"

"Good guess. Let me go over the administration of the drug again. Five times a week for two weeks, then three times a week for two months, then once a week?"

"Correct. Thirty-six waist, thirty"—she stepped back and appraised him expertly—"four leg, right?"

"Right again. That's very impressive. I wonder who came up with that schedule, and how closely it has to be followed."

"There're missed-treatment days built in, I know that much. The clinic's closed some holidays, and no one at Newbury seems to care if a patient misses one visit. We report it on a special form if someone misses two appointments in one week, or two weeks in any two-month period when they're on a weekly dose regimen. That's all. You're very nice to talk to, do you know that?"

"Thanks. So are you."

"You sure about that drink tonight?"

"Another time would be great. Don't you think we ought to get started? There're a couple of people in the waiting room."

Brian began seeing patients and setting them up for their Vasclear administration. The work was more demanding than he had anticipated. Many of them were quite ill from their coronary artery disease. All of the sick ones, he noted, were in the alpha or gamma groups. As he waited for the call from Jessup, it was all he could do to keep his focus on the business at hand.

But there was another reason he was having trouble concentrating. He had all but made the decision. If Jack was refused admission to the Vasclear study, or was randomized into any group other than beta, he was going to steal the first dose of beta tonight, and use various methods to continue to obtain beta doses until the code was broken, the tightly controlled study was ended, and the drug was released for general use.

It was, without a doubt, the most frightening, wrenching choice he had made since the onset of his recovery. But what options did he have?

There was, he knew, one other decision he had to make. For more than a year, Freeman Sharpe had been there for him—first as a guide along the often poorly marked path of recovery, and then as a friend.

"All I ask," Sharpe had said over and over, "is that before you drink, before you use, you call me."

Unspoken was the additional plea that until Brian's recovery was much farther along, he consult with Sharpe before doing anything emotionally risky. Would Freeman Sharpe try and talk him out of stealing the drug? Brian wondered. Was it worth putting the man in such a spot? At the moment, there was a thirty-three percent chance that Jack would be placed in the beta group and those questions would never have to be answered.

The first wave of patients were settled in and receiving their half-hour infusions. Brian took the opportunity to go over his plan one last time. There were two places the beta Vasclear for Jack could come from: the reserve supply and the doses set aside for IV infusion in the patients. As far as he could tell, the reserve supply wasn't counted, but it was disposed of frequently. If Lucy Kendall suspected medication was disappearing, controls would surely be tightened. He had decided that every third day, at least for the first two weeks, he would substitute normal saline for Vasclear for one of the beta infusions, rather than take a vial from the reserve. Lucy Kendall had made it clear that a missed-treatment factor had been built into the entire program. One missed dose was not harmful. No problem there.

God, but he hoped this whole exercise in deception-planning would be moot.

He wandered past the active-treatment rooms to make certain there were no problems, then slipped into the med room to try the keypad lock and count the number of beta vials on hand. The doorway was glass, so there was no reason to close it. Once inside the room, he glanced out at the corridor as he made a pretext of inspecting the shelves of various cardiac medications and the crash cart. He hated sneaking around like this.

"Eight, four, nine, oh."

Brian knelt by the small refrigerator and whispered the numbers as he punched them in. The door released instantly. There were three low cardboard boxes—two on the middle shelf and one on the bottom, each labeled with a Greek letter. The beta box had four vials in it, not as many as Brian had hoped. Still, if he juggled things around, he would be able to make it through the first five days. After that, he would—

"Dr. Holbrook?"

The man's greeting, from behind him, would have startled a weaker heart to an immediate standstill. Brian leaped and turned, closing the refrigerator door with the same movement. Dr. Art Weber stood just outside the doorway, smiling. He was in his early forties, and not as tall as Brian had thought from the video. But he was solidly built and undeniably good-looking, with sharp features and startling blue-gray eyes.

"Ah . . . yes . . . hi," Brian said, quickly regaining his composure. "It's Brian."

"Art. Art Weber."

His pronunciation of the *w* was a cross between *w* and *v*.

"I know," Brian replied. "I just finished watching you on the Vasclear video."

"And what was your impression?"

"Excellent. Just great. If Vasclear performs the way you say, cardiac medicine as we know it is about to change forever."

"There is no *if.*"

Brian stepped out of the med room and closed the door behind him.

"Well, Mrs. Nellie Hennessey is certainly testimony to that," Brian said cheerfully, trying to deflect some of the man's intensity. "I assisted at her cath this morning."

"Carolyn told me what you did today."

"I was lucky. The catheter fragment was in just the perfect position for the BIPAL forceps."

"No, I mean sending in a defective-product report to the FDA."

Brian groaned silently.

"I understand now that my doing so went against institute policy. I told Dr. Jessup it wouldn't happen again."

"Good. The same goes for Vasclear. We have encountered no significant problems, but if any do arise with any aspect of our program, I would expect you to report it to Dr. Jessup."

"No problem there."

"That includes our patients *and* our research animals."

Earl. Brian quickly decided not to pick up the gauntlet. The animal keeper clearly wasn't bluffing about having connections in high places.

"I understand completely," Brian said.

He sensed the moment he had been waiting for was at hand.

"Excellent," Weber said. "Excellent. We're getting closer and closer to being allowed by our statisticians to break the code of our double-blind study. From that point, we hope it will only be a short while before the FDA approves Vasclear for general sale."

"That would be wonderful."

"Yes, it would. And needless to say, to get a bureaucracy like the FDA to shortcut their prolonged evaluation process requires impeccable data and an impressive, irrefutable risk-benefit ratio."

"Which you have."

"Which we have," Weber echoed. "So, from now on, all reports of any problems go through us, yes?"

"Yes," Brian said, forcing himself to maintain eye contact.

"Now, I understand from Carolyn that you have expressed the desire to have your father included in the Vasclear study."

"Yes."

"She has gone over his history with me, including her recommendation that he undergo repeat bypass surgery."

"He had a terrible time with the first procedure. He's willing to endure almost anything not to have another."

"Well, he may want to reconsider, Brian. I felt deeply sorry for your father and his problem, and I did all that I could. I asked the statistician in charge of our double-blind study to randomize him into it, and this is the result."

He reached into his jacket pocket and extracted a small card, about three-by-five. Computer-printed on the card were Jack's name, birth date, sex, cardiologist's name, and a number, seven, reflecting the severity of his coronary disease. Below that information, in capital letters, was a single word: ALPHA.

Alpha. Almost certainly the placebo group. Brian felt himself sag.

"There's no way he can be put into the beta group?" he asked. Weber shook his head.

"I'm afraid not," he said. "I know it sounds absurd, but until we are statistically allowed to break the code identifying the doses received by alpha, beta, and gamma patients, we must behave as if we don't yet know which of the groups is which. At this point, with our results so striking, it seems like a charade. But we just don't have a large enough number of patients in our three groups to terminate our study unless we get FDA approval."

"Do you have any idea how long it will be before you break the code?"

"Soon. Maybe just a couple of weeks. The FDA is sending one of their people up to meet with me, Dr. Jessup, and our statisticians."

"Is there any sense in Jack participating in the study even in the alpha group? I mean, will that help your statistics?"

"The truth is, probably not. By the time his addition would matter, the study should be over. My suggestion is that you follow Dr. Jessup's recommendation and get your father in for surgery." Weber read Brian's disappointment and added, "I'm sorry. I truly am."

"Thanks," Brian said.

But the Vasclear project director had already turned and started off. Brian glanced back at the refrigerator, then checked the time and hurried to the phone in the dictation carrel. He had five minutes before the next wave of Vasclear patients, and he wanted to talk with Freeman Sharpe.

It took five rings before Sharpe came on the line. As always, his smooth baritone had an immediate calming effect.

"Freeman, it's Brian."

"Hey, my man. Is there a doctor in the house?"

"Oh, yes. The doctor is in. Got a minute?"

"You taking care of yourself?"

"Of course."

"Then I got a minute."

"They admitted Jack into the Vasclear study, Freeman, but he got randomized into the group I'm sure is getting the placebo."

"Too bad. Any chance they'll just change their minds and put him on the good stuff?"

"I don't think so, no. They want Jack to have the repeat bypass."

"And you think he should get the drug."

"This morning I helped do a cath study on a woman who's about five years older than Jack. She had coronary disease at least as bad as his, even though she never had a heart attack or bypass. She got randomized into the maximum-dose group, and now she's got arteries like a forty-year-old, and no symptoms."

Sharpe whistled softly.

"So we're thinking about what, stealing the drug?"

"I can't get it any other way."

"Can you get enough of it?"

"For two weeks, three at the very outside. But that may be all I need. I think the FDA's going to approve the drug soon. If it works on him even slowly, Jack could probably make it."

"If it doesn't?"

"According to the results they've gotten so far, he's got a seventy-five percent chance that it will. He likes those odds. So do I."

"You can do this without getting caught?"

"Probably."

"And without hurting anyone?"

"I think so."

"This is an old tape for you, I'm sure you know, rippin' off drugs from the hospital. Can you keep from dancing to it?"

"With your help."

"God's help, my man. Asking me is smart, but you'd best have a quiet chat with your higher power, too."

"I'll do that. Thanks, Freeman. You take care, now."

"You know what you're going to do?" Sharpe asked.

"I know," Brian replied.

Brian set the receiver down and made his way back to the med room. It took only a couple of minutes to empty two beta Vasclear vials into 10-cc syringes, make tiny marks on the vials, and refill them with saline. He then tucked the filled syringes into his clinic coat pocket and headed back to see more patients. An hour later, having put the syringes and an IV infusion set into his briefcase, he called home.

"Jack, how're you holding up?"

"Same old, same old."

"Well, I've got good news. You're going to start on high-dose Vasclear tonight."

"Hey, great. Dr. Jessup did that?"

"No. Another doctor. Actually, you've got to promise not to say anything to Dr. Jessup about it."

There was a prolonged pause.

"Whatever you say," Jack said finally.

"Perfect. I'll be home in a couple of hours. And Jack?"

"Yes?"

"I owe you ten bucks."

"For what?"

"I had a save today—two of them, actually."

CHAPTER THIRTEEN

BRIAN ADJUSTED THE MAKESHIFT IV POLE NEXT TO Jack's chair, took a syringe full of Vasclear, and shot it into a 250-cc bag of dextrose and water.

"Ready for another jolt of joy juice?" he asked.

Jack laughed sardonically.

"Some *joy* juice," he said. "It's not working, is it?"

"Hey, come on, Pop. At this point we shouldn't be forming any conclusions at all. Just don't get discouraged. You've only had six treatments. From what I've been able to learn, with most people, it's taken quite a bit longer than that for their symptoms to begin to improve. In fact, some people have continued to have symptoms for months even though their stress tests have returned almost to normal."

"Eight to five says I'm not going to make it."

"Dammit, Jack, stop talking like that. Your attitude has a lot to do with whether you make it or not."

"I'm tired, Brian. I'm tired of being sick."

"One more week, Coach. One more week and I'll bet you see definite improvement."

"And if I don't?"

"If you don't, we go see Randa." Seeing the bleak look on Jack's face, he added, "But I think this week it's going to start working."

For the past week, Brian had encountered no difficulties in manipulating the reserve supply of beta Vasclear in the clinic refrigerator. In addition, he had exchanged saline for Vasclear once with each of two patients. Both were well into their second year of treatment. It seemed impossible that there could have been any harm done to either of them. Still, doing such a thing at all went against every instinct.

He held on to the hope that if he could just buy a little time, the need for deception would soon be over. At noon tomorrow, White Memorial grand rounds was scheduled to be a Vasclear presentation by Art Weber and others, coupled with a response from a representative of the FDA. Brian anticipated getting some indication as to how soon Jack might legitimately go on full-dose Vasclear, provided, of course, the current treatment showed promise.

At work, his tumultuous first two days had mellowed into a comfortable, if busy, routine. He enjoyed managing the clinical ward and was regaining confidence in himself as a doctor with each new patient workup he completed and each crisis he dealt with. Phil Gianatasio was a huge help, and always seemed to show up just as a situation was getting tense. He was a bear of a worker, and had a tremendous attitude that included seeing the humor in almost any circumstance. He was also as cool and unflappable in a crunch as anyone Brian had ever worked with.

"Jack, any pain where that stuff is running in?"

"Nope."

Brian checked his father's blood pressure, which remained on the low side, and his pulse, which was fine. He had placed a thin catheter in a vein in Jack's forearm, capped it, and kept it open with anticoagulant between treatments. Although Jack kept maintaining he was feeling no better, Brian did notice that he might be using fewer nitroglycerins. In addition, he had gone out in the yard once with his granddaughters and once on his own.

Although these were encouraging signs, Brian knew that he should not make too much of them. Part of the problem with clinical medication research was the well-documented placebo effect. The more that patients, their loved ones, and treaters wanted a given therapy to work, the more the subject's symptoms suggested that it was working—at least up to a point.

Brian longed to discuss his father's case with Carolyn Jessup—to check on whether Jack's response to the drug was similar to that of other patients. But disclosing to her that he was stealing beta Vasclear would teleport him immediately back to No Job, No License-land. So, in terms of experience with the drug, he would simply have to fly blind. Soon, he kept telling himself. Soon, either through improvement in Jack's symptoms and the legalization of Vasclear, or through surgery, the secrets would end. Soon.

As good as the past week at the hospital had been, there *was* one unpleasant encounter. Brian had just set his tray on the conveyor belt to the dishwasher when he noticed Laj Randa approaching him, followed by his omnipresent pair of sycophant fellows. His turban this day was red, a color that seemed only to enhance his warrior's visage.

"So, Holbrook, how is it with your father?" he asked.

"He's home resting."

"I know that. Was he put in the Vasclear study?"

"No," Brian said, "but I'm hoping the drug will become generally available before too long."

"Answer me something, Holbrook. Why do you think Weber and his drug company are pushing and lobbying so hard to speed this product into the marketplace?"

"I don't know. Money?"

"No, not just money, my friend, a vast amount of money. A single dose of this medication is going to cost over one hundred dollars. That is one thousand dollars for the first two weeks per patient. A hundred thousand patients, a hundred million dollars. *In two weeks.* And a hundred thousand doesn't begin to touch the numbers who will be taking this drug inside of just a few months."

"So?"

"In their zeal to cash in on their product, Newbury Pharmaceuticals is making an all-out push to circumvent standard scientific practices. A limited double-blind study with no crossover at mid-point and no multi-institutional component. That's all they have. There is always something wrong with cutting corners like that, Holbrook. Always. You took biostatistics in medical school. You know that there is a reason that a study is not statistically valid until n in the equations—*number of cases*—has exceeded a certain minimum."

"Their results are very impressive."

"Their results are meaningless until the appropriate mathematics say otherwise."

Randa's voice was raised now, enough to attract the attention of those around them.

"Dr. Randa," Brian replied, "my father was in the hospital for nearly eight weeks after his last bypass. He was more dead than alive. And you know the numbers for repeat surgery as well as I do. The second time is more than twice as risky."

"Not in my hands."

"Tell me something," Brian ventured. "Does your bias against Newbury Pharmaceuticals and their drug and their methods have anything to do with how much Vasclear will shift the treatment of coronary artery disease away from surgery?"

The Sikh looked at him disdainfully.

"You're a fool, Holbrook," he said. "Your father needs surgery. He's not getting the operation he requires because of all the hype that has been generated over this drug. Until the scientific community gives the medication its blessing, it is only so much snake oil. You are making a mistake to wait for it to become available for him."

Without waiting for a reply, he stalked away.

The Hippocrates Dome was perched atop the five-story Pinkham Building at White Memorial. It was an amphitheater, built on the site where one of the first operations was performed under general anesthesia, and had quickly become known as the Hippodome. The four hundred sharply banked seats, still wooden with peeling veneer, were set beneath a striking stained-glass canopy consisting of scenes depicting various significant moments in medical history. After more than a hundred years, the dome was being refurbished, with scaffolding inside and out and a huge crane hovering above it like a giant mantis.

At twenty of twelve, when Brian arrived on the sun-splashed terrace just outside Pinkham 1, Phil was waiting for him with two cups of coffee.

"Still black with an ice cube?"

"Absolutely."

It was coffee resident-style, designed to be gulped on the way from one patient to another.

"I . . . um . . . didn't think you'd want a cruller, so I didn't get you one."

"Good move," Brian said, "as long as you didn't get me one *before* you decided I wouldn't want it."

"M'lord, thou cuttest me to the quick, wherever that is."

"So, what's your take on this dog and pony show?"

"I don't know. A representative from the FDA appearing on the stage alongside Ernie Pickard and Art Weber has got to be good news for the 'V' team."

"I certainly hope so. It'd be good news for my dad, too."

"How's he doing?"

Brian hesitated, uncomfortable at withholding the real story from an old friend. But in the end, it just wasn't worth putting Phil on the spot by telling him Jack was secretly on beta Vasclear.

"The truth is," Brian said, "he's not doing that great."

"Surgery?"

"The last time I mentioned it, he didn't refuse outright the way he usually does. I guess it depends on whether we get any indication today of when the FDA intends to move on Vasclear. Tell me something, Phil. In your experience, how long has it taken for beta Vasclear patients to start showing an improvement in their symptoms?"

"It varies. Some just a couple of days. Most within two weeks. Some a couple of months. But remember, a quarter of the cases don't get better at all. Most of those treatment failures have ended up in the OR. A few of them have ended up in the morgue."

Brian nodded. Phil knew as well as he did that except for simple treatments like penicillin for strep throat, almost no medication could boast that sort of success rate. Certainly no cardiac med. Brian checked his watch.

"Let's head up there, okay? I want to get good seats for this one."

A crowd was milling in front of the two Pinkham elevators. Protesting nearly every step of the way, Phil followed Brian up the stairs. The seats in the Hippodome were already half-occupied, and the rest were filling rapidly. Brian wasn't the least surprised. Vasclear coverage was now appearing in the *Star* and the *National Enquirer,* as well as on various evening newscasts. The drug was becoming a national celebrity.

They found two seats on an aisle toward the right, six rows back from the stage, which was a half-circle about twenty feet across and ten deep, raised three feet off the floor. Hazy sunlight filtered through the stained glass, painting the room. The huge screen behind the stage was down. Seated between it and the narrow lectern were Ernest Pickard, Art Weber, Carolyn Jessup, and, at the end nearest to where Phil and Brian were sitting, a woman in her early-to-mid-thirties.

"She's the FDA person?" Phil said, incredulous. "She looks like Jodie Foster on a good day."

"What's that disbelief in your voice supposed to mean, you sexist pig?"

"Hey, I am what I am, Bri. That woman up there not only has Jodie's looks, she's either an M.D., a Ph.D., or both. That impresses me as much as it intimidates me."

"Jodie Foster graduated from Yale, Phil."

"Well, *she* intimidates me, too. It's genetic. My mother used to scare the crap out of me."

Brian wasn't sure the woman on the stage resembled Jodie Foster all that much, but he would have been lying to say that her fine features and warm coloring weren't incredibly appealing to him. She was San Francisco to Carolyn Jessup's Upper East Side Manhattan. And at that moment, facing a full house in one of the nation's foremost teaching hospitals, she didn't look the least bit ill at ease.

At the stroke of twelve, Ernest Pickard approached the lectern.

Phil leaned over to Brian and whispered, "Distinguished Ernie, Elegant Carolyn, Leading Man Art, and Jodie. It's like a frigging casting call up there. The only thing missing from the group is you as mild-mannered reporter Clark Kent."

"Ladies and gentlemen," Pickard began, "welcome. These are exciting times for White Memorial Hospital and Boston Heart Institute. As you know, for the past several years we have been involved in a joint research effort with Boston-based Newbury Pharmaceuticals. Today, we would like to share the results of our investigations with you. But first, I would like to introduce those who will be conducting these rounds with me. Dr. Carolyn Jessup, professor of cardiology and associate director of BHI; Dr. Art Weber, director of the Vasclear project and liaison from Newbury Pharmaceuticals to BHI; and finally, our special guest, Dr. Teri Sennstrom, team leader of the cardiovascular drug evaluation unit of the Food and Drug Administration."

"Teri," Phil whispered. "I like that name. You must, too. You've been staring at her nonstop."

"Put a sock on it, Phil."

The first half-hour of Grand Rounds told Brian nothing new. It was a coming-out party for Vasclear, complete with a glossy slide show presented by Weber that chronicled significant milestones in its life. Following Weber, Carolyn Jessup got more scientific, with a discussion of dosage schedules and clinical results, as well as before-and-after arteriogram shots from several patients. She worked the stage, lectern, screen, and audience like a symphony conductor.

Throughout the presentations, despite his reluctance to prove Gianatasio correct, Brian had trouble keeping his eyes off Teri Sennstrom. But even more unsettling was that she often seemed to be looking straight at him as well. Their connections were brief and never acknowledged by either of them with so much as a nod. But they were real. Brian was certain of it.

Jessup wound down her presentation and entertained a few scientific questions, for which she was so well prepared that Brian wondered if they had been planted. Then she reintroduced Teri Sennstrom.

"You got her phone number yet?" Gianatasio whispered as Teri approached the lectern. "She looked like she was blinking it out to you in Morse code."

"Philip, will you grow up?"

" 'When the moon-a hits-a you eyes like a big-a pizza pie . . .' Hey, I don't see a wedding ring."

Brian was too proud to admit that he had noticed the same

thing. A list of his personal attributes would never have included dealing cheerfully with being teased.

"This is science," he shot back. "Pay attention."

Teri Sennstrom was wearing a brown gabardine suit with a cream-colored blouse. Her dark blond hair was held back in a tortoiseshell clip, revealing small pearl earrings. Facing four hundred souls in a steeply banked amphitheater, she appeared a bit more tentative than she had while sitting in the background.

Please, Brian thought as she set some file cards of notes on the lectern. *Please tell me what to expect for my dad.*

"Well, this is quite a day," Teri began, after thanking her hosts and conveying the best wishes and hopes of FDA chief Dr. Alexander Baird. "We appear to be at the leading edge of a miraculous advance in cardiovascular pharmacology. The data presented in brief here is a distillation of thousands of pages of reports and dozens of arteriograms, which my team at the FDA has been reviewing for over a year. We are impressed, Dr. Weber, with the care and thoroughness of your research design. We are impressed, Dr. Pickard and Dr. Jessup, with the scrupulous manner in which the research protocol has been carried out. And mostly, we are impressed with the results to this point.

"It is Dr. Baird's wish, as well as that of the President, that the patients in need of this drug receive treatment with it as soon as possible. To do so means that we will have to make concessions to the importance of Vasclear, just as our agency has done with other drugs in the past. Dr. Weber, Dr. Jessup, Dr. Pickard, we at the FDA believe that we are in the homestretch in our evaluation process. Dr. Baird feels that Vasclear deserves the status of a life-saving new drug, and it is his intention to move forward with its approval for general use."

A smattering of applause began and spread quickly throughout the hall, reverberating off the stained-glass ceiling until the Hippodome seemed to quake.

Yes! Brian thought. *Yes!*

"Our goal is to sign our approval of Newbury Pharmaceuticals' new-drug application for Vasclear in this historic amphitheater in two weeks."

Again there was applause. Gianatasio pumped his fist.

"You think you can keep your old man going that long?" he asked.

"We can try," Brian replied, suddenly wondering what preexisting factors might distinguish the twenty-five-percent failures from the rest. *Two weeks,* he was thinking. *We can do two weeks.*

"Now, however," Teri continued, "it is time for us at the FDA to ask a favor of you. As you know, our mandate is to protect the safety of the public while not unnecessarily delaying the release of any needed medication. I would like to encourage every one of you who has questions or information on Vasclear—positive or negative—to contact me. Dr. Weber and Dr. Jessup were aware that I planned to make this request, and it is to their credit that they stand by it one hundred percent. May I have the slide, please."

The lights dimmed, and a slide with Teri's name, the Rockville, Maryland, address of the FDA, and an 800 phone number appeared on the screen.

"She spells it with an 'i,' " Gianatasio whispered. "I like women who end their first names with 'i.' "

"Even when they have an M.D. or a Ph.D.?"

"I don't know. I don't think I've ever run into that combination before."

"Again," Teri Sennstrom was saying, "any of you who has worked with this drug or with patients who have received it are encouraged to call my office with reports of any adverse effects or unexplained symptoms. I promise that your call will be treated with the strictest confidence. I cannot stress enough that it is much, much easier to keep a drug off the market than it is to stop its sale and recall it once it is in general use. Several times over the next two weeks, I intend to be here at Boston Heart and White Memorial. I'll be happy to meet with any of you in person to discuss any aspect of Vasclear. Meanwhile, I think you can all share in the pride of what your institution has accomplished. Thank you."

The applause was vigorous, and for a moment, Brian thought the staid staffs of WMH and BHI were going to give Teri a standing ovation.

"Well, she's a winner," Phil said, as the crowd rose and began to file out of the dome.

"She is that," Brian replied, already planning how he was going to get the next two weeks' worth of Vasclear.

"You going to meet her?"

"Another time, maybe."

"How about now?"

Brian shook his head.

"Can't."

"Well, I think you should reconsider."

"Why?"

"Because she's about ten feet behind you and she's coming right this way. You're on your own, pal. I'll watch the master at work from afar."

Before Brian could respond, Phil was lumbering up the stairs. Brian, standing with a group of others, turned just as Teri Sennstrom arrived. She shook hands with each of them, but hesitated a second longer with Brian, and turned away from the group just enough so that she could speak to him without being overheard. Her eyes met his for a moment.

"Please call me at the Boston Radisson Hotel, room four-eighteen," she said softly before turning away with a bright smile for an approaching hospital official.

CHAPTER FOURTEEN

THE RADISSON HOTEL WAS LOCATED JUST A FEW blocks from White Memorial. Brian signed out to Phil for an hour and a half, and following Teri Sennstrom's instructions, took a circuitous route over Beacon Hill, past the State House, and back down to the hotel. He entered it through the main lobby, then took the stairs to the fourth floor and room 418. Teri had insisted that he tell absolutely no one about their meeting, including the friend who was covering for him. She had not backed down when he protested, and had promised him a full explanation for the cloak-and-dagger secrecy. And in the end, Brian told Phil Gianatasio that his therapist had found it necessary to switch his appointment.

It was two-fifteen when Brian reached the Radisson. The day, which had begun for him at six that morning, wasn't going to end until late the following afternoon. He had Vasclear clinic from four until eight, and then was scheduled to cover the clinical research ward throughout the night—his first night of being on-call in-hospital since his cardiac fellowship. His responsibilities would include carrying the Code 99 beeper for the entire hospital. Any crash emergency anywhere in BHI or WMH, and he would be part of the team. He would only be on in-house call every tenth night, so he was especially elated. In a hospital as large as White Memorial, it was almost certain there would be action.

He tapped on the door to room 418, and Teri answered in seconds. She was still dressed as she had been at Grand Rounds, although without her suit jacket. Her body was willowy, but her silky blouse highlighted her breasts, which were hardly boyish. Brian felt edgy at being alone in a hotel room with her, but if Teri was the least bit uncomfortable at the situation, she hid it well.

"Come in, come in," she said, shaking his hand once more. Her fingers, long and fine, were still completely enveloped by his. "I thought you might not have had a chance to eat, so I had them send up some food." She motioned at a room-service table to one side of the bed, set for two. "You okay with that?"

"If you only knew what I would have eaten at the hospital, you'd never bother with that question."

Teri Sennstrom didn't seem to be wearing perfume, but she carried a subtle, fresh, intoxicating scent that smelled to Brian like a spring rain. She took the chair closest to the bedside table, and he settled in across from her, determined to maintain decorum despite having eaten nothing all day but a bagel.

As if reading his mind, Teri took the pressure off by immediately uncovering the food then diving into her salad.

"I'm too nervous to eat for hours before a presentation like that," she said, not worrying that she hadn't completely finished chewing the mouthful, "and too wired to eat for hours afterward."

"Actually, you looked pretty cool up there."

"Thanks. I did a lot of theater as an undergraduate at Princeton. Little did I know that acting was going be more important for my career than all those science courses put together."

"You like working for the FDA?"

"I always had a thing for mathematics and statistics, as well as for biology. So in a way, the job is perfect for me. But my real moment of truth came on my first day on the wards as a third-year medical student, when an alcoholic with a GI bleed threw up a quart of blood on me. Oops, sorry, I forgot we were eating."

"I'm about as sensitive to that sort of thing as a yak," Brian said. "If some alcoholic threw up a quart of blood on me, there's a good chance I might not even notice. My life's goal was always to be a football player."

"Yes," she said. "I know."

Brian set his fork down and stared at her.

"A quarterback," she added. "And a very good one."

"I don't think I like this."

"I guess I wouldn't, either. Sorry for being so dramatic. Should I get started with some explanations, or would you like to finish lunch first?"

"We'd better do both. I don't have a great deal of time, and I have very poorly developed curiosity-management skills."

Teri Sennstrom's smile enveloped her ocean-green eyes as well as her sensuous mouth.

"Well, as you can probably guess," she began, "Vasclear is the hottest potato the FDA has had to deal with in many years, if not ever. My boss, Dr. Alexander Baird, is from Missouri—literally and philosophically."

"The Show-Me State?"

"Exactly. His mandate has been caution and strict adherence to procedure, but now, there's an enormous amount of pressure on him, political as well as medical, to do the one thing that comes the hardest for him—abandon scientific process. As I said at rounds,

Dr. Baird's agreed to approve the NDA for Vasclear—that's new-drug application—in about two weeks. But that doesn't mean he's giving up on our investigation of the drug. Questions?"

"None yet, other than why I'm here."

A well-traveled briefcase lay on the bed just to Teri's left. She snapped it open, took out a single sheet of paper, and set it on the bed beside Brian. He glanced down at it, but didn't have to pick it up. It was a copy of the MedWatch report he had filed on the defective Ward-Dunlop cardiac catheter.

"Everybody at the FDA knows the pressure Dr. Baird is under. You may have seen on the news the way he was ambushed by Senator Louderman at a public oversight-subcommittee hearing. We're trying to help him as much as possible. The head of the MedWatch program noticed that you work at Boston Heart Institute, and sent your report over to Dr. Baird, who insisted that I make a point of speaking with you when I came up here."

"But first he did a little checking up."

Brian emphasized his point by passing an imaginary football her way. She surprised him by catching it almost in tempo. Her eyes met his and held. Instinctively, he cleared his throat, swallowed against the sudden dryness there, and finally took a sip of Coke. She would never make the cover of anyone's glamour or beauty magazine, yet there was not one thing about her looks that didn't excite him.

"I'm afraid the phrase 'a little checking up' doesn't do our efforts justice," she said. "I hate this sort of thing, Brian, but once you've spent a little time working in Paranoington, D.C., you sort of get used to it."

She took a manila folder from her briefcase and then opened it up for him. The first thing that caught his eye was a photograph of him blown up from his high school yearbook.

"Lord," he said as he flipped through the papers.

There was a biography of him that filled three single-spaced sheets, along with numerous photographs and copies of newspaper articles, many of them from the sports pages. There were also his grades from high school, college, and medical school, a detailed credit report, which gave him a C-minus rating, reconnaissance-type photos of Phoebe and the girls, and the police reports, board rulings, and newspaper clippings surrounding his prescribing irreg-ularities.

"There's an agency in Washington that does this," she said. "I was as flabbergasted as you are to see how thorough they were. It's like all they have is an on-off switch. They either do you or they don't. Aldrich Ames, Brian Holbrook, it doesn't seem to matter to them. For all I know there's one of these in someone's file cabinet with my name on it. You've been through quite a lot. I really admire that you've made it back."

Brian looked up at her angrily.

"I'm surprised they don't have my discharge summary from Fairweather."

"If that's the hospital you were in last year, I think they tried."

"So?"

"One of the articles mentioned that your problems began after you got hurt playing football."

"It's not a good sport for anyone with knees."

"Dr. Baird doesn't like doing this sort of stuff, Brian. You'll have to take my word on that. But he's still very nervous over the step he's about to take with Vasclear. Remember, the evaluation of a new drug by the FDA requires an enormous amount of trust in the very company that stands to benefit most by its release. We just don't have the resources to conduct business any other way. And most of the time, the pharmaceutical companies are ethical. But we have virtually no experience with Newbury Pharmaceuticals, and there *have* been instances with other companies where information was conveniently omitted from reports, or numbers were changed to jack a result up from *probably* to *definitely* effective."

"Maybe you'd better get to the point."

"Brian, not everyone sends in a defective-product report the way you did. Most of the medical centers are conducting product research under some sort of profit-sharing agreement with the manufacturers or drug houses."

"So I've been told."

"Well, it turns out that in fact, one other person, at the university medical center in Wisconsin, encountered the same defect in that product as you did. The FDA is investigating now, but we've already come across what we think was a third case. That hasn't been confirmed yet, but the first of those other patients required surgery to get the catheter piece out, and the other one died. We're close to issuing an order to stop the use of the catheter until further notice. We can do that fairly easily because it hasn't been approved for general use yet. You may have helped save I don't know how many lives."

"I may have helped lose my job."

"I doubt it. I seriously do. The woman in Wisconsin who reported the incident is still working at the hospital there. Anyhow, you asked about the point of this meeting between us. Dr. Baird is looking for honest, committed people to help assure him that there's nothing he doesn't know about Vasclear. That report you filed puts you pretty high on his list."

Brian's shirt suddenly felt too tight. He loosened his tie and unbuttoned his collar.

"Let me get this straight," he said. "The head of the FDA wants me to spy on the people who have just hired me when absolutely no one else would, and who don't even know yet that my MedWatch report may have cost them millions of dollars?"

"Brian, we're determined to do the right thing with Vasclear. I know you feel you're being used, but as I said this morning, it's far easier to keep a drug off the market than it is to pull it once the pharmaceutical reps are brainwashing and courting the practitioners, and the prescriptions are rolling in."

Brian thought for a time, then said, "Teri, I'm not making any promises. None. But I will tell you that since I started working at

BHI, I've been especially interested in Vasclear. The woman in the MedWatch report I filed is a Vasclear patient, and I've seen dozens in the Vasclear-administration clinic. From what I've been able to tell, the drug is precisely as advertised."

"That's exactly what we hoped to hear. All Dr. Baird wants is for you to keep your eyes and ears open, as well as your mind. Talk to patients and staff. And if you hear anything, anything at all about this drug, report it to me." She wrote a number on her business card and passed it over. "That's my home number in Chevy Chase. I live alone, and I stay up quite late, so you needn't worry about disturbing anyone no matter what time you call. If you don't get me, just leave a message on my voice mail at home or the office. I check in with both frequently when I'm away."

Brian slipped the card into his wallet, wondering how he might ask if his call had to be limited to business. But he simply wasn't that slick.

Oh, yeah, Phil, I went up to her hotel room. First she massaged my body with warm oil. Then we made love for a couple of hours. Then we had room service and made love for a few hours more. . . . I know, I know. Alex Trebek and Joe Montana . . .

"I'm not guaranteeing I'll call," he said.

"I understand. You'll do what you think is best. Dr. Baird said he may actually be checking in with you himself. This business is that important to him. And please, don't be intimidated by him. He comes across as being reserved and even a little crusty, but he's great."

She stood, straightening her skirt, and set the manila folder back in her briefcase. Their meeting was over. Brian wanted to say something, anything that would prolong his time with her, but nothing in her manner had encouraged him to do so, and he needed to get back to the hospital. He also knew that the divorce and suspension of his medical license had rocked his self-confidence more than he liked to admit. The simple truth was that he just wasn't ready for a woman like Teri Sennstrom, if he was ready for any woman at all. The First Things First banner from his NA meeting fluttered across his mind. He could almost hear Freeman saying the words. This wasn't the time to be worrying about his social life.

Teri walked him to the door. As he opened it, he breathed her in one last time.

"Brian, listen," she said as he was stepping into the corridor. "I'm sorry if you've been placed in a difficult position. Dr. Baird wouldn't let me talk him out of doing this, and I really did try."

"Thank you for saying that."

"I . . . I'll be back in Boston in three days. If it's okay, I'd like to call you before I come. Perhaps we could have dinner together."

Brian felt his pulse stop, flip-flop, then start up again.

"Sure," he said, trying for some measure of aloofness. "I'd like that very much."

He grinned at her, turned, and walked into the chambermaid's linen cart.

CHAPTER FIFTEEN

B**RIAN** BEGAN HIS FOUR HOURS IN THE V**ASCLEAR** CLINIC by removing three days' worth of the drug for Jack—two from a new backup supply, and one from a long-term beta patient named Jessie Pullman, due in for treatment at six. He also had a single dose tucked away in the refrigerator at home in Reading in case, for whatever reason, the clinic supply became inaccessible to him. Two weeks. Assuming the drug began working for Jack, in two weeks they would be able to pop over to the local pharmacy and pick up a month's supply.

With thoughts of Jack, Vasclear, recovery, Teri, Freeman, the FDA, and the long night on-call competing for control of his head,

Brian picked up the first Vasclear patient's chart. It was Wilhelm Elovitz, the seventy-four-year-old who had walked away from an encounter with the high-voltage subway rail. A Phase One patient, Elovitz had started on Vasclear before the double-blind study was begun, and had now received two years of treatment with the drug.

"Mr. Elovitz, it's good to see you again," Brian said. "I'm Dr. Holbrook."

"Bill," Elovitz reminded him. "Everyone calls me Bill."

His silver hair was as uncontrolled as before, his smile just as engaging. Brian glanced at the cast on his left wrist, then noticed the row of blue numbers tattooed inside Elovitz's right wrist. He was a Holocaust survivor.

Distracted by the numbers and by his own concerns, Brian wasn't as sharp and observant as he usually was when approaching a patient. As a result, he was already seated at the small desk when he first appreciated the swelling in Elovitz's ankles. Then he remembered the shortness of breath he and Phil had observed in the ER. The dyspnea wasn't as easily discernible today as it had been then, but it was definitely still there. The man was almost certainly in some degree of gradually developing heart failure.

"If you could just give me a minute, Bill," Brian said, "I'd like to brush up on your medical history."

He opened the hospital record and flipped through it expertly. Elovitz, a Charlestown resident and one-time butcher, was referred to Carolyn Jessup by his GP because of typical cardiac chest pain. He was placed on Vasclear immediately, and it looked as if, for a time, he experienced some improvement in his symptoms, with much less pain and much more exercise tolerance. Then, week by week, month by month, his cardiac condition worsened again.

Eight months ago, he was hospitalized for two days for what appeared to be a small coronary. Since then, he had been coming monthly to the clinic for his Vasclear treatment, but the notes, mostly by various medical residents, nurse practitioners, and cardiology fellows, were rather sketchy. From what Brian could tell, there hadn't been a chest X ray or complete set of blood tests in over six months. Every one of his caregivers was treating Elovitz for congestive heart failure—a very common loss of heart-muscle pumping ability, usually caused by arteriosclerosis. It seemed that sometime along the way one physician had made that diagnosis, and everyone else had just assumed that it was correct. A bit sloppy for a place like BHI, Brian thought. Probably right about the diagnosis, though.

"So," Brian said.

"So?"

"So, how are you doing?"

"Ah, *that* 'so.' " Elovitz paused for a breath. "Well, the truth is, Dr. Holbrook, not so hot."

"Tell me why."

Elovitz patted his chest.

"It's my breathing. It never feels right."

"Do you sleep flat at night?"

"Oh, no. I feel like I'm suffocating when I do that. I sleep on three pillows. My wife doesn't use any."

"Can you make it up a flight of stairs?"

"I can, our home is up one, but I might have to stop once."

Brian scanned Elovitz's list of medications, which had been growing over the past six months; all were directed at arteriosclerosis and congestive heart failure. Digitalis, long-acting nitroglycerin, a vasodilator, aspirin as a blood thinner, a fairly powerful diuretic.

"When did your ankles start to swell like that?" he asked.

Elovitz shrugged. "When does anything really start?" he asked, stopping between sentences for some extra breaths. "It comes, it goes, you really don't notice it much. . . . It comes, it lasts a little longer, you still don't think much of it. . . . Then, one day, you realize it's come, but it hasn't gone away. It was like that with the ankles swelling, it was like that with the shortness of breath. . . . I've been through a great deal in my life, Dr. Holbrook," he said, nodding at the tattoo, "much of it unpleasant. If something doesn't really bother me, I usually wait until it goes away."

"But this breathing problem and the shortness of breath aren't going away?"

"No," Elovitz said sadly. "I'm afraid they aren't."

Brian glanced out the door and down the hall of the clinic. He knew he was behind schedule. He knew patients were waiting for his once-over so that they could be given their Vasclear and make way for the next hour's arrivals. But this man, who had endured so much, who had paid such unimaginable dues in his life, needed more than a once-over. He needed meticulous evaluation, and treatment that was carefully directed toward the underlying cause of his heart failure. The diagnosis of all the residents, nurse practitioners, and fellows was probably right, but the rather perfunctory care the man was receiving was not.

He moved Elovitz from the Vasclear-administration room with its contoured chair to one of the two rooms with a flat examining table. Then he asked Lucy Kendall to pick up two extra patients that hour.

"I'll make it up to you," he said, ashamed of himself for emphasizing the double entendre with a wink.

"When?" she replied.

Brian began Elovitz's workup with a careful vascular exam— blood pressures, lying and standing, in each arm; ophthalmoscopic examination of the arteries and veins along the surfaces of both retinas; careful inspection of the jugular-vein pulse pattern in the neck; and palpation of the arterial pulses in the neck, arms, groin, posterior knee, ankles, and feet. Finally, after a lung and abdomen exam, he turned his attention to Elovitz's heart.

Except for the difficulty he experienced lying flat for any extended period of time, Bill Elovitz was a perfect patient. For one minute, two, five, Brian listened, turning him on his left side, then his right, sitting him up, laying him down, then sitting him up again. As a medical student, Brian had learned the names and significance of the various normal and pathological heart sounds. As an intern and resident, he had begun to distinguish them. But it wasn't until his years of cardiac fellowship that his ear truly became trained. Now, as he completed his examination of Bill Elovitz and worked his stethoscope from his ears, he flashed on an exchange with the chief of pediatric cardiology during the very first day of his rotation through the man's service.

"Excuse me, sir," Brian had asked, "but I don't see how you can hear all that you just described when this baby's heart is going at one hundred and forty beats a minute."

"Son," the professor had replied patiently, "by the time you get finished with your training in this department, your ear is going to be so attuned that you're going to hear lub in a little one's heartbeat and get bored waiting for dub."

The cardiac exam of Bill Elovitz had not sounded normal to Brian at all. It included sounds that he would never have picked up even as a resident. An increase in the pulmonic component of the second heart sound. A fourth heart sound from the right ventricle. Soft murmurs suggesting abnormal turbulence through both the pulmonic and tricuspid valves. All this without evidence of much fluid in Bill's chest.

It was still quite possible that this was just what the residents had been saying—garden-variety congestive heart failure, caused by increasing hardening of Bill's coronary arteries. The medical maxim was, When you hear hoofbeats on the plains in Arizona, don't go searching for zebras. But based on Brian's cardiac findings, there *was* one possibility other than congestive failure—one zebra.

Congestive failure surely remained the most likely cause of the hoofbeats. But if it wasn't, then Elovitz's problem was almost certainly in his lungs, and the heart problems and ankle swelling were secondary to it. The zebra that kept galloping through Brian's mind was called pulmonary hypertension. PH, thickening of the walls of the arteries in the lung, caused breathing problems and increasing resistance to blood flow that would eventually put an enormous strain on the heart. The condition was very uncommon, initially subtle, and almost invariably fatal. Its causes were many, but included blood clots from the legs and pelvis going to the lungs, various infections, AIDS, certain degenerative lung diseases, and several different toxins and medications.

There was also an extremely rare version of PH called PPH— primary pulmonary hypertension—which seemed to have no detectable underlying cause at all.

Could this Vasclear patient have pulmonary hypertension as an explanation for his symptoms? It would be extremely taxing to find out. And it would be almost impossible to determine if the cause of the problem was an underlying lung disease, toxicity from some other substance, or a side effect of Vasclear. But it seemed crucial that he try.

"Bill, who came with you?" Brian asked.

"My wife. She went down to get a cup of coffee."

"Well, maybe I should wait until she gets back to tell you what I think."

"No," Elovitz said with some force. "That won't be necessary. . . . Devorah has a lot of trouble with her nerves. She's on medication. . . . I have no desire to upset her. . . . Whatever you have to say, you can say to me."

Brian shrugged.

"Okay," he said. "The doctors who have taken care of you here in the past think you have a condition called congestive heart failure. And they may well be right. But I find myself wondering if instead you may have a rather unusual lung problem called pulmonary hypertension. We call it PH. But I want to stress that PH is by no means a certainty in you. Because it is so difficult to make that diagnosis, and involves a fair number of tests, I would like to suggest strongly that you let me admit you to the BHI clinical-research ward for a few days."

The color instantly drained from Bill Elovitz's craggy face. He shook his head, at first a little, then more vigorously.

"You will have to find another way, Dr. Holbrook," he said.

"But why?"

Elovitz displayed his tattoo.

"*That* is why. That and concern about my wife. . . . I have no objection to coming in for tests, but in the Buchenwald camp there was a hospital. . . . It was a place as base, as depraved as you could ever imagine. . . . My friends, family, and I were taken there many times. . . . In fifty years since then, I have stayed overnight in a hospital only once, for two days when I had my heart attack. . . . Do your tests, Dr. Holbrook. Do whatever you want. . . . But do not put me in the hospital . . . unless it is something I would die without."

"At the moment, you're not in that kind of danger," Brian said. "But you'll need to come in several times to get all these studies done."

"It shouldn't surprise you that I have nothing else demanding my time. . . . Just tell me what to do."

Brian wrote out a stack of laboratory and X-ray requisitions: EKG, chest X ray, echocardiogram, ventilation/perfusion lung scan, arterial blood gas levels, blood chemistries, and a complete blood count. Once all the results of these studies were in, he would determine if the most invasive test, a pulmonary arteriogram, was also indicated.

"The secretary will schedule these tests for us, Bill," he said. "Most of the blood work can be done now. Meanwhile, I'm going to adjust your medications a bit."

"What about my Vasclear?"

"Excuse me?"

Elovitz grinned.

"My Vasclear. . . . That *is* one of the reasons why I came in tonight."

"Oh, yes. Well, Bill, with all that's going on, and given how long you've been part of the study, I think it would be better to hold off on your Vasclear until after the tests are back. Come, I'll help you get them scheduled."

As Brian walked Bill down the hall, he reflected on a massive outbreak of pulmonary hypertension in Spain in the eighties caused by tainted cooking oil, and another a few years later in New Mexico linked to the ingestion of L-tryptophan in an over-the-counter sleep medication. Then, more recently, there was the striking increase in PH associated with certain appetite suppressants. But except for those outbreaks, the condition was as rare as . . . as zebras on the plains in Arizona. And since his arrival at BHI, he had heard absolutely nothing about PH as a side effect of Vasclear, nothing at all.

It was entirely likely that he was orbiting Saturn on this one. And even if Bill Elovitz did have PH, his was a single, isolated case. There was no way to prove, or even infer, that Vasclear had anything to do with it. Still, Bill Elovitz was sick and getting sicker. Except for a little inconvenience to him and a modest financial hit for his insurance carrier, there really was no reason not to proceed with the workup. If he had PH, the quality and to some degree the quantity of his life could be improved, although the course of the disease would still be inexorably downhill.

As they turned the corner heading for the reception area, Brian saw a half-dozen huge balloons floating on ribbons over the secretary's desk. Getting closer, he realized there was a decorated sheet cake on the desk, large enough to feed a platoon.

"Hurry up," Lucy Kendall called excitedly. "We're all starving."

Brian was still several yards away when he was able to read the frosting inscription: *Thank You, Dr. Holbrook.*

Surrounding the words was an edible replica of the view up the main drive of White Memorial. As he approached, Lucy and the treatment nurse stepped aside. Standing behind them, beaming, was Nellie Hennessey. She was wearing blue jeans and a sun-yellow T-shirt proclaiming, I Walked the Charles For Hunger. Brian came around the desk and gave her a hug as the staff and several of the patients applauded.

"This cake is just beautiful," he said.

"Thank you. Decorating them is one of my favorite hobbies," she said simply.

Then she introduced Brian to her daughter, a buoyant redhead with Nellie's eyes and lively smile.

"If Megan wasn't married to the best man this side of heaven," Nellie said, "I'd insist she give you a try."

Again there was laughter and applause in the clinic. Lucy Kendall caught Brian's eye and gave him her most wicked smile. Anxious to remove himself from the center of attention as quickly as possible, Brian cut the first slice.

"So, Nellie," one of the patients asked, "exactly what did this tall, dark, handsome doctor do to save your life?"

For the briefest moment, Brian saw a look of confusion flash across Nellie's cherubic face.

"Well," she said, "I started having trouble with one of my arteries, and this lad opened it up."

Again, some people applauded, and that was that. No mention of the defective Ward-Dunlop product. No mention of the catheter tip.

Had Nellie been spoken to? Brian wondered. Bribed in some way? Or was she just incredibly intuitive about the need for discretion?

He led her over and introduced her to Bill Elovitz, then stepped back a pace as the two of them shared snippets of their stories. Nellie was one of the seventy-five-percenters. Get sick, get Vasclear, get well. Simple. Clean as a scalpel cut.

But what exactly was Bill Elovitz?

He had gotten fairly significant improvement initially, then had regressed. That pattern put him outside the twenty-five-percenters—the ones who simply had no response to Vasclear whatsoever. And now, there was the possibility that he had developed an extremely rare lung condition. Was the condition real or just a diagnostic stab in the dark? If it *was* real, was it a coincidence or a complication?

And what, if any, were the implications for Jack?

Even if Elovitz did test out as having PH, there was no way to link it definitely to Vasclear. And seventy-five percent success was seventy-five percent success. The findings in Bill were certainly no reason for stopping Jack's treatments.

"Nellie, tell me something," Brian asked. "Exactly how long after you started your treatment with Vasclear did it take for your symptoms to go away?"

"How long? Not very, darlin'. I can tell you that much."

"I remember exactly," Megan chimed in. "You had your first treatment on August tenth, and your pain was gone the day of my birthday. You decorated the cake with smiley faces and hearts, remember?"

"So how long was that?" Brian asked again.

"Oh," Megan replied. "My birthday's on the twenty-fourth. It was exactly two weeks later that your pain was gone. Two weeks to the day."

CHAPTER SIXTEEN

THE EVENING WAS FAR LESS EVENTFUL THAN BRIAN had anticipated. There had been no action on his code-call beeper, and following the Vasclear clinic, there had been only one admission to the ward, a thirty-eight-year-old man on an experimental drug for myocarditis, a viral infection of the heart muscle. The drug was still in Phase One trials—toxicity and dose adjustment. But from what Brian could tell, in this patient at least the treatment was a complete bust. The man's congestive heart failure was worsening, and he was being treated with more and more medications. He was a candidate for a transplant, but as with many others, he was mired so far down the list that it seemed likely his disease would take him before the call came in.

Brian took a history, did a physical exam, and wrote a set of admission orders. Then he headed to the on-call room to review the man's chart and type out his workup on the laptop that was bolted to the workstation there. On a busy service, typing admission workups was often simply too time-consuming, and the residents were forced to dictate. But by using the laptops, the case synthesis was generally more thoughtful and complete, the printout was in the chart immediately, fewer transcription secretaries were needed in the record room, and the possibility of a clerical error was eliminated.

Brian set the chart and a cup of resident-style coffee by the laptop, and had settled in the chair before he touched a key and saw the screen remain black. An attempt at restart, the limit of his ability to deal with any computer crisis, accomplished nothing. Dictation was a possibility, but he wanted to type out a review of the chart for his own study. He called a tape recording in the computer office and reported the malfunction. Then he decided to try the laptop in the dictation carrel in the Vasclear clinic.

He notified the nurses on duty where he'd be and let himself into the clinic using the keypad. The place was deserted, dark, and eerily quiet. The tiny, glass-enclosed carrel was situated just a few yards to his left. Without bothering to look for any light switches, he used his penlight to spot the door. He chose the cozier incandescent light of the table lamp, rather than the overhead fluorescent. Then he closed the door and pulled the drapes shut. A cocoon.

It was ten-thirty, but he knew there wasn't a chance in the world Jack would be asleep. The home health aide they had hired to fill in when the neighbors couldn't be with him answered on the first ring.

"So, how's he doing, Mrs. Rice?" Brian asked.

"No change from when you called at six. He just sits and watches sports."

She sounded frustrated, bored, or both.

"Well, he used to *play* them," Brian said with a deliberate edge to his voice, "and very well, too. Any chest pain?"

"Some when he got up to go to the bathroom. He put one of those pills under his tongue. I want to give him a back rub before my shift ends at twelve, but he won't lie down to let me do it."

"Could you put him on, please?"

"Hey, Bri."

"Hey, Jack, why're you giving Mrs. Rice such a hard time?"

"She's a nag, that's why. Besides, I don't need my back rubbed. I need some of that Vasclear."

"This is your off-night. I told you that a dozen times."

"Oh, I guess I forgot. I forget everything now. You know that. I wanted more of the Vasclear because I think it may be working."

Brian felt a rush.

"What do you mean? Tell me."

"Well, I can't explain it, but I just feel better tonight."

"Hey, that's great, Pop. That's really great. But Mrs. Rice said you took some nitro before."

"Just a couple. I'm telling you, Bri, the stuff is working."

"Well, that's wonderful news. I'll be bringing some more home for you tomorrow."

"You do that."

"I'll speak to you in the morning, Jack."

Brian set the receiver down, leaned back, and allowed his eyes to close. It was good to hear his father saying anything other than how miserable he was feeling. But he was still popping nitroglycerin just to make a twenty-foot walk to the bathroom. Was his sense of improvement merely a transient bump in his downward course, or did it represent a significant turn for the better?

He opened the thick myocarditis chart and had just smoothed it out beside the laptop when he heard the clinic door open. Moments later, there was the sound of voices. Through a small crack in the drapes, he could see the fluorescent overheads flicker on. He set his pen down and peered out through the opening. In seconds, Art

Weber and Carolyn Jessup walked past the carrel without glancing his way. They were on either side of a tall, robust, slightly balding man, who was dressed nearly as expensively as Weber himself.

Brian did not get a look at the taller man's face, but there was something familiar about him. The two physicians guided him into room 1, the administration room nearest to where Brian was working. Moments later, the lights in that room winked on. Brian inched the door of the carrel open just a bit. The voices from room 1 echoed out into the corridor.

"A quick exam to make sure everything's all right," he heard Jessup say, "then I think we'll run a cardiogram before giving you your treatment."

"How have you been feeling?" Weber asked.

"Great. The pain that brought me in to see Carolyn disappeared after just two or three weeks of treatments, and hasn't really come back."

The man's voice was familiar, too.

"That's excellent to hear," Weber said.

"You've got a winner in this stuff of yours, Art. A real winner. Not that there aren't occasional twinges in one place or another in my chest, but they don't last long."

"That's perfectly natural," Jessup said. "Everyone over the age of twenty feels an occasional twinge in the chest. The trick for a doctor is to separate true cardiac pain—angina pectoris—from a muscle spasm between the ribs, or extra acid washing up from the stomach into the esophagus, or a gas bubble trapped in the intestine beneath the diaphragm, or some inflammation of the lung, or even tendonitis around the shoulder. Sometimes it's not so easy to do. The list of possibilities goes on and on."

"There sure is a hell of a lot that can go wrong in that part of the body," the man said.

Who is that? Brian asked himself, now feeling that he was close to the answer.

"Mostly very minor and inconsequential problems, Walter," Jessup replied. "One might even say most chest pains are the body's normal response to the daily stresses of life. And that's the case with you now, because fortunately, thanks to Dr. Weber and the good folks at Newbury Pharmaceuticals, your coronary artery disease is virtually gone."

"Terrific," the man said.

Walter? Brian rolled his seat just a bit closer to the crack in the carrel door.

"This cardiogram looks like a teenager's," Jessup cheered. "You're getting an excellent response. Art, I think we're all set for the treatment. I'll slip the IV line in if you'll get the Vasclear."

"Glad to. One Vasclear cocktail coming up."

Weber emerged from the examining room and headed down to the medication room. Brian sat stunned, trying to sort out what he had just heard. Clearly, the man named Walter was a VIP—a VIP getting his heart disease cured by Vasclear treatments. Had he been randomized into the beta group? It seemed highly unlikely.

Weber returned from the med room in moments.

"Here you go, Senator," he said. "You did say high-test, didn't you?"

Walter Louderman! Brian caught his breath. He rarely voted Republican, but if the rock-jawed former linebacker did get his party's presidential nomination, he might well make an exception. There could be little doubt that Weber and Jessup had broken the code to ensure that the senator got "high-test"—the beta dosage. But almost as startling was the realization that Senator Louderman had heart disease—at least, he'd had it before his Vasclear treatment. Such a revelation would probably have put an end to his presidential aspirations.

They should have trusted me, Brian thought angrily.

His father's life was on the line. Everyone knew beta was the maximum-dose group. They were cheating with Louderman. Why couldn't they have just stowed all that randomization bullshit and put Jack on the drug, too? They could have done it in such a way that no one, not even Brian, would have ever known. Instead, Jessup had allowed the computer to randomize Jack into the damn placebo group. Then she had kept pushing for repeat bypass surgery.

Was it worth confronting them now? What would be gained?

Brian listened for another thirty seconds, then eased the door almost closed and pushed himself back to the laptop. He logged on to the record room and entered his password, *GODEEP*. After a prompt, he asked for the record of Walter Louderman. Not surprisingly, the record-room computer denied having such a chart. An alias of some sort seemed possible, but Brian doubted that a man with Louderman's lofty political ambitions would take even that chance.

He made a mental note to look through the film library adjacent to the cath lab. But he knew it was doubtful that Louderman's medical record or his cardiac-cath video would be anyplace other than inside a safe in Carolyn Jessup's office. She might even keep it at home. Suddenly he became aware of breathing and movement to his left. Art Weber was standing just outside the slightly ajar door of the carrel, peering in at him, his face an expressionless mask.

Brian glanced back at the laptop. From where Weber was standing, there was no way he could have seen that it was Walter Louderman's record Brian was searching for.

"Hi, come on in," Brian said with artificial cheer.

Weber pushed open the door with his foot, but stayed where he was.

"Have you been here since before we came in?" he asked.

"I . . . um . . . yes. The computer on the ward is down. I've been here for a little while working on a new-admission write-up."

"I see. And you saw us come in with our . . . patient?"

"I did, yes."

"And you recognized him?"

Brian still could read nothing in the project director's expression.

He debated, then discarded, the notion of lying to Weber. Finally, Brian nodded.

"Listen, why don't you stay right here and continue your work," Weber said. "I want to speak with Dr. Jessup."

Weber closed the carrel door behind him, then did the same with the door to room 1. Brian felt some measure of fear work its way into his anger. Could they fire him? Would they risk his telling someone what he had seen? The answers were, sadly, that he was totally expendable at BHI, and that addicts—recovering or not—were near the bottom of the world's credibility scale.

Carolyn Jessup emerged from room 1, tapped lightly on the glass door, then nudged it open and moved just inside the carrel. Brian warned himself to stay cool. He moved back and sat on the edge of the desk.

Eyeing him, she folded her arms across her chest. He noticed her makeup was understated and expertly applied. Her nails were manicured and polished a glistening scarlet. If Phil Gianatasio was intimidated by Teri Sennstrom, then this woman must be absolutely terrifying to him.

"Well, Brian," she began, clearly choosing her words carefully, "here we are again, talking about things that need to be done for the good of Boston Heart Institute."

"So it seems."

"Dr. Weber tells me you are well aware of the identity of our mystery guest."

"Senator Louderman is not easy to overlook."

Jessup's smile was noncommittal.

"Yes, I agree," she said, unfolding her arms, but never taking her dark eyes off his. "The senator was referred to me some time ago for ill-defined chest pains. I did a treadmill, expecting it to be negative, but it wasn't. He clearly had cardiovascular disease. Given the . . . *delicate* nature of his political position and plans, he was catheterized secretly by me, at which time a ninety-percent occlusion of his left anterior descending artery was documented, along with lesser blockages in the right and circumflex. He was begun on Vasclear immediately and has had such a remarkable result that I would doubt his health will be an issue at all—private *or* public—should he seek national office."

"Ninety percent," Brian said. "That's a fantastic result. I'm sure it means a great deal to have Vasclear work so well on a man as powerful as the senator."

"It always helps to have friends in high places," Jessup replied calmly. "A little like the BHI friends you have in Dr. Pickard and myself."

The threat was thinly veiled and Brian responded quickly.

"I told you before, Dr. Jessup, I'm very grateful to Dr. Pickard and to you for giving me the chance to get back on my feet. The last thing I would ever want is to jeopardize my position here. There's just too much at stake for me."

"Well said. In that case, Brian, in the interests of that career of yours and a great deal more, you must promise to refrain from mentioning Senator Louderman to anyone. And I mean *anyone*. Word getting out of his treatment here could be disastrous—to him *and* to us."

"I understand."

"Excellent."

Jessup glanced over her shoulder.

"Art, do you have anything to add?"

Weber stepped to the doorway of the carrel.

"I just want to applaud you, Brian, for appreciating the seriousness of this situation," he said. "If there's ever anything either of us can do to thank you, you need only say so."

Brian hesitated a moment, but knew he was not going to be able to remain silent.

"Actually, there is one thing," he said. "I . . . assume Senator Louderman wasn't randomized into the beta Vasclear group."

Weber and Jessup exchanged glances.

"Brian, we're talking about a man who might well be our next president," Jessup said. "There was no way we could take the chance of including him in the double-blind study."

"Right," Brian replied. "But as important as the senator is, the most important man in the world to me is my father."

"Of course. And you want him to be placed in the beta group."

"That was my desire all along, and it still is. But whatever your decision is about that, I want to assure you again that I understand the need for secrecy as far as the senator is concerned."

There was a surprising but unmistakable look of respect—of admiration—in Carolyn Jessup's eyes. *Welcome to the club, Dr. Holbrook,* they seemed to be saying. *It would appear you have what it takes to succeed here.*

"Well, Brian," she said, "that's not too much to ask, not at all. Suppose we start your father's treatment tomorrow afternoon, say, at five. I'll notify the nurses that he has been randomized into the beta group."

"I think the trip into the city may be a bit much for him right now. If it's all right with you, I'd like to start his treatments at home."

"As long as you know that my recommendation is still surgery, and as quickly as possible."

"I understand. I haven't looked at her films, Dr. Jessup, but from your description, Nellie Hennessey's arteriograms were just as bad as my father's. I saw her today in the clinic. She's nearly six years older than Jack and looks and acts a decade younger. I want to give him at least a reasonable try with Vasclear."

"In that case, beta Vasclear it is. Art will deliver a week's supply to you tomorrow."

"I'm very grateful."

The esteem in Carolyn Jessup's eyes yielded to a steely coolness.

"I hope so, Brian," she said.

CHAPTER SEVENTEEN

THE BOSTON GLOBE

Boston Pharmaceutical House Nearing Billion-Dollar Bonanza

Until this month, the largest profits realized by Boston-based Newbury Pharmaceuticals were from the export of vitamin products to Russia and the other breakaway republics of the former Soviet bloc.

Now, it appears, the privately owned firm is on the verge of a bonanza that experts say could easily reach ten billion dollars in the next three years. The impe-

tus for the huge windfall is the anticipated FDA approval later this month of
the drug Vasclear. The drug has demonstrated seventy-five-percent effectiveness
in melting away hardening of the arteries,
sources at the manufacturer report.

"The money will begin rolling in the
moment the trucks begin rolling out,"
one industry analyst reports. "The profits
could be unprecedented in an industry already famous for unprecedented profits."

UNTIL A SATURDAY IN NOVEMBER NEARLY EIGHTEEN
years ago, autumn had always been Brian's favorite season. Since
then, although the scent of mulching leaves and damp soil, the
splendid colors, and the cool, crystalline New England air still
pleased him, autumn inevitably brought bittersweet feelings as
well. From the beginning of his life, he had been raised to play
football, and it was rare that any experience off the field, even in
medicine, could match the rush of dropping back to throw the first
pass of a game.

Today, however, Brian was feeling everything special about autumn, plus an additional excitement as well. Teri Sennstrom had
called, and in less than an hour, he would be meeting her for
dinner. It was time for a break—time to put some things on the
back burner, if only for a few hours.

The days following Jack's official beginning on full-dose Vasclear had gone smoothly enough, but Brian seriously doubted that
his father had improved. And now, ten days had passed since he
had actually received his first beta dose. Brian had started keeping
a careful count of the nitroglycerin tablets and had set up a log
book so that the home health aides and neighbors could record
Jack's level of activity each day. The emotional ups and downs
were exhausting—grasping at the slim, subjective straws of improvement one moment, then fretting over the equally subjective
setbacks the next. Three more days, Brian had decided. Three
more days would bring Jack to Nellie Hennessey's magic mark of

two weeks. After that, he would begin pushing for a visit to Laj Randa.

Teri had requested that they meet someplace where it was unlikely anyone from BHI would be. Brian had chosen a small blues place that had just opened in Burlington, one town over from Reading. It was nearly six when he signed out at the hospital and made a check-in call to Jack.

"How're you doing, Pop?"

"Not so well tonight."

The roller coaster took a downward dip.

"Chest pain?"

"Not really. I don't know what's wrong. I just, I don't know—I feel scared."

Jack Holbrook, the undersized lineman who had once broken a bone in his leg during a game and played an entire quarter on it, was not only frightened about his condition, but was admitting it. He was wearing down.

"You want me to come home?"

"I thought you were going out to dinner with someone."

"I was. But it's not that important if you're not feeling well."

"Nonsense, I'm fine. Just a little bored and jittery is all. The playoffs are on in an hour. You have a good time."

"You sure?"

"Of course I'm sure. I have Sally from next door here, and a lasagna someone dropped off. As long as I get my Vasclear tonight—"

"As soon as I get home. Ten-thirty, eleven at the latest. Last chance. You sure you don't want me to come now?"

"Positive."

"I've got my beeper."

"Perfect. You don't have to worry. I won't be calling."

"Okay, enjoy the game. And Pop? . . . I love you."

There was a brief silence.

"You have a great time," Jack said.

Brian listened to the dial tone for half a minute before setting the receiver down. *I love you.* His recovery program encouraged fearlessness when it came to expressing feelings, but this was the first time, the absolute first time, he had said that to his father since . . . since ever, maybe.

I love you.

Why now?

Feeling excited at the thought of seeing Teri again, but at the same time strangely drained by the brief conversation with Jack, Brian changed into jeans and a plaid shirt, and headed for the hospital garage.

Teri was waiting for him at a table inside the Blues Barn, a rough-hewn space rehabilitated from what remained of an old farm. Looking absolutely at ease in a denim jacket and gold T-shirt, she greeted Brian warmly and kissed him on the cheek.

"No trouble finding the place?" he asked.

"Nope. You give great directions." She gestured at the crowded, gritty place. "This is just the sort of restaurant I wanted to be at tonight."

"The music starts at eight," Brian said. "I never heard of the group."

"It doesn't matter. I've been working nonstop on you know what. This evening is equivalent to a two-week vacation for me."

The bar waitress came over. Brian ordered his staple, Diet Coke with lemon. Teri ordered the same.

"I hope you're not avoiding alcohol because of me," he said.

"If I am, it doesn't matter. I can take alcohol or leave it."

"That's one thing I really can't say. I can't remember ever having a drink that wasn't a step on the pathway to a buzz, or, just as often, oblivion. That was true even before my problems with painkillers began."

"You're doing something about it with meetings and counseling. That's all that matters."

"Oh, yes, the file. You already know my life's history."

"I'm very embarrassed about that."

She brushed a wisp of hair from her forehead, but it instantly fell back. Brian had to battle his instinct to reach over and repeat the gesture for her.

"Well," he said, "maybe you should play catch-up. Tell me about yourself."

"If my file really does exist somewhere in D.C., it's much less interesting than yours. Younger of two girls from Indiana. First in my family ever to go to college, much less medical school. Father still works his butt off in a steel mill, drinks way too much, gets verbally and physically abusive when he does. Mother cooks and cleans and smiles a strained smile all the time, takes most of the abuse, and never has a harsh word for anyone."

"Mayhem and martyrdom. Sounds like a fun household."

"Oh, yeah. My older sister, Diane, was pregnant and married before she was eighteen. The old escape route."

"Nice guy at least?"

"What do you think? Give him thirty years and change his brand of beer, and he's Dad."

"And you?"

"I waited until I was almost nineteen to run off and get married. He was a med student. That's how I got interested in it all."

"What happened?"

"Everyone in a skirt happened. Peter was incredibly insecure. He needed more reassurance than he could get from me—or from the Rockettes, for that matter. I'd catch him, he'd lie, I'd catch him again, he'd get abusive and blame me. I had been accepted at Princeton out of high school and turned them down to go with Peter, work in a department store, and take courses on the side at the local community college. The admissions people at Princeton were kind enough to accept me again when I contacted them. They even offered me a scholarship. When Peter found out, he decided he needed someone with more time to fold his socks."

The waitress came to take their orders.

"You look too healthy for this," Brian said, "but I recommend the ribs."

She reached into her purse and held up a pack of chocolate chip cookies.

"For emergencies," she said. "In case I'm trapped in a mine cave-in. I'll take the ribs and an order of fries."

Waiting for dinner, they watched the band set up and talked about Boston and Washington, music, books, and movies, and traded stories about their jobs. Then, for a time, they ate in a pleasant, comfortable silence.

"So, what about you?" Teri asked finally.

"What *about* me? Isn't the file complete enough?"

"How did you get hurt?"

"Playing football. You know that from the file."

"No, I mean how? I think it's only fair to warn you that a girlfriend and I own two nosebleed-seat season tickets to the Redskins. I love the game."

"I believe I've died and gone to heaven."

"So, how did you get hurt?"

"First, you need to know that my father was my coach. In peewees, in high school, and in college. I went to UMass because they hired him. Black Jack Holbrook. I don't know how he got the name, except that he likes to bet on things."

"Father and coach. I imagine the line can get a little blurred."

"That's an understatement. I still don't even know what to call him. We were—*are*—both pretty headstrong. Sometimes, especially when I was younger, I'd purposely misthrow a pass if he said something that upset me. But mostly, I lived and died over what he thought of me and the way I played. I got hurt during homecoming my junior year. I was a preseason all-American mention in some magazines even though I didn't go to a big football factory.

And I was having a very good year and a very good game, even though we were losing by five points and there were only six seconds left in the game. . . ."

As he talked, in spite of himself, Brian's mind locked on to that perfect fall afternoon. He is having a typically brilliant day—three touchdowns, no interceptions. But now there are four yards to go for the winning score, and time for only one more play. Six seconds . . . five . . .

"Time-out," Brian cries.

He heads toward the sideline, wincing each time his right knee bears weight. Try as he might, he is unable to hide the limp. The instant he took the hit in the second quarter, he knew that something in the knee had stretched or frayed or popped. But he kept going, reminding himself over and over that Coach Holbrook had once played a quarter of a game on a broken leg. The coach pulls him aside.

"I don't like the way you're walking. Can you do one more play?"

"Why would you even ask that?"

"Because I'm your father, that's why. Okay, if you're going to stay in, I want you to take a three-step drop and get rid of the ball as quickly as possible. A quick-release pass to Tucker. Two-six-slant-eagle."

"Coach, Tucker has dropped two passes already. What about faking the pass and letting me run it in—a quarterback draw?"

"I don't want you putting that leg at risk. Two-six-slant-eagle. Is that clear?"

"Clear."

Brian walks back to the huddle.

"Loop left, z-out, patch QB draw," he tells the team. "On two."

The knee wobbles slightly as he approaches the center. A jagged spear of pain shoots up through the marrow of his thigh. But the leg holds. Brian glances over at his father. Their eyes connect. The coach claps once and gives a thumbs-up sign. It's time. As always at these moments, everything begins to move in slow motion for Brian. The sound from around the stadium grows faint, then mutes altogether. The position of each of his opponents, their eyes, their stances, their slightest movements, are cataloged in his mind. It is clear they have taken the bait—the deceptive offensive formation that says a pass is on the way. They are badly out of position for the play that is about to be run. The pass Coach wants him to throw might work or it might be dropped. But Brian's quarterback run is a lock.

"Down . . . set . . . hut one . . . two."

The ball snaps up into his hands. Brian holds it so his opponents can see that he is ready to throw. He takes two steps backward. In front of him now, a lane has opened up—a clear path to the goal line so wide that he almost smiles. He hesitates one more fraction of a second and then bolts forward. With the first plant of his right foot, two of the ligaments holding together his upper and lower leg rip apart. The lower leg bends outward at a grotesquely unnatural angle. Pain unlike any he has ever experienced explodes from the knee joint.

Brian begins screaming even before he hits the ground. He gasps and cries out again, then again. He grabs a fistful of turf and jams it into his own mouth, biting down on it with all his might. Even so, he can still hear his agonized groans. Through a sickening haze, he hears his father's voice calling his name.

"Brian . . . Brian . . ."

Embarrassed, Brian suddenly recognized Teri's voice. Her hand was over his, gripping it tightly.

"Whoa," he said, shaking his head, then brushing a bit of sweat from his upper lip. "I don't think we're in Kansas anymore, Toto. I sure haven't gotten lost like that for a while. Did I make any sense?"

"You made perfect sense, Brian. Perfect. Do you think if you had passed like your father wanted you to that you'd have ended up playing pro ball?"

"And not being strung out on painkillers? My father does, and that's really all that matters. He's never gotten over it."

He began drifting again.

The band, not half-bad, had started playing, and was into a slow, rumbling blues.

"You like to dance?" Teri asked, snapping him back.

"You know, that's the second time this week someone's asked me that question. You carry foot insurance?"

They joined three other couples near the band. Teri, very naturally, reached her arms around his neck and set her cheek against his chest. Brian was instantly lost in the sensations of her hair against his face, her body pressed against his, and his hands filling the hollow at the small of her back. He realized, perhaps for the first time, how tense his life had been since the moment of Jack's chest pain at the Towne Deli—a constant state of red alert. He closed his eyes. They were all still out there waiting for him—the job, the patients, the monitoring, the drug, his father. But gradually, there was only the music and the woman.

They held each other for a time after the music had stopped, then Brian led Teri back to their table as the band launched into an upbeat number showcasing the harmonica player.

"I don't think I'm ready for dancing to the up-tempo stuff," he said. "In fact, I don't think the *world* is ready for that."

"Nonsense. You're an athlete. Athletes have a special grace that translates well into any movement."

"Correction. I'm a cardiologist. And a six-foot-three-inch cardiologist with thirteen-D shoes at that. Could there ever be a more awkward combination?"

"Bah! I'll be patient with this misplaced modesty for now. But I warn you, with you or without you, I dance."

"Warning noted."

"And since you brought up cardiology," she added, "I really didn't want to talk business tonight, but I also don't want to stand in line waiting for my unemployment check—or worse, read head-lines proclaiming that a drug that I helped get into early release has wiped out the population equivalent of Iowa. Have you thought about my request?"

Brian sighed.

"Only constantly," he said. "I wish there were some way this process could go through Dr. Pickard and Dr. Jessup."

"That just wouldn't be wise. Brian, this is not the first time our agency has dealt with a drug or product that was going to make some people very wealthy. And it would hardly be the first time respected researchers had kept information from us. We have no reason to suspect anything is being held back from us as far as Vasclear is concerned, and Pickard and Jessup have spotless reputa-tions, but you know what's at stake as well as I do."

Brian flashed on the warning from Jessup following his filing of the MedWatch report, and on the realization that she and Weber had, in fact, lied to him. They had told him flat-out that "not once" in three years had protocol been broken.

"You did say that Jessup and Pickard agreed to the idea of confidential reporting to your agency?"

"Absolutely."

"Well, okay. I'll keep my eyes open." He hesitated, then added, "And I guess I should say that there's a potentially interesting case I'm looking at right now involving one of the early Vasclear pa-tients."

"Go on, please."

"There's not much to tell, yet. And I would never divulge his name, even to you, without a release."

"I understand."

"He's an older guy I just saw in the Vasclear clinic, one of the first treated with the drug."

"Phase One?"

"I think so, yes. It looks like he responded well initially, then he regressed. Now, after two years of treatment, he's quite ill. I haven't gotten any labs back on him yet, but I think he might have pulmonary hypertension."

Teri's eyes brightened with interest.

"Pulmonary hypertension. Has he been on diet pills? Or eating salad oil in Spain recently?"

Brian smiled.

"You know your medical-disaster history. No obvious precipitating factors that I can tell. But I've only just started the workup. For the moment, PH remains a long shot."

"When will you know something?"

"A few more days."

"And you'll keep me posted?"

"Provided I can do it in person."

"I promise."

"But Teri, there's one more thing I want to tell you. My father has bad coronary disease. He had a coronary ten years ago and the bypass he had six years ago is failing. I've gotten him into the Vasclear study. That's how much confidence I have in this drug."

"I hope he was randomized into the beta strength of the drug."

"Thankfully, he was. Hey, how'd you like to meet him? We live only a few miles from here. Meeting you would brighten Jack up considerably. I guarantee it. You can even watch me administer his Vasclear. I'm giving it to him at home."

"If you think he'd like it."

"He'd love it, believe m—"

"What's the matter?"

"My beeper! I just realized that I don't have it. I'm never without— Oh, I remember. I changed my pants at the hospital. The beeper's wrapped up in my bag in the car. I'll just call and tell him we're coming."

"I'll hit the ladies' room and meet you back here."

Brian found the pay phone in the front entryway. After four rings, he heard his own voice on their answering machine.

"Hello, you've reached the Holbrooks—"

He hung up, his heart beginning to pound, and waited an interminable twenty seconds for the machine to clear. Then he called again. Same result.

He raced out to the LeBaron and fumbled with the trunk. His beeper was hooked to the belt loop of his pants, inside his overnight bag. The LED displayed a call from home.

"Jesus," he muttered, racing back to the phone. "Come on . . . answer. . . . Answer, dammit!"

Three rings, then the answering machine again.

"Pop, I'm on my way home," he blurted after the beep. "I'm on my way right now!"

CHAPTER EIGHTEEN

BRIAN CHARGED BACK INTO THE RESTAURANT JUST AS Teri returned to their table.

"There's something wrong," he said. "There's no answer at home. Jack would never *not* be there and we had help tonight to boot. And he did try to page me. Dammit. I can't believe this. The one night I don't have my beeper."

He threw two twenties on the table, took Teri's hand, and hurried her outside.

"Do you want me to follow you home?" she asked.

"No! I mean, maybe you should. Sure."

Brian sped off with his focus alternating between the road and the rearview mirror. He squealed around the corner of his street expecting to see rescue squad vehicles parked outside the house. But except for the living-room light the place looked deserted. Without waiting for Teri, he raced inside. There was a note taped to the lamp beside Jack's chair—a note from the neighbor who was watching him.

Brian,

> 9:00 P.M. We tried paging you, but your beeper must be off. Your father is having severe chest pain and he's refused to call the ambulance because he wants to go to Boston Heart and he thinks they'll take him to Suburban. He was going to call a cab, so instead Harold and I drove him in. He said to tell you he took an extra aspirin just like you told him to.

Sally Johansen

Brian handed Teri the note and called the ER at White Memorial. It was several anxious minutes before a resident answered.

"Dr. Holbrook, I'm Stu Meltzer, first-year resident. Your father's here, but he's in tough shape. He's had an extensive anterior MI, and we're having trouble holding his pressure."

Extensive anterior MI—a massive coronary involving the muscle of the left ventricle, the major pumping chamber. Next to a rupture of the heart wall, it was just about the worst of all cardiac disasters.

"Damn," Brian said. "Is he conscious?"

"In and out."

"Who's with him?"

"Right now, the on-call team, but I've been told Dr. Jessup is on her way in, and Dr. Randa's just arrived down here."

"Thank you. Stu, tell my dad I'm on the way in."

"Will do."

"And Stu?"

"Yes?"

"Do whatever's necessary."

"I understand."

Brian looked to Teri.

"He's in big trouble."

"I heard. You go ahead in. I'll find my way to the Radisson. Call me as soon as you know anything."

"I can't believe this is happening! I just can't believe it. Oh God, poor Pop."

As he turned to go, she called his name. Then she reached up, pulled him down to her, and kissed him lightly on the mouth.

"Would it help if I drove you?" she asked.

"No, no. I'll do okay. If I can, I'll call you at the hotel as soon as I know how he's doing."

"Call later tonight or else first thing in the morning."

"Okay. Come on. Follow me onto the highway, then you're on your own. And Teri, thanks for tonight."

"Thank *you*," she called out as he raced to the LeBaron. "Be careful driving."

Brian waited until he heard the engine on Teri's rental turn over, then peeled away and sped toward I-93 and Boston. Extensive heart damage, blood pressure dropping, Laj Randa at the bedside . . . Brian had rolled the dice of his father's health at three-to-one odds. Now, it was clear, he had lost. The only question remaining was, how badly.

The White Memorial ER was in its usual state of hyperactivity. Brian knew exactly where to go and rushed to room 4 in the back. Nothing he had ever seen or done in medicine fully prepared him for the sight of his father at the center of the most extreme of medical dramas, a cardiac arrest.

"Clear!" Carolyn Jessup cried out.

Brian heard the pop of high-voltage electricity as the paddles discharged their energy into Jack's body. Through the crowd of fifteen or so technicians, nurses, and physicians, he saw Jack's arms flap upward, then drop. The cardiac tracing on the overhead monitor showed several seconds of an absolutely straight line, then fairly well-organized complexes began moving across the screen—very slowly at first, then faster.

"Looks like some kind of nodal rhythm."

"I've got a pulse. I've got a pulse."

"He's in sinus now. Regular sinus rhythm."

"Pressure's seventy."

"Up the Levophed," Jessup ordered. "Get an epi drip ready. Forget the cath. As soon as we can, we're going straight over to the OR at BHI."

Before Brian could get to the bedside, two of Laj Randa's surgical fellows charged into the room, bristling with authority.

"Dr. Randa wants an intra-aortic balloon assist put in right now," one ordered. "He says the heart-lung bypass pump tech is in and we'll be ready for this man in the OR in fifteen minutes."

Brian worked his way around rather than through the crowd. Carolyn Jessup glanced up from her work, spotted him, and shook her head. Maybe her expression was neutral, but Brian read his own grim thoughts into it.

You should have listened to me, Brian. I told you to go with Randa.

"Apparently your father was awake when friends got him here," Jessup said to him, as the surgical team got to work inserting the uninflated, sausage-sized balloon into Jack's right femoral artery and up into his aorta. "But he had a pressure of only ninety and evidence on EKG of an evolving extensive anterior MI. Shortly after they got him into bed, he began losing his pressure. Now his rhythm's unstable. This was the first time we've had to shock him."

"He's going to surgery?"

"If we can get him there. I wanted to try the cath lab and see if we could open the obstruction with anticoagulants or a probe. But I heard evidence in his chest that his mitral-valve function has been badly impaired by the coronary. Ultrasound confirmed mitral papillary-muscle dysfunction. The valve's going to have to be replaced along with the bypasses if he's going to make it."

If he's going to make it.

Brian stared down numbly at the narrow gurney where his father lay, his eyes closed, his rugged, angular facial features already beginning to puff. There was a nasogastric tube snaking up into his nose and down into his stomach, and a much larger endotracheal breathing tube through his mouth and down between his vocal cords into his trachea. His color was a frightening dusky gray.

Coach.

Randa's surgical fellows were quick and skilled. The intra-aortic balloon, wrapped around a thin catheter, was inserted and sutured in place in minutes. It was electrically synchronized to inflate in between each of Jack's heartbeats, forcing extra blood into the left ventricle—the pumping chamber. The small increase in filling volume kept the coronary arteries open as wide as possible and was often the difference between life and death.

Come on, Jack. Hang in there. Hang in there.

"We've got to get going," the surgical fellow said. "Dr. Randa's waiting."

The IV poles, monitor, and balloon assist pump were positioned for travel, and almost before Brian could react, Jack was gone. There was nothing he could do now but wait.

Immediately, the nurses began cleaning up the debris, which covered the floor. Room 4 had to be cleared out quickly and readied for the next crisis. Carolyn Jessup led Brian out to the hall. She had obviously raced into the hospital from home, and wore no makeup. Her shoulder-length ebony hair, which she invariably wore in a loose knot, was clipped back on each side. For the first time since Brian had met her, she was looking her age.

"We're doing everything we can," she said.

Brian looked at his feet.

"I know. Thank you. And thank you for not saying I told you so."

"I never thought your father had enough time to rely on Vasclear."

"I feel awful now that I didn't listen to you. He didn't want surgery, though, and everything I could find out gave reasonable hope the drug would work for him if we could ever get him on it."

"I understand. I want to be sure you know that even if we had started him on Vasclear a week earlier, as you requested, it wouldn't have been enough time."

Brian nodded. No point in telling her the truth now.

"Thanks for all you've done," he said.

"I wish it could have been more. I'll be up to observe in a few minutes. Then, once I know Randa's gotten him on the pump, I'm going to have to go home. I'll check on how Jack's doing as soon as I wake up in the morning."

Brian thanked her again, then made the incredibly lonely walk over to Boston Heart. On the way, he stopped and made two phone calls. The first was to Phoebe, who made him promise to call with the results of the surgery regardless of the hour. The second call was to Freeman Sharpe.

"Freeman, it's Brian," he said. "Jack's had a massive coronary and a cardiac arrest. They've just taken him to the OR at Boston Heart for emergency surgery."

"I'll be right over," was all Sharpe said.

Brian checked the time—nearly midnight. It was too late to call Teri, he decided. Instead, he left a message for her at the hotel that Jack was in surgery and he would call in the morning. Then he hurried to the OR observation area on the third floor.

Like everything else at BHI, the OR gallery was modern, plush, and high-tech. Observers could watch the surgery directly through Plexiglas canopies covering the two ORs or via TV monitors mounted on the wall. There were also high-powered binoculars on chains through which minute details within the incision could be observed.

Brian arrived just as Randa, standing on what looked like a hydraulic platform, had finished sawing through Jack's sternum to expose the heart. Randa's fellows had already placed the arterial and venous tubes used to attach Jack to the bypass pump, and were at work harvesting veins from the leg that hadn't been used in the first operation. The cardiopulmonary bypass technician had her heart-lung machine at the ready. In moments, Jack's circulation and oxygenation would be turned over to her. An icy potassium solution would then be infused into Jack's coronary arteries, paralyzing his heart.

From that moment on, there would be no reason to stop the surgery until it was completed. The critical variable, then, was Randa's skill and speed. The longer Jack was on the bypass pump, the more difficult it was going to be to get him off—provided, of course, there was enough heart muscle left to get him off at all. With numerous bypass grafts to be sutured in on the surface of his heart, and the mitral valve between the left atrium and ventricle to be replaced, the procedure would probably take at least four hours, or possibly even much longer.

This was one of dozens of bypass surgeries Brian had observed or scrubbed in on. From where he was standing, his father's head was screened from him by a surgical sheet. Deprived of that connection, Brian felt strangely detached from what he was watching. He thought about going over to the OR waiting room, but knew he couldn't leave this spot. As long as there was the procedure to focus on, he felt as if he could keep from exploding. At that moment, Randa glanced up and spotted him. Then, just as quickly, the surgeon turned his attention back to the operating microscope.

"It is not my custom to allow family members to observe the surgery on their loved ones," Randa said through the speakers, without slowing in his work.

"I'm okay, if it's all right with you, Dr. Randa," Brian replied. "I'd really be a mess pacing around the family waiting room."

"Very well. But I think you should know that I am not optimistic. I have no way of knowing how much heart muscle this man lost before we got him here."

"I understand."

"The papillary muscle holding his mitral valve in place is no longer functional. We are going to replace the valve."

"I know."

Randa was hanging crepe—preparing Brian for the very worst. Brian had done the same thing with patients himself, many times. Boldly promising good results in a difficult case was asking for trouble. Even a surgeon with Randa's hubris knew better.

Brian sensed what was coming from Randa next. But he had to wait several minutes for the delivery. By that time, Freeman Sharpe had been led to the observation area by a security guard, and was standing quietly beside him.

"So," Randa said coolly, "how long has it been since I recommended surgery for your father, three weeks?"

"Just about."

"And what have you been doing for him all this time?"

Brian had to clear his throat before he could speak.

"Standard medical management," he said, "plus Vasclear."

"Well, I can report unequivocally that your miracle drug did not work in this case. Your father's arteries are like rosary beads and his aorta is stiff with arteriosclerosis and calcium deposits."

"I feared that was the case."

"Going that route was a very unfortunate decision on your part."

Freeman grimaced at the surgeon's insensitivity. Brian, unable to respond immediately, shook his head helplessly and looked away.

"I took my father's desires and what I knew about Vasclear into consideration, and I made the choice I thought was right," he managed to say at last.

"The doctor who cares for himself or his family has a fool for a physician and a fool for a patient."

Freeman whispered into Brian's ear, "How do you turn this mike off?"

Brian pointed to a switch by the glass and Sharpe threw it.

"Where did you dig him up?" he asked.

"You don't need tact to make it into the Surgeons' Hall of Fame. Besides, he's right. I *am* a fool."

"I've heard your father talk about his last surgery. I don't think you're any kind of fool. How's he doing?"

"He's on a heart-lung bypass machine. It's going to be impossible to tell anything until the surgery's done and they try and get him off it. We've still got hours to go."

"You take anything?"

Brian looked at his sponsor incredulously.

"Freeman, why would you even ask that?"

"Well, believe it or not, taking drugs *has* been known to happen with addicts—in situations stressful or non. Besides, asking that question's part of my job."

"No. The answer is no. Freeman, I can't believe this is happening."

"I know, pal. What the little goon down there said before about your making the wrong decision—you believe that?"

"I don't know what to believe. In medicine, where someone's life is at stake, I'd always take doing the right thing for the wrong reason over doing the wrong thing for the right reason."

"And you told me yourself that patients who are reoperated on have a much poorer prognosis than they did the first time."

"Exactly. And this time I had the numbers—the statistics regarding Vasclear and re-bypass—to say nothing of Jack's history and his passion not to have more surgery. The choice seemed like a lock to me. . . . Freeman, thank you for being here with me. I feel so alone."

Sharpe put his arm around him.

"Well, you're not, pal," he said. "And as long as you have those beautiful girls of yours, and your faith, and me to keep you on the straight and narrow, you never will be."

"Five bypasses are done," Randa said. "We're moving on to the valve."

Brian glanced at the time. Less than an hour and a half. In a patient previously bypassed, *three hours* for this part of the operation wouldn't have been surprising. He closed his eyes. *Go ahead, Randa, feel free to be as much of an asshole as you want,* he was thinking, *so long as you keep going like this.*

The cardiac surgical fellows and Randa functioned like a finely tuned special-forces unit. The way they were huddled around Jack, there wasn't much to see without using the binoculars or checking the overhead monitor. Freeman chose to do neither.

"I saw enough open chests in Nam," he said.

Another hour passed as Randa worked on the mitral-valve replacement. For a time, Freeman tried diverting Brian's focus with small talk, then he simply sat back and let Brian dictate what little conversation passed between them.

For Brian, the detachment that had protected him from coming apart in the early stages of the procedure was rapidly wearing away. Replacing it was a kaleidoscope of images. The one that stuck out was of his dad's face at Brian's peewee games. Jack couldn't have been more excited if it had been the Super Bowl. It wasn't until Sharpe passed over some tissue and set his arm around his shoulder that he realized he was crying.

"Okay, everyone, heart's closed, let's get ready to come off the pump. Dr. Holbrook, you still there?"

Brian flicked on the microphone at the same time as he checked the clock. Not yet three hours. A repeat quintuple bypass and mitral-valve replacement in 175 minutes. The diminutive Sikh was a magician.

"I'm here," Brian answered.

"You have been very quiet."

"I'm very worried."

"You have every reason to be. The surgery has gone well techni-cally, but I cannot promise what we will find when we try to start your father's heart up again."

"I understand."

"And you want to stay?"

Brian glanced over at Freeman.

"I'd rather stay than wait someplace else," he replied.

"We have inserted an esophageal ultrasound probe to give us continuous monitoring of cardiac muscle contractility."

Brian picked up the binoculars and affirmed that he could get a good look at the ultrasound screen.

"Thank you for letting me stay," he said hoarsely, gripping the edge of his high-backed stool.

"Begin to slow the pump. Pacemaker on," Randa said.

"Coming off pump."

"Pacer at seventy-five. No capture yet."

"He's fibrillating. He's fibrillating."

"Bad sign. Turn the pump up. Paddles, please. Twenty joules. . . . Clear!"

"Flat line. . . . No, wait, there are complexes. Paced rhythm at seventy-five."

"Contractions minimal. No effective circulation."

Through the binoculars, Brian examined the ultrasound tracing and felt his hopes sink.

"Bypass pump up," Randa said.

The surgeon looked up at Brian and shook his head. Round 1 was over. Over and lost. Jack was not going to come off the pump easily. But even more disturbing was the ultrasound. There just didn't seem to be enough heart muscle left to generate a blood pressure. Fifteen eerily silent minutes passed before Randa ordered the pacemaker to be turned up again and the bypass pump to be geared down. Again Jack's heart fibrillated. Again it was shocked into a paced rhythm. Again there were weak contractions and no effective movement of blood. Again Randa called for the bypass pump to be turned up. Round 2, lost.

Twenty minutes more. Brian knew in his gut that this would be the last try. The ultrasound continued to show profound weakness of the pumping-chamber muscle. But a test was just a test, he thought. Every patient was different from every other, and Jack Holbrook had once played part of a football game with a broken fibula.

Come on, Pop. Come on, you can do it.

The voices transmitted from the operating room echoed through the observation area, as Laj Randa communicated with his team.

"Pacemaker up to ninety," he ordered. "Pump down slowly."

"Pacemaker at ninety."

"Minimal electrical activity," the first assistant reported.

"No contractions," the other surgical fellow observed.

"Volume okay?" Randa asked.

"Perfect."

"You're certain?"

"Yes, everything's working fine."

"Everything except this heart."

"Still nothing," the assistant said.

Laj Randa slumped visibly and turned away from the ultra-sound monitor screen. His coal-dark eyes gazed up at the observation gallery. Then he reached up his bloodied, gloved hand and pulled down his mask.

"I'm sorry," he said. "I'm very sorry."

PART TWO

CHAPTER NINETEEN

NBC NIGHTLY NEWS

The Medical Report

"The White House has confirmed that the President will be joining FDA chief Alexander Baird at the ceremony next week at which the highly publicized miracle cardiac drug Vasclear will be approved for general use. The drug, developed and manufactured by Newbury Pharmaceuticals of Boston, reportedly melts away the arteriosclerotic plaques that clog coronary arteries and cause heart attacks. According to sources

at Newbury, the drug has cured seventy-
five percent of test cases.

"White House Chief of Staff Stan Pomeroy says that the Vasclear ceremony will
take place at White Memorial Hospital
in Boston, site of most of the medication's clinical testing.

"Senator Walter Louderman, a vocal
advocate for early release of the drug,
has expressed surprise and pleasure at
what he calls the administration's 'sudden turnaround in policy regarding a
treatment so desperately needed and
awaited by so many Americans.' . . ."

BRIAN SAT SLUMPED ON THE COUCH IN THE LIVING
room, chewing on a piece of day-old pizza, barely cognizant of the
news program. The living room, dining room, and kitchen of the
Reading flat were filled with flowers and baskets of fruit in varying
states of decay, and the walls were covered with sad reminders of
good days and bad. Teri had sent both flowers and an assortment
of cheeses and crackers. She had called several times and expressed
her sorrow that her boss at the FDA did not feel it was appropriate
nor in Brian's best interests for her to attend the funeral. Brian
responded that her calls and concern meant much more to him
than her presence at any ceremony.

A week had passed since Jack's death—four days since his funeral. Except for the actual day of the funeral, the time had plod-
ded by for Brian. There was no way that anyone except Freeman
Sharpe could fully understand his inner turmoil and intermittent
despair.

One bittersweet note during the week was that Phoebe had been
a rock, bringing food over, tidying up the place, making certain
Becky and Caitlin were available to Brian as often as he could
handle them, and dealing with out-of-town visitors when he could
not.

"A very classy act," Freeman had called her.

"You mean very classy wreckage of my past," Brian had corrected.

Over the nearly two years since their separation and one since their divorce, this was the most time they had spent around each other. And there were moments during the week when the pain of realizing what he had lost in Phoebe and his family life hurt almost as much as did Jack's death.

Freeman emerged from the bathroom with his shaving gear and stuffed it into his overnight bag. Their NA group had made sure Brian had not spent a night alone in the flat since the funeral. But now, after staying with him for a day and a half, his sponsor felt he was ready.

"Did I hear something on the news about that drug?" Freeman asked.

" 'Miracle drug cures everyone on East Coast except one.' "

"Will you put a lid on it?"

"Sorry."

"Poor me, poor me, *pour* me."

"I know. I know."

"You've got to stop blaming yourself, Brian. You made a choice—an *informed* choice—and it didn't work out the way you had hoped. It isn't like you were showing off quick draws with your gun and it went off and shot your dad."

"I know. I'm just having trouble hanging on to it is all."

"You going to be okay if I go home?"

"Fine. I'm a little uptight about being on the schedule tomorrow at work, but I don't think they're ready for me to stay out too much longer."

Sharpe settled down on the far end of the sofa.

"You're better off at work than hanging around here, anyhow, that's for sure. Look at it this way—every meeting you've gone to this past year and a half, every minute you've spent meditating or talking with me or doing something else to take care of yourself and affirm that you're a worthwhile person, has been like putting money in the bank. Now, for a time, you're gonna be living off the interest on those deposits or whatever you need to withdraw."

"What if I don't have enough?"

"You do, Brian. I been around for quite a while, and you're just going to have to trust me on that one. You do. But you gotta stop beating up on yourself. That takes a toll. And for God's sake, whatever happens, remember that there is nothing so bad going on in your life that a drink or a drug isn't gonna make it worse."

Brian thought for a time, then crossed to the bookcase, pulled a thick volume out, and reached in where it had been. Then he flipped the plastic vial of painkillers over to Freeman.

"Jack's old cardiologist had prescribed these for him. I hid them in there after the funeral . . . just in case."

Sharpe glanced at the label on the vial, then calmly took the pills into the bathroom and flushed them.

"Good move, giving those to me," he said. "Especially before you took any of them. Believe it or not, that's the way it's supposed to work. I think you're gonna be just fine, my friend, as long as you promise to call me if you're feeling shaky. Any hour."

"I promise. And thanks, Freeman. Thanks for being there for me."

Freeman shook Brian's hand and patted him on the back.

"I only wish you could have met the badass dude who was always there for me when I was first coming around," he said.

For a time, Brian paced the apartment, feeling nearly overwhelmed by the oppressive silence. He played and replayed the years of Jack's illness over in his mind. Long before the decision to try Vasclear rather than surgery, there were so many steps, going back to the very beginning, where something could have been done differently. Would any of them have changed the ultimate outcome of his disease?

You made a choice—an informed choice . . . you gotta stop beating up on yourself. . . .

The phone had rung twice before Brian was even aware of it. For no other reason than self-pity, he decided to let the answering machine do its job.

"Brian, it's Teri. If you're there, please pick up."

Brian dove for the phone beside Jack's chair, taking out a brass table lamp in the process. Teri had called the day after the funeral, but they had not spoken since.

"Hey, it's me. I'm here. I'm here."

"Well, hi, there, Here. How're you doing?"

"The truth? I've been better. Lots better, actually. I've been trying to decide whether to run a few miles, run the tub, run away, or run my car into a bridge abutment. All in all, not my best night."

"Do you have company?"

"Not as of half an hour ago. My friend Freeman just left."

"Want some?"

"Oh, lady, your timing couldn't be better. I would like that very much."

"I just checked into the Newton Marriott on one-twenty-eight. The people here tell me I can be there in twenty minutes."

"You need directions?"

"I've bought a good street map. You're on it. Do you really run, even with your knee?"

"I lope. And my knee sort of decides whether it wants to come or not."

"Well, I brought my stuff along. Would you do a few miles with me?"

"That depends. Define *few*."

Forty minutes later, they were jogging side by side through the darkened, largely deserted streets of the town.

"I'm very flexible when it comes to distance runs," he had told her while they were stretching. "I have my two-mile, my two-and-a-half, my two-and-three-quarters, and my three with or without a rest stop. How far do you usually run?"

"It doesn't matter. Let's do the two-and-a-half."

"I can tell you want to go farther. Three. I'll be happy to do the three without a stop. Now, tell me. How far do you run usually?"

"Well, I don't run all the time. We have a sort of loosely organized running club at the agency and—"

"Enough said. I know those running clubs. Twelve miles over the lunch hour, then a raw-egg-and-liver shake, a shower for those few who broke a sweat, and back to work. We'll do the three."

Teri moved with the lithe, easy stride of a seasoned runner, relaxed and beautifully coordinated. Brian worked to keep up, but he knew she was holding back. It was a perfect autumn night, moonless, cool, and still. And from the moment they took their first steps he knew that this was exactly what he needed to be doing.

"You can go on ahead if you want," he said, slightly breathless after the first mile or so. "Maybe work up a sweat."

"This is fine. Stop me if I talk too much. When I run with the club, we sort of do it in twos and threes and gab all the way."

"So long as we don't talk about the hospital. I'm going back in early tomorrow. That'll be soon enough."

"Deal."

"You know," he said, "when my mother died, I was so worried about Jack that I really didn't have time to mourn her. Now, it seems like both their deaths have hit me at once."

"Well, Jack wasn't just your father, either. You took care of him. It was like losing a parent and a child at the same time. *Two* parents and a child, from what you say."

"I'm really glad you're here tonight. And I'm glad we're doing this. It bothers me, though, that your shoes barely make a sound when they strike the pavement. Mine sound like a pair of beavers slapping out the warning of an approaching wolf."

"Ten," she replied.

"What?"

"Ten. That's how many miles we usually run over lunch. Not twelve. If you ran that much, your feet wouldn't make any noise, either."

Throughout the three-mile loop, Brian's feeling of connection to Teri deepened. And somewhere during the last mile, he realized that, purposeful or not, running together at night this way was foreplay. Two blocks from home, he sprinted past her.

"Hey, what's the rush?" she called out.

"Guess," he yelled back.

Teri beat him to the porch by ten yards, then had to hold him up by the waist and help him into the living room while he caught his breath.

"You are good," he panted.

"You don't know that, yet," she said, as she made him bend over and peeled off his sodden shirt.

"I'm totally gross."

"It's okay," she replied, raising her arms over her head so that he could do the same for her. "I'm a doctor."

She slipped off her running bra, then knelt in front of him and untied his running shoes. Then slowly, slowly, she pulled down his shorts and his jock. He was instantly rigid.

"In case you can't tell," he said, "I'm a little out of practice and easily excited."

She ran her lips up his body to his mouth. He hooked his thumbs in her waistband and lowered her shorts.

"I'm not so used to this myself," she said, pressing his face against her damp hair. "I don't know if I should be proud or embarrassed about how long it's been for me."

Standing there in the living room, their clothes still around their ankles, they kissed again and again, exploring each other with their fingertips. Finally, they kicked off their running shoes and rid themselves of the rest of their clothes.

"The moment I saw you at the hospital I wanted this to happen," he said.

"So did I, in case you couldn't tell. I'm just so sorry I couldn't be with you this week until now."

"You've made up for it already. But if you function better from guilt, feel free to hang on to it."

He led her into the bathroom Jack had remodeled just a few years ago. The floor was carpeted. There was a good-sized, clawfooted tub and across from it a large stall shower, done in light blue ceramic tile. They chose the shower.

"Cold, warm, or hot?" he asked, unable to keep his hands off her.

She held his erection in both her hands and stroked him as she kissed his lips again.

"Whatever temperature will keep you just like this," she whispered.

They soaped each other front and back, and shampooed each other's hair. As the steaming water cascaded off them, he drew her up to him and kissed her deeply. Slipping his hands beneath her thighs, he lifted her up. She wrapped her legs around his waist and her arms about his neck.

"Can you do it like this?" she whispered.

"I don't know. But as long as there's no Romanian judge giving out style points, I can try."

He lowered her down onto him.

"A perfect fit," she said dreamily. "And look, there's a little Romanian-looking guy standing over there behind you, holding up a card with a ten on it."

CHAPTER TWENTY

BRIAN ARRIVED AT THE HOSPITAL BEFORE SEVEN DE-
spite staying up much of the night talking with Teri and making
love with her. He still knew much less about her than she did
about him, but he *had* learned that a long-term relationship with an
Air Force pilot had soured about a year ago, and that since then she
had spent more time avoiding men than she had dating them.

"I'm looking for quality," she said. "Not quantity."

Brian was missing her already.

He went directly to the ward and began his first day back by
reviewing the charts of the seventeen patients being treated there.
The staff was concerned and supportive toward him. Everyone, it

seemed, knew the circumstances of his father's death. When Brian
finished his chart review, patient rounds were not yet ready to start.
He went down to the mail room to claim the stack of mail they had
been saving for him. Then he hauled it back to the ward and
dropped it onto the coffee table in the small faculty lounge. Between Jack's death and his newfound lover, he was having a tough
time concentrating on much of anything. Maybe opening a few
dozen envelopes and reports would bring him in for a landing.

Simple tasks, he reminded himself, repeating advice he thought
he might have learned from his father. When all else fails, break
life down into simple tasks and do them one at a time.

The mail pile included some dictations to be reviewed and
signed, hospital bulletins, two thank-you notes from patients, and a
dozen cost-free magazines, newspapers, and journals, all of them
subsidized in one way or another by the pharmaceutical houses. In
addition, there were a number of computer-generated laboratory
and X-ray reports. Brian worked his way through the results one at
a time, having learned from one bitter experience early in his residency the danger of losing focus, however briefly, when reviewing
test reports.

There was nothing at all notable until he came to a sheet of labs
on Bill Elovitz. With all that had transpired over the past week, he
hadn't given the Charlestown man a thought. There were no blood
tests that were specifically diagnostic of pulmonary hypertension,
but because of the variety of the potential underlying causes of the
condition, any findings were possible. He scanned the chemistries.
Cholesterol and triglycerides, the lipids that contributed to arteriosclerosis were, not surprisingly, elevated. There were also some
mild liver-function abnormalities, which could have been due to
almost anything, but were most likely due to congestion of the liver
from the back pressure of blood trying to make it through mal-
functioning lungs, heart, or both. Nevertheless, Brian noted down
the abnormal results on a card destined for Teri.

One of the unit nurses knocked and poked her head in.

"Everyone's here," she said. "Phil says we'll be rounding in five minutes."

"I'll be there."

With a few minutes remaining before rounds, he turned to the second page of Bill Elovitz's labwork: hematology—the blood-cell counts. Immediately, one test caught his eye. The eosinophil cell count was elevated—quite elevated, actually. The so-called eos were a type of granular white blood cell that appeared red under the microscope with the most commonly used blood stain. They were abnormally increased in a number of disease conditions, including parasitic infections such as hookworm and trichinosis, and allergic reactions such as asthma, eczema, and hay fever. But also among the more common causes of eosinophilia was reaction to medication.

Brian stared at the result, then circled it, and noted it down on the Elovitz file card. Clinical findings consistent with pulmonary hypertension, coupled with marked eosinophilia in a patient taking an experimental drug. Maybe nothing, maybe something. No matter what, he still didn't feel as if he were trying to force the square peg of Elovitz's physical findings and eosinophilia into the round hole of the diagnosis.

He shoved the reports and a few journals into his briefcase and went out onto the ward. Phil Gianatasio, the teaching visit on the unit for the month, was in the process of herding the students, residents, fellows, and nurses over toward the first patient. Phil had been at the funeral, and had been a concerned friend as well, calling to check in, stopping over at the house twice, and once managing to talk Brian into going out for lunch.

Brian fell in with the group, but only heard a fraction of what was being said. Bill Elovitz's shortness of breath and ankle swelling might never be proven to be anything other than congestive heart failure due to hardening of the coronary arteries. But now there was another finding to explain—an abnormal eo count.

Brian's mind began ticking over the possibilities. As far as he could remember, the cases of PH associated with the toxic oil in Spain, as well as with the L-tryptophan and diet pills, all featured eosinophilia in the majority of the patients. Antibiotics, iodides, even aspirin—the list of drugs that produced reactions accompanied by some degree of elevation in the eo count was almost as extensive as the entire pharmacopoeia.

Freeman was right. The hospital was a much better place for him to be than stewing around alone at home.

"What do you think about that possibility, Brian?"

Phil stood across the bed from him, waiting. Brian grinned sheepishly.

"Lost in space," he said. "I'll try to be less distracted. Sorry."

"As long as you're there when my next case of thyroid storm comes walking in," Phil replied.

The rest of patient rounds was uneventful. Brian did manage to stay better focused on the cases at hand, but at times he still couldn't keep his mind from wandering to Jack, to Teri, or to Elovitz. Finally, the last case examined and discussed, Phil sent the team off to their various jobs.

"You're covering the ward today?" he asked Brian.

"Yes."

"You okay to do that?"

"I'm fine, really. I'm sorry for zoning out on you like that. I do have a lot on my mind. But I can handle the ward."

"I trust you on that. Anything you want to talk about?"

"Actually, if you have time, there is. There's some coffee in the pot in the lounge."

"In that case," Phil said, "I'm all over it."

They settled in easy chairs opposite each other in the small lounge.

"Phil, I want to tell you about a case, and I want your opinion."

"Shoot."

"This is the man, Bill Elovitz, that you fixed me up with in the ER."

"Miracle Man?"

"Exactly. I saw him in the Vasclear clinic just before Jack died. He's a retired butcher and has a tattoo on his arm from the Nazi death camps. He was one of the prestudy Vasclear patients."

"Phase One, right?"

"Yes, I believe so."

"Proceed."

"He was referred here a couple of years ago with classic cardiac history and findings. His course is that he got much better for a while after receiving Vasclear, then he started getting symptoms of coronary artery narrowing again. Finally, he had a small MI eight or nine months ago, for which he spent two days in the hospital and then signed out. He's had a thing about hospitals ever since he was in the concentration camp."

"I understand. Tell me more."

"Well, he's been coming to the clinic once a month for Vasclear treatment, but over the last four or five months, he's developed ankle swelling and shortness of breath. He's been treated for congestive failure with the usual stuff, but he's been getting progressively worse. He's still pretty mobile, but now he can't always make a flight of stairs without stopping."

"Okay," Phil said, "I'm ready. You didn't call me in here to present a run-of-the-mill case of congestive heart failure. What's the catch?"

Brian took a sip of coffee, then said, "My ears may be a little out of practice after a year and a half without a stethoscope in them, but there's the possibility they may be rested, too. I heard a loud right-ventricular fourth heart sound, an increase in the pulmonic component of the second sound, and murmurs of both pulmonic and tricuspid insufficiency."

"Pulmonary disease?"

"Phil, he sounded exactly like the one pulmonary hypertension patient I've ever diagnosed."

Gianatasio's expression seemed to tighten, though almost imperceptibly. He turned and set his coffee on the table, but a bit sloshed onto his hand. He wiped the drop off with his other hand, and when he turned back to Brian, he was the old Phil again.

"PH is a tough call to make without a shitload of studies," he said. "Even *with* them sometimes. But hey, would I question the ears of the man who diagnosed Stormy from the bedside in the heat of battle?"

"There's more," Brian said, still wondering about Phil's queer reaction and whether it had even happened. "I just found some bloodwork in my pile that was drawn on the guy ten days ago. His eos are fourteen percent. His total white-cell count is normal—ninety-five hundred."

"Fourteen percent of ninety-five hundred's not that much of an elevation when you consider the actual number of cells."

"Phil, zero to three percent is normal."

"I know. It still doesn't impress me. I'd check it again. And I'll bet you a pan pizza it comes back under five. Eo counts bounce all over the place. The first thing to do with an unexpected abnormality in a lab test is to repeat it."

"I will. You sound like you don't make too much of this."

"Too early to tell, Bri. I assume you ordered a few gazillion dollars' worth of tests."

"Something like that."

Brian was beginning to feel some irritation at his friend's flippancy. Then, suddenly, Phil was on his feet.

"Well," he said, "I gotta go earn a living. Brian, there have been over two hundred cases treated with beta Vasclear since the double-blind study began, to say nothing of the two hundred in the gamma group that got the lower dose. None of them has had so much as a rash that's been pinned on the drug. I think you're on a zebra hunt with this PH stuff. Keep me posted, okay?"

"I'll do that."

Brian stayed in the lounge for several minutes, feeling annoyingly unfulfilled by the exchange. Then he took his briefcase to the computer terminal in the on-call room. He was able to get Bill Elovitz's home number off the man's front sheet without going through anyone at the record room. An older woman answered on the fourth ring.

"Hello, Elovitz residence."

"Hello," Brian said. "This is Dr. Holbrook calling from White Memorial Hospital. I wonder if I could speak with Bill Elovitz, please."

There was a prolonged silence before he heard the woman's partially muffled voice say, "Devorah, it's a doctor from White Memorial. He wants to speak to Bill."

A woman responded in the background, but Brian could not make out anything she was saying.

"Doctor, what was your name?"

"Holbrook. Dr. Brian Holbrook. Look, if you want to call me here at the hospital to verify that's where I'm calling from, the number is—"

"That won't be necessary, Doctor. I'm Mrs. Levine, the next-door neighbor. I . . . I think I met you when Bill got hurt." She began to sob. "Bill Elovitz is dead, Doctor. He was killed five days ago—shot during a holdup at the little market down the street from here."

CHAPTER TWENTY-ONE

THE MORNING WAS PAINFULLY LONG. SEVERAL TIMES, Brian simply asked the nurses to handle as many of the problems as they could, and went to lie down in the on-call room. Maintaining enough energy at work had never been a problem for him. But now, the raw wound from Jack's death, the night just past with Teri, and the disturbing news about Bill Elovitz had him feeling drained.

Maybe Freeman had been wrong about his returning to work this soon.

As a murder victim, Elovitz would almost certainly have been autopsied. Brian made a note to check with the medical examiner's office about the results. Next he called the record room and found that none of the important tests he had ordered had been done before Bill's death.

Finally, he dozed off and floated through a disturbing, disjointed dream involving, as best as he could piece it together, football, death camps, the Blues Barn, and his tenth-grade geometry teacher. He was awakened not by his pager or the phone, but by a soft knock on the door—once, then again.

"It's okay, come in," he called out, wondering illogically if it might be Teri.

The door opened partway and Phil poked his head in. He looked clearly troubled. Brian had called him immediately with the news about Bill Elovitz. There had been nothing the least bit flippant in Phil's reaction—just a soft whistle, a prolonged silence, and a few words of genuine dismay.

"You got time to talk?" he asked now.

"Am I in trouble?"

"Why do you ask that?"

"I don't know. Just paranoid, I guess. The last time someone knocked on my door like that asking if I had time to talk, it was the DEA."

"Well, you're not in trouble that I know of. But I do need to talk with you. Chris Glidden has agreed to cover the ward for an hour."

"Sounds serious. Just give me a little time to put my body back in working order."

"How about meeting me in my office in, say, ten minutes?"

Phil was gone before he could reply. Brian pulled himself together and tried calling Teri at the Marriott, but she had checked out as she had told him she was going to. She must be somewhere in the hospital going over records, or else over at Newbury Pharmaceuticals. Word was out in the papers and all over the news that the President was planning to come to White Memorial for the Vasclear signing ceremony. Time was running out for Teri to find any reason to postpone the event.

Phil's office on the seventh floor was very much junior-faculty—tight space, metal shelves for bookcases, and a view not of the Charles, but across the center of the hospital, including the skeleton of a building under construction and the latticework of scaffolding around the stained-glass Hippocrates Dome. Brian had stopped at a machine canteen on the way up and bought a couple of nondescript, sugar-coated, cellophane-wrapped pastries. He tossed one on Phil's desk.

"Here," Brian said. "This is a bribe in case you were lying about my not being in any trouble."

Phil set the pastry aside—a bad sign.

"I didn't lie about that," he replied, "but I did lie about something else. Sit down, please."

Brian cleared some papers off a Scandinavian Design–type chair and settled in. Phil, usually a fairly natty dresser, and always composed, looked haggard and stressed. His tie was loosened, and there was a small coffee stain by the collar of his shirt.

"Easy does it, Phil," Brian said. "Short of wasting someone, there's not much you could have done that I haven't done in spades. Regardless of what you have to tell me, I'm not into judging people anymore."

Gianatasio composed himself with a deep breath.

"I'm sorry I acted so detached earlier when you told me about that poor guy you thought had pulmonary hypertension. The truth is, I didn't know what to do with the information. You see, a couple of years ago, back when Vasclear was still in Phase One trials, I encountered another Vasclear patient I thought might have pulmonary hypertension. I scrounged around and found his name. It was Ford, Kenneth Ford. I saw him only once in the clinic, but I keep a little card file on interesting cases I see, and he was in it. His physical findings were almost identical to the ones you described hearing and seeing in your man—ankle edema, shortness of breath, tricuspid- and pulmonic-valve insufficiency, everything."

"What happened?"

"I . . . I did what we're supposed to do. I spoke to Art Weber about him. He told me there had been several allergic-type rashes with the drug, which he and his chemists had determined were due to an ingredient used in the chemical-stabilization portion of the synthesis. After that, the process had been overhauled, the contaminant removed, and no problems had been reported until this Ford guy. Weber and I checked his record carefully, and sure enough he had started on the drug before the synthesis was modified."

"So what happened to the guy? How has he done?"

"Brian, listen. I've been on a tenure track since I arrived here. Now I'm just about to get approved. Tenure at Boston Heart and the medical school. The plum of plums, every academic cardiologist's dream, and I'm about to realize it. You know as well as I do that I'm not the brightest bulb on the academic light board by any stretch, so I've had to resort to working that much harder than anyone else, keeping my nose clean, and most of all, playing by the rules. And at Boston Heart, one of the biggest rules of all is not going off half-cocked when it comes to research results on any BHI product or drug. I've really got to be careful."

"I understand, Phil. I really do. Tell me, though, this Ford fellow, did they ever definitively diagnose pulmonary hypertension in him?"

Phil looked up at the drop ceiling.

"I . . . I don't know," he said. "Weber promised me he'd speak with Carolyn and that she would take over Ford's care and decide whether his situation was reportable or not. I never made any effort to follow up on the case, and then I sort of forgot about it—until this morning. Bri, I feel like shit about this. I really do."

"I can tell. You did right to get it off your chest, Phil. And the truth is, we really don't know whether either of these guys actually had PH."

"That *is* true. And maybe we should let sleeping dogs lie. I think you know, Brian, but I want to warn you again. This drug is their baby. I can't even begin to estimate how much is riding on it. The first thirty seconds it's on the open market, it will probably bring in more money than they pay the two of us together in a year."

"I know."

Brian left it at that, sensing his friend was just too tense right now to handle any witty remarks about their salaries.

"Pickard, Jessup, Weber—they all seem to like you a lot," Phil went on. "And you've done a couple of stellar things since you got here. But they're all tough as nails when they're cornered in an academic argument, or when someone makes trouble for them or threatens to cost them money. I've seen examples of it a number of times since I've been here. You have no way of knowing this, but Pickard and Jessup came to me after you admitted sending in the FDA report on that Ward-Dunlop catheter. Brian, they were going to can you. Right then and there. No second chances. No concerns about your future with the Board of Medicine, your kids, nothing. Here you saved my thyroid lady and Jessup's patient, and they were prepared to send you into medical purgatory just for not making a team-oriented decision."

"What saved me?"

"Probably a little of everything. I said my piece on your behalf. And you made a hell of an impression on Pickard. I think he finally persuaded Jessup to give you another chance. But it was touch and go for a while."

"So, it would seem we've both got reasons for thinking things through pretty carefully."

"That depends."

"On what?"

A bit more relaxed, Phil could resist the pastry no longer. He opened it and took a big bite before answering.

"On how much you enjoy renting cars and how much I would want to be working the counter alongside you."

Brian thought about Teri and her boss, searching for anything that they might use to postpone the general release of Vasclear. He thought about her warning that it was much more difficult to pull a drug off the market than it was to keep it from getting there in the first place. And finally, he thought about the hundreds of lives that might be saved every single day Vasclear was being prescribed.

"Phil, we can't just let it drop," he said.

"Why not? We've got two hundred cases with virtually no problems from therapeutic doses of the drug, one hundred and fifty of whom have been cured of a lethal disease. You've seen the patients. You've seen their results. And you heard Jodie Foster, M.D., up on the stage in the Hippodome saying how anxious the FDA was to get something, anything on Vasclear before it was released."

"I don't know, Phil."

"Brian, I promise you. If we report these cases to anyone other than Jessup, Pickard, and Weber, and we get caught, or even if we go poking around and they get wind of it, we are finished. Here, there, and everywhere. Finished."

Brian was still uncomfortable with letting the possibility of an unknown drug-toxicity just slip away. But everything—absolutely everything—Phil was saying made sense. Every single drug on the market had toxicities—many of them lethal. Risk-benefit ratio was the very backbone of clinical pharmacology.

Fatal aplastic anemia has been reported in less than one percent of patients taking drug A. . . . Hepatitis has occurred as a complication of therapy with drug B, liver-function tests should be monitored frequently throughout the course of therapy. . . . Cases of irreversible hearing impairment have been reported. . . . Drowsiness . . . Fever . . . Renal shutdown . . . Blindness . . . Convulsions . . . Encephalitis . . . Paralysis . . . Sudden death. The list of warnings and adverse reactions to FDA-approved medications filled much if not most of the three thousand or so pages in the *Physicians' Desk Reference.*

So what if a small percentage of patients who received Vasclear developed a serious complication?

Risk-benefit ratio? No contest.

This was a case of miracle cure versus a couple of old men with commonplace symptoms that might or might not have had an uncommon cause. And, Brian reminded himself, Ford and Elovitz had received their Vasclear before the chemical-synthesis process had been modified. For the past two years, there had been no problems with Vasclear—none at all.

But still, he wanted to know more. He had chosen Vasclear as the linchpin of his father's therapy, and now his father was dead. He needed to find out all he could about the drug. But at what cost?

"Look, Phil," he said. "Supposing we poke around very quietly and see what we can learn about both Ford and Elovitz. If we don't come up with anything more, we'll just keep our mouths shut and let the chips fall where they may."

"I don't like it."

"All right, all right. How about you just call up your man's record and see if he had an elevated eo count? That can't possibly hurt."

Almost all White Memorial charts had been scanned into the record-room computers. Phil shrugged, turned to his terminal, and logged in. Brian came around the desk and stood behind his chair. It took less than a minute for the record to be electronically retrieved.

Two and a half years ago, when he was first seen at Boston Heart, Kenneth Ford was a sixty-nine-year-old black divorced laborer from the Dorchester section of the city. He was referred to one of the staff cardiologists for evaluation of chest pain, found to have moderately advanced coronary artery disease, and started on Vasclear as part of the Phase One study. He showed excellent early response to his treatment, but then began to experience increasing chest pain, shortness of breath, and ankle swelling.

They scanned the visits to doctors and to the Vasclear clinic.

"There," Phil said, pointing at the screen. "There's my dictation."

Brian scanned the two pages, which were a near double for the ones he had done on Elovitz.

"There's your plan," he said. "Chest X ray, EKG, cardiac ultrasound, chems, CBC. Nice going. Find the CBC."

Phil scrolled through the rest of the chart. There were plenty of lab tests, including some complete blood counts, but none at or after the date on which he had seen Kenneth Ford.

"Strange," he said.

He returned to the clinic notes. Ford was seen one more time, by a resident who either had not reviewed the chart or hadn't bothered to write down a summary of the case. There was no mention of Phil's extensive note nor of the recent lab work. Congestive heart failure, the resident concluded, making what was obviously a rubber-stamp diagnosis. Cause: arteriosclerotic cardiovascular disease.

Phil scrolled through the rest of the record and stopped at a letter written four months after he had seen Kenneth Ford in the Vasclear clinic. The letter was from a general practitioner in Dorchester to the cardiologist to whom Ford had been initially referred, sadly informing the specialist of the death of Mr. Kenneth Ford at Boston City Hospital. The cause of death was pulmonary edema—overwhelming congestive heart failure—secondary to arteriosclerotic cardiovascular disease.

"Damn, but I wish I knew if he had an elevated eo count or not," Brian said.

"What difference does it make? That test's totally nonspecific."

"Come on, Phil. You know as well as I do that the test is abnormal in allergic reactions and normal in most cardiac conditions. It's certainly not something you'd expect to find in run-of-the-mill congestive failure from arteriosclerosis."

"I'm telling you, Brian, let it drop."

Brian snatched up the phone and tried calling the record room at Boston City Hospital. As he had expected, there was no way anyone would speak with him without a signed release from Kenneth Ford or his legal representative.

"Damn," he murmured, setting the receiver down. "Phil, any thoughts as to why the CBC you ordered isn't in Ford's chart?"

"None."

"Do you, um, think you might call the hematology lab and see if they can come up with it?"

"Brian, you're fucking around with our future, here. And for what?"

"I don't know, Phil. I don't know for what. Why is that test missing?"

Phil called the heme lab. No CBC on Kenneth Ford after Phil had seen him in the clinic.

"Shit," he whispered. "Brian, I don't know what in the hell is going on, but I think you're blowing this whole thing way out of proportion. People with heart disease have congestive failure all the time. Lab reports don't make it into charts every day. Patients are always having unexplained elevations in their eosinophil count from nothing more malevolent than a virus. And we are getting in over our heads."

"I'm sorry," Brian said, settling himself down with a bite of his machine-canteen pastry.

"Thanks, pal. Look, I don't know the reason you're acting like a terrier on a rat about all this. Maybe you're just angrier than you realize at Vasclear because it didn't work for your father. But I do know that you're overthinking this whole business. Overanalyzing it."

"Maybe."

"Well, thank you, Jesus, for that 'maybe.' My pulse rate is beginning to recede."

"So, what are we going to do?"

"Do? Why, nothing, Bri. That's the point. We have nothing, we do nothing."

"Maybe."

"Amen to another 'maybe' from the lad. Please, let's call it a day. My conscience is clear. Your conscience is clear. And we're both still employed."

"What do you want to bet Kenneth Ford had an eo count above ten percent?"

Gianatasio's expression became an awkward, flushed mix of fear and anger.

"Enough, Brian, please," he said. "I'm telling you, these are not people you want to cross—especially when you have absolutely nothing to gain."

"How are they going to find out if I go over to Boston City and try to get hold of Ford's labwork?"

"I don't know. How did I hear from someone who heard from someone else that you nearly had a fistfight with that drunken cretin who runs the animal room?"

Brian stared at him.

"What? What did I say?" Phil asked.

"The animal room! Phil, the fight I got into with that jerk Earl was over a monkey—a chimp that I thought had massive fluid retention and some degree of pulmonary edema. I wanted to know what experimental study he was part of, and that doofus nearly tore my head off."

"Oh, come on. Don't add a fucking monkey to the conspiracy theory."

Brian fished a paper out of his wallet.

"Four-three-eight-six," he said. "That's the chimp's number. Wanna really make yourself some money? I'm going to make it a three-horse parlay. If any one horse loses, they all lose."

"I don't get it."

"First, Kenneth Ford's going to have elevated eos. Second, monkey number four-three-eight-six is going to turn out to be part of the early Vasclear studies. And third, he's got some monkey version of pulmonary hypertension."

"If you decide to go after this," Phil said, "just do me one favor."

"Namely?"

"Save me a luxury low-mileage sedan, and don't bother with the insurance waiver."

CHAPTER TWENTY-TWO

We have been informed by hospital administration that the President of the United States will be at White Memorial Hospital on Friday October 18 or Saturday October 19 to preside over a ceremony, which will be held in the Hippocrates Dome. Also present that day will be Dr. Alexander Baird, commissioner of the Food and Drug Administration, and Senator Walter Louderman. Because of limited seating, admission to the Dome will be by guest list only.

Security around the Pinkham Building will be tight. Only those with essential patient-care tasks will be permitted in the building. Those who do not receive a formal invitation to the ceremony from White Memorial administration, Boston Heart Institute, or New-bury Pharmaceuticals, may have the chance to meet the President in the hospital cafeteria.

Details of the President's trip to Boston have not yet been made public, nor has the exact date and time of the ceremony at White Memorial. Thank you in advance for tolerating any inconvenience our increased security and crowd-control measures may cause you. Any questions may be directed to this office.

BRIAN SIGNED OUT AT FOUR O'CLOCK, CLAIMING EX-haustion and a headache, and battled rush-hour traffic through the Callahan Tunnel to Logan Airport. Teri was waiting for him in one corner of a small bar in the B terminal.

It had been less than twelve hours since they had last made love. But sitting there in her business suit and glasses, hair up, briefcase open, reading a document, she looked light-years from the woman who had straddled him in his bed, crying out softly as she had first one, then another orgasm.

For a few moments, he paused by the doorway of the bar, watching her, aware of the bewildering, paradoxical feelings of connection and detatchment, of intimacy and distance. He had touched every millimeter of her body, shared incomparable feelings with her. Yet he did not even know what her apartment looked like. Was this the beginning for them? Were they destined to be-come the love of one another's lives?

Thank God it's a day at a time, he was thinking. Otherwise the twists and turns would simply be too tight to negotiate.

For Brian, the Vasclear situation was still very much up in the air. But Phil had placed himself unambiguously on the sidelines. The two of them had spoken by phone a few hours after their meeting in his office. Brian had made the call.

"Phil," he said, "I just wanted you to know that I haven't gone racing off half-cocked about this Vasclear thing. And I wanted to tell you how much I appreciated your trusting me and my judgment by sharing what you knew with me the way you did."

"I'm glad you called to tell me that. The truth is, I've been nervous since we spoke, thinking that if I had just kept my mouth shut about the Ford case, you wouldn't be in danger of upsetting the applecart around here and getting yourself canned. I really do enjoy having you around, pal."

"Thanks. Believe me, I'm in no mood to be back working behind the counter of Speedy Rent-A-Car, either. But Phil, you shouldn't feel any responsibility for me no matter what happens. I'll admit I'm curious about these little chinks in the Vasclear armor, but I assure you I am not about to self-destruct over them. So, stop worrying about me."

"Okay. Presto change-o. I'm not worried about you."

"I'm serious. I mean, what do we know, anyway? There were how many cases that received Vasclear during Phase One trials, do you suppose?"

"I'm not certain, but I think I once heard eighteen humans plus the usual array of four-legged subjects."

"Okay, eighteen. Two out of eighteen may or may not have developed PH. One of those maybes had a single elevated eosinophil count. That's it. That's all we know."

"That's it," Phil underscored. "And besides, Weber's people modified whatever was causing the rashes in patients anyway. If that part of the drug was causing PH as well, it's been fixed."

"Exactly."

"So, you're going to let things drop?"

Brian hesitated before saying, "Probably."

"We don't do *probably* here at Boston Heart," Phil said. "I want *definitely*. Because Brian, I'm telling you, we've got nothing to gain and I really can't chance losing everything. I just can't."

"Hey, I understand. That's why I called just now, to tell you that

I didn't even want you doing anything about these PH cases. You're right. There's too much at stake."

"Thank you. Now, I only hope *you're* listening to what you're saying."

"I am, Phil. You take care, now."

"I will. Listen, there *is* one thing. That monkey you mentioned—the chimp in the animal lab?"

"Four-three-eight-six? What about him?"

"He doesn't exist."

"What?"

"And as a matter of fact, that animal keeper, Earl, is gone, too."

"Tell me."

"There's nothing to tell. I went down to tend to my hamsters, and there was a new guy down there. Andrei, I think his name is. Speaks with some kind of accent, Russian, maybe. I asked him about Earl, and he said he had no idea who he was or why he didn't work there anymore. Then I sort of sauntered past where the primates are kept. There's one chimp there, but his number's not four-three-eight-six, and he sure doesn't seem to have anything wrong with him that I could see. He was jumping all over a swinging tire, and making faces at me like Joanne used to."

"Did you ask what happened to the other monkey?"

"Hell, no. I'm telling you, Brian, the walls have ears around here, and I am out of the loop."

"Out of the loop," Brian echoed.

Teri glanced up and spotted Brian as he approached. Her smile lit up the dim corner. They had agreed that she would have him paged at the hospital at noon, just to check in. By then, he had decided to share with her what he had learned about Bill Elovitz and Kenneth Ford. She promised to check with her office to review exactly what had been reported on the two Phase One patients, and to fill him in at the airport.

"Hi, there," she said. "I was wondering if you were going to make it before my flight."

She rose and kissed him on the mouth, adding that she had thoroughly surveyed the bar patrons and determined she could risk it.

"In that case, risk it again," he said. "God, you smell good."

"I smell like Newbury Pharmaceuticals because that's where I've spent most of the day. Here, I ordered your usual. I'm doing chardonnay."

"How goes everything?"

"Well, I think this is it, actually. I have amassed as much information as I could."

"And?"

"And I think we're a go for Saturday. Let the Vasclear games begin."

"What about those two cases?"

"Well, I checked with my office. The patients from Phase One and Phase Two are identified by initials only. Patient K. F., who I assume was Kenneth Ford, was reported as having died of congestive heart failure. But there was also a note from the team at Boston Heart saying that he was being evaluated for pulmonary hypertension at the time of his death. My people didn't think much of that one case, especially since there have not been any others."

"Until now."

"Without divulging your name, I actually mentioned your second man—the poor fellow who was killed in the holdup—to Dr. Baird. He thought your findings were as consistent with congestive heart failure as they were with pulmonary hypertension. And before he came to take over the FDA, he was a professor of medicine. But even if it was PH, there's no easy way to connect it to Vasclear. Besides, these men were part of Phase One studies. The chemical process used to make the drug was modified before Phase Two. Since then, nothing. Dr. Baird doesn't feel we have any cause for concern or alarm. And the truth is, neither do I."

Brian shrugged and took her hand.

"Hey, fine with me," he said. "I was just doing what I promised to do—keep my eyes and ears open and report to you."

"And I hope you know how grateful I am. Brian, I'm finally excited about Vasclear. After all this work, I think this drug is the real deal. I think it's going to save lives—many, many lives."

Memories of his father made it hard for Brian to share her enthusiasm.

"In that case, I'm excited, too," he said. "I'm also glad your part in this is coming to an end."

"I guess in a way it is. But we have a very active postmarketing surveillance program. If any problems crop up with the drug, we'll be on top of them. And one really good thing about Vasclear getting approved is that I'll have more time free to spend with you. In fact, I have a couple of weeks of vacation coming to me. How about we go someplace?"

"Unfortunately, I'm a newcomer at BHI. I don't get any vacation for six months, and by agreement with Dr. Pickard, I can't be away from my periodic random drug tests for a year, which means no travel away from Boston."

"So, I'll come up. I'd love to meet your girls."

"Now you're talking."

"Two weeks from now I should be able to get away. Maybe you could fly down for a weekend before that."

"Maybe I could."

Teri checked her watch.

"Meanwhile, I'll be pretty tied up with the pomp and ceremony. But I'll be up again in five days. Let's plan to speak every day until then. If we miss connections, I'll page you. You can leave messages for me at home or at the office."

Brian took her in his arms.

"I really loved last night," he said. "And I hope it's the start of something very special."

"It is," Teri whispered, her lips brushing his ear. "Believe me,

Brian. I know now why I've been ignoring the phone and keeping to myself for so many months. I've been waiting for you."

Brian ransomed the LeBaron from the airport parking garage and began the drive home to Reading. His thoughts were only of Teri Sennstrom—her voice, her poise, the scent of her hair, the feel of her waist, her body pressing against his. They had kissed good-bye in the bar, deciding it was still too chancy to walk together through the terminal to the security checkpoint. After Vasclear had been released to the world, there would be no problem in their going public. But for now, it was better for both of them to be discreet.

Teri was right, he thought, as he headed north on 1A. It was over. Despite his suspicions regarding Ford and Elovitz, Vasclear had proven to be incredibly effective and squeaky-clean in a reasonably sized, carefully controlled double-blind study. There was nothing he could do about Jack's failure to respond to the drug. Of every million patients worldwide who would be treated once the Hippodome ceremony was over, two hundred and fifty thousand weren't going to respond to Vasclear, either. Two hundred and fifty thousand total treatment failures. And at this point, from all anyone could determine, there was nothing more than the fickle finger of fate at work deciding who was going to be cured by the drug and who was not. A lethal combination of factors unknown plus plain old-fashioned lousy luck—that's what had conspired to bring Jack Holbrook down. There was nothing more Brian could have done.

It was time to let the whole business rest. Phil had said it perfectly. They had nothing to gain and everything to lose by infuriating the powers that be at Boston Heart over this one.

Time to let the whole business rest. The words were still reverberating in Brian's head when he reached Bell Circle, the rotary off of which one of the exits led to the highway home. Before he even fully realized what he was doing, he had sped past the turnoff, gone completely around the rotary, and was heading south on 1A, back toward the city—more specifically, back toward Boston City Hospital.

The secret of moving freely about a hospital was simple: Look and act like you belong wherever it is that you are. In a huge hospital like Boston City, with its many buildings, enormous international faculty, inner-city patient population, and chronically overworked staff, the task was easy.

Brian's neat appearance, clinic coat, stethoscope, and plastic ID card got him into the record room, where he soon had the librarian helping in his search for the record of Kenneth Ford, deceased. It took considerably longer to get a security officer to come and lead him into the dusty bowels of the hospital to the locked storage room where the so-called inactive records were kept.

Not surprisingly, the carefully numbered cardboard file cartons, like the records inside them, seemed to be in no consistent order. After ten minutes of standing around, the guard became impatient and left, instructing Brian to lock up after himself when he was finished.

We Respect Patient Confidentiality. The signs were up in every elevator in every hospital Brian had ever known. Yet here he was, armed with only his clean-cut looks, a plastic ID from another hospital, and some of the accouterments of a physician, alone with thousands of medical records.

It took nearly forty-five minutes and half a dozen cartons to find the file on Kenneth Ford. And for a time, Brian had wondered if it would be among the missing, like the White Memorial labwork and chimp 4386.

Kenneth Ford had been admitted to Boston City Hospital on August 3, two years before, and had died on the sixth. Admission diagnosis: congestive heart failure, severe. Discharge diagnosis: same. His EKG showed changes consistent with both cardiac and pulmonary disease, and his chest X ray showed too much fluid in his lungs to make possible a diagnosis as subtle as pulmonary hypertension.

Brian felt a strangely pleasing tension as he turned to the hematology section of the lab reports.

White Blood Cell Count 13,300/cu. mm (elevated)
Differential Cell Count:
Granulocytes: 45%
Bands: 3%
Lymphocytes: 33%
Monocytes: 5%
Eosinophils: 14% (elevated)
Basophils: 0%

Brian tore the page out and folded it in his pocket. He would leave Phil out of this from now on; it wasn't fair to involve him. He would have to be extremely careful and tread softly. But Jack was dead, and directly or indirectly, Brian's treatment choice of Vasclear had helped kill him. No matter what, there was no way he could let the matter rest until some gnawing questions were answered.

CHAPTER TWENTY-THREE

The Oprah Winfrey Show

Oprah: Do you believe in miracles? Today we're devoting this program to people who have had their lives saved by so-called miracle cures. But before we begin with our very special miracle-cure guests, I would like to introduce to you Mr. Al Morgenfeld, a man with a history of two heart attacks and severe coronary artery disease, who is living life as what is known as a cardiac cripple. Also with Mr. Morgenfeld is his wife, Julia, and his cardiologist, Dr. Susan Norman, who has promised Mr. Morgenfeld he will be on the new wonder drug

Vasclear the very day it is released for general use . . . which could be as soon as next week.

BRIAN STOOD AT THE REAR OF THE SMALL CROWD IN the Vasclear-clinic waiting room and watched the initial portion of the TV program that everyone at the hospital had been anticipating. Patients and staff alike cheered and applauded at the mention of the drug that had brought them all together. Lucy Kendall, resplendent in pink cashmere, had positioned herself just to Brian's left and a half-step behind him, and continued her assault on his arm and back with her breast.

"Isn't it wonderful?" she said.

"It is that."

"My only big concern is how long the clinic is going to remain open," Lucy said.

"I never thought of that."

It made sense that once the drug was in general use, the care of most Vasclear patients could be turned back over to their own doctors. Any physician with access to a pharmacy or a UPS truck would have access to Vasclear. *Time, Newsweek,* CNN, evening news programs, now Oprah. . . . How desperate everyone had been for a drug like this one. And how many hundreds of millions watched those shows and read those magazines? It would be a medical gold rush.

Brian flashed on what Laj Randa had told him about the cost of a course of treatment with the drug. One hundred dollars a dose, fifty or so doses in a full course. And what's more, the managed-care people and insurance companies, the real controllers of cost in the country, would gladly pay. One quintuple bypass was the equivalent of how many doses of Vasclear? And, Brian reflected sourly, if the patient happened to be a nonresponder like Jack, and that patient was one of those who happened to die before he got into the OR, so much the better.

"Well, the drug still has to be given IV," Brian said. "For all we know, Vasclear-administration clinics will become all the rage over the next few years, like surgicenters. And even if that doesn't happen, you're an excellent nurse, and I'm certain you won't have any trouble landing something new."

"Thank you for saying that. Are you okay, Brian?"

"What do you mean?"

"You just seem distracted. Distracted and sad."

"I have a lot on my mind."

"Your dad?"

"Yeah, him. Some other stuff."

"Anything I can do?"

The question was punctuated with a less-than-subtle mammary nudge. Brian considered asking if she knew the names of the eighteen patients treated during the Phase One evaluation, but thought better of it. Just a word from her to Art Weber, and the fuse would be lit beneath one B. Holbrook.

"Thanks, Lucy," he said, "but it's stuff I've got to work through for myself."

On the overhead TV, a barber named Al Morgenfeld from Moline, Illinois, was telling a hundred million people what it had been like to live with severe angina, knowing that each twinge in his chest or shoulder or jaw could be the start of what he called the Big One.

"Dr. Norman," Oprah then asked, "tell me something. Why haven't you sent Al for coronary artery bypass surgery like so many thousands of others have had?"

"Well, for one thing," the doctor replied, "he already had bypass surgery once, seven years ago. Repeat surgery would be riskier. I got wind of Vasclear over a year ago and have been in constant touch with the people at Newbury Pharmaceuticals. We've been holding out for a nonsurgical cure of Al's disease."

"What you mean to say is that you've been holding out for a miracle."

"Exactly. And I think we've got one."

Brian turned and headed off toward the physician's office.

"Hey, I almost forgot," Lucy called after him. "Your girlfriend is in room two."

"Girlfriend?"

"Nellie—the woman who was willing to turn her daughter over to you"—she ran up and whispered the rest of the sentence in his ear—"as your sex slave."

"Oh," Brian said with far less enthusiasm in his voice or expression than he had intended, "thanks."

He went back to the office, purposely avoiding room 2. It wasn't Nellie who had him upset. She was a delight. It was what she represented—a Vasclear cure—that upset him.

Why not Jack? he asked himself for the millionth time. *Why not my father?*

Finally, after a few minutes of shuffling papers, he headed in to see her. Nellie seemed, if anything, even more full of life than when he had last seen her at the cake cutting. But she was also very upset.

"Dr. Holbrook, the nurse just told me about your father's death," she said. "I'm so sad for you."

"Thank you."

"Was it his heart?"

"It was, yes."

"That must have been very frustrating for you as a cardiologist. I'm so sorry."

Impressed as before with her intuitiveness, Brian thanked her again, then conducted a fairly brief physical exam, which showed a normal heart and excellent arteries.

"How old were your parents when they died?" he asked.

"Parent," she said. "My mother is ninety-three and still bright as a penny and living by herself, thank you very much." It was clearly a question she enjoyed answering. "My father died three years ago at eighty-nine. Believe it or not, he fell off a ladder and broke his hip. The operation did him in. A blood clot in the lungs, they said."

A pulmonary embolus, Brian translated to himself—an avoidable complication of not mobilizing the man early and often enough, and inadequately thinning his blood post-op. To all intents, Nellie's father hadn't even died of natural causes. Her parents had essentially both lived into their nineties! Usually the most common predictor of cardiovascular disease—positive and negative—was family history. What had happened to Nellie?

"Well, Nellie, the nurse will be in to hook you up," he said. "Afterward, you can see the secretary about next month's appointment."

"Wait, I almost forgot." She fumbled in her purse and handed him an unsealed envelope with *Dr. Holbrook* printed on the front.

It was a neatly typed letter announcing a twenty-mile charity walk for the homeless and requesting sponsorship for each mile. An attached page summarized a number of similar events in which she'd participated.

"This is wonderful," Brian said, scanning the list, wondering what his father would have been like with a clean set of arteries. "I'll be happy to sponsor you."

He wrote in a pledge, tore off that portion of the letter and gave it to her, then dropped the rest of the announcement into his briefcase. For a decade or more, the battered case had served as his combination medical bag, library, portable desk, and even closet. He would next see Nellie's papers when he cleaned the thing out, as he was forced to do every week or two.

"Will I see you before I leave?" Nellie asked.

"Only if the secretary has a problem making your appointment. Otherwise, she has all the schedules, and you can just pick a date."

She has all the schedules. The image sent Brian suddenly hurrying to the front desk, where the receptionist, Mary Leander, was filling out an appointment slip for a patient.

"Can I help you, Dr. Holbrook?" she asked.

"Ah . . . yes. Yes, you can." Brian realized that he should have taken a minute or two to prepare for this performance. "I was asking Mrs. Hennessey when it was that she shifted from receiving treatments every two weeks to every four and she couldn't remember. I was thinking the answer might be in the clinic appointment book, but I didn't know how far back they go."

Brian hoped his explanation made sense to Mrs. Leander, because it made absolutely none to him.

"Well, I don't know," she said. "I think we get a fresh book each year. I have no idea where the old ones are kept, or even if they're kept at all. Maybe somewhere in the office here."

She gestured behind her at the ceiling-to-floor shelves of forms, ledgers, procedure manuals, papers, and the like—far more than Brian had time to sift through at the moment. But if there was an appointment ledger from the first year of the clinic's existence, then maybe he could find the names of the other sixteen patients from the Phase One trials.

"Thank you, Mrs. Leander," he said. "I'll check some other time when I have the chance."

That evening, Brian's first night duty since before Jack's death, was blessedly quiet. He had decided to wait until eleven before searching for the first Vasclear-clinic appointment book. At exactly five of, he checked on the two sickest patients on the ward, reassuring himself that they were reasonably stable. Then he told the charge nurse he'd be on-beeper, left the floor, and slipped into the clinic through the same door Jessup and Weber had used to bring in Walter Louderman.

The place, as before, was eerily dark. Brian decided to keep it that way. He used his penlight to negotiate the long corridor to the receptionist's office, wondering if, perhaps, the glass-fronted room might be locked.

Despite being alone, Brian moved cautiously. If the door was locked, the game was over and he would return to the ward. But he could see immediately that it wasn't even completely closed. He slipped inside, hesitated, then flicked on the overhead lights. In the nearly total darkness, the sudden fluorescence was blinding. He allowed his eyes to adjust, then explored the drawers of the metal desk behind the receptionist's station. Nothing. Next he turned to the bank of shelves.

It took just a few minutes to find them—two thin volumes, leather-bound, obviously purchased from the same stationer, identical to the one lying closed on the receptionist's desk. Each had a year embossed in gold on the cover. Brian pulled the first one out and settled down on the receptionist's chair. The appointments were widely scattered at first, but then rapidly filled in. Brian reasoned that what he was seeing was the transition between Phase One patients, who may have been seen initially in their cardiologists' offices, and the larger double-blind study, Phase Two, which soon grew to over six hundred cases. The clinic, itself, seemed to have been opened two and a half years ago, about halfway through Phase One.

He found early appointments for both Bill Elovitz and Kenneth Ford. Using them as a marker, he began to scratch down names and follow them through the ledger, searching for those who did not have the two weeks of almost-daily treatments demanded by Phase Two. After twenty minutes the list, counting Elovitz and Ford, had grown to ten. Brian felt reasonably certain that most, if not all, of the ten were Phase One patients. Then, he heard the tones of a keypad being punched, followed moments later by a door opening. A faint shaft of light pierced the darkness in the hall.

On a sudden adrenaline rush, Brian cut the lights in the office, thrust the list of names into his pocket, dropped to his knees, and crawled as quickly as he could out through the darkness to the waiting room. The lights in the hallway flared on. Brian inched toward the patients' entrance, then ducked behind a sofa as he sensed the intruder approaching the reception area.

Only now did Brian curse himself for overreacting. He had dived for cover like a prowler about to be caught in the act. He was on the faculty of the institute and on duty that night. He also possessed the keypad access code to the clinic and a perfectly legitimate reason for being there—a reason he had established earlier in the day during a conversation with the receptionist, Mrs. Leander. Now, however, it was too late.

The piece of furniture he had flattened himself behind— wooden arms and frame with loose cushions on top—offered some, but not total, cover. Brian lay on the floor looking under the furniture and wondering if all of his seventy-five inches was hidden. He reached down slowly and shut off his pager. But he decided against disabling the code-call beeper. If there was a cardiac arrest somewhere in the hospital, however, his own might follow close behind.

The door to the waiting room was maybe six feet away, but there was no way he could chance going for it. The noise of opening it would probably get him caught, and there was also the possibility it was locked. He pressed the side of his face onto the heavy-duty carpet and breathed silently.

Suddenly the fluorescents flickered on in the waiting room. Beneath the furniture, Brian could make out the pants legs and sneakers of a man standing across the room. Sneakers? He wondered whether hospital security allowed such dress. The sneakers turned one way then another as the man scanned the room. Then, after an unending two or three minutes, the overheads went off.

Brian sensed more than heard the man retrace his steps. The hallway lights were turned off, and once again the clinic was thrown into pitch darkness. A door opened and shut. It sounded as if it was at the end of the hallway.

Brian waited. Five minutes. . . . Ten.

Finally, he inched his way to the door and gently tested the knob. No problem. He was about to open it when he remembered the appointment book. He had left it on the receptionist's desk. He had no stomach for resuming his search for the remaining Phase

One patients tonight, but assuming the clinic was empty, there was no sense in leaving the book there to invite questions. Still on his hands and knees, his senses alert for any hint that the intruder hadn't really left, he inched his way across to the office door and stopped. The silence and darkness were total.

For several minutes, he lay there, listening. Finally, he pushed himself up, opened the door, and turned on the light.

The appointment ledger was gone.

He rushed to the shelves, but only the year 2 book was there. He checked the floor and the desk drawers. Nothing. Once again, his pulse was hammering. Why had the security guard, or whatever he was, thought to take the book? The situation made no sense, but was terrifying nonetheless.

He could not think of a thing to do except return to the ward and worry. Then, just as he was about to cut the light, he glanced up at one side of the office and groaned out loud. A black nozzle protruded from a corner where the bookcase wall, another wall, and the ceiling met—a security camera focused on the glass and the counter of the receptionist's area, not exactly concealed, but not that easily noticeable, either.

Brian stared at it for a few seconds, wondering who was watching him, and from where. Then, feeling absolutely helpless, he snapped on his beeper, turned off the lights, and left the clinic.

If anyone confronted him about the late-night foray, he still had an excuse, albeit a bit feeble, that Mrs. Leander would support. But no matter what, he couldn't shake the dreadful feeling that the fuse beneath him had just been lit, and that he had struck the match.

CHAPTER TWENTY-FOUR

By three-thirty in the morning, Brian was physically and mentally spent. Action on the ward had picked up
around midnight, with one patient dropping her blood pressure,
and another going into a series of difficult-to-manage cardiac ar-
rhythmias. Neither patient was part of the Vasclear study. It took
several hours to stabilize the two women, and Brian was forced to
slip a temporary pacemaker into one of them. Finally, all was calm,
although by now the muscles in the back of his neck were like
braided ropes, and those in his legs ached unremittingly.

The emergencies did have the beneficial side effect of keeping
Brian's mind off the debacle in the Vasclear clinic. There wasn't

much more he could have done wrong there. Worst of all was losing control of the clinic appointment book. But getting himself videoed on someone's security system was certainly a close second.

What to do? As he made a final check of each patient on the ward, the question began reverberating in his head.

He splashed some water on his face, signed off the ward and on to his beeper, and headed down to the security office in the basement of the Pinkham Building. The guard on duty there was a crew-cut bull of a man whose name tag read *JIM UNDERHILL*. He wore the standard blue wool uniform of his department, and was sitting behind a waist-high counter reading a Stephen King paperback.

On the wall to his right was a bank of eight monitor screens, with the scene on each of them changing every ten seconds or so. Brian tried to pick out the Vasclear reception area, then remembered that he had left the clinic completely dark.

Brian held up his photo-ID card, while at the same time angling to get a look at the man's shoes.

"Yes, Dr. Holbrook," Underhill said, "I've heard of you. What can I do for you?"

I heard you was comin'. Hadn't those been animal-keeper Earl's exact words?

Unlike his exchange with Mary Leander, this time Brian was prepared.

"I'm sorry I couldn't get down sooner," he began, "but we had a couple of emergencies on my floor at Boston Heart. I was one of the last ones to leave the Vasclear clinic tonight around eight-fifteen. Before I left, I went into the reception area to check on some appointments. Then I got an emergency page to the CCU and had to run out. About an hour later I realized I had left my little black medical bag on the receptionist's desk. But when I went back for it, it was gone."

"Couldn't someone have just found it and put it away for you?"

"Maybe. But Lucy Kendall, the charge nurse, and I were the last ones there, I think. I called her at her home when I realized what had happened, and she didn't know anything about my bag."

Wearily, the guard pulled a clipboard out from under his desk. As he did, Brian moved to the end of the counter, feigning watching the screens, and got a clear glimpse at his shoes. Black leather, polished to a high gloss. Almost certainly, the intruder at the clinic wasn't one of the hospital's regular security force.

"Okay, Doc," Underhill said wearily, "fill out this incident report."

"Actually, Jim, I've never had much faith in filling out forms. But while I was in the receptionist's office looking for my bag, I noticed a surveillance camera sort of hidden away beside the bookshelf. I wondered if maybe you picked up something here—a video of whoever took my bag."

Underhill squinted as he probed his memory. Then he gave up and took a laminated sheet from a clipboard hanging beneath the screens.

"Just as I thought," he said after a minute's perusal of the paper. "There's no screen listed that includes the Vasclear clinic."

Brian felt a sudden chill.

"Well, what do think that surveillance camera is for?" he asked.

The guard shrugged.

"No idea. Maybe it ain't hooked up."

"Maybe," Brian said, though he didn't believe that for a moment. "Are there any other security cameras around the hospital that aren't projected here?"

"No idea, although I don't see why there would be. The head of my department, Tom Dubanowski, probably knows. You might ask him. He'll be here around seven."

"Thanks," Brian said.

He left the security office weighted down by a feeling of impending disaster. Someone had seen him via the office surveillance camera. That same someone had sent the guy in the sneakers up to investigate. And now, whoever it was had the appointment ledger and with it at least a few concerns about what Brian had been looking for. He spent some badly needed mental energy trying to work out who that might be. Newbury Pharmaceuticals could have installed the cameras, but the plant was several miles from the hospital. How could they have gotten someone up to the clinic so quickly? Or maybe Jim Underhill had lied. Maybe he kept a pair of sneakers under his desk for dashing about. The guard certainly wouldn't have been the first one in the hospital to withhold the truth from him.

The hour—it was after four A.M., now—didn't contribute to clear thinking. Ward rounds would be starting up in less than three hours. Brian knew he was nearing what he thought of as the point of no return, the point where he would be worse off trying to get his mind and body functioning after a couple hours of sleep than he would be by simply pouring down some residents' coffee, summoning up the adrenaline of utter fatigue, and attempting to go the distance—twenty-four hours plus the following workday. It would certainly make for an adventurous ride home.

Heads you go to bed, tails it's the machine canteen, he decided, reaching into his pocket for a coin. What his hand landed on instead was the list—ten names hastily printed on a small, crumpled piece of paper.

Before he was fully aware he had made a decision, Brian was at the door of the record room in the basement of the building adjacent to Pinkham. Every computer log-on to the record room was recorded somewhere. It seemed logical that from now on, the guy in sneakers or his boss would be keeping close tabs on charts released to Brian. Sooner or later, he would probably have to resort to an electronic review. But before that happened, he might be able to get a look at one or two charts in their original form.

The door was closed, but there was a phone on the wall beside it with instructions. Brian explained who he was to the Hispanic woman who answered, and that he wanted to review the hard copy of a chart he couldn't seem to call up on his laptop. Moments later, the door opened the length of a chain and a young woman peered out. Brian showed her his ID badge and said he'd be happy to get security to accompany him if she would feel more comfortable.

"That won't be necessary," the woman said. "The security guard is already here."

The door was eased shut to release the chain, then opened fully. The woman, in her early twenties, was slender, raven-haired, and lovely. Her clothes and hair seemed just a bit askew, and her lipstick a bit smeared. A man and a woman behind a locked door in a hospital in the early-morning hours. Brian groaned inwardly. And to make matters worse, the man was another security guard. He and Jim Underhill would be comparing notes before long. Brian stood outside the door, considering just mumbling some excuse and leaving. But the woman had already seen his ID. At this point, *not* entering might actually arouse more suspicion in the guard.

It took just a minute for the young attendant to return with the chart of the first name on Brian's list, a woman in her mid-seventies named Sylvia Vitorelli. Brian set the record in a small dictation carrel. Aware that the young woman and the guard were watching and waiting, he flipped through the chart as quickly as possible. Because Vitorelli had been a longtime WMH patient, with a hysterectomy, gall-bladder removal, surgically repaired ankle fracture, and cardiac problems, the chart was a weighty one, perhaps an inch and a half thick. Finally, though, he was able to piece together her story.

A resident of the North End, not far from the hospital, Vitorelli was a married mother of four and a grandmother, who at one time had smoked more than a pack of cigarettes a day. She began having chest pains and was referred to Carolyn Jessup, who treated her with traditional medical therapy for over a year until making her part of the Vasclear Phase One trials nearly three years ago. Brian reviewed Vitorelli's stress test, cardiac ultrasound, and other EKGs. Her cardiovascular disease was fairly extensive, though not as extensive as Brian's father's.

It sounded from Jessup's notes as if Vitorelli had had an excellent early response to her Vasclear therapy. Then, suddenly, the chart simply ended. No more notes, no laboratory reports, nothing. Brian skimmed through the pages searching for a section that might have been out of order.

"You going to be much longer, Doc?" the security man called to him. "Elana wants to go for her break, and we can't leave you in here alone."

"One more minute," Brian said.

He turned to the lab-report section. There were none after the first three months of Vitorelli's Vasclear therapy. Absolutely none.

He made a photocopy of the front sheet of the chart, thanked the eager Elana, and headed back to the ward. Unless he was way off-base, the final pages of Sylvia Vitorelli's chart had suffered the same fate as Kenneth Ford's. Did the woman represent a third case of Vasclear failure followed by signs and symptoms that might have been pulmonary hypertension? Was it worth trying to prove his suspicion?

If he was right about Sylvia Vitorelli, Phase One testing seemed to have an inordinate number of problems, yet Phase Two was nearly perfect. Had the modifications in the chemical synthesis of the drug made that great a difference?

The questions seemed endless.

But there was another question of even more immediate concern to him. How long did Brian Holbrook have left at Boston Heart?

CHAPTER TWENTY-FIVE

THE BOSTON GLOBE

Vasclear Orders Flooding In

Boston-based Newbury Pharmaceuticals confirmed that orders for its new, as-yet-unapproved drug Vasclear have been pouring in not only from all over the country, but from all over the world as well. The medication, which comes in 10-cc vials and must be diluted and administered intravenously, has been reported to eliminate the plaques that cause heart attacks in as many as seventy-five percent of patients.

Dr. Art Weber, Vasclear project director for Newbury, says that the overwhelming demand for the drug is almost
certain to create initial shortages and
drive up the price.

AT SEVEN-FIFTEEN, WHEN PHIL CALLED PATIENT ROUNDS
to order, Brian was just stepping out of the on-call-room shower.
He had done his best to stay awake until the morning crew arrived,
but with no specific emergencies to pump him up, he hadn't stood
a chance. When the nurse's call woke him at six-thirty, he had been
flat on his back in a deathlike sleep for two hours. Within seconds
of her call, he was out again. By agreement, fifteen minutes later,
she called a second time, not letting him leave the phone until he
could recite the Pledge of Allegiance and the names of all the
chambers, valves, and arteries of the heart.

Brian toweled off and dressed, furious with himself for having
placed his job, his future, and the immediate security of his daughters in jeopardy. But in truth, what had he done? An elderly survivor of the Holocaust had come to see him with a serious medical
problem. In investigating the problem, he had stumbled onto a
similar case. It was only natural for Brian or any decent doc to
want to get to the bottom of the situation.

He hurried out to the ward and caught up with the gang that
surrounded the bed of the patient in 514.

"Sorry I'm late, Phil," he said.

"No problem. Looks like you had a busy night."

You have no idea.

"Busy enough for these old bones. I didn't schedule Mrs. Cam-
eron for a permanent pacer, but she's going to need one."

"I'll take care of it."

Rounds were scheduled to last until nine-thirty—ten at the latest. Technically, as the teaching visit for the month, Phil was not
only charged with educating the nurses, students, residents, and
fellows, but he was legally responsible for signing off on all the

patients on the service as well. Brian watched his friend function in the role, working on the staff with just the right combination of questions, cajoling, inoffensive humor, and medical wisdom. In Brian's opinion, Phil's assessment of himself was far from the mark. He was a hell of a doc. But Brian knew that what might have been respected, even revered, in a faculty member at many hospitals, was the norm at Boston Heart.

Midway through rounds, as they were approaching a string of student cases on whom Brian had nothing to report, he cut away, went to a secluded phone across from the nurses' workstation, and dialed Sylvia Vitorelli's number. A woman answered.

"Hello?"

"Hello, Mrs. Vitorelli?"

"Who?"

"I'm calling Mrs. Sylvia Vitorelli."

"There's no one here by that name. You must have the wrong number."

"Wait, please don't hang up."

Brian read off the number he had dialed.

"I'm sorry," the woman said. "That's my number, but there's no one here by the name you said."

"Please," Brian said. "I'm a doctor calling from White Memorial Hospital and I'm trying to find this woman. The number I dialed is the one that's listed in the hospital record for her. How long have you had it?"

"More than six months."

"Thank you," Brian murmured, setting the phone down.

He made it back to rounds for another twenty minutes, then escaped again to the phone. This time the call was long-distance, to the man listed as Sylvia's next of kin, Richard Vitorelli in Fulbrook, New York. Brian, now more careful than he ever would have been before the near disaster in the Vasclear clinic, used the outside operator and a credit card rather than going through the hospital operator. A woman answered.

"Who did you say you were again?" she asked.

"Dr. Holbrook from White Memorial Hospital in Boston."

"Did you take care of my mother-in-law?"

"I . . . no . . . not exactly."

"I think you should speak to my husband. He'll be home late tonight. You'll have to call tomorrow."

"Well, could you just tell me how Mrs. Vitorelli is?"

There was a prolonged pause before the woman answered.

"She died," she said finally. "She collapsed here in this house and died at the hospital about two years ago."

Brian felt his pulse respond to the news. Sylvia's chart ended not too many months before that.

"I'm sorry," he said. "Could you tell me any of the details of her death—any at all?"

"I . . . think you'd better call back when my husband's here."

"Okay, but please, just tell me, do you know the cause of death?"

"It was her heart. Now please, call back tomorrow."

Sylvia's daughter-in-law had hung up before Brian could ask her another question. But he was asking himself plenty. Was Sylvia hospitalized anywhere before her death? Did she have a cardiological evaluation at any point? A blood count? An autopsy? And perhaps the two biggest questions of all: Was it too late for him just to let the Vasclear matter drop altogether? Was he even capable of doing that?

"Well, another riveting set of rounds, eh?"

Brian hadn't even noticed Phil approaching.

"Sorry I kept leaving the group. I had a couple of calls to make."

"Hey, no problem. You just keep putting in the pacemakers and saving the lives. I'll take care of the theoretical stuff."

"You really are a very good teacher, Phil."

"Aw, pshaw."

"Seriously. I can tell you really love doing it, too. Not everyone does, you know."

"Well, the truth is I *do* love it. I love everything about what I'm being paid to do here. That's why I'm willing to put up with some of the bullshit and the unwritten rules. It goes with the territory. It's also why I can't be of any more help to you with this Vasclear thing, and why I'm begging you to be careful."

"Do you know something I don't?"

"About what?"

"Nothing, nothing. I'm just a little paranoid and a lot overtired."

"I can understand both. Bri, if I sound preachy, I apologize. But it's a fact of life that every place that has more than one person working in it has a set of egos that the lower-downs like you and me have to deal with. In places where those people are doctors, the personalities are just . . . more sharply defined, that's all. Once you get used to who has the fragile egos around here and what you have to do to stay on their good side, it really is a decent place."

"Hey, you don't have to tell me. I'm the one who was pulled off the medical scrap heap, remember?"

"Yeah. Well, I wanted to thank you for not pushing matters."

"No problem."

Brian could see the discomfort in his friend's face. The decision to remain uninvolved wasn't an easy one for him.

"Well," Phil said awkwardly, "see you later."

He backed off a few steps, then turned and hurried away.

Brian opened his briefcase and took out an envelope on which he had written Phil's name. Inside it was a copy of the list of the ten Phase One patients. Brian had intended to see if Phil would feel comfortable searching out the records of some of them. Instead, he tore up the copy and dropped the bits in the trash. Phil was officially out of the loop. Now, Brian thought, if he could only be as definitive about himself.

"Dr. Holbrook," the ward secretary called out, "do you have a second?"

"Sure."

Brian snapped his briefcase shut and crossed over to her desk.

"Dr. Holbrook, I just noticed this envelope on the corner of my desk had your name on it. I don't know who left it there or when. I just looked and there it was. I'm sorry."

"Nonsense. That's fine, thanks. It looks like nothing important, anyway. Probably fell out of the pile I lugged up from my mailbox."

He didn't believe that explanation for a second, but it was the best he could do on the spur of the moment. He took the envelope from her and retreated as nonchalantly as he could manage to the lounge.

The envelope was plain white, and sealed, with *DR. BRIAN HOLBROOK* carefully printed in block letters. Brian tore the envelope open, but even before he unfolded the single sheet, he knew it was trouble.

WHITE MEMORIAL HOSPITAL DIAGNOSTIC LAB
Patient: 1744   SPECIMEN DATE: 10/15

Test Name	Result
Ethanol (Urine)	NEGATIVE

Drugs of Abuse Screen (Urine)

Tetrahydrocannabinol (THC)	NEGATIVE
Amphetamines	NEGATIVE
Barbiturates	NEGATIVE
Benzodiazepine Metabolites	NEGATIVE
Cocaine and Metabolite	NEGATIVE
Methadone and Metabolite	NEGATIVE
Opiates	POSITIVE
Phencyclidine	NEGATIVE
Propoxyphene and Metabolite	NEGATIVE

Comments

—The specimen processed under chain of custody

—Positive opiate results confirmed by gas chromatography

—Quantitative result to follow

Patient 1744. Brian's number. But the date was today's. He hadn't even given a urine today, much less one that was positive for the opiate narcotic group—the class of drugs for which he had gotten in trouble. He sat there staring across the tiny lounge at a framed print of Hippocrates pouring something from a clay bowl down a patient's throat. It felt as if a barbell had been dropped on his chest. According to his agreement with Ernest Pickard, just one positive test confirmed by gas chromatography was it. No excuses, no alibis, no protestations of innocence, no hiding behind lab error, no second chances. *It.* Termination at BHI. Immediate report to the Board of Registration. Humiliation. Suspension. Forget about doctoring. Forget about unsupervised visits with the kids. *It.*

The clinic where he had his urine testing done had a log book— a hedge against someone blaming the lab or the collection procedure for a missing specimen. Had whoever sent this bogus report also forged his name in the book? Brian wondered why they had picked a day when he hadn't been ordered to get a test, rather than wait until he had actually gone and simply alter the results. If they could do this with an official report, they could do anything.

Suddenly, he realized his beeper had gone off. The LED displayed *OUTSIDE CALL.* Brian stuffed the bogus report into his pocket and dialed in. The caller was a man with slow, deep, almost guttural speech . . . and some kind of accent.

"You have the envelope, Dr. Holbrook?"

"Who are you?"

"Today, this is only a warning. A show of our capabilities. If you continue trying to cause trouble with the FDA or anyone else, we will find out about it. I promise you we will. And if we do, the next report will be on a urine sample you dropped off. Your name will be in the log book. The test will be positive, and you will be finished. Have I made myself clear?"

"Who are you?" Brian blurted again.

The caller hung up.

Brian stared at the phone, wondering why he was being given a second chance at all. Surely, with a positive urine, the credibility of anything he had to say would be badly tarnished. It had to be that he had stumbled onto something important and potentially damaging to Vasclear's squeaky-clean image. Teri had said it any number of times. Alexander Baird was looking for something, anything, that would offset the incredible hype surrounding the drug, and enable his office to delay its release to an all-too-eager public. The caller and his people wanted Brian quiet and were willing to trade him his career for that absolute silence. Brian tore the report into tiny pieces and sprinkled them into the trash. He was being given one last chance—but by whom?

Numb, bewildered, and distracted, he left the lounge and nearly collided with Ernest Pickard. During the weeks Brian had been on the service, not once had he seen the institute chief on the ward. Yet here he was. Coincidence?

Pickard was dressed immaculately in a blue double-breasted suit. A stethoscope protruded from one pocket, although Brian doubted the man got to use it very much anymore.

"Well, well," Pickard said, with his usual cheer, moving Brian to a spot far enough away from the workstation counter so they could talk, "how's the quarterback doing?"

Brian studied the man as hard as he dared, trying to pick up any intonation that this was a follow-up visit to make certain the Vasclear message had gotten through.

"I haven't taken too bad a hit yet," he said.

"The reports that have reached me are quite a bit more glowing than that. Well, I dropped by because I wanted to make certain you were all right after the tragedy."

"Tragedy?"

"Yes. Your father."

"Oh, yes. Yes. That's very kind of you, Dr. Pickard. The truth is, I feel like I'm just going through the motions right now."

Pickard put a hand on his shoulder.

"That's a perfectly normal reaction. I know it's hard to keep your concentration. Well, don't let it get you down too much."

"I'm trying not to."

"And for God's sake, don't allow yourself to have a relapse. You are still going to your meetings?"

"Absolutely."

"Excellent. Because you seem to be fitting in quite well here, and I would certainly hate to lose you."

Without waiting for a response, Pickard patted Brian on the shoulder again, smiled toward the nurses and secretary, who were gathered behind the counter ogling him, and left.

Brian wandered back to the lounge. It was impossible to tell if Pickard knew what was going on with him or not. But one thing was clear. With only four days left until the Vasclear signing ceremony, he was a marked man. He glanced out the door to be certain there was no one about, then called the one person he could completely trust. Thank God, Freeman was in his apartment.

"Freeman, I called to see if there are any meetings around, say, three this afternoon, that you might be able to make."

"Let me check my trusty meeting-list books. I see nothing in the NA department until this evening, but there's an AA meeting at eighteen Stiles Street in Brookline. Four to five. Discussion."

"Can you meet me there?"

"Hey, if you need me, you got me. Especially at a meeting. That's in the sponsors' handbook."

"Thanks. Well, I need you and the meeting. One other thing. Do you have any idea how to find out who owns and is on the board of directors of a company?"

"No, but I can tell you that between AA and NA there is always someone who knows whatever it is you want to know, whether it's business, rap music, home repairs, or neurosurgery. It's just a matter of trackin' down the right dude."

"Could you try?"

"Of course, provided you're gonna tell me what this is all about."

"I'm going to tell you, Freeman. I promise."

"Okay, then. What's the company?"

"Newbury Pharmaceuticals. I want to know who runs Newbury Pharmaceuticals."

CHAPTER TWENTY-SIX

FREEMAN SHARPE ARRIVED AT THE CHURCH IN BROOK-line fifteen minutes after the AA meeting had started, but Brian was there saving a spot for him. They sat together for a time, listening to a lawyer talk about the mistakes he had made in his practice over the years because of his drinking, and the changes that had occurred during the eight years since he had stopped. In addition to doing volunteer work answering the phones once a week at AA central service, he had resigned from his high-pow-ered firm, exchanged his BMW for a Tercel, thrown away his Maalox, and begun doing legal-aid work for the inner-city poor.

The glow off the man's craggy face lit up the hall.

"Sounds like he's pretty well got it," Sharpe leaned over and whispered.

Brian looked up at a stained-glass window.

"Yeah," he said flatly.

Sharpe sighed.

"Dr. Brian, I think maybe we should go outside and talk."

"Go outside? Sharpe, you've never left in the middle of a meeting in all the time I've known you."

"Well, my special spider sense is tingling and it says that you're a mess."

They stopped at the pot for coffee and carried the cups out with them to the street. The late afternoon was cloudy, but warm, and Brian was grateful he had changed into jeans and a T-shirt before leaving the hospital. In silence, they wandered down a block, then across a deserted ball field to a concrete bench. Freeman packed his corncob pipe.

"I'm in trouble," Brian said.

"Seems like you've been in trouble almost since the day you went to work at that place."

"Renting cars was a lot simpler, I'll grant you that. Freeman, Jack died in part because I chose not to push him to have surgery. And the main reason, hell, the *only* reason I didn't was because I had him on Vasclear. Now I'm starting to find some things out about the early patient trials with that drug—things that the drug company never knew or else never told the FDA."

"Is there something wrong with the drug?"

"I can't say that for sure. Not now, anyway. But two and a half years ago, they did some preliminary testing on eighteen people. I've only located three of those eighteen, but they're all dead. Two of them had a weird blood test and the kind of symptoms that might have been caused by the drug. The third one I just found out about. She died at her son's place in upstate New York. I don't know any of the details. But her hospital record and the record of one of the other patients both look like they've been tampered with. Pages are missing."

"But the drug's working okay now?"

"Yes. It still doesn't work for everyone, but it doesn't seem to harm anyone, either."

Freeman lit his pipe. The cherry tobacco smoke blended perfectly with the scents of autumn.

"So?" he said.

"Last night I got caught on a video-surveillance camera in the clinic, getting the names of some of the early patients so I could check up on them."

"Why did you do that?"

"I don't know. I . . . I can't shake the feeling that I didn't push Jack hard enough about the surgery. I wanted so badly to believe that Vasclear was the answer."

"A crusade. I just love crusades. All them horses, those little white capes with the red crosses."

Brian managed a brief laugh.

"You know," he said, "maybe it is a crusade. But the question is, who am I fighting against? The deeper I get into this thing, the more I think I'm battling against myself—my own arrogance. It almost destroyed my life twice—once when I tore up my knee, and later when I refused to get help for an addiction problem that was eating away my soul. But I thought that after all my work in NA and therapy, I was on top of that part of me, had it under control. Then, all of a sudden, I decide I know what's best for my father and override the recommendations of his doctor and one of the foremost cardiac surgeons in the world."

"So that's why you won't let this thing drop?"

"Maybe. Yes. Yes, I think that's a lot of it. I can't face what my own ego led me to do, so I'm looking to punish the drug and the people who make it. But Freeman, I also think there was something wrong with the drug. I don't have any idea what, but I think this problem with the Phase One patients has been swept under the rug. The doctors involved with Vasclear are respected researchers, but they already lied to me once about something that's crucial to the study."

"And these respected researchers are getting upset with you?"

"Maybe them, maybe someone else. This morning someone left me a urine report with my case number on it. It looks authentic, but it's not. It's positive for narcotics. I didn't even *give* a specimen today. A few minutes later a man called and implied that unless I stop trying to cause trouble, next time the report would go to my boss."

"So, what sort of advice do you want from your sponsor?"

"I want you to tell me that I just started back in medicine after eighteen months, that this whole Vasclear thing amounts to nothing but my overripe imagination, that I really have no concrete proof there's anything wrong with the drug, that the FDA isn't the least bit interested in what I've found so far, and that I had better tend to my own business."

Sharpe sent a smoke ring swirling skyward.

"Why do you think they threatened you with that fake urine?" he asked.

"I'm not sure. Either they're afraid I'm going to stumble onto a skeleton in their closet, or they're just being cautious with the approval of the drug only a few days away. If it turns out they knew something about Vasclear in Phase One and didn't report it to the FDA, even if they subsequently fixed the problem, that would probably be sufficient grounds for the FDA to postpone the approval indefinitely."

"Even if the drug has worked fine since then?"

"I think so. And there's a tremendous amount of money at stake."

"So, the best you could hope for would be postponing the release of a medication that seems to be working perfectly well and could save thousands of lives. And trying to accomplish that dubious feat might cost you your career as a doctor."

Another smoke ring.

"When you say it that way, it sounds pretty foolish," Brian said.

"It sounds like a guy who cared a lot for his father and is feeling very guilty, angry, and frustrated about his death. That's not foolish."

"So, you think I should forget the whole thing."

"Not really, no."

Brian did a double take.

"What do you mean?"

"Well, you asked me to do some digging into Newbury Pharmaceuticals, right?"

"That was just this morning. You've got something already?"

"Maybe. First of all, the company's privately held, and spotless on the surface." He pulled a piece of paper from his windbreaker. "The secretary of state's office at the State House doesn't demand much information from privately held companies, and that's precisely what they've got on file for Newbury." He handed a list of four names to Brian. "A CEO, a treasurer, a clerk, one name from the board of directors. Those and a mission statement are the minimum requirements. None of these names mean anything to me, and I doubt they'd mean anything to you."

"They don't."

"Remember when I told you that in AA, whatever it is you want to know or you want done, there's someone who knows it or can do it? Well, I got to thinking that if there was anything off-center about this company of yours, Cedric L. would know. You know him? Probably the only Chinese guy in the world named Cedric. He belongs to the downtown Friday-night group. He also belongs to a social club in Chinatown that's really a hangout for one of the toughest gangs in the city."

"And here you were worried about me walking off with a few vials of medicine."

"Cedric's got twenty years of solid recovery in," Freeman replied. "Maybe more. When you got that long, you can make informed choices. Anyhow, I called ol' Cedric, and it turns out he knows quite a bit about your Newbury Pharmaceuticals."

"Such as?"

"Such as for the last ten years they've been a front for laundering money."

"Drug money?"

"Is there any other kind?"

"The Mafia?"

"Not the one you're thinking of. According to Cedric, the Russians own the place. Owned it even before the Berlin Wall came tumblin' down."

Brian glanced at the list of four names.

"Then who are these people?"

"Don't know. People who have had their names changed. People who get paid off to put their names on corporate documents. Probably something like that. The company makes vitamins."

"I know."

"Well, Cedric says the word is they buy the raw ingredients for their vitamins from someplace over in Russia, then sell the finished products back there. Somehow, the money makes it from here to there as fives, tens, and twenties, and comes back as bank notes and electronic deposits."

"Now they make Vasclear?"

"So it would seem. And if that stuff is worth as much as the papers say, they ain't gonna have to peddle vitamins or dope much longer."

Brian whistled softly.

"Freeman, the guy who called me this morning and threatened me had a Russian accent. I'm certain of it."

"In that case, my man, I would say that you have gotten yourself into some deep, deep shit. When you do something to cross these guys, they don't usually slap you on the knuckles with a ruler. I'm surprised that all you were threatened with was a positive urine test."

Brian sat stunned, gazing across the field at two boys who had begun tossing a football through the gathering dusk.

"This Cedric, is he someone you trust?" he asked.

"He's a gangster. How the hell should I know? But yeah, I believe him. What reason does he have to lie to me?"

"I staked my father's life on a miracle drug that's controlled by the Russian Mafia?"

"So it would seem. But that don't change that the drug works."

"Yes, that's right. Seventy-five percent of two hundred cases. Freeman, what should I do?"

"Don't drink, don't drug, go to meetings, and ask for help."

"Generic advice."

"Ah, but the right advice for this or any situation. Brian, I got more than a year invested in you. You may be right that the Newbury people are covering something up, or you may be wrong. At this moment, I really don't give a rat's ass which. I just don't want to see you hurt."

"So, you're saying I should go along with what they're demanding, and not do anything?"

"Maybe."

"But the thing is, Freeman, I haven't done anything anyhow—certainly nothing to deserve this kind of reaction from them. They're using the fact that I'm in recovery against me, threatening to destroy my life as a doctor, and I haven't really done a damn thing but check some records."

"It does seem a bit like they're trying to kill an ant with an elephant gun."

"Why?" Shaking his head, Brian stood and started across the field. Sharpe followed, tapping ashes from his pipe.

"Why?" Brian asked again.

They neared where the teens were playing catch. Brian clapped his hands for the ball, and one of them dutifully tossed it over.

"Go deep," Brian said, motioning the boy away. "Deeper," he called out. "Deeper still."

"Mister, come on," the youth hollered back.

"Okay, suit yourself!"

Every bit of confusion, doubt, and fear went into Brian's throw. Although the boy was a good forty yards away, the perfect spiral was still rising when it sailed over his head. The ball landed more than sixty yards from Brian, bounced once, and disappeared into a low tangle of bushes.

"I can't quit on this, Freeman," he said. "I just can't."

CHAPTER TWENTY-SEVEN

FULBROOK, NEW YORK, WAS A SLEEPY, POSTCARD-PRETTY village in the foothills of the Catskill Mountains. The drive there from Boston was three and a half hours through intoxicating autumn foliage. Brian made the trip with the top down on the LeBaron, usually a tonic for any inner turmoil. But today, nothing was going to be able to distract him—nothing except some answers.

Richard Vitorelli had been as suspicious and reluctant to speak to Brian as had his wife. Finally, he agreed to meet with him in person, provided he brought proper identification, and they could do it at the office of his family doctor—the man who also doubled as the county medical examiner. Brian was more than happy to oblige.

Following nearly thirty-six hours on duty, Brian was off-call for the entire day. After speaking with Richard Vitorelli and getting directions to Dr. Samuel Purefoy's office, he had called Teri from the flat. The sound of her voice made everything else seem less important.

"I was just about to call *you*," she said.

"What about?"

"I don't know. Phone sex, maybe? I really miss you, Doc."

"And I really miss you, Doc. Can you get up here before Saturday?"

"I really don't see any way. There's a tremendous amount of stuff still to be gone over here. Dr. Baird and I are flying up early in the day Saturday by government jet."

Brian had already decided that without specific proof, he wasn't going to share any of the information Freeman had gotten from Cedric L. It was likely that the FDA was familiar with the officers and principal researchers of Newbury Pharmaceuticals, and that they had checked out above any reproach. Making unsubstantiated charges would only diminish his own credibility.

"Have you come across any disturbing information about Vasclear?" he asked Teri.

"None, except for what you told me about the two cases of heart failure that might have been PH."

"And Dr. Baird didn't make anything of those."

"Not really. Remember, the patients in Phase One were all pretty sick to begin with. It seems only natural that some of them would die from their cardiac disease."

"What about the pulmonary hypertension?"

"Brian, there's no proof that either of those patients actually had it. And only one of them died of heart failure. You said the other man was shot during a holdup."

"He was. I've been meaning to get over to the medical examiner's office to see if the autopsy on that guy showed any evidence of PH in his lung vessels, but there just hasn't been time. And there's another Phase One patient I want to learn about—a lady named Vitorelli. Like the other two, she's dead. I think she died from cardiac disease, but I want to find out whether she might have had PH. I have the day off tomorrow, and I have nothing planned. So I thought I'd put the top down, drive over to her son's place in New York State, and speak with him and the medical examiner."

"I won't try to talk you out of it, Brian, but I will tell you that we're satisfied the drug is safe and effective."

"But you said you'd be checking on Vasclear right up until the last minute."

"And I meant it. If you find anything concrete, anything at all, Dr. Baird will evaluate it. He has the President's word that the signing ceremony can be called off even at the last minute."

"In that case, I'm off to Fulbrook. You sure you don't want to fly up tonight and drive over there with me tomorrow morning? It's about a four-hour trip and I have this car fantasy—"

"Oh, not *that* one. All you men have that one."

"Oh yeah? Well, it just so happens that mine has to do with orange marmalade, a Ouija board, and my medical bag. Just so you know what you're missing."

"Now that does sound intriguing. Brian, we really are satisfied we've done all we can. You don't need to stick your neck out."

"You should have thought of that before you invited me to your hotel room. Now I'm obsessed."

"In that case, can I take a rain check on the Ouija board and marmalade?"

"Absolutely. I'll call you when I get back." Brian heard a click on the line. "Do you have call waiting?" he asked.

"No, why?"

"I just heard a sound—a click."

"I'm always hearing weird stuff on my line, but nothing this time. Are you okay?"

"Huh? Oh, sure. I'm tired and a bit stressed from work, is all. And I miss my dad."

"I would think those feelings might soften, but they'll never go away."

"Yeah. . . . Well, I've got to get to the store for some marmalade."

"I miss you, Brian."

Dr. Samuel Purefoy, the Greene County medical examiner, was a jovial bowling ball of a man. His office was in a small sky-blue bungalow at the foot of a low mountain ablaze in fall colors. There was an old buggy, freshly painted, on the front lawn—a reminder of the simpler, gentler days of medicine.

Brian arrived fifteen minutes earlier than promised, and Purefoy used the time to brew them a pot of tea and benignly grill him about medicine, White Memorial Hospital, and BHI.

"I've never encountered a scene quite like the one in that woman's bedroom at Ricky's place," the aging GP said finally, the information acknowledging his acceptance of Brian. "There was blood-tinged pulmonary edema fluid everywhere. God, how that poor woman must have suffered before the end. She drowned. Pure and simple. We did what we could for her, but there really wasn't any chance."

"She was alive when you got to her?"

"She was, but just barely. It was a Sunday. My home is just a mile or so from the Vitorellis' place, and my back was acting up so I decided to pass on church. I made it over there right when the rescue squad arrived. We actually got a tube in her, and got her over to our little hospital. It's small, but it's a damn fine place."

"I'll bet it is," Brian said.

"She never made it out of the ER, though. With all that fluid in her chest, we just couldn't get enough oxygen into her blood."

"Did you consider doing an autopsy?"

"Not really. She was a White Memorial cardiac case. Her medications bore that out. I didn't see any sense in putting her or her family through the trauma of a post. What brings you all the way out here from Boston two years after the fact?"

"Mrs. Vitorelli was one of the first patients to be treated with Vasclear."

"Ah, the wonder drug. I've already got half a dozen candidates lined up for it. I heard it was going to be available this weekend. That right?"

"I think so. Dr. Purefoy—"

"Sam. Please call me Sam."

"—Sam, I've bumped into a couple of cases of patients who were part of the early Vasclear studies and who had something that looked and acted like severe pulmonary hypertension. Is that much of a possibility in Mrs. Vitorelli, from what you could tell?"

"Pulmonary hypertension, huh. I'm not sure I've ever seen a case. Or if I did, I didn't diagnose it. Her ankles were terribly swollen, about as bad as I've ever seen. That's part of pulmonary hypertension, right?"

"Absolutely, although it's not specific to PH."

At that moment, Richard Vitorelli came in, looking and smelling like a man who spent his life in the fields. He was broad-shouldered with thick, curly black hair and an extremely kind face. He tentatively shook a callused hand with Brian, then turned to Purefoy.

"This guy legit?" he asked, his expression suggesting that trust didn't come easily to him.

"Oh, he's legit all right," Purefoy replied. "White Memorial Hospital, just like he said. He's checking up on that drug Vasclear your mother was taking."

"What about it?"

"Well," Brian said, "in just a couple of days, people all over the world will be taking it."

"Including a bunch right here in Fulbrook," Purefoy interjected.

"I'm checking on people who were taking Vasclear and died. Your mother was on my list."

Vitorelli looked again to Purefoy, who nodded that it was okay to say anything he wanted.

"My mother was never sick until my father died of a stroke four years ago," he began. "Then, just a few months after he died, she started getting pains in her chest."

"That's when she was put on Vasclear," Brian said.

"Yes. She took it for almost a year," Vitorelli said. "At first, it looked like it was going to be really good for her. Her chest pains pretty much went away, and she perked right up. Then she started complaining again. When she came up here and I got a look at her legs, I was scared. I was gonna call Doc Purefoy, but it was Sunday and I . . . I thought it would keep until the next day."

He rubbed the back of his hand at the sudden moisture in his eyes.

"It wasn't your fault, Ricky," Brian said, more sympathetic than either of the other men would ever know. "If your mother had the lung problem I think she had, no one could have saved her—not me, not Sam here, no one."

"She was a very good woman," Ricky said. "Is there anything else you want to know? If not, I'd better get back to the tractor."

No questions about the possible link between his mother's death and Vasclear; no sudden interest in a big lawsuit. Richard Vitorelli hadn't been raised to think *sue* first, ask questions later. Silently, Brian vowed that if Vasclear had harmed Sylvia Vitorelli and Newbury Pharmaceuticals knew about it or had tried to cover it up, he would be back to visit with her son.

Ricky shook Brian's hand more forcefully this time. Brian stood to go, then he thought of something.

"Sam, it just occurred to me," he said. "Did they ever do a blood count on Mrs. Vitorelli?"

"I don't really know. I would imagine we sent bloods off, but then she . . . she didn't make it."

"Could you find out? I'm specifically looking for her total white-cell count and the percent of eosinophils."

"If it's there, I don't see why not. Ricky, I know it was two years ago, but do you by any chance remember the exact date your mama died?"

"It was two years ago this month. October the fifth."

Sam Purefoy called the hospital, spoke to the lab, then hung up. They didn't have to wait two minutes for the results, which came in via a printer tucked into the corner of his office.

"Well," he said, scanning the sheet, "the eosinophils are up, but just a bit. Seven percent of a total white blood cell count of twenty thousand."

He passed the sheet over. Brian studied the numbers excitedly. He didn't bother to point out that stress and maybe even dehydration had artificially elevated Sylvia's white-cell count. If it had been the normal 5,000 to 10,000, the eo count would have been between fifteen and twenty percent—strikingly elevated.

"Can I keep this?" he asked.

"Of course," the GP said.

Three Phase One patients, two dead of heart failure, a third *with* heart failure, and all with an elevation in eosinophils. It certainly sounded as if there had been a drug reaction of some sort going on.

Brian was about fifteen minutes outside of Fulbrook, cruising through a late-afternoon canopy of red, orange, and gold on a largely deserted, winding two-lane road. Distracted by the Vasclear puzzle and by his interaction with Sam Purefoy and Ricky Vitorelli, he didn't notice the brown unmarked sedan in his rear-view mirror until the red strobe on the dash began flashing.

Reflexively, he glanced down at the speedometer. Forty-five.

Maybe he had missed a microscopic twenty-five-miles-per-hour sign and had gone through a small-town speed trap, he thought.

Annoyed, he pulled off onto the narrow, soft shoulder. The sedan rolled up behind him, and the dashboard strobe was cut off. There were two men in the front seat, both with sunglasses on. The one on the passenger side got out. He was under six feet and trim, but he moved with the looseness of an athlete. He was wearing slacks and a dress shirt with an open collar. He also had a shoulder holster under his left arm.

He circled to Brian's side and flashed the badge in his wallet.

"License and registration, please," he said, his tone perfunctory to the point of boredom.

"What seems to be the problem?" Brian asked, rummaging through the glove compartment for the registration, then handing it over along with his license.

"Speeding," the policeman mumbled.

He turned and ambled back to the sedan. A minute later he was back.

"Would you mind stepping out of the car, please, Doctor."

Doctor? How could he— Then Brian remembered that on his first driver's-license renewal after his graduation from med school, he had insisted on adding M.D. after his name. Deduct one more point for arrogance. The fine he was going to be asked to pay had probably just doubled. Next renewal—

"I really don't think I was speeding," he said as he opened the car door.

The policeman glanced back at the other officer, who had Brian's license and registration, and nodded. The man opened his door and stepped onto the pavement. Unlike the first officer, he *was* physically imposing—six four, narrow waist, massive shoulders.

It took Brian only moments to place where he had seen him before. The high cheekbones and badly pockmarked face were not easy to forget.

CHAPTER TWENTY-EIGHT

BRIAN'S ENTIRE FOOTBALL CAREER AND MOST OF HIS time in the cath lab had been guided by one rule: Evaluate. React. Now, 175 miles from Boston, as he watched the man he had seen in the White Memorial basement emerge from the bogus police car, his evaluation took less than a second. He was going to be badly hurt . . . or he was going to die.

In the three or four minutes since they had pulled him over, not a single car had passed. And even if one did, the chance of the driver stopping, or even realizing something was wrong, was remote. In a few more seconds, Brian would be disabled on the floor of the sedan or in the trunk, headed for someplace where he could be patiently and persuasively grilled about Vasclear—what he had learned and whom he had told. There was nothing appealing about the prospect. Assuming Cedric L. was right about the Russian mob controlling Newbury, these two were almost certainly professional killers.

Nothing in the huge man's manner suggested that he realized he had been recognized, or even that he remembered those fifteen seconds by the basement canteen. But he had eased the sedan door closed and was turning in the direction of Brian's car. Brian knew he might be killed outright if he tried to run. But doing nothing, placing himself at the mercy of these two, was an even more frightening option. He was taller by six inches than the man standing just three feet from him. If he had any chance, it was now.

He brought his left foot up with all the strength he could muster, and kicked the man squarely in the groin. Brian was tempted to hit the gunman as he sank to his knees. Instead, he whirled and bolted down the road. From behind he heard a firecracker snap, then another, followed immediately by the soft thud of a bullet slamming into the pavement just ahead of him.

Brian zigzagged as much as he dared, cursing himself for not changing into his sneakers for the drive home after the Purefoy interview. Another gunshot, this time accompanied by a sharp sting across his deltoid muscle. *Was that it? Was that what it felt like to be shot?*

He had been running for no more than fifteen or twenty seconds, but already he felt his wind beginning to go. Six foot three, 215, and slowing down—he was about to become a hell of a target. Staying on the road was suicidal. There was a small opening up ahead between the trees to his right. He feinted once to his left, then charged into the woods, glancing back just long enough to check on his pursuers. The linebacker with the gun was closer to him, maybe twenty yards away. Behind him, the smaller man, moving with an awkward gait, was trying gamely to catch up. Neither of them wore sneakers, either.

Arms flailing at branches, Brian thrashed through saplings and bushes, frantically trying to put some distance between himself and the two men. One of them called out to the other in a language other than English. Russian? There was another gunshot, but no sound of an impact. Brian, now battling a fierce stitch in his side, lost his footing and tumbled down a steep, shrub-covered embankment. Scraped, scratched, and bleeding from the backs of both hands, he scrambled to his feet and risked a check behind him. He could hear the two men, but couldn't see them. Then suddenly, there was only silence. They had lost sight of him, too, and were waiting for a telltale sound.

Brian crouched down, fighting the urge to suck in air too greedily. It was after five now, and the gathering dusk was his ally and their enemy. If he could only find a place to hide. . . .

He dropped onto all fours and slowly, quietly began inching his way along the gully at the base of the embankment. Suddenly, from above and behind him, one of the gunmen cried out. It was the smaller of the two, hanging on to a tree at the top of the embankment about thirty yards away, visible through a perfect corridor in the foliage. The only word Brian made out clearly was Leon, the name of the taller man.

As the killer reached for his gun, Brian pushed off and started running again—a steeplechase this time, hurdling fallen logs and splashing across a narrow streambed. Slipping on the slick rocks, he barely managed to keep his balance. Another shot. Then another. Brian knew the trees and shadows were making him a tougher target. His knee was beginning to worry him, though. Running on the roads, with no twisting, no torque, the knee had felt reasonably solid and secure. But now, sprinting on sodden, leaf-covered, uneven ground, over bumps, rocks, and branches, he knew a disaster was only an unlucky misstep away.

As he ran, in spite of himself he wondered how the two men had known he would be in Fulbrook. It was possible they had followed him from Reading. When he was cruising through the magnificent autumn colors, lost in thought, he hadn't been paying much attention. But he didn't recall noticing their car, even on the mountain roads. Then he remembered the strange click on the line when he was talking with Teri. He had actually mentioned the sound to her, just as he had mentioned he was going to Fulbrook. His phone was tapped. That had to be it. They didn't follow him to Purefoy's office. They were already there, waiting.

He sensed that he was opening some ground on the two thugs. As he pushed deeper into the forest, huge granite boulders and outcroppings became part of the landscape, offering him even more protection. Gasping for breath, he stopped, leaned against a massive boulder at least ten feet high, and listened. He could hear one pursuer behind him, and another to his right, both closer than he had expected. If he moved, they were almost certain to hear him. If he stayed and tried to conceal himself at the base of the boulder, he might luck out. Being passive, doing nothing, had never been in character for him. He decided to keep running.

He took another few moments to gauge the two men's positions, and decided to bolt up the hill to his left, away from at least one of them. He whirled, but as he planted his right leg, his knee popped out, then back. There was an immediate dull shock all the way up to his hip. But just as quickly, most of the pain vanished. He took a tentative step. There was discomfort, but he had no trouble bearing weight. A slight sprain—the sort that would slow him down some. *Now what?*

The rustle made by the man behind him sounded closer. Brian wondered why in the hell he hadn't listened to Phil, and simply let the whole matter drop. He was about to get tortured and probably killed, and for what? Even if they had left him completely alone, he still hadn't come across anything significant enough to interest Teri and her boss. Apparently the Russians didn't care.

A branch snapped not too far away. It was almost over, Brian thought. Two professional killers, two guns against one unarmed doctor with a gimpy knee. He thought about Caitlin and Becky.

The idea of never seeing them again, the notion of their pain should anything happen to him, forced him into action. Running seemed out of the question. But there was a large rock by his foot. If he could loosen it enough to pick it up, and somehow manage to haul it up on top of the boulder . . .

Without the time to reason his actions through too carefully, he dug his fingers beneath the rock, pried it up from its muddy bed, and filled the hole with leaves and soil. The rock was twenty, maybe twenty-five pounds of absolute dead weight, but Brian found a balance point beneath one arm, and using the other to brace himself, inched his way around to a spot where he could gain some purchase on the boulder. He made the tough first step up, clutching the rock in the crook of his arm like an oversized, prehistoric football. Then he had to set it down to maintain his balance. The boulder sloped just enough, though, so that he could inch the rock along ahead of him as he climbed.

Then, just when he needed a break, the man closer to him called out to Leon again. He couldn't have been more than a dozen yards away. The pockmarked linebacker responded with a short, angry burst from somewhere to Brian's left—probably ordering the first man to shut up. They were both closing in. Brian sensed that before much longer it would be over for him. Using the rock as a weapon had been a stupid idea. Now, essentially trapped, he had no choice but to go through with the effort.

Lances of pain shot up from his knee as he forced himself in an awkward duckwalk to the crest of the huge boulder. Once there, he flattened his body against the cool, smooth gray stone and listened. If the man came up behind the boulder, Brian was finished. If he passed below, on the same natural trail Brian had taken, there was a small chance. A branch cracked. Then, to his right, Brian saw some leaves move. He eased the rock ahead another inch. A direct hit from this height could easily crush the man's skull. The notion of killing someone, even someone bent on killing him, made Brian queasy. But if it happened, it happened.

Again the trees moved. This time, with his cheek pressed against the boulder, Brian saw the top of the smaller man's head. He was ten feet away if that, moving stealthily through the gray silence. Unless he turned and started around the boulder, he was going to pass directly below where Brian lay. Moments later, the killer stepped out from the trees, his gun, a snub-nosed revolver, at the ready. *Five feet. . . . Three. . . .* Brian was going to have to rise to his knees to achieve any accuracy and force. It would all have to happen very quickly, and there would be no retakes—no second try. *Two feet. . . . One more step. . . . Just one more step and—*

Now! Brian braced himself, rose to his knees, held the rock at the level of his face, and hurled it almost straight down with all the force he could manage. The man was starting to turn just as the rock caught him—a sickening thud against the hairline between his ear and eye. He dropped with a soft grunt, and the rock clattered away. The gunman, Leon, was immediately alerted.

From somewhere ahead of Brian, bushes began to thrash. He scrambled down the boulder and hobbled in the opposite direction, deeper into the forest. He half-ran, half-stumbled for nearly five minutes with no notion of whether or not he was still being pursued. Finally, the stitch in his side competing with his knee for possession of his mind's pain center, he burrowed beneath some gnarled roots overhanging a dry streambed, pulled in a small wall of sticks and brush to cover his position, and waited for night to fall.

Freeman Sharpe lived in a neat four-room basement apartment in one of the Roxbury buildings he looked after. He was watching the eleven-o'clock news with his wife of three years when the phone rang. As the handyman for fifty units, and the recovery sponsor for half a dozen men, he was used to late-night calls.

"Freeman, thank God you're home."

"Doc, what's the matter?"

"Only everything. Freeman, could you come and pick me up?"

"Of course."

"I'm at a phone booth by a gas station."

"Where's the station?"

"New York."

CHAPTER TWENTY-NINE

IT WAS JUST AFTER SEVEN IN THE MORNING WHEN Freeman rolled his Chevy van into the small windowless garage that also doubled as his workshop. Brian awoke from a heavy sleep and set a battered hand across the LUCK tattoo on his friend's knuckles.

"Thanks," he said hoarsely. "Except for family, I don't think there's ever been anyone in my life who would have done for me what you just did."

"I'm only glad you finally fell asleep. How're you feeling?"

"A lot sorer than I used to feel at football training camp. And I know it'll be worse tomorrow."

"A hot shower, some eggs, and some of Marguerite's home fries ought to help get you back on the right track. Plus you've got to get out of those clothes. I have a sweat suit one of my NA pigeons left here. It ought to fit."

Brian worked himself creakily from the van and tested his knee, which did not feel that sore. Then he motioned Freeman to stop.

"I'm still trying to figure out when they might have started tapping my home phone, and if there's any chance they would know about you. As far as I can tell, this trouble all started when I got the abnormal blood test back on Bill Elovitz. I don't see how they could have been at all concerned about me until then, so there's no way they could have someone watching your place now."

Freeman grinned at him through the darkness.

"For their sake I hope they don't," he said.

Brian remembered Marguerite telling him something about Freeman's decorations in Vietnam. Such honors were nothing his sponsor would ever talk about himself.

"I don't want you getting involved in this any more than you have already," he said.

"Oooh," said Sharpe. "Suddenly we forget that after twenty years of recovery, our sponsor ought to be capable of making up his own mind about such things. Don't worry, Doc, I don't like getting hurt any more than the next guy. But I also don't like seeing my friends getting walked over. Now, come on in and let's get you cleaned off and fed. Then we'll talk about what's next."

Brian had stayed concealed beneath the overhanging roots in the forest outside of Fulbrook for almost an hour, until it was too dark to believe anyone might still be looking for him. His sense of direction was never going to win any prizes, but after forty-five minutes of wandering through the pitch-black woods, he heard the sound of a speeding car. A short time later, he dragged himself onto what looked like the same road on which the Russians had originally stopped him. A farmer in a pickup brought him to the police station in the next town over from Fulbrook.

The police knew nothing of a brown sedan or a red LeBaron convertible parked on Route 213. A patrol car had made that drive not an hour before, he was told, and saw no cars at all on the soft shoulder. To Brian, the fact that both cars were gone meant the recipient of his rock bomb had probably survived in decent shape. It also meant that the LeBaron was probably at the bottom of some thousand-foot-deep, water-filled quarry. The image of it floating down, down brought him close to tears.

It was the policeman's theory that the two men were nothing more nor less than professional car thieves, perhaps coming up from New York City to work their scam on a few small-town hicks. When they saw they had a live one in Brian, they chased him around for the fun of it, without any intention of seriously injuring him. Brian had no desire to counter that hypothesis with *his* theory, which, though much more likely, would sound significantly more far-fetched. He filled out the required forms as quickly as he could manage, and went down the street to a pay phone to call Freeman.

Marguerite Sharpe was a petite Haitian woman with a knowing smile and a practical intelligence. Freeman called her an unmerited gift of his recovery. And having spent many hours at their place during his first few months back from Fairweather, Brian considered her an unmerited gift of *his* recovery as well. She worked as a counselor at a halfway house for women and was the best cook he knew.

Even through the steam of the shower, Brian could smell sausage and onions grilling. He gingerly soaped the dirt and dried blood from the scrapes and cuts on his hands, face, and arms. His pants had been torn at the knees, although he had no recollection of when that could have happened, and a layer of skin over both kneecaps was being replaced by scab. In addition, there was a deep, linear gouge across his right upper arm—probably from a bullet.

A bullet. Brian recalled how ecstatic he had been when Ernest Pickard notified him of the job at BHI. Now, he was washing out a bullet wound, mourning the loss of the only physical possession that mattered to him, and wondering what he was going to do with his life once the Board of Registration was informed he had a positive urine test and was back on drugs again.

Was there any way out? Was there any way to stop—to acknowledge to himself and notify his pursuers that he had gotten in over his head and was willing to let the whole Vasclear matter drop? Whom could he even deal with? Art Weber? Pickard? Jessup?

He toweled off and pulled on the gray sweat suit Freeman had left for him. Sharpe's NA sponsee was an XXL—if not a lineman for the Patriots, a candidate. Brian settled in across from Freeman and sipped gratefully from a cup of rich, aromatic coffee. Marguerite set a pitcher of orange juice and a huge platter of eggs, pan-fried potatoes, and sausage links in the center of the table and joined them. For a few minutes, no one spoke.

"I'm very glad you weren't hurt badly, Brian," Marguerite said finally, in her melodic island accent. "Freeman has told me some of what is going on. It must be very frightening for you."

"And confusing," Brian added. "I don't even *know* what's really going on. Even after all this, I don't know."

"Freeman says the Russian crime syndicate is involved. That's bad. That's real bad."

"But even if they are, their drug has the potential to save hundreds of thousands of lives. That's already been proven. I've been trying to figure out what they've really done that's wrong, or what they're planning on doing. The best I can come up with is that they're planning on holding Vasclear for ransom against the entire world, like the villains in a James Bond movie."

"Ah, SMERSH," Freeman said in a theatrical accent. "Please give us your report on the nuclear warheads project, Number Two. . . . Except I read somewhere that the income from this Vasclear drug could approach one billion in the first year alone. It doesn't sound like our friends at Newbury would have to do anything shady. Just send out the trucks and cash the checks."

"I don't know," Brian said again, running his fingers across the wounds on the backs of his hands.

"Are you supposed to be at work today?" Marguerite asked.

Brian looked up at the kitchen clock.

"Jesus, it's eight-thirty. I completely forgot about work."

He snatched up the phone and called the ward.

"Clinical ward, this is Jen speaking."

"Jen, it's Dr. Holbrook."

"Oh, Dr. Holbrook, everyone's been looking for you. For Dr. Gianatasio, too."

"What do you mean?"

"Neither of you were here for rounds. Dr. Cohen's on the ward now, leading them."

"Have you heard from Phil?"

"No. I don't think anyone has."

Brian felt a sudden chill.

"Well," he managed to say, "I overslept because I'm sick. It's just the flu. I might be able to make it in this afternoon. I'm only on second call, so you can reach me by beeper if whoever's on gets in trouble. I'm scheduled in the clinic later today. I should be in for that."

"Okay."

"And could you do me one other favor, Jen? Could you have Phil page me as soon as he checks in or shows up? It's very important."

"Of course, Dr. Holbrook. Do you think something's wrong?"

"No. I'm sure he just forgot to tell anyone he wasn't going to be in."

"Thank goodness," the woman said. "We were worried about you both, and now you've called in. Maybe Dr. Gianatasio will check in soon."

Brian set the receiver down.

"You look upset," Marguerite said.

"The only other person at the hospital who knew something might be wrong with Vasclear hasn't shown up for work. He's an old friend of mine who helped me get my job."

"Was he investigating the cases like you were?"

"No, no. At least I don't think he was. He's up for academic tenure at the hospital and so we decided he was better off staying out of it. I don't like this. I don't like this at all."

"Eat some more," Marguerite said. "I have a feeling you're going to need the energy."

Brian forced down another couple of mouthfuls, then took up the phone again.

"Who now?" Freeman asked.

"My machine. Listen, you guys, if you have to get to work, just go. I'll be okay here."

"Marguerite starts at nine-thirty," Freeman said. "I start whenever I want."

"Okay. Just don't let me put you out."

Brian dialed his home, feeling squeamish and angry at the notion that someone was probably listening in.

". . . Hello, Brian, it's me—" *Phoebe.* "—You're scheduled to come out on Sunday. I forgot Becky has a dance recital at two. Can you take her? Let me know. I hope I'm not messing up any plans, and I hope you're okay. Bye." . . . "Hi, Doc. Two more days. I miss you. Keep thinking about that vacation." *Teri* . . . "Hey, Bri—" Phil. "—I thought I might catch you in, being as you're too virtuous to date. Listen, I've got news. I found another case. One of the residents saw him in the clinic a couple of weeks ago and this afternoon she asked my advice about the case in passing. Phase One patient, bad shortness of breath, bad ankle edema. I decided to check on the guy's chart even though I said I wasn't going to. Couldn't help it. I was curious. There was no blood count in the chart, but I asked myself, if I were The Brian, what would I do? So I called the lab and tracked one down from three months ago.

Fifteen percent eos, pal. One-five. The guy's name is MacLanahan. Angus MacLanahan. I'll tell you more when I see you tomorrow morning. Stay loose."

The final call was from the ward secretary, wondering where Brian was.

"You look pale, son," Freeman said as Brian hung up. "Bad news?"

"Maybe. That old friend at the hospital I mentioned to you left a message last night that he had found out about another possible case. He changed his mind about helping me and reviewed this guy's chart."

"And now he hasn't shown up for work," Freeman said.

"Exactly. Freeman, I have this feeling that my phone is tapped. That's how those guys knew where to find me in New York. If it *is* tapped, they must have heard Phil's message as well. Or else he didn't cover his back when he went after those patient records. Newbury has eyes and ears all over the hospital."

"I don't blame you for being concerned. I'm worried, and I don't even know the guy. So what's next?"

"I want to try and call Phil's girlfriend at the hospital."

Brian made the call, but hung up after a brief conversation.

"She's on vacation for a week," he said.

After Marguerite had left for work, the two men sat silently at the table. Then Sharpe sighed.

"It's hard to remember sometimes that things have a way of working out the way they're supposed to," he said. "But they generally do."

"Maybe. It's just that at the moment, I feel like I'm stuck in a vise, and it's getting tighter and tighter, and I don't have a clue how to stop it."

"You just got to put one foot in front of the other. You do have some options."

"I thought about the police and rejected that possibility. Why in the world would they believe me? My connection at the FDA says they can't make any move at all against Vasclear without absolute proof. I don't know who at the hospital I can trust—or worse, who I could get hurt. I still don't have anything concrete, so the newspapers are out of the question. Exactly what options are we talking about here?"

"Well, let's see. You need to get some clothes. You need to rent a car. You need to report yours stolen to the insurance company. At some point you need to show up for work, assuming you're going to do that. Or, you can just roll over and play dead until you actually are."

"Point taken," Brian said. "The truth is, I *am* feeling pretty sorry for myself right now. Jack would have kicked my butt for whining."

"You can pretend he did."

"They might be watching my house."

"I'd be surprised if they weren't."

"Do you have time to help me get some stuff from my place?"

"No problem. And you can stay here until things settle down. Maybe after the President comes and makes their drug legal, they'll leave you alone."

"I hope so. Freeman, thank you. There's one other thing. I'd like to try and speak with the guy Phil called me about."

"Name?"

"Angus MacLanahan."

Sharpe pulled a Boston phone directory from a drawer.

"Here he is," he said. "Joy Street. That's over on Beacon Hill."

"Not too far from the hospital."

Sharpe dialed MacLanahan's number and handed the phone over.

"One step at a time," he said.

"Out of order, no other information," Brian said. "What do you make of that?"

"Typical phone company customer, I'd say. You want to go by there on the way to your place?"

"If you have the time. We've got to be careful, though. His name was on my answering machine. Somebody might be watching his place."

"They may be looking for you," Freeman said, "but they ain't looking for me."

Angus MacLanahan's apartment was halfway up a narrow street on the side of Beacon Hill, not far from the State House. Freeman double-parked the van in front and was entering the building when Brian first noticed the plywood covering the windows of one of the apartments on the second floor. Sharpe was back in just a few minutes. He walked calmly to the van, then jumped in and sped away.

"MacLanahan's dead," he said grimly. "The lady in the apartment beneath his told me. That was his place up there on the second floor. There was a gas explosion three weeks ago."

"I knew it," Brian said. "The moment I saw those windows boarded up I knew it was his apartment."

"And the other man you told me about, the concentration-camp survivor?"

"Shot to death in a convenience store holdup."

Freeman pulled away from the curb and headed toward I-93, the highway north to Reading.

"If those two men dying so violently is a coincidence, it's a damn ugly one," he said. "What are you going to do?"

Brian rubbed at the fatigue still stinging his eyes.

"After I get my stuff, I think I want to talk to Bill Elovitz's wife," he said.

CHAPTER THIRTY

Talk of the Town With Pat Carson

WBZ-TV, Boston
Pat: Boston has long been recognized as the mecca of medicine for the country, and indeed for the world. But never has there been so much focus on this city as during this week, when the President will travel to Boston in just two days to preside over ceremonies approving the Boston-developed and -tested drug Vasclear. In honor of that occasion, on today's _Talk of the Town,_ we'll be speaking with Dr. Art Weber, Vasclear project director from Newbury Pharmaceuticals,

based right here in Boston. But first, we have a very special guest, Mrs. Hermione Goodman, who is one of the lucky ones to have been part of the experimental group receiving Vasclear for the past year and a half. Mrs. Goodman, welcome to *Talk of the Town*. Tell us first how you came to be put on Vasclear.

Hermione: It all happened very rapidly, actually. I was never really sick until one day I began having pains right here under the base of my breastbone.

Pat: What were the pains like?

Hermione: They were sharp and sort of gassy. At first I thought it was indigestion. But I decided to see my doctor, just in case. Because I had a family history of heart trouble and some minor changes on my electrocardiogram, he sent me for a checkup by Dr. Jessup at White Memorial. I had a treadmill test, then a catheterization. I was real surprised to find that I had quite a serious heart condition.

Pat: That's when you were put on Vasclear.

Hermione: Exactly.

Pat: And how quickly did you respond?

Hermione: Oh, it was just a few weeks. Maybe a month. My discomfort went away, and I've been fine ever since.

BRIAN SAT IN THE PASSENGER SEAT OF THE VAN, HIS feet up on the dashboard, a spiral notebook propped on his lap. Along the margin of the page, spliced among a dozen geometric shapes, were his trademark doodles—an Indian headdress, a speedboat, a pig face, a volcano, and a football, each of which looked remarkably like the others. In the center he had printed:

Kenneth Ford—probably PH; eos 14% . . . dead
Sylvia V.—possible PH; eos 15–20% . . . dead
MacLanahan—possible PH; eos 15%—violent death
Bill Elovitz—PH; eos 13%—violent death

Underneath the list, he had sketched the words *Russians . . . Pharmaceutical House . . . Vitamins . . . Drug $$ Laundering . . .* and finally, beneath those, a single word: *Vasclear.*

"Freeman, I'm missing something," he said. "It's like you said before. I'm an ant, and yet they're going after me with an elephant gun. And now Phil. God, I hope he's all right."

Suddenly, he cursed and pounded his fist.

"What is it?"

"Teri—the woman I told you about from the FDA. I spoke to her the night before last. If the Newbury people were listening in, she may be in trouble. I've got to call her and at least warn her to be careful."

"Just don't do it from your phone."

They cruised off the interstate in Reading and made a slow pass of the streets for two blocks around the flat that would be Brian's as soon as his father's will was probated. In this quiet, residential neighborhood it would be difficult for strangers to remain unobserved while they kept up their surveillance.

"Duck down!" Freeman ordered as they finally cruised past the house.

Brian quickly folded himself on the floor and seat.

"Do you see something?" he asked.

"A gray sedan parked between two other cars half a block down and across the street. Just one man inside from what I can tell."

Freeman kept driving, then pulled to the curbside several blocks away.

"How badly do you want to get inside your place?" he asked.

"Some clothes would help, but my briefcase is what I really need. It has my ID badge and a ton of papers from work in it, to say nothing of my stethoscope."

"Then let's do it."

The plan they came up with was simple. Brian would be dropped off a block away and would approach the house from the rear through a neighbor's yard, over a low fence, then across the backyard. Meanwhile, Freeman would pull up next to the driver's-side window of the sedan to ask directions. He would then stall as long as he could, blocking the view from the car as he tried to learn something of the man inside. From what they could tell, the driver seemed to have a clear line of sight into the living and dining rooms on the street side of the house, so Brian had to stay away from those windows.

"How're you gonna get inside?" Sharpe asked.

"There's a spare key under a rock by the back porch."

"Get in, get out. A rule to live by straight from Nam."

"Get in, get out," Brian echoed.

Freeman dropped him off, watched while Brian began cutting through a neighbor's yard, then drove away. Brian leaped the low picket fence with ease and dropped to a crouch, pleased that his knee had handled the jolt. Through the space between houses, he could see Freeman approaching the gray sedan. He crossed the yard, located the key, crept onto the back porch, and quietly opened the back door. His briefcase with his hospital ID inside was right on the kitchen table where he had left it. He retrieved a nylon gym bag from beneath his bed and stuffed it with underwear, socks, T-shirts, jeans, and a pair of sneakers. Then he took a few hangers' worth of dress clothes from the closet.

He was just glancing around for anything else he might need when the toilet in the hallway bathroom outside the kitchen flushed. He dropped the clothes on the bed and flattened himself against the wall, breathing deeply in an effort to overcome the burst of adrenaline that had at least doubled his pulse. A few seconds later, the bathroom door opened. Brian glanced about for a weapon. The best he could find was a marble-based trophy on the bureau by his right hand—an overflow from Jack's living-room collection, New England College Player of the Year.

He clutched the trophy with the stylized passer and watched as the intruder entered the living room. It was the thin man from Fulbrook. Clearly, the rock hadn't injured him nearly as badly as Brian had believed. Beyond the man, through the living room window, Brian could actually make out Freeman's van. There was no way his friend could stall much longer.

The intruder wore his shoulder holster over a plaid shirt. He paced around for a time, glanced out the window, and then used a two-way radio, presumably to call the car outside. The conversation was in rapid-fire Russian. Now, the man was no more than ten feet away. His back was to the bedroom and his concentration on the radio call, but Brian saw no chance of slipping past him to the kitchen. He tightened his grip on the trophy, took a single breath, held it, and charged. As the man turned and cried out, Brian could see that the rock had in fact done considerable damage to the side of his head and face. He brought the marble base down with as much force as he could muster, connecting squarely in the center of the massive, raw bruise. The man grunted and instantly went rag-doll limp.

Through the window, Brian could see Freeman's van still parked by the sedan. He imagined the other thug now screaming for Freeman to pull forward so he could get out. The man at Brian's feet was still breathing, but there was no way to tell if the wound oozing blood onto the oak floor was mortal or not.

Brian snatched the revolver from the man's shoulder holster, threw it in the nylon bag, then raced with the bag and his briefcase out the back door. He was vaulting over the neighbor's fence when he heard the squeal of Freeman's tires as the van sped around the corner. Sharpe slowed, but didn't come to a full stop. Brian dashed along the sidewalk, then out onto the road. He opened the van door, threw his things onto the floor, then scrambled onto the passenger seat as Sharpe accelerated. They were a mile away, approaching the interstate, before his breathing had calmed enough for him to speak.

"This is crazy," he said. "The guy in the car outside, real big? Scarred face?"

Freeman shook his head.

"Squat, broad shoulders, mustache," he said. "His English wasn't that bad."

"Jesus. Freeman, they've got a whole army. The guy I left bleeding on my living-room floor is the same one I hit with the rock in New York. This time I used one of my old trophies. I'm afraid I may have killed him."

"Practice makes perfect," Freeman said. "I hope you're not feeling sorry for the guy. They've declared war on you, Doc, so you better be ready to do whatever it takes to survive. First thing is we're gonna find a phone booth so I can make one of those anonymous calls to the Reading police and report suspicious activity around your address. With any luck, they'll get there just as Trotsky is dragging Lenin out to the car. Wouldn't that be something?"

"Yeah, terrific. Freeman, I'm going crazy with this. I'm really not a baby, but these bastards are trying to kill me, and I don't know why. Now the only guy I could trust at the hospital hasn't shown up for work. Do you think I should go to the police and tell them what's going on?"

"If you believe that will do you any good, that's what you should do."

Brian buried his face in his hands.

"I don't see how I could do it without mentioning Vasclear, and at this point, I still don't have anything that even resembles proof. No one would listen. Everyone would think I'm nuts, or back on drugs, or both. I'd get fired at work if I haven't been already. And the Russians will probably still kill me."

Freeman pulled up beside a pay phone and put a calming hand on Brian's shoulder.

"Easy does it, pal," he said. "Those banners you been looking at for the past year and a half at the meetings aren't just words. Easy does it."

"Maybe I should just go into hiding until the signing ceremony's over and Vasclear's on its way around the globe."

"Hey, great idea. Not showing up for work should help your job situation a whole bunch."

"At least I'd still be alive." Brian managed a tense smile and then squeezed Freeman's hand. "I'm okay. Scared is all. But I'm really okay. Go make your call, then I'll make my two."

Brian sat alone while Sharpe went to call the police. His thoughts were mostly of Phil. He tried to concoct a persuasive scenario in which his workaholic friend wouldn't show up for rounds on a day when he was acting as ward visit, and wouldn't call, either. Nothing worked—at least nothing that didn't involve the sort of people who had just tried to kill him.

"Well," Freeman said, reentering the van, "your crack Reading police force didn't sound too eager to be dealing with an anonymous tip. But they might look into it."

Brian hurried to the phone and called Teri's office, then her home. He got her voice mail in both places, and left identical warnings.

"Teri, I know it sounds crazy to you, but I'm hitting a raw nerve by poking into these early Vasclear cases. All of a sudden, people are trying to hurt me. My phone may be tapped, and they might know I've been talking to you, too. So until the ceremony, please be very careful. Stay with friends if you can. Don't do too much alone. I miss you. I miss you like crazy."

After recording the second message to Teri, he called information and got the number of Wilhelm Elovitz in Charlestown. This time, Elovitz's widow, Devorah, answered herself.

"Oh, yes," she said in an accent not as thick as her late husband's. "Bill said you were the finest doctor he had ever had."

"He seemed like a very decent man, Mrs. Elovitz. I'm sorry I didn't get to know him better."

"Yes."

Brian could tell that she was beginning to cry.

"Mrs. Elovitz, I'm sorry if my call is upsetting you. Perhaps I should call back at another time."

"No, no. I'm fine. Tears are not the worst thing in the world. Please, tell me what I can do for you."

"I know Bill was shot during a holdup, but I don't know any of the details."

"It was in all the papers and on TV."

"I'm sorry I didn't hear anything about it. I was having a tragedy of my own at the time. My father died suddenly."

"Oh, dear. I'm very sad for you."

"Thank you. Perhaps I could stop by and speak with you, rather than ask you questions over the phone."

"If you want to stop by, that would be fine. But I think you should be talking to Sid."

"Sid?"

"Sid Mastrangelo. He owns the market where Bill was . . . was shot."

"And he was there when it happened?"

"Oh, yes. They shot Sid, too."

CHAPTER THIRTY-ONE

SID'S MARKET OCCUPIED THE FIRST FLOOR OF A RED-brick tenement in a gritty section of Charlestown, not far from the berth of the USS *Constitution*. Devorah Elovitz's directions were reasonably good, but they weren't needed.

"After I got back from Nam," Freeman explained, "I spent a good deal of time engaged in commerce on these streets. I actually remember Sid's Market from way back then."

"And do you remember Sid?"

"It's been about twenty years, but if he's as wide as he is tall, I remember. I think he threw me out of his place more than once."

On the ride to Charlestown from Reading, they kept the radio

tuned to the all-news station. Although there were two items related to Vasclear and the President's impending visit to Boston,
there was nothing about an anonymous call to the Reading police,
followed by the discovery of a bludgeoned body in the home of a
physician who, until recently, had lost his license because of drug
use.

"Too soon," Freeman said. "Besides, I don't think your crack
police force believed me. How're you doing there?"

"Shaken but no longer shaking would about describe it. I can't
believe that bastard was waiting inside my house."

"They had your key. Hiding someone inside meant that the
dude outside could drive away from time to time. You were just
lucky Mr. Inside was heeding nature's call."

"I have the feeling my luck may be running out."

"That's the old recovery spirit."

Sid Mastrangelo was indeed as Freeman remembered him. He
was egg-bald except for a graying monk's fringe, and would have
gotten consideration in any casting call for Friar Tuck. He wore a
canvas apron, untied at the waist, and had his right arm in a sling.
Brian introduced himself and Freeman.

"Bill Elovitz's wife called a little while ago and told me you
were coming," Mastrangelo said.

"Did she say what we wanted?"

"She said something about the shooting. She also said you were
Bill's doctor."

"I was. One of his cardiologists at Boston Heart."

"And what are you?" he asked Freeman.

"Just a friend."

"Yeah? Well, you look like a punk from a long time ago who
used to hang around this corner too much."

"I look after a couple of apartment buildings in Boston," Freeman replied calmly. "Married, member in good standing of the
Elks, buddies with doctors like this guy. Couldn't be me you're
thinking of."

"Good," the grocer said, his eyes sparkling. "Because the punk I remember had *Hard Luck* tattooed on his knuckles just like you."

"Mr. Mastrangelo," Brian cut in, "would you be willing to talk to us about what happened?"

"Bill's wife asked me to, so I will."

An elderly woman came in for milk and cigarettes. Mastrangelo rang her charges up on an ancient register, handed over her change, and then warned her about the danger of her continuing to smoke.

"Before we begin," Brian said, "do you have a phone I could use? I need to call the hospital."

Mastrangelo reached beneath the counter and passed over a portable handset.

Praying silently, Brian called the ward. Still no word from Phil, he was told.

"Do you know if Dr. Pickard is aware that Phil hasn't shown up?" he asked Jen, the unit secretary.

"Oh yes. In fact, Dr. Pickard was here asking questions just a little while ago. Wait a minute, he's still here. He's just going down the hall."

"Can I speak to him?"

"Hang on, Dr. Holbrook. I'll see if I can get him."

Brian glanced to his right where Freeman was paying for some mints, a Coke, and a pouch of pipe tobacco.

"I don't inhale," he heard his sponsor say just as Ernest Pickard came on the line.

"Brian," he said. "We've been terribly worried about you and Phil. Are you okay?"

"Yes, sir, I am. I was up half the night with a GI bug and I forgot to set the alarm. But I'm much better now, so I was planning on being at work within the hour."

"Good. Excellent. Do you have any idea where Phil might be? He missed the rounds he was scheduled to conduct this morning, and didn't call."

"That's certainly not like him. Have you sent someone over to his place?"

"I believe the police are on their way now. Brian, two of our fellows are on vacation. Phil was actually scheduled to cover the ward in-house tonight. Is there any way you could do that?"

"I'll be in by two," Brian said, thinking about using the night on duty to get back to the record room and continue down his list of Phase One patients, "and I'll be happy to cover if you want me to."

"No news?" Freeman asked.

"None. I'm going to cover for Phil tonight."

"You think that's wise?"

"You're the one who thought I'd be making a mistake to vanish."

"That's true. Go in to work, but stay in the main corridors, away from the nooks and crannies. And Brian? Think of some reason why you look like you've been thrown in the briar patch."

"Sorry for talking around you like that, Mr. Mastrangelo," Brian said. "There's been a lot of turmoil at the hospital, and I seem to be right in the middle of it."

"Does it have anything to do with the shooting?" he asked.

Freeman and Brian exchanged glances. *The truth,* they decided.

"It might," Brian said. "That's why we wanted to see you. I was hoping you might go over exactly what happened when Bill Elovitz was killed."

"I can do better than that," Mastrangelo replied. "I can show you."

"Show me?"

"I have a copy of the video my security system took that night. My place is just upstairs if you want to see it."

Sid Mastrangelo set a Closed sign in the window and led Brian and Freeman up the back stairs to the full-floor apartment he shared with his wife.

"I have a friend in the security business," he explained. "Triple

A Security right here in Charlestown. I was being shoplifted to death and got broken into a couple of times. Manny set up a system for me. After the holdup, before he turned the tape over to the police, he made me a copy. The two guys who did it had ski masks on. I've watched the tape three or four times, trying to see if there was anything about them I could connect with someone I knew."

"And did you?" Brian asked.

Mastrangelo shook his head.

"Not a thing."

As they settled down before a large-screen TV in the comfortable, slightly musty apartment, Mastrangelo's wife—a feminine version of the grocer—waved cheerfully to them from the kitchen.

Sid turned on the set then cued the VCR and handed the remote to Brian.

"Stop it anyplace you want," he said. "Ask any questions that come to mind."

A few seconds of electronic static were followed by a grainy black-and-white view of the interior of Sid's Market.

The camera, located above, behind, and to the left of Mastrangelo, had a fish-eye lens that distorted the scene somewhat, but enabled the camera to pick up a wider field. Seen from above, the figures in the drama appeared compressed. And without sound, the ghastliness of what was being recorded seemed strangely muted.

Empty store except for the back of Sid's head as he moves back and forth behind the low counter . . . 2048 hrs, a time stamp in the lower-right corner says. 8:48 P.M. . . .

"I close at nine on Fridays," Mastrangelo commented.

Front door opens and Bill Elovitz enters, wearing a beltless trench coat . . . His left wrist is in a cast . . . His rich silver hair glows in the grayish recording. . . . His puffy ankles are actually visible over the tops of his Top-Sider–type shoes. . . . He waves familiarly to Mastrangelo and smiles in the bittersweet way that had first drawn Brian to him. . . . He heads to the back of the store and vanishes from the screen. . . . Moments later the door opens and two men come in. . . .

Both are wearing dark windbreakers and ski masks. . . . One is carrying a handgun, the other a sawed-off shotgun. . . .

Brian hit the pause button. Although the physiques of the gunmen were distorted, one of them—the one carrying the shotgun—was clearly much taller and more broad-shouldered than the other. Freeman looked over at him quizzically and Brian nodded. He would bet the ranch that the face beneath that mask was deeply scarred. Leon. Whether the other gunman was the man he had possibly killed just a short time ago, Brian could not be certain. He hit the play button.

The shorter man gesticulates at Sid with his gun and seems to be doing most if not all of the talking. . . . Leon leaves the screen and returns seconds later, pushing Bill Elovitz ahead with his shotgun. . . . Elovitz is talking and does not seem overly frightened. He has experience with armed bullies. . . . The shorter man orders the cash register opened, takes what bills are there from Sid, and stuffs them into his pocket. . . . The gunmen back toward the door. . . . They have reached it. . . . They begin to turn away. . . . Suddenly, Leon whirls back. . . . He is no more than six or seven feet from Bill. . . . Without hesitating, he fires. . . . Elovitz appears to take the full force of the shot in the center of his chest. . . . He flies backward as if scooped up by a tornado, hits a set of shelves, and crumples to the floor. . . . The intruder with the handgun whirls on Mastrangelo and fires from seven or eight feet away, but Sid is diving for cover behind the counter when he is hit. . . . The two gunmen do not go to finish him. Instead, they flee. . . . Seconds later, Sid's hand appears on the counter as he pulls himself up. . . . The time stamp reads 2052. . . . Four minutes.

Brian clicked off the VCR and nodded grimly at Freeman. *It's them.* He set the remote down.

"Mr. Mastrangelo," he asked, careful to avoid providing any clues to the answer he expected, "the man who shot you, was there anything unusual about him—anything at all?"

"He spoke with some sort of accent," Sid said without hesitating. "I don't know what kind. German, maybe."

"And the other man?"

"Godzilla? I don't think he said a word. Did seeing that video help you?"

"Maybe. There's a lot I don't understand yet."

"But you don't seem like you think Bill was shot as part of a holdup."

Brian shrugged his shoulders, then stood and shook the store owner's hand.

"I don't know for sure, Mr. Mastrangelo," he said. "But I didn't see anyone take Bill's wallet."

CHAPTER THIRTY-TWO

Brian left his gym bag in the van and had Freeman drop him off at White Memorial. He entered the hospital lobby on full alert, scanning the crowd for anyone who seemed to be scanning the crowd for him. He was clutching his briefcase, which, in addition to the usual papers, medical instruments, Kit Kat bars, and change of underwear, had a single white gym sock in which was concealed the snub-nosed revolver he had taken from the unconscious man bleeding on his living-room floor.

Brian had never fired a gun except for a BB gun and once a .22 rifle. He hoped he wouldn't ever have to. But two thugs from Newbury Pharmaceuticals had murdered one elderly Phase One patient, and had probably murdered a second. Now, the killers were after him, and Phil had disappeared.

Was there anyone besides Teri he could trust? Would she be willing to go out on a limb with nothing more substantial than his word? How much time did he have before Pickard's office called him to go for a sure-to-be-positive urine test? Perhaps Pickard was someone he could turn to.

"Dr. Pickard, I don't have any proof, but I want you to know that the company you've been working hand-in-glove with for the last five years or so is controlled by the Russian Mafia. My source? Oh, a Chinese mobster named Cedric who goes to NA meetings. Now, for some reason, even though the drug you've developed with Newbury will save tens of thousands of lives and make your institute millions of dollars, the pharmaceutical company's hired killers to murder your patients. . . ."

Would the story play any better with the police? With Carolyn Jessup?

Brian took the wide corridor to the BHI lobby, flashed his ID at the guard, and headed up the stairs to the ward. What else was there to do except to keep on picking up scraps of data, piece them together, and hope that at some point they might suggest an explanation that made sense? Of course, he would have to do so while steering clear of the professionals who were trying to kill him.

Pop, where are you when I need you?

Brian trotted up the five flights of stairs, pausing at each landing to listen for footsteps. He changed into scrubs in the on-call room. Jen, the usually perky unit secretary, brightened considerably as he came on the ward.

"Oh, Dr. Holbrook, I'm so glad to see you," she said. "What an awful day this has been. What happened to you?"

"Just a touch of the GI flu."

"No, I mean to your face and hands."

"Oh . . . ah . . . gardening. I really get into my gardening sometimes. Any word on Phil?"

She shook her head grimly.

"Nothing. Dr. Pickard just left for his office. He's been caring for the patients on the floor. I never knew he was such a good doctor."

"One of the best anyplace."

"Dr. Holbrook, he said you were on-call for tonight, and he left you the code-call beeper."

She passed over the emergency pager and Brian hooked it to his belt. Then he handed her a slip of paper with the name **ALLISON BROUGHAM** printed on it—the next of the Phase One patients on his list.

"Could you call down to the record room and have them send this woman's chart up here, please? Better still, if you can leave your post long enough to go down and get it, that would really help."

"I shouldn't leave the desk unattended, but Beverly is coming in at three to take over. I'll go down then."

"Perfect."

The clinical-research ward was in reasonably good shape. Fifteen patients, all fairly ill, but none critical. By three-fifteen, when he was summoned to the front desk, he had been in to check on nine of them. Each had a meticulously written progress note from Ernest Pickard. Brian saw that he had described his boss well. Despite all the nonmedical responsibilities of his job as head of Boston Heart, Pickard was a truly outstanding cardiologist. With two of his junior staff missing, and the President's visit just two days away, helping the cardiology fellows care for patients was probably the last thing the man wanted to be doing. But from what Brian could tell from his progress notes, the chief had been thoroughly briefed and had gotten involved with each case.

"There's a phone call for you from Jen," the new ward secretary said, handing over the phone. "She's calling from the record room."

"Jen, it's Brian."

"Dr. Holbrook, I'm here in the record room. There's no Allison

Brougham, B-R-O-U-G-H-A-M, in their computers. No one by
that name has ever been a patient here."

Oh, yes she has, Brian wanted to say. But there was no point.
Loose ends were being tied up. No more missing pages of lab
reports. The Phase One patients were being systematically eliminated from the hospital's data banks.

By the time Brian left Freeman, he had written down everything
he had learned, along with what amounted to a few meager conclusions. Freeman was annoyed at Brian's "If anything should happen to me" speech, but in the end, he took the papers and promised
that one way or another, the powers at the FDA, the newspapers,
and anyone else who might listen would get them.

Before returning to make rounds on the last six patients, Brian
paged Phil and called his apartment. Nothing. Carrie Sherwood
was out, too. Could she and Phil have married? Would Phil have
gotten so swept up in the spontaneity, romance, and sex that he
decided to abandon his workaholic, responsible persona for this one
day? The explanation might have temporarily assuaged some of
Brian's fears, if only Phil hadn't left that message on his answering
machine about Angus MacLanahan.

It was after four when Brian finished seeing the last of the
patients. Just in case, he selected another name from his Phase One
list, and asked the evening unit secretary, Beverly, to send down for
the chart. Then, realizing that he hadn't had a thing to eat since
breakfast, he signed off the ward and headed for the cafeteria. He
reached the stairway door, then stopped, returned to the on-call
room, and withdrew his briefcase from under the bed. He was
wearing a knee-length lab coat over his scrubs. The revolver,
wrapped in his sock, felt awkward and a bit frightening in his coat
pocket. Instead, he returned it to the briefcase, which he decided to
carry with him.

The cafeteria, the pride of White Memorial, had a number
of small public and private dining rooms surrounding a vast,
horseshoe-shaped central eating area. At the open end of the

horseshoe was the serving area, with a salad bar, pizza kitchen, grill, full-meal section, and dessert bar. With a thousand or more employees working any number of shifts, the cafeteria was almost always busy.

Clutching his briefcase and constantly vigilant, Brian joined the human stream entering the massive restaurant. There was no one in the line he even recognized, let alone anyone he knew well enough to sit and dine with. He flashed briefly on the Suburban Hospital days, when there was always an animated group in the physicians' dining room and there was not a soul, from housekeeping to the CEO, with whom he didn't have some sort of history. Now, he was virtually anonymous, and the one person he was close to had disappeared.

After a brief feint toward the salad bar, he settled in the line headed toward the grill. He was just about to order a half-pound cheeseburger with fries, when he noticed a man some distance away, heading out of the cafeteria with a loaded tray. Brian's vantage point was at a sharp angle from behind, but the height, thin waist, and powerful shoulders were a giveaway—especially since Brian had just watched a video of him murdering an old man in cold blood.

Brian bolted from the line, trying to move quickly without calling attention to himself. Leon was wearing the same outfit—jeans and a blue dress shirt—he had worn that evening by the machine canteen. Whether he was checking to see if he was being followed, or searching for Brian, there was no way to tell, but he stopped a couple of times to look around. He moved into the main corridor and turned in the direction of Boston Heart—back toward the spot where Brian had first seen him. Brian hung back a good distance, now almost certain that Leon was headed toward the staircase to the subbasement.

As they approached the basement of Boston Heart, the corridor was virtually deserted. Brian had to hold back so far that he actually lost sight of the killer. Finally, he reached the stairway to the subbasement. To his right was the stairway up to the ground floor of BHI, and thirty or forty feet past it were the cath lab, the cath film library, and the elevator doors. Ahead and to the left was the machine canteen, and at the far end of the hall was the animal facility. Leon was nowhere in sight. Almost certainly, he had headed down.

Brian descended the staircase cautiously, expecting at any moment to have Leon appear below him, pocked face grinning, gun leveled. Hospital subbasements frequently housed the laundry, central equipment supply, and some portion of the power plant. Leon could be working in any of those units, although Brian couldn't see why they would be located in the BHI subbasement and not beneath the main hospital.

The subbasement of Boston Heart was somewhat dimly lit by incandescent bulbs set into the concrete ceiling and diffused by opaque, flush-mounted plastic covers. The hallway itself was unpainted cement, and completely unadorned. There were no doors except for the one from the stairwell and a steel door some distance away on the right, at a spot roughly beneath where the cath lab was. The elevator apparently stopped at the floor above.

Brian took a few tentative steps forward. The steel door had a recessed grip that suggested it slid open. Two more steps, then Brian hesitated, opened his briefcase, and removed the snub-nosed revolver from its covering, dropping it into his coat pocket next to his stethoscope. He was no more than twenty feet away from the door now. The corridor beyond it seemed to dead-end at what would correspond to the animal facility a floor above. If someone came down the staircase now, he would be trapped. He slipped his hand inside his pocket and gripped the revolver. *Did it have a safety*—something he had to release to fire it? This was a hell of a moment not to know, he thought. Flattened against one wall, he took another step.

Suddenly, his code-call beeper began sounding, nearly startling him into a coronary standstill. Somewhere in the hospital, there was a cardiac arrest or dire emergency. His hand shot down and quickly deactivated the sound. Then he risked glancing down at the LED display.

BHI-7, it read. The cardiac surgical floor of Boston Heart. There was a cardiac crisis in Laj Randa's kingdom. Of all the places in the entire hospital, BHI-7 was the one where Brian knew he would be the most superfluous at a Code 99. Randa had a virtual army of postdoctorals, fellows, and surgical residents. Besides, Randa had so little respect for him, it was doubtful the man would even want Brian anywhere on his service.

He hesitated. One possibility was watching the doorway from the stairwell. Another was going over and trying the door. The options rumbled through his head, but he could not seem to get past the issue of whether he was capable of ignoring a code call. No, he decided—not even one for which they probably didn't need him.

He turned to head back to the staircase and froze. Behind him, mounted on the ceiling, virtually concealed in the corner between the ceiling and a concrete support, was the nozzle of a small video-surveillance camera, virtually identical to the one in the Vasclear clinic.

At that moment, the metal door behind him began sliding open.

CHAPTER THIRTY-THREE

BRIAN MOVED QUICKLY BACK TOWARD THE STAIRWELL, passing beneath the overhead camera, then out of its range. Even though he felt certain the person about to emerge from behind the sliding door was a 230-pound professional bent on killing him, he had the irrational urge to stand his ground—to pull the revolver from his pocket, gain an advantage on the man, and demand some answers. The code-call page on his belt sounded once again, snapping him back to reality. Without waiting for Leon to show himself, he whirled and bolted up the stairs, expecting any moment to hear the crack of a gun and feel an explosion of pain from the small of his back.

Breathless, Brian reached the main lobby of BHI. There were still seven flights to go to the surgical floor. His knee was beginning to throb. The elevator was the obvious way to go, but the notion of being trapped in a steel box with Leon somewhere in pursuit made him uneasy.

Yielding to his own imagination, he hurried back to the stairwell. He made the seven flights with a single stop on three to catch a few extra breaths and listen for footsteps. Nothing. But now, thanks to the subbasement surveillance camera, they knew he was getting closer. Maybe it was for the best, he thought. He was armed and had no intention of going anywhere in the hospital that wasn't full of people. There was no way Leon, or whichever killer was emerging from that door, would be able to take him by surprise. And if they acted hastily and took risks to stop him, there was a heightened chance they would make a mistake.

Who was that guy in the TV series trying to convince people that there were aliens infiltrating Earth in human form? . . . Vinson. That was it, Roy Vinson.

All Brian needed was one captured alien—one of Newbury's Russian killers trying to explain to the police what he was doing behind a steel door in the Boston Heart Institute subbasement, and why he or one of his pals had murdered Angus MacLanahan and Bill Elovitz and was trying to murder Brian Holbrook.

The surgical unit was identical in its layout to the medical one except that the nurses' station was larger and the rooms had glass walls and doors on the hallway side.

The crisis, evidenced by a crash cart and two medical students by the door, was at the far end of the corridor in room 703. Brian was relieved he had answered the page when he saw that inside the room there were three nurses, a lab technician, and only one physician—a resident. On the bed was a middle-aged man, supine and naked, who appeared near death. He had a recent sternotomy incision running from the top of his breastbone to the bottom. The skin was held together by a railroad-tie arrangement of dozens of two-inch paper-tape strips, stained with dry blood. A similarly closed incision ran down the inside of the man's right thigh—the site where a vein had been harvested for bypass grafting.

Two or three days post-op, Brian thought immediately, noting that the chest tubes, routinely inserted at the time of surgery, had already been removed. The heart rate on the monitor screen was quite rapid—130, 135—but the cardiographic pattern of the beats looked surprisingly regular. The man's color was awful—his skin mottled, his lips purplish. His breathing was labored. *Severe shock.*

Brian identified himself to the resident, who was clearly rattled.

"I'm Mark Lewellen," the man said. He looked to Brian like a teenager. "I'm a first-year resident and I'm really glad you're here. Usually there are lots more surgeons on the floor. One of our teams is at the main hospital in the OR. Dr. Randa and the rest of the staff were at a conference at Boston City, but it ended fifteen minutes ago, so they've gotta be on their way back."

"I'm not getting any pressure," the nurse kneeling by the bed said.

Brian had already checked the pulses at the man's neck, elbows, wrists, and groin. Now he pulled out his stethoscope and listened briefly.

"Get a catheter in him, please," Brian said evenly to the nurses. "Hang a dopamine drip, open his IV wide, and have someone call down to see if there's any blood still cross-matched for him. If there's just a unit or two, we need four more stat. Make that six." He turned to Mark Lewellen. "Okay, talk. Quickly."

The resident cleared gravel from his throat.

"Mr. Paul Wilansky," he began, "is a fifty-five-year-old married accountant who—"

"I'm going to need the condensed version," Brian said, continuing his examination.

At that moment, Carolyn Jessup entered the room, breathing hard. She was dressed identically to Brian—scrubs, sneakers, and a knee-length coat.

"I was just finishing a case when the clerk here called down looking for help," she explained. "The elevator took forever."

"I'm glad you're here," Brian said. "Go ahead, Mark. Hurry, please."

"He had a semi-elective quadruple bypass done by Dr. Randa two and a half days ago. No complications. Moved here to the step-down unit last night. Scheduled for discharge the day after tomorrow. He was fine. Then suddenly, his pulse started going up and he complained about feeling light-headed and nauseous. A few minutes later he lost consciousness."

"How long ago?"

"Five minutes," a nurse responded, indicating the code clock on the wall over the bed.

Brian slipped on a rubber glove, worked his hand between the man's legs and under his scrotum, and did a rapid rectal exam. Then he smeared a bit of stool on a chemically impregnated card and added a drop of developer to test for blood.

"Negative," he said to Jessup.

Sudden intestinal hemorrhage was moved well down the list of possibilities, although a massively bleeding stomach ulcer could still cause this kind of shock before the blood had time to reach the man's rectum.

"Just in case this is *upper* GI bleeding," Jessup said to one of the nurses, "please slip a nasogastric tube down into his stomach."

"Still no pressure," the nurse at the bedside called out.

"Dopamine's up and wide open," the third nurse said.

Brian scanned Wilansky's EKG, then passed it over to Jessup.

"Some strain, some old damage, nothing new," she said.

"Agreed."

With no obvious acute damage on the cardiogram, a heart attack, highly unlikely in view of the recent bypass surgery, seemed more unlikely still.

"Mark, do you want us to run this code until the surgeons get here?" Brian asked.

"Sure. I mean, please, go ahead."

"I think we've got to start pumping until we get this thing sorted out. He's got to be bleeding someplace."

Jessup checked the patient's carotids and listened to his chest.

"I would think so, Brian," she said, totally calm, totally focused. "Nothing else makes sense. When were his pacemaker wires taken out?"

The wires! Brian thought. *Of course.*

The pacer wires, inserted routinely during bypass surgery, were at one time removed as late as five or six days postoperatively. But in the era of managed care and shorter hospitalizations, two to three days had become the norm. Removing the wires that early was fine, Brian had often said sardonically, unless, of course, the patient subsequently needed them.

"The wires?" Lewellen replied. "Oh, Dr. Randa left orders to have them removed. I pulled them about an hour ago."

"Bingo," Brian said, nodding his appreciation of Carolyn's assessment.

"We'll see soon enough," she said coolly.

Brian and she were standing elbow-to-elbow, functioning perfectly in tandem, each backing up the other, making certain no possibilities or actions were being overlooked.

"Mark," Brian said, "I think you'd better start pumping on this man's chest right now. Is anesthesia coming? If not, we need to intubate him."

"Can you do that?" Carolyn asked Brian.

"I can do that."

The resident moved to the bedside and began doing closed-chest compressions. The mottling of Paul Wilansky's skin had given way now to a deep violet. With no blood pressure, he was on the edge, the very edge. And most disturbing was that there was no abnormal heartbeat rhythm for them to correct.

"Anesthesia is tied up in the OR," the nurse said.

"Miss—" Brian read the head nurse's name tag, "—Dixon, we

think that while the pacemaker wires were being removed, one may have gotten tangled around the branch of a vein graft. If that's the case, and this man is bleeding rapidly from a torn graft into his chest, we're going to need an operating room and a bypass pump on standby for your surgeons. In the meantime, I need a seven-point-five endotracheal tube and a laryngoscope. Be sure to check the balloon on the tube for leaks."

Brian pressed his fingers down on the patient's groin, trying to feel if Mark Lewellen's closed-chest compressions were pushing blood around forcefully enough to generate a pulse in the femoral artery.

"I'm not getting anything," Brian said.

"The heart's empty," Carolyn said. "We need more volume. Use a large syringe to push in the Ringer's lactate. Dr. Lewellen, can you do your cardiac compressions any harder?"

"I think I've already torn apart the wires that were holding his sternum together."

The resident was unable to keep the panic from his voice.

"That's okay," Brian said reassuringly. "The surgeons can fix those."

They can't fix dead, he wanted to add but didn't.

Like Jessup, he appreciated that the patient lying there had little chance of making it. And like the resident, he was feeling enormous tension. The trick was not letting that anxiety show too much, or more importantly, not letting it get in the way of thinking clearly. Whatever had to be done they would do. Having Carolyn Jessup working alongside him was like bringing a ship through treacherous waters with the help of a seasoned pilot.

Brian knelt at the head of the bed. He had moonlighted in various ERs for most of his medical career, and despite the eighteen-month layoff, intubating a critically ill patient was still second nature. He shifted Wilansky's tongue aside with the lighted blade of the laryngoscope and then smoothly slipped the clear polystyrene breathing tube in place through his vocal cords.

"Nice shot," Jessup said.

Brian attached the end of the tube to a breathing bag and began rapid, one-a-second ventilations to try and replace built-up carbon dioxide in the accountant's lungs with oxygen.

Jessup checked Wilansky's neck and groin for pulses and then shook her head. Still none.

Brian could tell what Carolyn was thinking. He was thinking the same thing. Wilansky was in EMD—electromechanical dissociation—the gravest of all cardiac emergencies. The cardiogram pattern said that the natural pacemaker and nerves in his heart were appropriately delivering electrical impulses to the muscle, but the muscle wasn't responding with a contraction forceful enough to circulate blood. The explanation had to be that much of the man's blood was in his abdomen or chest cavity. They had to buy some time until the underlying problem, which Brian assumed was a torn graft, could be corrected. And Lewellen's external compressions, though technically well performed, weren't doing the trick.

They had done almost everything they could do to save this man . . . *almost* everything.

"Have you ever done open massage?" he asked her.

She sighed deeply and shook her head. "Maybe way back in the old days when we were just switching over to closed-chest compressions. You?"

"Just once," Brian replied, "but it was a few years ago. A gunshot wound I treated in the ER. Gang fight. Opening the guy's chest went well enough, so did sewing up the two bullet holes in his heart."

"And?"

"He never made it to the OR."

"Well, Brian, maybe this man will."

Shit.

Brian wasn't certain whether he had spoken the word or just thought it. The way they saw it, there was simply no option left other than to open the man's chest where he lay, clamp the bleeding bypass graft, continue massive fluid-volume replacement, and squeeze the heart manually until the surgeons could get him to the OR and onto a heart-lung bypass machine. The chance of Paul Wilansky surviving the chest crack would be slightly more than zero—especially with a nonsurgeon performing it. But without control of the bleeding site and manual compressions of the heart, the EMD would soon degenerate into lethal ventricular fibrillation.

Brian thought about saying that he wasn't up to trying the procedure, that Carolyn's overall experience as a cardiologist more than offset his single, unsuccessful case. Instead, he checked the man's pupils, which were not especially dilated, and bit the bullet. Maybe there was still time.

Brian's mouth was desert-dry. Every muscle was tensed. Thoughts of Leon and the incident in the BHI subbasement were forced to the back of his mind.

"Miss Dixon, get set to open his chest, please," he heard himself saying.

"Right away."

"Chest set's ready," the nurse called out.

Brian slipped on a mask and gloves and picked up a scalpel. Then, suddenly, there was commotion and loud voices from the hall. Moments later, Laj Randa stormed into the room. His small black eyes were those of a hawk about to strike.

Randa quickly took in the scene surrounding his patient. Mark Lewellen was still pumping on Wilansky's chest, but Randa ignored him. He turned to Brian.

"Why are you up here on my service?" he asked.

Brian felt foolish, standing gloved, gowned, and masked, scalpel poised in hand before one of the great surgeons in the world. In spite of towering over Randa, he felt himself shrink before the man's obvious disapproval. What would have happened, he wondered, if he had cracked Wilansky's chest and the man had died? Or worse still, if he had cracked Wilansky's chest, their assessment of the situation had been wrong, and the man had died? Actually, he realized, nothing worse than what was probably going to happen anyway.

"I had the code-call beeper," he replied with some defiance.

Randa evidently had heard enough from him.

"Carolyn. What's going on?"

"Sudden shock less than an hour after his wires were pulled," she said. "He's essentially in EMD. You can see what we were getting prepared to do. Dr. Holbrook has some experience with the procedure, so we—"

Randa stopped her with a raised hand. He had heard and seen all he needed to.

"Chest tray," he ordered. "Quickly, now. Quickly. If Mr. Wilansky appears to need it, give him some IV Demerol."

He motioned Lewellen away from the bed with a shake of his head and, with a similar movement, ordered one of his cardiac surgical fellows to take the young physician's place.

Without having to be asked, the nurse helped Randa slip a surgical gown over his street clothes, and stretched open a pair of gloves, into which he thrust his hands. His movements were rapid and smoothly precise.

"Scalpel," he said. "Have the spreader ready."

Without another word, the cardiac surgeon sliced through the paper tape and the incision with the same stroke. The sternum had been split down the middle for Wilansky's surgery, after which the bone had been wired back together. Only the middle one of the three wires had broken during Lewellen's closed-chest massage. Randa snipped the remaining two while his surgical fellow worked the spreader into place.

"Tamponade," Randa said, speculating that they would find the heart constricted by hemorrhage.

The gush of blood from the cardiac cavity confirmed his prediction, as well as the diagnosis Carolyn had made. The pacemaker wire had caught on the vein graft and pulled it free of the aorta.

Except for his own commands, Randa worked in absolute silence. In less than a minute, the bleeding was stemmed. He slipped his left hand beneath Paul Wilansky's heart to cradle it while he performed downward compressions from above with his right. Brian noted, without surprise, that Randa's technique was perfect. The two-handed compressions would keep the surgeon from squeezing with one hand and inadvertently perforating the thin right atrial wall with his thumb.

"Good pulse," Brian risked saying, his fingers pressing down over the femoral artery.

"We need an OR," Randa said to the nurse, blatantly ignoring Brian.

"They'll be ready for you by the time you get there," she replied. "The pump team should be there by now."

"Who ordered that?"

"Dr. Holbrook. We also have two units on the way and he ordered another six cross-matched."

Randa continued his rhythmic massage. Then he turned to Mark Lewellen, who looked as if he were trying to melt into the wall.

"You nearly killed this man, Lewellen, by not recognizing EMD and its cause," he said icily. "You have only these doctors to thank that he's alive. I want you off my service immediately and I don't want you back."

"But—"

"Now!" Randa snapped the word like a whip.

Complete, painful silence accompanied the shattered young resident from the room. Brian managed a glance at Jessup, who looked furious, but she just shrugged and tightened her lips.

"So," Randa said to his staff, "let's unhook this man from the monitor and get him down to the OR. My hands are getting tired."

Without another word, Randa and his entourage quickly maneuvered themselves out the door of the room and down the hall.

Brian, Carolyn, and the two remaining nurses stood silently amid the debris that was the typical aftermath of a Code 99, sharing exhaustion and lingering uncertainty, as well as dismay over the way Mark Lewellen had been expelled. The twenty minutes just past had been frantic, gut-wrenching, challenging, and up to now at least, triumphant. And during that time, members of the hastily formed team had been bound to one another in a way unique to a crisis in a hospital.

Finally, the nurses thanked the doctors for their help and assured them that their obligation to the surgical service did not extend to helping to clean up the room. Brian followed Jessup to the hallway.

"That was a really great pickup," he said, "diagnosing a torn bypass graft that quickly."

"Thank you, Brian. I was going to tell *you* how much confidence I have in you, having seen you in the cath-lab emergency and now here."

"What a team."

Brian held out his hand. Almost hesitantly, Jessup took it.

"A team," she said softly. "Well, I'm late for an appointment." She turned quickly and headed down the hall.

"Dr. Jessup?" Brian called after her.

She stopped and turned slowly back to him.

"Yes?"

"You are really a terrific doc."

Even at a distance of ten feet or so, Brian could see a dark sadness in her eyes.

"That's nice to hear," she said.

CHAPTER THIRTY-FOUR

THE SCENE WAS ALL TOO FAMILIAR FOR BRIAN AS HE stood on the observation floor above the cardiac surgical OR, watching Laj Randa and his team perform. Just ten days earlier it had been his father lying there on artificial life supports, living out the final minutes of his existence.

Before heading down to watch the surgery on Paul Wilansky, Brian had done a quick run-through of the patients on the ward, and then made another unsuccessful attempt to contact Phil Gianatasio. With each ring, he became more and more certain that something bad had happened to his friend. He had no luck in reaching Teri, either, and was beginning to worry about her as well. He left urgent messages on her voice mail and at her home, imploring her to page him as soon as she got in. Finally, he called the Reading police. A squad car had been sent to his home, he was told, but when nothing was seen through any of the windows, the patrolman elected not to break in.

How in hell had all this happened?

Brian felt as if he had stepped into quicksand and was now up to his chin, with no rope, no rescuer, in sight. He had gone up against a company with billions of dollars at stake and with the resources and depravity to do whatever was needed to protect their investment. Elovitz, MacLanahan, maybe Phil, and God only knew who else. Even the drunken animal keeper Earl and his poor chimp. None of their lives mattered to the pharmaceutical juggernaut.

Brian feared what was in store for him, but he was angry and frustrated as well—angry that there was no one he could safely turn to for help, and frustrated that there were still so many unanswered questions. From what he could tell, during Phase One trials, Vasclear worked well for a while in at least some of the patients, but soon their arteriosclerosis began recurring. Worse, although there was no solid proof in any one case, a number of those patients developed what looked like drug-induced pulmonary hypertension.

A drug with modest, short-lived benefits, complicated by a frequently occurring lethal side effect. *What combination could possibly have been worse?* And yet, the scientists at Newbury had persevered, had modified the drug, and had ultimately emerged victorious. Brian had seen the clinical successes firsthand. Seventy-five-percent success. No significant side effects. A miracle cure. Why, then, were the Newbury powers still out to destroy the ants?

Brian felt a bit nervous about being alone in the dimly lit surgical-observation suite, but there was a security man on duty at the door, as there was whenever the operating theater was in action. And tucked in his lab coat pocket, beneath a washcloth he had taken from the on-call room, was the snub-nosed revolver. From what he could tell, the gun was strictly point-and-shoot—no safety, no special features. But he wasn't certain. He had come close to wrapping it in the mattress in his room to try firing it, but feared the noise might attract someone's attention, or else that he would do something wrong and blow off his own hand.

Brian stood back a bit from the Plexiglas canopy over OR 1. He had endured enough of Laj Randa's pomposity for one day. Once it was clear Paul Wilansky was going to make it, he was out of there. Below him, the operation to repair the accountant's bypass graft seemed to be progressing smoothly, although there was no way to tell what kind of intellect would emerge once the anesthesia was turned off. Wilansky's blood pressure had been extremely low for some time, and he was on CPR for the better part of fifteen minutes before Randa opened his chest. Had they managed to keep his brain adequately perfused? The operation was a success, but—

"Nice of you to stop by, Dr. Holbrook," Randa said suddenly.

As far as Brian could tell, the surgeon hadn't once looked in his direction, nor was he looking up now.

"How's it going?" Brian asked.

"Perfectly well."

"How do you think he'll do?"

"I have no reason to believe this man won't make it intact."

Unlike the one I killed, right? Brian thought.

"That's great," he said.

There was a prolonged silence during which Randa's attention once again seemed focused on the motionless, artificially chilled heart before him.

"My nurse tells me you performed quite admirably during this man's crisis," he said suddenly. "You have my gratitude and at least some of the respect you lost by hanging your father's life on the Vasclear thread."

"That's a cruel thing to say," Brian managed.

"But it is true nonetheless." Randa worked on as he talked. "You bought into the hype, Dr. Holbrook. Instead of waiting for the verdict of reason and scientific process, you chose to believe what you read in *Time* magazine and saw on TV."

"That's not true. I made inquiries. I read reports. I spoke with my colleagues, I examined patients. My father had nearly died after his bypass operation. For him, Vasclear was plainly the preferable option."

"And I tell you, Dr. Holbrook, anything that seems to be too good to be true invariably *is* too good to be true. Mark my words on that. There is no Santa Claus. And you ultimately cost your father his life by believing there was."

"Dr. Holbrook did nothing of the kind, Randa!"

Startled, Brian thrust his hand around the revolver and whirled, stumbling several steps backward in the process. Art Weber stood less than ten feet away, looking not at Brian, but at the scene below.

"Ah, if it isn't the guru of Vasclear, himself," Randa said. "Your man there helped save this patient's life. I was just thanking him."

"I heard what you were doing," Weber shot back. "Randa, you're just terrified of losing a huge chunk of your precious bypass empire. From the day you first realized that Vasclear was curing people, you've been on a mission to keep it from the public. Well, Laj, you've lost. Beginning Saturday, those kings and sultans who have been flying over here to pump up your already-bloated ego will be able to sit back on their thrones and get treated with nothing more invasive than an IV."

"Get out!" Randa shouted. "Get out of my operating room!"

Brian was shocked to see the Sikh lose his composure, let alone be at a loss for a counterpunch. Even at a distance, swathed in his surgical garb, Randa seemed deflated. The only possible explanation, Brian realized, was that the surgeon sensed Weber was right. For all his railing against the way Vasclear had made an end run around the scientific community, Randa had no reason to believe there was any problem with the drug.

But Brian had more immediate concerns than Randa's bruised

ego. People were out to kill him. And as far as he could tell, the
man at the heart of that threat was standing just two paces away.
Brian kept his grip on the butt of the revolver and worked his
finger through the trigger guard. If necessary, he could fire
through his pocket. The muscles in his shoulders and neck were
tense almost to spasm. He expected at any instant to have massive
Leon come bursting through the door, gun blazing.

Instead, Art Weber reached over calmly and flicked off the microphone. Then he moved out of the sight line of the OR and
motioned Brian to do the same.

"I ran into Carolyn," Weber said. "She told me what a great job
you did with Randa's patient. She said that she thought you might
be here in the observation suite following up on him."

Brian inched backward, putting more distance between the two
of them. Weber appeared relaxed, almost euphoric—the look of a
man about to make medical history and come into several hundred
million dollars at the same time.

"Where's Phil?" Brian asked.

"Gianatasio?"

"Yes. Do you know what's happened to him?"

"I had no idea *anything* had happened to him."

Brian tried to see behind the man's words. Nothing. But Weber
was Vasclear. If Newbury Pharmaceuticals had anything to do with
Phil's disappearance, he had to know.

"He's been missing all day," Brian said. "We've all been worried
about him."

"Now I am, too. Have the police been called?"

"By Dr. Pickard, yes."

Brian loosened his grip on the revolver, but kept his hand in his
lab coat pocket. Even if Weber did know where Phil was, there
was no way he was going to blink.

"Brian, I wanted to speak with you about Vasclear. I understand
you've been making some inquiries about some of our Phase One
patients. I believe their names are Elovitz and Ford."

"Were," Brian said.

"Pardon?"

"*Were* Elovitz and Ford. They're both dead."

Brian held back from saying anything about MacLanahan and Sylvia Vitorelli.

"I don't think I knew that," Weber said. "Well, I wanted to ask you to back off on any further investigation of our drug until the ceremony on Saturday is over. After that, you're free, in fact you're *encouraged* to pursue whatever investigations you wish."

"I don't understand. You *want* me to investigate Vasclear?"

Weber nodded.

"We've been very impressed with some of the things you've done around here, Brian. Your performance today is a case in point. Just because Vasclear is being approved for general use doesn't mean our responsibilities are over. And frankly, I have a number of other projects that need my attention. I need a close associate to supervise the postmarketing evaluation of Vasclear and to troubleshoot should any problems arise. I think you could do that job, and do it well."

Brian stared across the dim light at the man. Through the corner of his eye, he could see Laj Randa back away from the table as his fellows began closing Paul Wilansky's chest. The operation was over.

"I . . . I'm not sure I believe what I'm hearing," he said. "You're offering me a job at Newbury?"

"The pay would start at, say, a hundred and fifty thousand. But after six months we can renegotiate."

"A hundred and fifty thousand is . . . is very generous."

"You don't have to let me know right away, but I will have you put on the payroll as soon as you do. Of course you can stay at Boston Heart as long as Ernest needs you. For however long that is, you'll actually be collecting two salaries."

"I . . . don't know what to say."

"You don't have to say anything right now, Brian. I would hope, though, to hear from you within the day. And of course, I would strongly urge you to hold up on any communication with the FDA. They are still quite jittery about speeding Vasclear into the world market. Any delay at this point would be extremely costly to Newbury and to thousands of needy patients."

"You have my word."

Art stepped forward and reached out his hand. Brian was reluctant to take his from his lab coat, but finally did.

"I'm looking forward to having you on our team," Weber said. "I know the arrangement will be mutually beneficial for years to come."

So, Brian thought, watching the man walk away, in one week he had learned what it felt like to be hunted, shot at, and now bribed. Art Weber and the folks at Newbury had given him an out—the chance to back off his crusade with honor and profit, and, of course, with his life. A hundred and fifty thousand for starters. Maybe it was worth it, he thought. He had nothing on Vasclear— less, even, than Weber might be fearing. A hundred and fifty thousand plus the forty-five or so he was earning at BHI. He closed his eyes for a moment, somewhat giddy with thoughts of what nearly two hundred thousand dollars would do for him and the kids. But those thoughts were quickly replaced with another image, the image of Bill Elovitz slamming against the shelves in a Charlestown convenience store, his life gone even before he hit the floor.

Brian moved over to the Plexiglas and watched as Paul Wilansky, his heart working satisfactorily, was transferred to a gurney for the trip up to the recovery area in the surgical ICU. Randa, mask now down, was standing off to one side of the OR. Brian turned on the mike.

"How did he do?"

Randa looked up. For a moment, Brian thought he was simply going to ignore him.

"His pupils are down and reactive. It will be some time before we know if there has been brain damage, but I think he'll be okay," the surgeon replied.

"Excellent."

"Your friend Weber is an insolent ass."

"Perhaps. But you were attacking his life's work."

"The race is not always to the swift," Randa replied. "In science, the ultimate victory always goes to the steady performer who walks the distance, rather than to the sprinter."

Brian smiled inwardly at Randa's analogy. Nellie Hennessey, the poster child for Vasclear, was a long-distance walker.

"I'll keep that in mind," he said.

Suddenly, Brian went so cold, it was as if he had been slammed with a blast of arctic air. But he knew that what he had really been hit with, finally, was understanding. Involuntarily, he shuddered. Randa had given him the answer. His hands gripped the brass railing that surrounded the canopy and squeezed until his knuckles were white. The explanation—the elusive answer to so many questions—had floated past him again and again, but never in a form concrete enough to grasp. And each time, he had missed it—he had missed it completely.

Now, suddenly, he knew. He knew the secret of Vasclear.

"Yes!" he said. "Oh, God, yes!"

He whirled around and charged back to the on-call room.

CHAPTER THIRTY-FIVE

VISITORS' HOURS WERE JUST ENDING WHEN BRIAN BOLTED through the door to the clinical-research ward, startling an elderly couple on their way to the elevator.

"Crisis," he said, racing past them and into the on-call room.

If he was right, the key to unlocking nearly everything was a single sheet of paper in his briefcase. He pulled the battered case from beneath the bed and dumped its contents out on the white cotton spread. For a moment, he thought his memory had failed him, but then he found what he was searching for, caught between the pages of a journal article. It was the letter Nellie Hennessey had given him requesting support for her latest walk for charity—

more specifically, the portion of the solicitation that included a list
of the previous walks she had done.

Nellie, tell me something. Exactly how long after you started your
treatment with Vasclear did it take for your symptoms to go away?

How long? Not very, darlin'. I can tell you that much.

Brian recalled the conversation with Nellie and her daughter,
Megan, almost verbatim.

I remember exactly, Ma. You had your first treatment on August
tenth, and your pain was gone the day of my birthday, the twenty-
fourth. It was exactly two weeks to the day.

August 10, two years ago. The day Nellie started treatment.
Brian ran his finger down the list. The walk he remembered noticing had been right around that time.

JULY 27 — 25-MILE WALK FOR AIDS. 25 MILES
COMPLETED. $2,600 RAISED.

Brian stared at the date. Why hadn't he thought to question it
before? Within two weeks of walking twenty-five miles in July
heat, Nellie was on the cath table at Boston Heart, being diagnosed
with end-stage arteriosclerotic heart disease.

Other pieces began drifting into place as well. Nellie's symptoms, as described in her chart, were classic angina. But her own
description of the pain was far from typical. Why hadn't that registered? Her parents both lived into their late eighties or nineties.
When was the last cardiac case he had seen who could boast that?
Never, that was when.

Nellie's phone number was on the solicitation sheet.

"Hello, Nellie Hennessey here," she answered.

"Nellie, it's Dr. Holbrook calling from the hospital."

"Oh, yes, dear. Is everything all right?"

"Fine. Everything's fine. I was just looking at the list of walks
you gave me, and I realized that you went on a long one just before
your heart trouble was diagnosed."

"That's right," she replied without a hesitation. "Twenty-five miles for AIDS."

"Do you remember if you had any chest pain during the walk?"

"Not really. Not that I remember. But don't forget, Dr. Holbrook, I never had any real chest pain to begin with. It was all in my shoulder and sort of up into my neck. In fact, by the time I had that positive treadmill test with Dr. Jessup, it seemed like my problem might actually be getting better."

That's because it was never cardiac pain to begin with! Brian wanted to scream.

"Nellie, you've helped me a great deal," he said instead. "I hope your next walk is a huge success."

"It's not *that* one you should be cheering for," she said. "It's the one after that."

"Oh?"

"December twenty-first I'm doing the annual Boston Christmas walk. The benefit charity changes every year."

"And what is it this year?"

"I'd have thought you would know, dear," she replied. "It's Boston Heart Institute."

Brian repacked his briefcase and sat for a time absently polishing the revolver with a washcloth. If he was right—and his theory was the only one that fit the facts—seventy-five percent or so of the Phase Two beta Vasclear group didn't have cardiac disease to begin with. The seventy-five percent that "improved" so dramatically. The pains that brought them to the attention of Carolyn Jessup were bursitis or esophagitis or gastritis or pleurisy, or any of the other myriad masqueraders of cardiac disease. As a cardiologist in private practice, he had seen at least as many patients whose symptoms turned out to be noncardiac in origin as those with bona fide heart disease.

It would have been easy enough for an EKG machine to be electronically "adjusted" to print out the pattern of coronary artery disease during a stress test. But what about the arteriograms done in the cath lab? Jessup wasn't the only one watching the monitor screen. There were, at a minimum, two sharp, well-trained nurses and an experienced cath tech, to say nothing of the students, residents, fellows, and private cardiologists who frequented the lab. Among the entire group, they had observed thousands of caths. They would certainly be able to tell if a study was abnormal or not, and to what degree.

Could a cardiac cath possibly be faked on the spot? Was there any way to alter a patient's arteriogram at the moment he was having it?

No, Brian concluded. There was no way, unless . . . unless the arteriogram being viewed on the monitor screen during the initial cath wasn't the patient's at all.

Brian took a pad of progress-note paper from the drawer of the small writing desk and began composing a letter to Teri, detailing what he believed was going on with Vasclear. Then, after a couple of sentences, he stopped writing and tried one last call to her at home. She answered on the first ring.

"Hey, it's me," he said.

His relief at hearing her voice instantly lifted the apprehension that had been stifling him.

"Oh, Brian, I just came in and got your messages. I was about to have you paged. Are you okay? Has your friend Phil shown up?"

"Not a sign of him. Teri, there's big trouble here and I believe Vasclear and Newbury Pharmaceuticals are right in the middle of it. When are you coming up?"

"Not until Saturday morning."

"Can you make it up tomorrow?"

"Brian, I'd love to, but that would be impossible."

"Okay. In that case, can you stay by your phone for a while right now?"

"Of course. But what's going on?"

"I think Art Weber and Carolyn Jessup have been forging the

results of the Phase Two Vasclear study. I don't think most of the patients in the beta group ever had heart disease. And I don't think they've been getting Vasclear, either."

"That's impossible. We've reviewed the arteriograms and cardiograms. We've even interviewed the patients. Do you have any hard evidence at all?"

"I'm going down to the video library to try and get some right now. I'll call you as soon as I do."

"Okay. I'll be right here. Just be careful, Brian. Don't do anything dangerous."

Brian slipped the revolver back into his lab coat pocket, hurried to the desk, and told the ward secretary he would be on-page for the next hour. Less cautious than he had been, he ran the six flights down to the cath-lab film library—the only place where he might find tangible proof of his theory.

Art Weber seemed smugly confident that Brian had been bought—at least until after the ceremony. It stood to reason, then, that Leon and his friends might have been taken off their search-and-destroy status. With any luck, by the time Weber realized his miscalculation, Brian would be somewhere safe with the documentation he needed to blow the lid off a billion-dollar scam.

The basement was totally deserted and eerily silent. At the far end of the long hallway, past the machine canteen, the lights in the animal facility were off. Determined not to repeat his earlier mistake, Brian remained in the safety of the stairwell and scanned the ceiling and walls of the corridor for cameras. Convinced there were none, he moved to the cath-lab door. It was strange and frightening to think that Leon, and possibly others from Newbury, might be just a few feet directly below him.

The video library could be reached either through the lab itself, or directly from the hallway. Brian chose the hallway door. Like most of the secured rooms in BHI, the library had a keypad entry system. Brian tapped in his code and quickly slipped inside the totally dark, windowless space. Before turning on the lights, he used the illumination from his penlight to make a careful scan of the walls and ceiling. There were no surveillance cameras that he could see, but there was a grate—probably air-conditioning—in the center of the ceiling. He quietly climbed on a chair and tried to peer behind it. If there was a camera there, it was too far back to see. He hesitated, then shrugged and flicked on the overhead light. Having gotten this far, he wasn't about to wait.

The room was long—twenty-five feet or so—and narrow. The rear two-thirds was occupied by shelves of catheterization videos in individual cardboard containers, the front third by the two Vangard viewers. Brian flipped both of the viewers on and used a log book to obtain Nellie's film numbers. In all, she had been catheterized four times: pretreatment, then at six months, one year, and two years after the onset of Vasclear therapy.

Brian had no difficulty finding all four films. He set the pretreatment video in one Vangard and the two-year film—the one on which he had assisted—in the other. Then, slowly, he advanced each film to the first view, the left anterior oblique shot taken immediately following an injection of dye into Nellie's right coronary artery. When viewed individually, there was nothing unusual about either film. The pretreatment video showed extensive arteriosclerosis throughout the branches of the right coronary. The two-year film, while not completely free of blockages, showed excellent vessels for a woman Nellie's age.

It was only when the films were studied carefully, side by side, that the secret became apparent: The arteriograms were not from the same patient. Brian scanned the initial and latest videos, then briefly ran the other two, which were identical to the most recent one. The pretreatment video—the one that had pointed Nellie Hennessey toward the Vasclear study—was bogus. It was a damn close match, chosen by someone who had access to a large number of abnormal cases and knew cardiovascular anatomy well. But the pattern of each person's cardiac vessels, if mapped out carefully, was unique. And Nellie Hennessey's pre- and posttreatment patterns were clearly different from each other. Somehow, during the initial study, a video of the catheterization of a diseased patient was fed into the system and projected onto the monitor screen in the cath lab.

"Remarkable," Brian whispered. "Absolutely remarkable."

He sat there for a time, nearly consumed by a mix of anger and regret. If he was right, he had deprived his father of potentially curative surgery and had put his own recovery on the line in order to treat Jack with nothing more potent than intravenous water. No wonder Carolyn Jessup kept pushing Jack into Laj Randa's court. She knew all along that the Vasclear being given to the test subjects was useless. Vasclear's success stories had never had cardiac disease to begin with.

Brian rewound the films, slipped them back in their boxes, and replaced the six-month and one-year films in their slots. Then, cradling the other two videos in his left hand, he snapped off the viewers, cut the lights, and carefully opened the door to the hallway an inch.

While not irrefutable, the Hennessey films would definitely be enough evidence to postpone the Vasclear signing and bring Teri, her boss, and their cardiology experts down to the viewing room to look for other instances of fraud. If Brian was right, they would find another 170 or so cases where the pretreatment and posttreatment films had anatomic discrepancies. Art Weber and the other powers at Newbury Pharmaceuticals didn't know it, but they were on the ropes.

All was quiet in the corridor. Brian leaned his shoulder against the door and eased it open a bit more. Nothing. All he had to do now was make it to the clinical unit and hide the two films in the on-call room. In the morning, with the crush of staff and visitors, he would have no problem getting them out of the hospital.

He pushed the door open all the way and stepped into the corridor. The heavy pistol butt cracked down on his left wrist like a jackhammer. Electric pain exploded through his hand, paralyzing his fingers. The video boxes clattered across the tiled floor.

Clutching at his wrist, Brian stumbled backward and hit the wall, narrowly keeping himself from falling. Standing just a few feet away, leering at him, was an apparition—the thin gunman who had absorbed bludgeonings first in the New York woods, then in Brian's living room. A grotesque violet bruise now extended from his hairline to the corner of his mouth, puffing his eye and discoloring his cheek and the side of his nose. A swatch of hair had been shaved away, exposing a nasty gash that had been closed with rows of neatly placed stitches.

The man called out in Russian to someone who was inside the cath lab, covering Brian's other route of escape. Brian, still trying to shake some feeling into his hand, knew he had only moments to act. In one motion, he thrust his good hand into his lab coat pocket, pointed the pistol in the direction of the gunman, and fired. The bullet caught the Russian squarely in the center of his chest. His eyes widened in terror, pain, and disbelief as he lurched sideways. There was a sudden gush of blood from between his lips, and he was dropping to his knees when the cath-lab door opened.

Brian, the gun now out of his coat pocket, fired again and again at the doorway. Then he took two steps backward, fired once more as he was turning, and sped off down the hallway.

A gunshot echoed down the corridor, then another. Concrete chips sprayed from a spot not far from Brian's face. His lab coat billowing behind him like a cape, he rounded the corner and headed down a long, straight passage toward the main hospital. There were footsteps pounding after him. In seconds, whoever it was would have a clear shot. Reacting instinctively, Brian cut to his right, down a flight of stairs to the subbasement. The unfinished concrete tunnel was deserted. He bolted past the laundry, which was closed for the night with a steel accordion gate. Footsteps were echoing down the stairs behind him, but now, running in sneakers, he thought he might be opening some ground.

A tunnel marked Power Plant branched to the right off the main corridor. With no idea where he was, Brian raced down it, searching frantically for someplace to hide. What he saw instead was a tall, narrow, unlit staircase going up. At the top, there looked to be darkness enough to conceal him. He would also have the advantage of shooting down at his pursuer if he had to. He took the concrete stairs two at a time, trying to re-create how many shots he had fired and guess at how many bullets the revolver might hold.

He reached the top of the flight and crouched in the blackness. The stairs ended at a small landing and beyond that, a heavy steel door. Fighting air hunger and an icy tremor that he didn't seem able to control, he flattened his body tightly against the door. Could he be seen from down below? He didn't think so, but there was no way to be sure. Of one thing he was certain—he had just shot a man to death. He searched his feelings for any sense of remorse, but he found none. His father was dead because of the remorseless greed of these people—so were Bill Elovitz and Angus MacLanahan. If he had to kill again, he would.

He sat in the darkness, still pressed back against the steel door. There was no sound from below. Was someone there, waiting? How in the hell had they known where he was? There had to be a camera behind the ceiling grate. No other explanation made sense. One minute passed. Nothing. Brian slipped out of his lab coat and rolled it into a ball beneath him. Dark green scrubs might be harder to spot through the gloom than the white coat. Then, from the hallway, he heard a radio crackle to life and a brief exchange in Russian. Moments later, Leon passed by below him, pistol at the ready, glancing only briefly up the stairs.

Brian held his breath, reached above him, and grasped the metal bar that might open the door. Slowly, silently, he pushed it. The door gave just a bit. Fresh, damp air wafted toward him. Was it possible the door opened to the outside? He pushed a bit harder. There was a clank of metal as the door popped free of its casing. The sound echoed down the stairs. In an instant, Leon was below him, gun drawn. Brian fired first. The killer backed away, but then reached around the corner and fired wildly up the stairs. The bullet careened off the wall and slammed into the door. Still in a crouch, Brian pushed the door open and fired twice down the stairs. The first was a shot, the second an impotent click.

Leon stepped out and fired, but Brian was already outside. A chilly rain was falling. He was in a shallow stairwell in an alley between buildings at the very fringe of the hospital. To his left, the alley appeared to dead-end. To the right, he could hear traffic noises. He dropped the revolver and ran down the pavement in that direction. Chest burning, he splashed across the deserted, rain-slicked street and past a construction site. There was no way he could keep running like this for much longer.

A shoulder-high row of dense hedge surrounded an apartment building ahead of him and to his right. He summoned all his remaining strength and hurled himself in an awkward roll, attempting to clear the bushes but missing badly. The dripping branches at the top of the hedge tore at him as he crashed through. Soaked and bleeding from a new set of scratches and gashes on his arms and face, he fell heavily to the ground on the other side, gasping for air.

CHAPTER THIRTY-SIX

HIS SCRUBS SOAKED THROUGH, BRIAN LAY IN THE RAIN on the sodden ground for another fifteen minutes, peering through the hedges at the hospital two hundred yards away. There was no sign of Leon, but he knew that meant nothing. The Newbury Pharmaceuticals goons would already be mobilized and searching the area for him. Trying to make it back into White Memorial was out of the question. Weber and the powers at BHI would have the hospital's own security force looking for him, and maybe the Boston police as well.

By now, some story about the man shot to death in the basement of BHI would have been concocted, and in all likelihood, Brian would be at the center of that tale.

He pushed himself to his feet and tried to flex some of the achiness from his arms and back. His knee was throbbing from the pounding run through the concrete tunnels. Rain spattered on the shallow gouges on his arms, keeping them from clotting over. At that moment, his beeper went off. The clinical ward was calling him. In addition, he realized he had the code-call beeper for the entire hospital. Luckily, he also had his wallet in the back pocket of his scrub pants.

He made it to a nearby convenience store and ignored the curious looks of the clerk while he got change for a dollar. Then he called the unit secretary on the clinical ward.

"I'm out of the hospital and won't be in again tonight," he told her. "Notify the cardiology resident on-call at White Memorial. Tell her she'll have to function without the code-call beeper."

He hung up without giving the secretary a chance to reply, then he flagged a cab and took it to Freeman Sharpe's place. His ring of keys, including the ones the Sharpes had given him to their apartment, was in his briefcase in the on-call room. If Freeman and Marguerite were out, Brian would be wandering around the tough Roxbury section of the city at night, soaked to the skin in a surgical scrub suit. At that moment, the boredom of his year at Speedy Rent-A-Car didn't seem all that bad.

The street outside the apartment building was deserted.

"Hello?" Freeman said through the intercom.

"Freeman, it's Brian."

"Uh-oh."

Freeman buzzed him in. Marguerite clucked at Brian's appearance.

"Someday you're going to show up at my door in a nice business suit," she said. "They'll have to revive me with smelling salts."

Brian showered and donned the jeans and sweatshirt he had

taken from his place. Then he sat in their living room wrapped in a blanket, clutching a cup of steaming coffee, still trying to expunge the chill from his bones.

"I killed a man tonight at the hospital," he said simply.

"One of them?" Freeman asked.

"The one from my house. I shot him in the chest with the gun I took from him this morning."

"At least his head won't hurt him anymore. I told you, Brian. These people have no soul, and they're waging war on you. You've got to wage war right back at them; play by their rules, or lack of. Do you at least have a better understanding of what's going on— why they're so threatened by you?"

"Understanding, yes. Proof none. As for being threatened by me, they have every right to be."

"Tell us."

"There are still a few pieces missing, but basically, the key to the whole thing is that once a drug is on the market, it's extremely difficult to get it off. And it's virtually impossible to get a drug recalled just because it doesn't work. In fact, most of the drugs on the market today don't work all that well. Some of them don't do anything at all. And the truth is, nobody cares. Nobody in research or even at the FDA has the time or the interest to run studies or follow-up research on most of those medications as long as they don't hurt anyone. That's the key. *Primum non nocere* is the Latin phrase they teach us in medical school—'First do no harm.' Most people get better from whatever's wrong with them *regardless of* or even *in spite of* the medicine they take. Others, whose condition is more serious, are always on multiple treatments. It's almost impossible to tell what's working and what isn't."

"But this Vasclear drug does work," Marguerite said.

Brian shook his head.

"That's just it. It doesn't," he said. "The researchers at BHI have been faking their results. Vasclear doesn't work at all. In fact, it did bad things to people who took it. Some of the earliest patients who were put on it got better at first, but then they developed a fatal lung problem.

"So, why did they push ahead?" Freeman said.

"I think you know the answer as well as I do. It costs a hundred million dollars or more to develop a new drug, test it, and get it to the marketplace. If your pal Cedric is right about the men behind Newbury Pharmaceuticals, and I have no reason to think he isn't, I don't think they'd take a hundred-million-dollar hit with much grace. All they have to do is get the drug on the market, and the money will start rolling in. It will be a year, maybe more, before people even begin to suspect that the drug isn't working, and years after that before it gets pulled."

"As long as nobody gets hurt," Marguerite said.

"They don't count people like my father, who end up not getting the surgery they need because they've hitched their wagon to the Vasclear star, but yes—as long as nobody gets hurt."

"And the people from Phase One? The ones who got sick?" Freeman asked.

"Loose ends. The longer they hung around, the more likely it became that someone was going to start questioning their strange lung conditions and the role Vasclear played in their illnesses. So I think someone, probably Weber, has been monitoring the Phase One blood tests. As soon as patients' counts begin to get wacky, they have an accident."

"But you have no proof at all?"

"I had proof in my hand—two films from the cath-lab library at the hospital." He told them about Nellie Hennessey's faked pictures. "That's when I almost got killed. Speaking of which, we should turn on the news."

"I'll do it," Marguerite said, "although the news doesn't come on for fifteen minutes yet."

There was no need to channel surf or wait the fifteen minutes. There was a news special on the first Boston channel Marguerite turned to. *Mayhem at Boston Heart,* the headline above the anchorwoman read. Brian and his two friends sat in bleak silence, watching as the coverage was turned over to a reporter on the scene.

"This is Lina Fallin reporting live from White Memorial Hospital in Boston, where two men have been shot to death and a portion of the Boston Heart Institute has been destroyed by fire. White Memorial is where, in just two days, the President is scheduled to sign approval of a new wonder drug developed and tested at Boston Heart. It is unclear whether these murders are related to that presidential visit or not.

"The identity of one of the victims, a security guard found in a basement hallway, has not yet been released. But the other, burned almost beyond recognition in the fire, is believed to be Dr. Philip Gianatasio of Boston, a cardiologist at Boston Heart who was reported missing earlier today. Although there has been no official confirmation of this, one policeman on the scene said that Gianatasio's death appeared due to a gunshot wound, and not the fire, which completely destroyed the cardiac film library in the basement of the institute. The fire was apparently contained in that one area."

"Oh, Jesus, no," Brian said, burying his face in his hands. "Oh, Phil. Oh, shit. No!"

Marguerite squeezed Brian's hand and pulled him close to her. None of them doubted what was coming next.

"Lina, do police have a suspect and a motive?" the anchorwoman asked.

"Details are sketchy, Paula, but police say they're looking for a physician, also a cardiologist, named Dr. Brian Holbrook, who was on duty tonight at the hospital, but who called in a couple of hours ago to say he had abandoned his coverage at the hospital and wouldn't be coming back."

Brian changed the channel.

". . . Superintendent of Police Dracut is on the scene now and will be making a statement to the media in just fifteen minutes.

But to repeat, police have found what they believe may be the murder weapon—a handgun possibly dropped by the killer while fleeing the scene. There is a search underway for Dr. Holbrook, who apparently has had problems in the past with drugs, and who only recently got his medical license back from the Board of Registration in Medicine."

"Bill, is there any word on whether the White House has been informed of this tragedy and how it will affect Saturday's ceremony?"

"No. No word yet . . ."

Brian shut off the set, too shocked and too angry even to cry.

"Unlimited money, no regard for human life," Freeman said. "It's a bad combination."

"Drug-crazed doctor goes berserk," Brian said. "How perfect. You really have to hand it to them. You also have to believe that the moment I'm captured by the police, Weber and his friends will find some way to get to me."

"I wish I could disagree with you," Freeman said. "Do you have any cards to play? Any at all?"

"The charts are gone. The films are gone. Phil's gone. And before I could ever get anyone to believe my story, I'll be gone."

He snatched up the phone and called Phoebe, who was asleep.

"Do your best to protect the kids," he said, after begging her to believe that he wasn't in relapse and had done nothing more than shoot a gunman in self-defense. "I'll be in touch as soon as I can. I'm sorry this is happening."

There was a shocked silence, but at least she wasn't hurling accusations at him.

Brian watched for another hour and a half, but learned little more. The fire in the video library had been carried out with calculated skill. The smoke detectors had been taped over, then hundreds of angiograms had been dumped from their containers onto Phil Gianatasio's body and set ablaze.

Around midnight, Ernest Pickard read a brief statement deploring what had happened and urging Brian to come forward. Later, White House Chief of Staff Stan Pomeroy read a statement saying that unless more information surrounding the double murder came to light, the President expected to go through with Saturday's ceremonies as planned. However, he added, additional security measures might be taken.

At twelve-thirty, Freeman and Marguerite went to bed. Brian switched off the set and called Teri. She was wide-awake.

"Brian! I've been worried sick about you. I just got a call about what happened."

"I didn't set that fire, Teri, and the only man I killed was someone who was trying to kill me."

"Well, then, who set the fire and killed your friend Phil?"

"The people from Newbury Pharmaceuticals."

"Brian, what are you talking about?"

He recounted the evening's events for her. She listened patiently, but when she responded, her tone was urgent.

"Brian, you've got to turn yourself in," she said. "If what you're saying is the truth, people will believe you."

"I have no proof. None at all."

"I can order random samples of Vasclear to be pulled and analyzed. Would that help?"

"Maybe, but I suspect there'll be some chemical close to the original in the vials. These people are very careful."

"I don't know what to say, Brian. We've only known each other a short time, and . . . I'm not sure what to think. I still say you've got to turn yourself in."

"I'm not turning myself in. If I do, they'll get to me, I know they will. Teri, you've got to convince people to believe me."

"Do you have any proof? Anything at all?"

"No, but—"

"Brian, please. Don't put me on the spot like this. Turn yourself in."

"If I do get proof, how can I get it to you?"

"Just bring it down to Maryland."

"When will you be up here?"

"Saturday. The ceremony will be at eight in the Hippocrates Dome."

"I'll try to make contact. Teri, I didn't do anything wrong. You've got to believe me."

"I'm trying," she said.

Brian set the receiver down and slumped across the couch. Five hours later, when he awoke, he was covered with a blanket. The aroma of fresh coffee and frying sausage filled the apartment.

"Hey, I'm glad you got some sleep," Marguerite said. "Freeman's just showering."

"Thanks. Do you have the morning paper?"

"I do, but I'm not sure you want to see it."

"If it's the *Globe,* I'll look at it. If it's the *Herald,* I don't know."

"It's the *Globe,* but the boundary between the two papers is sort of blurry with stories like this one."

Brian poured a cup and stared down at his picture on the front page. Ironically, it was the photo he had submitted with his application for staff privileges at White Memorial.

"And to think, when I was playing ball, I used to be upset if I didn't get enough press coverage," he said. "This is going to be awful for the girls."

Freeman, in his robe, emerged from the bedroom, toweling his hair.

"So," he said, "another day."

"I know the old AA saw—any day you don't drink or drug is a good one—but I have serious doubts about yesterday."

"I know. Have you got a plan yet?"

"Not really. But I've got to do something."

Freeman sat down beside him and sipped at some juice.

"Is there anyone at your hospital you can trust?" he asked.

"Only Phil." Brian gestured toward the news photo of Gianatasio. "And maybe that egomaniac surgeon who tried to save

Jack. Everybody else has an enormous professional or financial stake in Vasclear. Why do you ask?"

"Well, I know the Russian Mafia is capable of gunning down a guy in a market, or blowing up a sick old man in his apartment. But it's a little hard to believe that all these high-powered doctors are capable of it, or even condone it."

"Or even know about it!" Brian said suddenly.

"What do you mean?"

Brian didn't respond right away. If Freeman was right, there might well be a chink in the Vasclear armor—someone who knew part of what was going on, but not everything, especially not the part about the murders of the Phase One patients.

"Freeman, you keep saying that whatever it is you need, there's a person somewhere in AA and NA who can get it."

"That is true."

"Well, if I gave you the name of a person with an unlisted phone number, do you think you could come up with somebody who'd get that phone number for me and the address that goes along with it?"

"You mean, like someone who works for the phone company?"

"Exactly."

Freeman and his wife exchanged knowing grins.

"What's the name and town?" Freeman said.

"She lives on the North Shore—Salem, Marblehead, Beverly, Gloucester—one of those. I'm not sure which."

"And her name?"

"Dr. Carolyn Jessup."

"I'll see what I can do. It may take a while."

"That's okay. It's not like I have anyplace to go. And Freeman, if you can manage it, there are three other things I'll need."

"As long as one of them isn't a gun."

"Actually—"

"I'm serious, my friend. If you're thinking about going up against the Newbury people, I want you to take your chances with the police first. You get hold of a gun at this stage, and the only person I'm absolutely certain will be killed is you."

"Okay, okay. Forget the gun."

"In that case, just tell me what you need for your grand plan, and I'll see what I can do."

"Nothing that exotic, actually. I need a rental car, three or four overnight-mail envelopes, and a cellular phone . . . plus a lot of luck."

CHAPTER THIRTY-SEVEN

BOSTON HERALD

**Drug Doc Wanted for
Double Murder
President Still Coming to Hub**

Murder arrest warrants are out for former UMass football star Brian Holbrook,
who is currently on the staff of Boston
Heart Institute. Holbrook, who lost his
medical license for eighteen months because of fraudulently prescribing narcotics to support his own drug addiction, is
the prime suspect in a bizarre shooting
spree at White Memorial Hospital, which

left a part-time hospital guard and a prominent cardiologist both dead. The cardiologist, Dr. Philip Gianatasio, was also on the faculty at Boston Heart Institute.

In a related story, sources close to the President report that there are no plans to change the ceremony scheduled for tomorrow night at White Memorial.

BRIAN SPENT THE ENTIRE MORNING AT FREEMAN'S computer, typing out a detailed report of everything that had happened from the day Jack was brought to the White Memorial ER.

The hospital charts are missing, he wrote, *and most, if not all, of the Phase One patients are dead. But I believe a close review of the autopsy of Wilhelm Elovitz will reveal the changes of pulmonary hypertension in the arteries of his lungs, just as a careful review of the convenience-store video will show that his murder was deliberate and premeditated. . . .*

It was almost one in the afternoon before he began printing out the eleven-page document. One copy to the *Globe,* one to the *Herald,* one for Phil Gianatasio's parents, and the final one for Teri. He would not give a copy to Freeman and Marguerite. They had already put themselves on the line for him. As Freeman said, this was war. There was no way Brian would allow any more of his friends to become casualties.

An eleven-page report to the *Globe* and the *Herald* from a drug addict wanted for murder, backed up by nothing tangible, accusing the developers and manufacturers of a proven miracle drug of fraud and multiple murders—how crazy did that sound? The ramblings of a nutcase—and a dangerous nutcase at that. *No chance,* Brian thought. There was absolutely no chance anyone would take him seriously. And if someone did, a judiciously placed bribe or threat or bullet would surely take care of matters.

Outside, the steady rain continued into a second day. Five to seven days altogether, the forecasters were predicting. The rain, the sun, autumn, the kids, his one night with Teri, Freeman and Marguerite, his patients . . . they all seemed so precious now. Throwing a football . . . listening to a heart . . . breathing in the seasons. Brian wondered how differently he would have approached many things in his life had he known it was the last time he would ever be experiencing them.

How many *last times* with Jack passed by unappreciated during those final, frantic weeks?

The phone was ringing. Brian hesitated, then answered it. It was Freeman. A pipe had burst in the other building. He would be home within the hour with everything Brian needed.

"Once you turn those over to me," Brian said, "I'm out of here and you're done."

"Hey, if you think I'm gonna argue with you about that, you're wrong," Freeman replied. "I ain't the hero type."

Brian dressed and pulled on his still-damp sneakers. It was time to begin preparations. If he was wrong about Carolyn Jessup, if she could not be swayed, he would have to be ready to turn himself in . . . or to run. The one remaining thing he needed to do was speak with Teri once more. He couldn't leave her in the dark. But neither could he expect her to risk her credibility and even her career for him. He would take care of this business himself. And if he failed, he would fail alone.

He found her at her desk.

"Teri, I'm going to overnight you a complete summary of everything I think is going on with Vasclear. I'm sending copies to the papers up here as well. Maybe someone will sense I'm not crazy."

"But you still have no proof?"

"No. Not really, but I'm going after that tonight. I worked with Carolyn Jessup on a difficult case yesterday, and she took care of my father before he died. She really is a very good doctor. Even though I kept refusing surgery for Jack, she kept pushing to have him operated on. I think it was because she knew the Vasclear he was getting wasn't ever going to work. I don't know how she's gotten mixed up with these Newbury people, but I'm hoping she'll come forward when she hears what they've been doing."

"For your sake, I hope so, too. Is there anything I can do to help?"

"Where are you staying here tomorrow?"

"I'm not. We're flying back right after the ceremony."

"That's just as well. I think you'd best keep out of this anyway. Phil didn't, and look what happened to him."

"Brian, are you sure you're okay? The papers down here have had some pretty unkind things to say about you."

"I'm sure they have. Teri, I wish this weren't happening, but unless I see it through somehow, I don't have a chance. The envelope should be at your office by ten tomorrow. Read what I have to say, and then see how you feel."

"I will. You take care. Don't do anything foolish."

Brian set the receiver down and closed his eyes. He was beginning to drift off when the sound of the key in the lock startled him. The aroma of Freeman's pipe preceded him by several seconds.

"One cellular phone. One set of keys to a Ford Taurus," he said, ceremoniously depositing each on the table. "Express mailers from your post office. Street address and phone number of one Dr. Carolyn Jessup. Street-map book of metropolitan area including the town of Nahant."

"Nahant," Brian said. "I heard her talking about living on the North Shore, but I didn't think Nahant."

The one-time island was now connected to the mainland by a mile-long causeway. It consisted primarily of hilly neighborhoods of closely packed clapboard houses, but it also boasted many beautiful oceanfront homes, most with views across the harbor to Boston. Actually, now that he thought of it, Nahant—remote, pristine, interesting—seemed a perfect match for Carolyn Jessup.

It was midafternoon when Brian sealed the last of the envelopes and left them on the kitchen counter.

"Thanks for all you've done for me, Freeman," he said, taking his sponsor's hand. "And look, you've been a total success. Through everything that's happened, I haven't touched a drug or a drink."

"Just don't lose that priority," Sharpe said. "You've always got a place here, my friend. And I expect a call as soon as you've seen this woman on Nahant. Use that phone, then keep it as long as you need to. And as for the car, well, I signed up for all the insurance waivers and also took the liberty of having an extra key made. That leaves me with the original set in case someone happens to steal the poor thing. And here, just in case it's not safe for you to hit a money machine."

He passed over an envelope.

"I owe you," Brian said without looking inside it. "Big time, I owe you."

"Just don't get killed. That'll be payment enough."

Brian packed his gym bag with some clothes, the cell phone, and the street-map book.

"If this doesn't work out," Freeman asked, "are you planning on turning yourself in?"

"I don't know. Maybe I'll rent *The Fugitive,* then decide."

"At your size, you're a little more conspicuous than Harrison Ford."

"Tell me about it."

Brian hugged his sponsor and held the embrace for a time.

"The car's right out front," Freeman said finally. "I thought you'd want black."

"Perfect."

"Just remember, pal, God doesn't give us more than we can handle."

"Freeman, pardon me for saying it," Brian replied, "but with my father and my friend both dead, and me wanted for murders I did and didn't commit, this isn't such a great time to be talking to me about God."

CHAPTER THIRTY-EIGHT

THROUGHOUT THE FORTY-FIVE-MINUTE DRIVE TO NA-hant, made in early rush-hour traffic, Brian was on high-tension alert. The slightest fender bender or illegal lane change could mark his last minutes of freedom.

Would he really have to go on the run? Once he started running, he knew there would be no sudden salvation, no triumphant vindication as the credits rolled. Vasclear would be released—or rather, some harmless, chemically related placebo *labeled* Vasclear. Years and maybe billions of dollars later, Vasclear would simply slip from the marketplace, another promising drug that just didn't pass the test of time. But hey, no harm, no foul . . . except, of course, for Jack Holbrook, Bill Elovitz, Phil, and a few others.

Brian headed up the Lynnway, a two-mile eyesore of automobile dealerships, restaurants, car washes, power lines, and gas stations. It was after four now and, for the moment at least, the rain had yielded to a pale wash of late-afternoon sun. Even the Lynnway looked fresh. An apartment complex, one final restaurant, and he was at the causeway to Nahant. A cruiser sped up behind him, strobes on, sirens blaring. Brian felt his heart stop dead. He meekly pulled over, ready to surrender, as the black-and-white sped past. This was how it was going to be for the rest of his life if he ran.

Thanks to Freeman's map, he had no trouble negotiating the tangle of narrow streets that made up most of the town. Carolyn Jessup's place was on the water at the end of a small side street on the southeast end of the peninsula. The lot was modest, but completely secluded from her neighbors and much of the street by carefully trimmed eight-foot-high hedgerows. The house itself, a ranch with a single-car garage attached, was back from the road, on a small promontory above the water. The street-side windows of the place were unimpressive, but Brian suspected that those facing the harbor and the city skyline provided a spectacular view.

Unwilling to stay too long in one place, he made several passes around the town. By the time the streetlights winked on, he had found a dark side street where he could leave the Taurus without the local police taking undue notice. A face-to-face meeting was the only chance he had of getting the truth from Jessup.

The causeway was a problem. If Jessup was determined to protect herself and Newbury, and she knew he was nearby, one call to the police would have the mainland end of the mile-long road sealed off before he could ever get off the peninsula. Another problem was his reluctance to stay in the car on the side street. A routine patrol wouldn't pay any attention to the Taurus unless they noticed someone inside it. For the next hour, he cruised onto the mainland and back several times, once risking a stop at a burger place for takeout. Twice he passed a Nahant cruiser.

It was nine o'clock when Brian realized that new lights were on in Jessup's home. Wearing a dark windbreaker, he took the cell phone, left the Taurus, and hurried across the deserted street to the safety of the hedge. Next he worked his way around to the water side. There was a narrow, well-maintained lawn behind the house, and then a rocky slope of twenty feet or so to the ocean. The dense overcast helped keep the entire yard in darkness, but there was some glow across the water from the city.

As Brian had anticipated, the south side of Jessup's house was almost entirely glass, with a ten-foot-square deck off the kitchen. He made his way to the edge of the yard, then dropped down and maneuvered himself over the embankment and several feet down the sea-smoothed rocks. From that vantage point, he had a clear view into Jessup's kitchen and living room. He fished out her phone number, then stopped as she entered the kitchen.

He was fifty or sixty feet away, but even at that distance, he could tell she was agitated. She was still dressed in her skirt and blouse, pacing about the room. Then suddenly she stopped, took a bottle from a cupboard, splashed some liquid in a tumbler, and drained it in a single gulp. She poured another but left the drink on the counter as she crossed to the sliders and gazed out across the water at the city.

Brian slid farther down the wet, rocky embankment. It felt uncomfortable to be spying on her this way, but at this point, the more connected he was to her, the better. Jessup appeared drawn and very tired. She loosened her dark hair and shook it free. It was time, Brian decided. He punched in her phone number and watched with relief as she reacted to the ring. Freeman's NA sources had come through again. Her phone was a portable on the built-in desk in one corner of the kitchen.

"Hello?"

"Dr. Jessup, it's Brian Holbrook."

She stiffened at the mention of his name.

"How did you get my number?" she asked.

"My back's against the wall. Desperate people can be very resourceful. I'm sorry to call you like this, but as you know, I'm in a great deal of trouble. And the truth is I have no one to turn to."

"You need to be turning to the police, not to me."

"Dr. Jessup, yesterday you and I worked together to save the life of a man on the surgical service. I think you're a remarkable doctor. I also think you're fair enough at least to hear what I have to say. And one other thing."

"Yes?"

"I think you tried to save my father's life by insisting he have surgery instead of Vasclear."

During the few seconds of silence that followed, Brian watched her retrieve the tumbler of liquor from the counter and drain it.

"I don't know what you're talking about," she said.

"Dr. Jessup, I didn't kill Phil Gianatasio. He was my friend. But I did have to shoot the man the papers are calling a part-time security guard for the hospital. He might have worked part-time for the hospital, but he worked full-time as a hired gun for Newbury Pharmaceuticals. I shot him because he was about to kill me. And he was about to kill me because I was leaving the film library at the cath lab with the before-and-after angiograms of Nellie Hennessey. I know the before film wasn't hers, Dr. Jessup. I didn't check any other patients, but I'd bet whatever you like that close study of their films would reveal the same thing. Phil was beginning to realize what was going on, too. That's why they killed him. That's why they burned the films."

"Who are *they*?"

"The people at Newbury. I think Art Weber is at the center of what's going on, although I don't believe he controls the whole company."

There was another telltale hesitation. Jessup was braced against the refrigerator.

"I don't believe you," she said. "If you have accusations to make, you should go to the police. Now, I'm going to hang up—"

"Please! Please, Dr. Jessup. Just listen. My life depends on you. So do a lot of other lives. I can't believe you wouldn't at least listen."

"Go on," she said finally.

"Thank you," he said. "I don't know how you got into all this so deeply, but I don't think you fully understood what these people have done. All those Phase One patients—the patients who started developing pulmonary hypertension from their Vasclear treatments—Newbury has been arranging accidental deaths for those of them who didn't die of PH. While you were creating a phantom medical miracle by curing patients who had no heart disease to begin with, Newbury has been eliminating anyone who could possibly slow down the approval process for Vasclear. *Killing* them."

"You have proof of what you say?"

"You're my proof, Dr. Jessup. You could have just let my father die, but you tried to save him. If you had known what Newbury was doing to the Phase One patients, I think you would have come forward. I need your help. I need you to do what's right."

In the silence that followed, he watched her once again take a drink.

"I . . . I don't know if I can," she said finally.

She had sunk onto a kitchen chair now, and was staring, unseeing, out the sliders.

"Will you at least talk to me in person?" he asked. "I need you to fill in some gaps for me. Then, if you don't want to do any more, that's up to you. I'll take my own chances."

Jessup was beaten—exhausted. Brian could see that now.

"When?" she asked.

"Right now. I left instructions just under the stairs off the deck in back of your house. They'll tell you where to meet me."

Brian had come up with the lie as a way of neutralizing the danger of Jessup calling the police and getting the Nahant causeway sealed off. She still had no idea he was on her property. If she hung up on him now, or made a phone call to anyone, he would simply leave. If she came directly out onto the deck and then later refused to help him, he would have to tie her up so he could get away.

Keeping Jessup in his line of sight, and staying low, he moved to a spot where he could insert himself between her and the sliding doors. In the kitchen, she cradled the phone as she mulled over his request. Finally, after an interminable minute, she opened the sliders and stepped out onto the deck. Brian forced himself deeper into the shadows. She looked around cautiously, then moved to the stairs and stepped down to check beneath them. Brian bolted from his concealment and leaped up onto the deck.

"Dr. Jessup, please don't be frightened," he said quickly. "I'm not going to hurt you. I just want to talk."

Jessup stumbled backward a step and glared up at him, her lips pulled tight in a startled snarl. For a moment Brian thought she was going to charge him.

"How dare you sneak in here and spy on me this way," she said, her voice raspy.

He had to hand it to her. He held the advantage in size and position, yet she looked completely unintimidated.

"Dr. Jessup, my father died because I believed what I read and was told about Vasclear. Now my friend is dead, I've had to kill a man, and my own life is going down the drain. It's got to end. Fabricating research results is one thing. But people are getting murdered. You can't let it go on any longer."

Jessup continued glaring up at him, but Brian could see the fatigue and confusion in her eyes. Finally, she let her breath out in a long, defeated sigh.

"Do you want to go inside?" she asked.

"I'd rather stay back here."

He motioned her to a spot on the edge of the deck and set his windbreaker down for her to sit on.

"I really am deeply sorry about your father's death," she said.

"I know you are. At least now you've got a chance to do something about it."

"I'm very frightened."

"So am I."

Jessup rubbed wearily at her eyes.

"Okay," she said finally, "where do you want me to begin?"

"It doesn't matter. I need to know about Vasclear. I need to know how this could have happened."

"A number of years ago, Art Weber was working with an international medical group at a clinic in the Amazon River basin in Columbia. That's where he discovered Vasclear. Or thought he did, anyway. There was a tribe of primitive meat eaters that chewed some sort of boiled bark every day and lived to be a hundred or more with no sign of hardening of the arteries. Art believed he had found the fountain of youth, but he needed money to analyze the contents of the bark, isolate the bioactive substance, synthesize it, and test it. And he wanted to retain as much control and profit as possible. I don't know how he knew the people who own Newbury, or what sort of deal he made with them. But I'll tell you this, he could talk a frightened rabbit out of its hole."

"He made a deal with the devil," Brian said. "They're Russian Mafia."

Jessup looked over at him, impressed.

"Actually, they're *Chechen* Mafia," she said, "although I didn't know anything about them at all until things began to go wrong. According to Art, even the *Russian* Mafia is scared of the Chechens."

"I believe it."

"The people behind Newbury anted up an enormous amount of money, but Art had made clear to them how much they had to gain. It took three years of chemistry and animal work just to isolate the bioactive substance they named Vasclear. I was made director of clinical research, and Newbury began funding a number of BHI projects in exchange for the work I was doing. Everything seemed fine with Vasclear until we began our Phase One testing. The drug showed some initial promise. But first the animals got in trouble, especially the primates, then some of the patients."

"Eosinophilia followed by pulmonary hypertension."

"Exactly. Art told his partners at Newbury that they had to go back to the drawing board. They said that would be fine with them as long as he repaid the tens of millions of dollars they had already laid out, plus interest."

"But how did he get you to go along with the hoax?"

She looked away. Even in the semidarkness, he could see her cheeks flush. She and Art Weber were lovers!

"There . . . there was a great deal at stake for me," she said, carefully choosing her words, "financially and otherwise."

"I understand," Brian said, sparing her the humiliation of spelling things out.

"Art was genuinely panicked. He said the people at Newbury wouldn't hesitate to kill both of us unless we found a way to recoup their money. That was when I came up with the idea to create fake heart disease in patients, then cure it. Yes, the idea was mine, almost all of it. Art made some refinements, but I set up the framework. We even calculated how long the drug would have to be on the market before we were safe from Newbury."

"I'll bet it wasn't that long," Brian said.

"The key was that the FDA would never conduct their own research."

"And as long as no one got hurt by Vasclear, no one would pay much attention to it."

"But the cases and the research results had to look good," Jessup added, a note of proud accomplishment in her voice.

"And they did."

"Reprogramming an EKG machine to print out abnormal stress tests was relatively easy. The caths were the challenge. I chose a storage area that had been built beneath the cath lab. We built an apartment down there for our technicians as well as a sophisticated electronics center linked to the video monitor in the lab."

"I know where that room is," Brian said. "The killer I shot must have been hiding out there, if not living there."

"I didn't know that," she said. "You have to believe me. I didn't know."

"I believe you. Go on, please."

"Well, I put together a set of twenty abnormal caths—enough of a selection so that one of them would come close to duplicating the anatomy of almost any patient."

"The one you used for Nellie Hennessey was a very close match."

"And it wasn't even the best we had."

"So what was it, an electronic switch somewhere?"

"Beneath the foot pedal I used to control the camera. With the switch thrown, which I usually did the evening before the cath, the dye injection that was projected on the monitor when I hit the pedal came from downstairs. It had to correspond exactly to the view we were doing in the cath lab."

"But it wasn't the patient's."

Jessup stared out at the water, utterly deflated. But Brian also sensed some relief.

"No," she said. "It wasn't."

"Pardon me for asking, but are you and Art still . . . as close as you were?"

"He seems to be gradually pulling away, if that's what you mean. But yes, we're still lovers. There was a time when I think I would have done almost anything for him. But don't get me wrong. I was going to benefit, too. Two million or more in just the first year if all went well. I have money, but not that kind of money."

Brian rubbed at the strain and exhaustion that were burning his eyes.

"We have to come up with a plan," he said. "What do you think we should do now?"

"Do?" the man's voice behind them said. "Why, I would expect you to do nothing."

Brian and Jessup spun to the voice. Art Weber stood by the edge of the deck, eyeing them calmly through the gloom. Fanning out from him in a semicircle were Leon and two other men, all of them holding guns.

Brian glanced over at Jessup to see if she was as shocked at the arrival of the intruders as he was. He didn't have to wait long to find out.

"Art, he knows everything," she said hoarsely. "Absolutely everything."

Weber stepped forward and smacked her viciously across the face with the back of his hand.

"He does now, you stupid bitch!" he snapped.

CHAPTER THIRTY-NINE

MINUTES? . . . HOURS? . . . DAYS? . . . FOR BRIAN, time was completely lost within a swirling haze of drugs and pain. He was on a wooden chair in a spare, windowless room, his arms lashed together at the wrist and his legs at the ankles. His ribs, separated if not broken from the pounding he had taken to his abdomen and chest, made each breath a grunting, agonizing effort.

Now, for the first time, his head was beginning to clear. He remembered being pummeled by Leon in Carolyn Jessup's back-yard—sharp blows with fists and feet to his face and belly. He remembered the sting of the first injection, given deep into the muscle at the base of his neck while he was still lying on the wet grass. He remembered being zipped into a plastic body bag. He remembered his tall frame being folded into the trunk of a car. Then, he remembered nothing.

He blinked rapidly, trying to focus his vision. His eyes felt puffy, the muscles in his face stiff and swollen. His tongue probed the fleshy cavity where a front tooth had once been. His nostrils were thick with dried blood.

"Water," he croaked. "Bring me water."

There was movement behind him. Moments later a plastic cup was pushed against his mouth. He drank gratefully, rinsing before he swallowed. His vision slowly cleared. The man holding the cup reeked of bad cologne. He was short and stocky, with a thin mustache and vacant brown eyes—the driver Freeman had confronted outside Brian's home in Reading. The room was a combination living area and small kitchen, the furniture utilitarian. There were no pictures on the whitewashed walls. A TV and VCR stood over to one corner.

Even though there were no definite clues, Brian felt certain he was deep in the belly of the hospital, in the subbasement space Carolyn Jessup had helped to create. Somewhere, possibly just beyond the gray-painted fire door facing him, was the control room used to transfer videos to the cath-lab monitor screen one floor above. He wouldn't be surprised if that room was also outfitted with surveillance screens keeping watch on the corridors, rooms, and clinic areas involved with the Vasclear program.

Brian thought about his capture by Weber. Carolyn must have been followed home from the hospital by one of the Chechens. No other explanation accounted for Weber's timely arrival on the scene. Now Weber was determined to learn the names of everyone to whom Brian had given information regarding Vasclear. He had used drugs—Ketamine and something like Seconal, Brian thought. He had used physical punishment—in addition to the aching throughout his body, Brian felt certain the little finger on his left hand was broken.

Was the torturing finished? . . . Was Weber convinced he knew all Brian had to tell him? . . . How much time had gone by? . . . Was the Vasclear ceremony over? . . . What had happened to Jessup? . . . Had he broken down in some dark moment and mentioned Teri? . . . Freeman and Marguerite?

The questions roiled in his brain. One thing he knew with certainty. He was never going to leave this spartan little place alive. The door to his left opened, revealing a second room—a sleeping area about half the size of the room he was in. He could see one bed and the edge of another. Seated on the side of the bed was Carolyn Jessup. Her face appeared to have absorbed a battering to both sides, but her hair was neatly tied back, and otherwise she still seemed amazingly composed. At some point she had changed into scrubs—Brian couldn't imagine why.

"I'm not going to tie you down anymore, Carolyn," he heard Weber say, "but you know what will happen to you should you or our friend in the chair out there cause them the least bit of trouble. These men have their instructions, and they will enjoy carrying them out. Is that clear? . . . Is it?"

"Yes."

"And is that clear to you, Dr. Holbrook?" he asked, backing out of the room, then turning to Brian. "It will be on your head if Dr. Jessup gets hurt."

"It's clear," Brian managed. "What day is it?"

"Day? Why, it's Christmas. My, my, my, it appears you *have* had a rough go of it. I'm afraid Leon has taken what you did to his friend very personally. Is that so, Leon?"

The huge killer stepped around from behind Brian and slapped him violently across the mouth. Brian's lips, already cracked and clotted, split open again. He sucked at the blood and glared up at Leon's hideously marked face. Feral eyes glared back at him.

"Stop it!" Carolyn screamed.

Weber pointed a manicured finger at her.

"Shut up!" he snapped. "This a warning. A final warning."

He turned back to Brian.

"I'm afraid I'm not through with you," he said. He glanced theatrically at his Rolex and for the first time Brian registered that Weber had changed into a beautifully tailored suit and conspicuously expensive silk tie. "However, as you might by now realize, it is the nineteenth of October. I have pressing business with the President of the United States. The names you have given us include two newspapers, and the father of poor, ill-fated Phil Gianatasio. We can handle all of those. But I can't shake the feeling you're holding out on us."

"You've had my phone tapped," Brian said hoarsely. "You should know everything."

"Dr. Holbrook, except for the few minutes we all know about, you haven't *been* home in several days. But, rest easy, Doctor. Your little peccadilloes are safe. We've never tapped your line."

"But—"

"I don't have the time to discuss anything with you right now. But when I return, I promise you discussions aplenty, painful and otherwise. In the meantime, Leon, I don't want either of them harmed unless one of them causes you trouble. Then, take it out on her. She can come in here to watch the show on TV if she wants, even to speak to him. But I don't want either of them left alone— not for a second. Yes?"

Leon grunted and nodded.

"Okay," he said.

"Leon's English speaking leaves a bit to be desired," Weber explained, "but I promise you, his comprehension is perfect. Right, Leon?"

"Perfect."

Leon's smile bared cigarette-stained teeth.

Weber crossed to the TV and clicked on a local station.

"If my information is correct," he said, "Channel Seven will be covering the proceedings upstairs live. Our crack Newbury sales force has been very busy taking orders for Vasclear from around the world, and the trucks are ready to roll. Within minutes of the end of the ceremony, they'll be on the road."

"You're still an asshole and a loser," Brian said.

Weber stepped back and allowed Leon another roundhouse, open-hand slam on Brian's face. His head snapped against the chair back. His broken nose began oozing blood. His eyes glazed over and teared.

"We'll see who the loser is," Weber said. "I'll be back in a few hours. I've got a presidential signing to attend, and some rumors about the two of you to begin spreading. Holbrook, I'll expect some satisfactory answers from you."

He turned, blew a kiss to Carolyn, and left. Brian sat motionless, trying to clear his thoughts. Was Weber telling the truth about not having his phone in Reading bugged? If so, how had—

"Brian, are you all right?"

Carolyn had come out of the bedroom. The bruises about her eyes were ugly. Her lower lip was split.

"I've been better," he managed to say. "How did you get the scrubs?"

"I . . . I threw up. They made me watch while they beat you."

"I'm glad I wasn't there."

He was about to say more, but he was stopped by a sudden thought. Maybe Carolyn had been given promises by Weber if she could accomplish with Brian what the drugs and the beatings had not.

She crossed to the sink, wet a towel, and gently cleaned him off. Then she pulled a chair over from the small dining table and set it a few feet away, where he could see her face. Brian sensed her thoughts were scrambling, as his were, for some way to escape. If he couldn't trust her, he decided at that moment, he had no chance at all. But he wasn't going to mention Teri or the Sharpes. He noticed a man in the bedroom to his left and another, the man with cologne, behind him and to the right. Leon, now standing close to Jessup, made three of them, all with shoulder-holstered guns. Bad odds.

"I'm sorry about this, Brian," Jessup said, maintaining steady, level eye-contact with him, and speaking deliberately—too deliberately, he thought. "I'm sorry about everything. You know, I've been thinking, as one physician to another, about how many wonderful medical cases we've shared together over the years."

What in the hell are you . . . ?

The intensity in Jessup's eyes kept him silent.

"Yes," he said, still nonplussed. "I remember."

"I was especially impressed with that wonderful gentleman you helped me take care of in the clinic one night. Walter something."

Louderman. Brian glanced over at Leon, who was leaning against the kitchen counter three or four feet away. He looked indifferent to their conversation.

"He was a fascinating case," Jessup went on. "A bit like that Hennessey woman—the woman with the incredible films whose life you saved that time in the cath lab."

Louderman . . . films like Nellie's . . . Suddenly Brian understood. All the proof of the Vasclear hoax had not been destroyed in the film-library fire. There was still one set of videos—one that had been carefully hidden from prying eyes—the films of the man who had designs on becoming the next president of the United States.

Brian nodded to let her know that he understood. He glanced over at the TV, where a game show was on. Nothing happening yet in the Hippodome.

"Are you sure we saw him in the clinic?" Brian asked.

"Actually, now that I think about it, it was in my office," she replied. "We took his cardiogram with that special EKG machine I have there—the one I invented. The one next to the file cabinet."

In Jessup's office. Louderman's films were in the file cabinet, along with the rigged EKG machine. It was the proof for which he had so frantically been searching—the proof that could stop Vasclear, shut

Newbury down, and go a long way toward clearing him of murder charges.

Leon seemed to be paying more attention to their conversation now, but if he realized the medical aspects of their exchange were total nonsense, he hid it well. Brian had no idea how they might get free, but if he made it upstairs, he wanted to know the keypad entry code to Jessup's office.

"I remember that case very well," he said, wincing at the pain in his chest. "He and I waited for an hour in the hallway because *we couldn't get in.*"

Jessup nodded.

"Yes," she said, "I thought he was having trouble with his lowest cervical vertebra."

C-7—the lowest cervical vertebra.

"Yes," he replied, "but that wasn't it."

"No. And as I recall, we checked all of his EKG leads, too."

Twelve leads . . . 7-1-2 . . .

"I'm surprised you remember."

"It's hard to forget. You did a great job on him. Especially evaluating his major coronary chambers."

Four . . . 7-1-2-4 . . . Brian indicated that he knew the keypad combination and tested the clothesline binding his hands. There was no give. If he bent his knees to his chest, he could probably get off a kick, or he could even use his head to butt, but the rope around his ankles meant there was no way he could stand up straight and keep his balance. And he didn't know how much more pounding his damaged ribs could take.

"How is your heart holding up?" Jessup asked, her expression suggesting that he needed to pay attention.

"Some pain," he replied.

"Well, as long as you don't have any V. fib."

V. fib—ventricular fibrillation . . . It was a lethal heart rhythm, usually accompanied by collapse and a seizure. Carolyn wanted him to be ready to fake a cardiac arrest. But when?

He watched as she stood and paced around the room. There was a half-filled vodka bottle on the table. She took a sip—no one tried to stop her—then set the bottle back down. A weapon. Next she turned her attention to the TV. Still no ceremony. Brian had once been driving into Boston from the airport at almost the same time as the President. The entire mile-long tunnel into the city had to be closed and emptied of traffic. Two ambulances, half a dozen motorcyclists, several patrol cars, and six or seven limousines made up the motorcade. It was a wonder they ever got anyplace on time.

Jessup looked in the refrigerator and cupboards, which were virtually empty. Finally, she loosened the drawstring on her scrub pants and slowly, theatrically, tucked her top in. Then she tightened the cord around her narrow waist again. It was a movement that any man with a molecule of testosterone, regardless of his age, would have found seductive. Brian could tell that both the gunmen in the room were paying close attention to her. She glided over to Leon, doing her best to keep him interested in her body, and complained about being starved. Just a doughnut and a cup of coffee, she cooed, brushing against his arm. It was an impressive attempt to narrow the odds.

Not a chance, Brian was thinking, although he gave her points for courage. Then suddenly, Leon broke into a broad grin and patted her on the bottom.

"Doughnuts," he said, laughing out loud.

He snapped off some machine-gun orders in Russian to the man with the mustache, who quickly came around to face Brian. Then he yelled to the man in the bedroom. The third gunman, much younger than the other two, immediately emerged and took a position by the outside door. He was tall and well-built, but looked to be only about twenty, if that. Finally, Leon took Carolyn by the arm and set her down on the couch across from the television.

"Stay," he ordered.

Then, with a final set of instructions to his men, Leon left. They had five minutes, Brian thought. Ten at the most. If it was going to happen, it had to happen right now.

"Hey," Brian said to the man now in charge, "do you speak any English?"

"I speak English good," the stocky guard said, warning as much as bragging.

"Well, I'm not feeling so good."

Brian waited another thirty seconds. Then he doubled over and began moaning and gasping for breath.

"What?" the gunman asked. "What is it?"

"Brian, is it your heart?" Jessup cried out, leaping up from her seat.

Brian moaned even louder, then threw himself on the floor, shaking his head violently, and doing what he could, within the constraints of his bonds, to look like a man having a seizure. Jessup rushed over to him.

"It's his heart!" she exclaimed. "Quickly, untie him so I can work on him."

"No. Wait for Leon."

"By that time he'll be dead, you fool! Look at him."

"No," the man said again.

"You, over here!" Jessup demanded of the young thug. "Turn him on his back."

The two guards, more bewildered each second, exchanged rapid-fire Russian while Brian continued moaning and rhythmically jerking his legs.

Finally, the younger man bent over and turned Brian onto his back. Brian could see that Jessup had stood up, stepped away, and now held the vodka bottle behind her back.

"Now!" he heard her say.

Jessup exploded the vodka bottle over the stocky man's head, dropping him in a hail of glass and booze. The younger guard turned away from Brian toward the commotion. Although Brian's movements were slowed by the clothesline and the pain in his side, his attack was still quick enough. He swung his hands over the man's head. The clothesline binding Brian's wrists caught the guard around the throat. Brian snapped the cord taut and threw himself backward. The Chechen fell heavily on top of him, his face to the ceiling.

Ignoring the pain boring into his chest from the guard's weight, Brian pulled down with all the strength left in his arms. The young man thrashed wildly but there was no way he could turn over. His elbow was a spear, thrusting again and again into Brian's injured side. Then suddenly the blows stopped. The man's body went limp. Brian, blood streaming into his eyes from his nose, kept intense pressure on the rope.

"You can stop, Brian," Jessup said. "He's dead."

Brian shoved the corpse aside, unable to avoid staring at the protruding violet mass that was its tongue. He was surprised at how little remorse he was feeling at having killed for a second time. Carolyn, still breathless, knelt beside him and undid the knots.

"Is the other guy dead?" he asked.

"No. Actually, I think he's waking up."

Brian helped roll the semiconscious man onto his stomach. They lashed his arms and ankles behind him.

"Do you want to stay and try to ambush Leon?" she asked.

"I want to get out of here. I'm in no shape to get the better of Leon."

"In that case, we have to get to my office as fast as we can," she said. "If we can get those videos over to the Hippodome and show Alexander Baird what we have, we could still stop the ceremony."

"I promise I'll tell anyone who will listen about how you saved my life," Brian said as she helped him stand. "It will help."

Jessup bent over, took the revolver from the shoulder holster of the corpse, and offered it to Brian.

He shook his head.

"A dear friend wisely told me just yesterday that my having a gun greatly increases the odds that someone will choose to shoot me first and question me later."

"I don't care if they shoot *me,*" she said, cradling the gun. "I've never even held one of these. Any tricks?"

"Point and shoot, just like the camera."

They cautiously opened the door to the communications center. The room was just as Brian had imagined—state-of-the-art recording equipment, half a dozen monitoring screens on the wall.

The corridor outside was deserted.

"Let's go to the first floor and take the elevator up to the fourth floor from there," Jessup said.

"Looking like we do, I think we'd be better off sticking to the stairs."

Carolyn pulled a tissue from a box on the counter and wiped some of the blood from his face.

"Stairs it is. Hang on, Brian. It's almost over."

"I hope so," he said. "Tell me something," he added as they hurried down the hall to the stairwell. "How do you think Art got to your place last night the way he did? Do you think you were followed?"

Jessup considered the question for a few seconds.

"I don't know," she said finally. "I stopped for a while at the beach by the end of the causeway, and the place was absolutely deserted. Mine was the only car in the little parking area. If someone was following me, I don't know how they kept me from spotting them. Why?"

"It's bothering me," Brian replied. "That's all."

CHAPTER FORTY

WHDH-TV

Channel 7

"This is Kimberly Herrera reporting
from the venerable Hippocrates Dome
amphitheater at White Memorial Hospital where moments ago, the President of
the United States entered to enthusiastic
applause from the four hundred or so
packing this beautiful auditorium. Accompanying him was FDA chief Dr. Alexander Baird, and waiting to greet them
were Massachusetts Senators Sal Giglia
and Walter Louderman.

"The atmosphere here is electric. In just a short while, Dr. Baird and the President will sign the necessary documents approving the cardiac wonder drug Vasclear for general use. The drug was developed by Newbury Pharmaceuticals of Boston and tested right here at the renowned Boston Heart Institute. After that portion of the ceremony, the President will issue and sign a proclamation declaring this National Cardiac Health Week.

"The crowd, studded with local dignitaries, has not only been awed by the atmosphere surrounding the Presidential visit, but also by the massive stained-glass dome overhead, depicting great moments in medical history. The dome is now in the final phases of a two-year restoration that will end up costing over five million dollars, all of which, we are told, has come from private sources. As you can see, the dome still has some scaffolding in place around its base. It is stunningly backlit by eight spotlights brought in just for this occasion.

"Well, the house lights are dimming. The dome is glittering. And the President has finished shaking hands and has taken his place on the platform. This is a great day for medical care in Boston, generally acknowledged to be the best in the world. . . ."

FUELED BY ADRENALINE BUT SLOWED BY INJURIES, BRIAN followed Carolyn Jessup up to her fourth-floor office. Getting in enough air was a problem for him. His nose was completely clogged with drying blood and his ribs were painfully monitoring every movement. Still, he made the six flights from the subbasement without stopping. As Carolyn had said, it was almost over.

Not surprisingly, given the hospital's guest of honor, the stairway was deserted. They reached Jessup's office without encountering a soul. Jessup punched in the code and unlocked the outer door to her darkened suite. She led Brian quickly through the reception area into the inner office. The EKG machine was right where she said it would be. Alongside it was the four-drawer oak file cabinet. Jessup groaned.

"The key's on my ring," she said.

"No backup?"

"My secretary has one, but I think she keeps it on *her* ring."

Brian searched the receptionist's desk and came up not with the key, but with a fairly sturdy letter opener.

"Having Senator Louderman referred to me for a cardiac evaluation was a totally unexpected godsend," Jessup explained as Brian worked at prying open the drawer. "Straight out of the blue. Once we made him a believer, the entire Vasclear timetable was accelerated."

"But he didn't have heart disease."

"No. Plain old esophagitis."

She still couldn't keep a note of smugness from her voice, Brian noticed. At the moment he was certain the opener was about to snap, the drawer popped free. Louderman's films, properly labeled, were in a small soft-leather valise.

"We have to hurry," Brian urged. "Leon's probably returned with that coffee by now. They've got to be looking for us. Come on."

As they started toward the door into the reception area, Brian said, "I'm not sure I'm presentable enough to meet the—"

The spit of a silenced pistol stopped him in midsentence. He whirled just in time to see Jessup, clutching at her upper chest, spin fully around and fall heavily by her receptionist's desk. Standing by the doorway, guns drawn, were Leon and the stocky killer they had tied up. Brian groaned as he remembered Carolyn suggesting that they go directly to her office, not thinking the man on the floor was conscious. *Stupid!* But not nearly as stupid as failing to take the man's gun.

Desperate, Brian looked toward the window as the two killers moved into the reception area. Jessup's office was on the fourth floor, but one story down, maybe twelve feet, was a roof—the roof of the surgical-observation unit, Brian figured. Was there any way he would have the nerve to plunge headfirst through the plate-glass window? Could he survive such a move?

"Naugh-ty doctor," Leon said, grinning grotesquely through the office door at Brian. "Stay here," he ordered to his man in English.

He took a single step forward. Behind him, Brian could see Carolyn begin to move. Her guard was paying no attention to her, but instead was looking past Leon at Brian. His inattention was quickly fatal. Carolyn's shot, from an awkward angle, caught the man squarely in the forehead. He was stumbling backward when Jessup fired again. This time, *Leon* cried out and clutched his shoulder. Carolyn, on her knees, managed to scramble behind the desk as Leon fired at her.

Brian knew this was his moment. He dove for the door from the office to the reception area, slammed it shut, and bolted it. From beyond the door came another shot, then another. He considered calling the hospital operator for help, but just as quickly changed his mind as first one, then another bullet shattered the wood around the lock. Instead, he lifted Jessup's heavy leather desk chair over his head and hurled it with all his strength through the window. Cool, wet night air flooded the office. Outside, a wind-driven rain was falling through a pitch-black sky. Another shot. More splinters.

Brian kicked out a few remaining shards of glass, slipped his hand through the handle of the case with Louderman's films, and lowered himself out the window until his arms were at full extension. The throbbing in his chest and finger made the effort excruciating. The roof seemed farther down than he had estimated, but what difference did that make now? At the moment the door above him shattered open, he let go.

Give and roll, was his only thought as he fell through the rain. *Give and . . .*

He hit the gravel roof with his legs virtually straight, and pitched awkwardly to one side. No give, no roll. Air exploded from his lungs. Already-damaged ribs separated even further. His bad knee popped out, then back. He hit the wet stones with his shoulder and the side of his face, tearing away skin that was already badly bruised. The blow stunned him, but he managed to respond to the voice shrieking in his head.

Move! . . . Move!

Brian rolled away from the building as a bullet snapped into the gravel not far from his neck. Leon, at the window above, fired again. This time the shot tore through the muscle of Brian's thigh. He cried out but kept rolling across the roof. He looked back just as Leon, able to use only one arm, lowered himself out the window.

Clutching Louderman's angiogram films, Brian forced himself to his feet and, dragging his injured left leg, hobbled across the roof toward what he prayed was some sort of fire escape. What he found instead was a broad scaffolding coming off the roof, and pressing flush against the next building. Ahead of him, maybe fifty yards, the night was awash in light. Spotlight beams from several buildings shimmered down through the rain, focused on a single area. The dome!

If he could get close enough, he could throw the case with the films through the glass, and then try to make it down the scaffolding alongside the Pinkham Building. At least the proof would survive. The drop to the amphitheater floor was perhaps twenty-five or thirty feet, but the videos seemed reasonably well protected.

Brian glanced over his shoulder just as Leon hit the roof. Despite his wounded arm, the killer rolled with expert grace and leaped catlike to his feet. No linebacker Brian had ever played with moved like that. He dragged himself painfully out onto the scaffolding and hobbled through the downpour toward the light, knowing it would not be much longer before Leon caught up with him. The brilliant colors of the dome were growing closer. Brian heard the pounding footsteps behind him. He had just seconds now. There was no hope of getting off the scaffolding; no hope of finding a way to the ground. Quickly, he folded the soft leather valise around the film boxes, then hefted it in his hand. He passed it like a football at the moment Leon's gun hammered down on his back. The pouch crashed through the stained glass about halfway up the dome.

Brian could hear screaming from below as he stumbled forward several more steps and fell, not a foot from the edge of the glass. Instantly, Leon was on him. Furious, he grabbed Brian by the front of the shirt, pulled him to his knees, and rammed the barrel of the silenced pistol into his mouth. Brian could only close his eyes and wait for the end.

"Secret Service! Drop it, right now!"

The voice came from the window of the building behind Leon and to Brian's left. Brian could see the Secret Service man, rifle aimed, perched on the window ledge. Leon's grip on his shirt loosened. Slowly, he drew the gun barrel back. Then suddenly, he swung his arm around toward the Secret Service agent and fired. There was an immediate burst of gunfire from the window. Brian could feel the slugs as they hammered into Leon's body. The behemoth, still gripping Brian's shirt, toppled forward onto him, forcing him over backward onto the stained glass.

There was shrieking from beneath him as Brian crashed through the glass, with Leon's deadweight on top of him. He girded himself for the fall to his death, but the drop ended after just a few feet when he slammed onto the narrow metal scaffolding inside the dome. Leon's full weight hit him from above, driving rib into lung in an explosion of pain. Then slowly, exquisitely slowly, the huge killer rolled off to one side and vanished from Brian's sight. An instant later, Brian heard the thud of Leon's body on the seats below.

"Move and you're dead!" a man screamed up at him.

Brian smiled weakly and closed his eyes.

Don't worry, he was thinking. *I'm not movin' for a while.*

Brian had no idea how long he lay there. When he opened his eyes, he was still on the scaffolding. A man in a dark blue windbreaker was standing over him, keeping a pistol leveled steadily at a spot just between his eyes.

"I'm Secret Service, Holbrook. Don't even think about moving. They're getting a ladder in place now. We're going to strap you to a board and lower you down. Can you hear me okay?"

Brian just nodded, concentrating on getting air in past the intense pain in his chest. Moments later, the ladder clanked against the scaffolding. A second Secret Service agent and an EMT scrambled up carrying a body board.

"Just lie still, fella," the EMT said. "We're going to carry you down."

"There'll be guns on you every inch of the way, Holbrook," the Secret Service agent warned.

Brian blinked up at the rain falling through the huge hole in the stained glass.

"I hear you," he murmured.

The men lashed him to the board, lowered him down, and placed him on a hospital stretcher. The amphitheater was largely empty now. Two doctors and two nurses from the ER immediately began working on him. One of the nurses bent down beside him.

"Brian, it's Sherry," his friend from Suburban said. "Sherry Gordon."

"Hey."

"Don't try to speak. I just want you to know that Dr. Jessup's in the ER. She's been shot a couple of times, but she's conscious. She's been asking about you. The surgeons say she'll make it. They're taking her to the OR now."

Thank you, Brian mouthed.

A uniformed policeman replaced the Secret Service agent and handcuffed one of Brian's wrists to the safety rail of the stretcher.

"You don't have to do that," Sherry said.

"You do your job and let me do mine," the officer replied.

Moments later, Sherry moved aside to make room for Laj Randa. The Sikh, splendid in a dark suit and orange turban, listened to Brian's chest, then gently squeezed his hand.

"I believe your right lung has collapsed," he said. "I will accompany you down to the ER and put a tube in. Then we will see what else needs to be done. You picked a hell of a way to demonstrate you have come over to my way of thinking about Vasclear," he said.

"Believe me, I have."

They started moving the stretcher away, then stopped.

"Can I speak with him?" he heard a familiar male voice say.

"Just for a few seconds, Senator," the policeman replied. "No more than that. And stay on this side of the stretcher. This man's wanted for murder."

"I know."

Walter Louderman's face appeared above Brian. It was flushed with concern.

"What about those films, Holbrook?" he asked. "Why are you doing this to me?"

Brian did his best to smile, aware of his missing front tooth. He reached up a bloodied hand and patted the senator on the sleeve. His voice was hoarse and strained.

"You won't be upset with me for long," he said.

EPILOGUE ONE

ONE WEEK LATER

A SERIES OF THUNDER SQUALLS HAD LEFT MIAMI IN-
ternational Airport even busier than usual. Art Weber was irritated
about the delay in his flight to Bogotá, but he was equally grateful
for the milling crowds. Anything to stay inconspicuous. That was
the reason he was flying coach.

The moment Leon Kulrushtin's body had come exploding
through that stained-glass dome, landing like a sack of cement on
the amphitheater seats, Weber knew that his own plans for the
future and life as he had come to know it were over. In fact, if he
failed to act quickly and decisively, his life might be over in a much
more literal sense. In the confusion and panic, he had slipped out of

the amphitheater and hurried directly to a studio apartment he had been keeping in Cambridge, across the river from his Back Bay penthouse.

He used the apartment sparingly, usually for exotic sex with women he bought through high-priced escort services. But in the main, the place was his hedge against just the sort of disaster that Brian Holbrook had brought down upon him. It contained clothes, luggage, three passports with corroborating IDs, several handguns, and $100,000 in twenties and fifties. He had skimmed off more than three million from Newbury Pharmaceuticals over the years of their association, but that money was already in a Grand Cayman bank.

Weber figured he had several days to put as much distance between himself and the Chechens as possible, while they were scrambling to distance themselves from the authorities. After that, the search for him would be on. Favors would be called in. Rewards would be offered. Bribes would be paid. In the years since the collapse of the USSR, the loosely connected Chechen mob had spread over much of the U.S. And they seldom went after anyone they didn't ultimately get. But they had never gone after a man as resourceful and intelligent as Art Weber.

Planning was the key. Long before he needed it, Weber had mapped his route to Colombia and had begun funneling money to men who would help him disappear for as long as he felt necessary. Now, as he stood in the line to check his baggage, he congratulated himself on his quick action and the flawless design of his escape. In less than five hours, he would be heading out of Bogotá toward the jungle.

A suitcase nudged him in the back of the leg.

"Perdone usted, señor," the embarrassed young woman behind him said.

Weber turned. She was in her early to mid-twenties, dressed in the white pleated blouse and colorful skirt of a peasant, and she was absolutely ravishing—copper skin, thick jet hair, wide dark eyes, and a body that made his mouth go dry.

"Please, think nothing of it," he replied in near-perfect Spanish. "Are you going to Bogotá?"

Before she had even responded to the question, Weber had mentally undressed her.

"It is my home," she said, somewhat shyly.

"And it is about to be mine," he said, forcing his eyes from the cleft between her magnificent breasts. "My business will be keeping me there for many months."

"Your Spanish is excellent."

Her name was Rosalita and she was returning home from visiting her sister in Miami. By the time Weber had checked his bags, she had agreed to take the seat next to his on the flight. He stood by as she checked her tattered canvas suitcase. Before they touched down in Bogotá, she would be resting her head on his shoulder, her hands wrapped tightly around his. And by tonight . . . ?

There was still over an hour to kill before the flight. The woman was his now—a reward for his thoroughness. Fifty million and Carolyn Jessup in Boston, or three million and this incredible jewel in the tropics. The choice, had it been his to make, would have been a tough one. He suggested a drink and took her arm as they found an out-of-the-way bar. A booth was vacant in the most dimly lit corner of the wood-and-leather room. Weber couldn't take his gaze from her breasts and was now considering the giddy notion that she might even be a virgin—clay for him to mold.

They talked for a time about nothing in particular. Weber tried unsuccessfully to keep his hands off her. Finally, he put his arm around her narrow waist and was ecstatic when she let it stay there.

"You really are very beautiful," he whispered.

"And you are very handsome and very persuasive."

She turned fully to him. Her scent was intoxicating. Her breast, now pressing against him, was as firm as a teenager's. Her eyes widened. Her lips beckoned. Weber glanced furtively around to see if it would be too outrageous to kiss her. None of the few patrons in the place was paying the slightest attention to them. He pulled her toward him and set his mouth against hers. Her lips parted and her tongue sought his.

By the time Weber felt the pain beneath his ribs and realized she had stabbed him, the eight-inch stiletto was through his diaphragm and well into his heart. The woman twisted the blade expertly to enlarge the hole, while she pulled his mouth so tightly against hers that it was impossible for him even to speak. Then she released him, positioning his body to remain seated. Finally, she knelt on the seat beside him, put her lips to Weber's ear and one hand on his groin.

"No hard feelings," she said.

EPILOGUE TWO

ONE MONTH LATER

THE FOOD AND DRUG ADMINISTRATION HEADQUARTERS was a massive thirteen-story structure, gray and grim, sprawling over a two-block square in Rockville, Maryland. Beneath a cloudless November sky, Brian parked his rental car and entered the Parklawn Building.

It was time to face Teri. Still conscious of his limp, Brian crossed to the guard in the main lobby and was directed to her fourth-floor office. He could tell when he had spoken to her by phone that she was bewildered by his request to meet in her office and not at her home or someplace else away from work. But she certainly had to know things had changed. Except for a brief conversation when she called the day after his emergency surgery, they had not spoken. He hadn't phoned her since then, nor had he accepted any of her calls.

He left the elevator and entered a modest reception area serving a dozen offices. While the FDA might be guilty of inefficiency, he thought, as he checked in with the receptionist, no one could ever accuse them of overspending on their physical plant. He settled into a threadbare Danish-modern chair, ran his tongue over the bridge that held his temporary front tooth in place, and thought about what he was going to say to her.

You're the most exciting lover I have ever been with and probably ever will be with. That would be the truth, but that was not what Teri was going to hear today. The receptionist called him over and pointed toward an office door indistinguishable from any of the others except for the *T. Sennstrom, M.D., Ph.D.* stenciled on it. Brian knocked once and stepped inside.

The office was small, perhaps twelve feet square. The walls were lined with gunmetal-gray steel shelves, filled to overflowing with manuscripts, texts, and journals. Teri had chosen to greet him from behind her government-issue desk, but extended her hand across it to him, and he took it. She was wearing a black straight skirt and lavender blouse—a simple outfit that on her looked sensational. Brian took the chair directly across the desk. This conversation was not going to be easy, but he wanted to do it right.

"You look good," Teri said. "Being cleared of murder charges agrees with you."

"Thanks. My nose is finally approaching its former size, although I think it will never be its former shape. You look pretty fine yourself."

"I was upset that you never returned any of my calls."

"I know. Phoebe started coming to see me every day in the hospital. I spent a couple of days recuperating at her house. We've . . . we've started talking about getting back together."

"Oh? That's why you never called me?"

Brian hesitated but forced himself to maintain eye contact with her.

"Actually, no," he said. "That's not why. Some things have been bothering me, Teri—bothering me a lot. I wanted to share them with you to see what your take on them might be."

She looked at him queerly, coldly.

"Go ahead," she said.

"Well, when he thought I was never going to leave his little dungeon in the hospital alive, Art Weber assured me that my phone line had not been tapped. I'm certain he was telling the truth."

"So?"

"So, his man, Leon, and another guy were waiting for me in New York State. Fulbrook. If my phone wasn't tapped, how did they know where I was going?"

"Maybe they followed you."

"I don't believe so, Teri. I thought and thought about who I might have told about the trip. You were the only one."

"That's nonsense," she said, but her color had drained.

"I don't think so. You see, there's more. There was a nice old guy named Elovitz. Bill Elovitz. He survived the death camps in Nazi Germany but he couldn't survive the folks at Newbury Pharmaceuticals. He was killed because I thought he had pulmonary hypertension. But how did they know about his PH almost as soon as I did? I'll tell you how, Teri. I told you, and you told them."

"But—"

"And then Art Weber shows up at just the moment Carolyn Jessup had agreed to help me. She's certain she wasn't followed home from the hospital. I searched my memory for who could have known I was going to her house. There were only two. One was my NA sponsor, who would walk into the fire for me. The other was you. Teri, how much was Weber paying you to spy for him?"

"Brian, please. This is ridiculous!"

"No. I'm afraid it isn't. I've gone over the facts a hundred times. You were on Weber's payroll."

Her eyes glazed over with tears.

"I had no idea what was going on. You have to believe that. Weber was paying me simply to pass on information. That's all. I didn't know what they were doing with it. I had no reason to believe there was anything wrong with Vasclear until . . . until you began reporting things to me. By the time I realized what kind of a person Weber was, he had videos of . . . of me accepting money. I was frightened. I didn't know what to do."

Brian shook his head.

"People died because of you."

As quickly as the tears had formed, they were gone. Teri Sennstrom lifted her chin.

"How dare you lay that kind of guilt trip on me," she snapped. "I didn't kill anyone. In fact, I didn't even do anything that illegal. You know, I work my ass off in this job for lousy civil service pay. I made more from Art Weber in a few months than I've earned in my entire career here. I *deserved* that money."

"I'm going to tell Dr. Baird what I know," Brian said.

"You bastard! Go ahead. You tell him, and I'll deny it. He loves me. He knows the kind of work I do. Go ahead."

Brian sighed. The face he had fantasized about, dreamed about so many nights, was pinched and ugly with anger.

"Actually," he said wearily, "it's not going to be your word against mine, Teri. It's going to be your word against yours."

He stood and opened the door. Then he turned back to her, unzipped his leather bomber jacket, and showed her the tape recorder he had strapped onto the lining.

"This is closure for that patient of mine who got gunned down," he said with no joy, "and for my father, and especially for me."

Teri shrieked at him loudly enough to bring the receptionist running. But Brian merely strode past the woman to the stairs.

Teri's invectives were still echoing through the reception area when the stairwell door closed behind him.

On the way back to D.C. where he'd meet Phoebe and the girls, he stopped at a small park where a group of teens was just choosing sides for a game of touch.

"You guys need a quarterback?" he asked.

ABOUT THE AUTHOR

MICHAEL PALMER, M.D., is the author of *Critical Judgment, Silent Treatment, Natural Causes, Extreme Measures, Flashback, Side Effects,* and *The Sisterhood.* His books have been translated into twenty-six languages. He trained in internal medicine at Boston City and Massachusetts General hospitals, spent twenty years as a full-time practitioner of internal and emergency medicine, and is now involved in the treatment of alcoholism and chemical dependence. He lives in Massachusetts.